THE SHORT STORIES OF CHEN RUOXI
TRANSLATED FROM THE ORIGINAL CHINESE

A Writer at the Crossroads

Chen Ruoxi

Edited by
Hsin-sheng C. Kao

The Edwin Mellen Press
Lewiston/Queenston/Lampeter

Library of Congress Cataloging-in-Publication Data

Ch' en, Jo-hsi.
   [Short stories. English. Selections]
   The short stories of Chen Ruoxi, translated from the original
Chinese : a writer at the crossroads / Chen Ruoxi ; edited by Hsin
-sheng C. Kao.
      p.   cm.
   Includes bibliographical references and index.
   ISBN 0-7734-9190-2
   1. Ch' en, Jo-hsi--Translations into English. I. Kao, Hsin-sheng
C. II. Title.
PL2840.J6A25 1992
895.1'352--dc20   92-29960
                                                             CIP

Art work by Andrew Chao
Chinese calligraphy by San-pao Li

A CIP catalog record for this book
is available from the British Library.

Copyright © 1992 The Edwin Mellen Press.

The Edwin Mellen Press   The Edwin Mellen Press
      Box 450   Box 67
Lewiston, New York   Queenston, Ontario
   USA 14092   CANADA L0S 1L0

                  Edwin Mellen Press, Ltd.
                   Lampeter, Dyfed, Wales
                 UNITED KINGDOM SA48 7DY

           Printed in the United States of America

陳若曦短篇小說

CONTENTS

Acknowledgements v

Foreword to the English Edition by Chen Ruoxi vii

Preface 1

Prologue: Chen Ruoxi on "Homeland and the New Land" 11

Short Stories:

 The Crossroads 15

 On the Other Side of the Pacific 77

 Suyue's New Year's Eve 153

 The Woman from Guizhou 173

 Guest from the Homeland 201

 Green Card 233

 Morning Encounter with a Stranger: A Monologue 263

 It's Your House, But It's My Home! 283

 Twenty Thousand Dollars Less. . . . 299

 Ah Lan's Decision 311

Short Biography of Chen Ruoxi 321

Glossary 325

Bibliography 331

ACKNOWLEDGEMENTS

The ten short stories and novellas in this translated collection were originally written in Chinese and published separately in books, periodicals, magazines, or newspapers. I am greatly indebted to Chen Ruoxi for her generous permission to translate and publish these stories. Without her encouragement, her detailed illumination of numerous passages from her stories, and her reading and rereading of the entire manuscript, this project would not have been possible.

For critical acumen on creative writing issues, I am grateful to Yu Lihua and the Overseas Chinese Women Writers Association. Special thanks go to C. T. Hsia for inspiring the title of this short story collection; to Angela Jung Palandri, Leo Ou-fan Lee, Samuel H. N. Cheung, Charlotte Furth, and Sung-sheng Yvonne Chang for their advice and encouragement; to the translators of six of these stories: Tammy C. Peng, Shiao-ling Yu, Feng-ying Ming, Zelan D. Sang, Shu-mei Shih, Adam Schorr, and Xincun Huang; and, to Robin W. Stevens for her astute and assiduous editorial assistance and thorough proofreading.

Finally, I wish to thank Yuanliu Publishing Company and Shibao Publishing Company of Taibei, Taiwan, for their kind permission to use excerpts from *Guizhou nuren* (1989), and *Chengli chengwai* (1983), respectively, by Chen Ruoxi; and, to California State University at Long Beach for providing me the two research grants and assigned-time release needed to complete this translation project.

September, 1992
Hsin-sheng C. Kao

FOREWORD

At the Crossroads Again!

By

Chen Ruoxi

Ten years ago I wrote *The Crossroads* commemorating human rights activist Wei Jingsheng, a young worker who posted an article on the Beijing Wall. His article demanded that "democracy" be added to Deng Xiaoping's "Four Modernizations"[1] reform program. For that, he was sentenced to fifteen years in prison. At the time, it was believed that China was at the crossroads of either moving toward reform, possibly leading to a pro-capitalist and, hopefully, democratic future, or returning back to the old authoritarian ways. Therefore, many Chinese-Americans wrote to Deng on Wei's behalf, but to no avail. Deng, however, did choose to initiate some reforms, and as a result of his "open-door" policies, the Chinese enjoyed a period of political and economic relaxation.

In the spring of 1989, Wei Jingsheng's name once again resurfaced.

---

[1] This term refers to Premier Deng's policy to modernize China's industry, agriculture, science and technology, and national defense by the year 2,000. This modernization plan was first announced by the late Premier, Zhou Enlai (1898-1976), to the Fourth People's Congress (January 13-17, 1975). It has been a dominant policy of Deng's regime since the late 1970's.

This time it was the scholars and writers in Beijing who wrote to Deng pleading for Wei's release. Overseas Chinese followed suit. Then, on April 15, 1989, the liberal Communist Party leader Hu Yaobang passed away. Following his death, a gathering in Tiananmen Square, eulogizing Hu, was transformed into a massive pro-democracy movement. Soon after, martial law was reinstated, and the Square was emptied in a bloody massacre on June 4th, 1989.

The shocking incident touched the entire world. Now, with most of Eastern Europe having already abandoned communism, or on the brink of it, China is again at the crossroads. They must decide whether to continue the current reform policy and risk the ideological collapse of communism, or to go back to the old iron-fist rule of Mao Zedong's days.

It is said that history repeats itself. Not quite. Ten years ago, when the term "human rights" was first introduced, the Chinese people did not think it had anything to do with them. Now, it is a popular term and many people are demanding it. We, on the western hemisphere, may think that is a small accomplishment for ten long years, but for one billion Chinese people, this is where their hopes lie.

March, 1991
Berkeley, California

EDITOR'S NOTE ON THE TEXT

As evidenced by the *Bibliography*, there is no definitive Chinese edition for some of Chen Ruoxi's novels and short stories. Due to political reasons or others, there are some omissions from her works published either in China, Hong Kong, or Taiwan, with slight errata or inconsistence. The only criteria adopted here are the stories furnished by Chen Ruoxi herself. The sources were selected from Chen Ruoxi's own recommendations. Acknowledgements for the Chinese sources are made on the first page of each translated story.

Except for proper names or places, the Pinyin romanization system has been adopted throughout this book. In the *Bibliography* and *Glossary*, both the Pinyin romanization and Chinese characters are given.

All translations in this book are from the writings of Chen Ruoxi and are translated from the Chinese original for the first time. Individual acknowledgements are made on the first page of each short story concerned. Unless otherwise stated, all other passages, comments, and translations in this book are my own.

September, 1992
Hsin-sheng C. Kao

PREFACE

It has been over twelve years since Chen Ruoxi made her explosive debut on the world literary scene with the English publication of her *The Execution of Mayor Yin and Other Short Stories of the Great Proletarian Cultural Revolution* (1978)[1]. Her work is one of a handful of Chinese women writers to be published by a major academic press, and the first Chinese woman writer to be extensively reviewed and acclaimed by literary critics from virtually every major national publication and newspaper. Frederic Wakeman, Jr. set the tone of the critics' responses with his thorough review which appeared in *The New York Review of Books*[2]. He saw her stories as authentically inspired accounts of the determination and will of the Chinese people to survive and transcend political repression. Echoing the same voice, Western critics and Chinese scholars such as Richard Bernstein, Mark Elvin, C. T. Hsia, Kai-yu Hsu, David Lattimore, Joseph S. M. Lau, Leo Ou-fan Lee, Timothy Light, Bonnie S. McDougall, Pai Hsien-yung, Wai-lam Yip, and others, in books, reviews, and articles were equally as enthusiastic and

---

[1] Chen Jo-hsi, *The Execution of Mayor Yin and Other Stories from the Great Proletarian Cultural Revolution*. Translated from Chinese by Nancy Ing and Howard Goldblatt. Bloomington: Indiana University Press, 1978.

[2] See Frederic Wakeman, Jr., "The Real China", in *The New York Review of Books*, xxv, no.12 (July 20, 1978): 9-17.

2

favorable with their comments, a few even comparing her work to the great tradition of Orwell and Solzhenitsyn.[3]

Although considered a pioneer in the "literature of the wounded" (*shanghen wenxue*), and a dissident-exile writer by others, Chen Ruoxi is now most widely recognized as a forerunner in the realms of overseas Chinese literature. In her writings of the eighties, she has shifted her focus away from the soil of mainland China to the plight of overseas Chinese and the criticism of human rights violations allegedly committed by both the Chinese Communist and Taiwanese Nationalist governments. Motivated by her desire to influence other overseas Chinese, she urges her compatriots to unite and form a strong influence outside China and Taiwan, and to even get involved in politics, as other minority groups have done. She encourages her readers not to yield to the dogmatic ideology presented by either side, nor to allow themselves to fall into the traps which both extremes may proffer. Of the many novels and stories she has written over the past ten years, the following are just a few examples of her works written along this new thematic line: *Chengli chengwai* (In and Outside the Wall, 1983*)*, *Tuwei* (Breaking Out, 1983*)*, *Yuanjian* (Foresight, 1984*)*, *Er Hu* (The Two Hus, 1985*)*, *Zhihun* (Paper Marriage, 1986), and *Guizhou nuren* (The Woman from Guizhou, 1989*)*. In

---

[3] Cf. Richard Berstein, "Mao's Misfits", *Times* (June 26, 1978): 60 and 64; Mark Elvin, "Tales of the New China", *Times Literary Supplement* (June 9, 1978): 629-630; C. T. Hsia (Xia Zhiqing), "Chen Ruoxi de xiaoshuo" (The Fiction of Chen Ruoxi), in *Chen Ruoxi zixuan ji*, 1-31; Kai-yu Hsu, "A Sense of History: Reading Chen Jo-hsi's Stories"; in *Chinese Fiction from Taiwan: Critical Perspectives*, ed. Jeannette L. Faurot, 206-233; David Lattimore, "Chinese samizdat", in *The New York Times Book Review* (July 30, 1978): 10-11 and 20-21; Joseph S. M. Lau (Liu Shaoming), "Chen Ruoxi de gushi" (The Story of Chen Ruoxi), in *Xiaoshuo yu xiju*, 83-98; Leo Ou-fan Lee, "Dissent Literature from the Cultural Revolution", in *Chinese Literature, Essay, Article, and Review*, no. 1 (1979): 59-79; Timothy Light, review of "*The Execution of Mayor Yin and Other Stories from the Great Proletarian Cultural Revolution*", in *CLEAR*, no. 1 (1979): 131-134; Bonnie S. McDougall, review article on "*The Execution of Mayor Yin and Other Stories from the Great Proletarian Cultural Revolution*", in *Harvard Journal of Asiatic Studies* 39, no. 2 (1979): 469-474; Pai Hsien-yung (Bai Xianyong), "Wutuobang de zhuixun yu huanmie" (The Pursuit and Dissolutionment of Utopia", in *Zhongguo shibao* (November 1, 1977); Wai-lam Yip (Ye Weilian), "Chen Ruoxi de lucheng" (The Journey of Chen Ruoxi), in *Lianhebao* (November 7-10, 1977), and others. For further details, see *Bibliography*.

these stories, Chen's stress on the distinctive features of Chinese-Americans is an expression of the authenticity of overseas Chinese-American culture. At the same time, she reasserts her belief that if they show collective strength and establish credibility, their conviction will lead to a brighter future for Chinese people everywhere.[4]

The pluralism of modern Chinese literature is undeniable. Since 1949, when the Communists assumed power over mainland China and the ousted Nationalist government fled to Taiwan, Chinese literature has progressed and developed in a diversified manner. The variety and treatment of its subject matter reflects a broad spectrum of styles from Marxist dogmatism to daring modernism, from socialist realism with its glorification of the proletariat to explorations of an individual's search for identity at home or abroad. Chinese literature is commonly divided into one of three distinct political and geographical categories: Communist Chinese or PRC, Nationalist Chinese or ROC, and overseas Chinese. However, regardless of which group they belong to, or in which country they reside, many of today's Chinese writers continue to write using the Chinese language.

It was not until the sixties that an outpour of literature written by overseas Chinese intellectuals, immigrants, and exiles developed into what is termed *Haiwai wenxue*, or overseas Chinese literature.[5] Attempting to

---

[4] For further details, see *Yuanjian* (Taibei: Lianjin shudian, 1984), p. v. However, there are other examples echoing the same statement scattered throughout Chen Ruoxi's latest publications, especially in the short stories collected in *Chengli chengwai* and *Guizhou nuren*.

[5] For discussion on early overseas Chinese intellectual literature (liuxuesheng wenxue), see Pai Hsien-yung, "The Wandering Chinese: The Theme of Exile in Taiwan Fiction," in *The Iowa Review* 7, nos. 2-3 (Spring-Summer, 1976): 205-212. For a comprehensive study of the same overseas Chinese writers, see Yan Huo, *Haiwai huaren zuojia lueying* (Brief Interviews of Chinese Writers Overseas) (Hong Kong: Joint Publishing Co., 1984). For comparative studies of overseas Chinese writers and the concept of *diaspora* or voluntary dispersion, see Zhang Cuo's article, "Guopo shanhe zai--haiwai zuojia de bentuxing" (Divided Nation, Undivided Land: On Overseas Chinese Writers' Nativism) appeared in *Unitas*, vol. 7, no. 3 (January, 1991): 24-

illustrate the experiences of overseas Chinese, writers of this genre emphasize the effects of cultural assimilation, resistance to assimilating foreign influences, identity crises, and the varying adaptive lifestyles immigrants lead. In a broad sense, these works often describe the fusion of several nations such as China, Taiwan, the United States, Hong Kong, Southeast Asia, and elsewhere, and the cultures of their people. Akin to such writers as Saul Bellow, Joseph Heller, and Vladimir Nabokov, these Chinese overseas writers endeavor to give meaning and justification to their emigre characters' existence in a new country through an examination of values common to both their old and new cultures.

In the sub-genre of overseas Chinese-American writings, two discernible paradigms exist describing the problems of integration and rejection experienced by Chinese-Americans. First, the hyphenated identity associated with the term "Chinese-American" still remains a central issue in comprehending the roll and place of overseas Chinese in American society. This label not only signifies "dialectical" tensions between the dominant society and "traditional" culture; but it also implies that there are two ways of perceiving reality and values. Thus, the label forms a binary pattern of opposition which is ultimately brought about by the interaction between different cultures and the peoples involved.

This labelling leads to a second common trait: utilizing the Chinese language as a mode of communication, as well as the coded filter through which a world view of culture is presented. The choice to write in Chinese, in a way, can be understood as a form of self-exile and cultural defiance against the United States, a nation that is often intolerant toward the use of foreign languages. Well known bilingual writers Bai Xianyong, Nie Hualing,

---

28. This particular issue also contains articles related to literary topics of exile, and Chinese uprootedness, among others.

Yang Mu, Yu Lihua, Zhang Ailing, and Zhang Cuo, all consciously follow this trend because of the relevance they see in developing works from their own Chinese cultural viewpoint. This sense of nonconformity is transformed into an aesthetic and authentic force seen as essential to the new poetics of Chinese overseas literature.

Since her arrival in the West, in 1978, Chen Ruoxi has joined the above mentioned overseas Chinese writers and others, focusing her writings along these main lines. As Kai-yu Hsu points out, Chen Ruoxi writes in Chinese with a sense of her Motherland culture and history, sensitizing us to the strains a person feels living in this strange and yet familiar world of ours.[6] Her characters, like herself, are either repatriate or expatriate immigrants, originating from Taiwan or mainland China. The physical and geographical separation from their home soil has made them suffer keenly, not only from their confrontations with a new and alien culture, but also from the loss of their heritage and customs. This disjunction and breaking away, in turn, leads to a series of emotive and perceptual transformations. It is a vertical rather than horizontal transformation -- a process that leads to an existential ascent into the self, or an expansion to new psychological and moral planes.

Conceptually, Chen draws these transformations into her writing from the collective layers of her Chinese-American compatriots. As satirically indicated by one of her characters, Lina, in "On the Other Side of the Pacific", Chinese-Americans perpetually suffer from disenchantment and isolation, mainly due to their self-imposed attitudes rather than the newly adopted society. Long-term residency or even permanent status as a naturalized citizen is not sufficient enough to be considered full-fledged assimilation.

---

[6] For details, see K. Y. Hsu, "Sense of History: Reading of Chen Jo-hsi's Stories", *ibid.*, pp. 206-33. Hsu writes on the historicity of Chen Ruoxi's fictional text, and addresses the complex role of her works in history and historiopolitical criticism, thereby reinforcing his belief that readers have much to learn from modes of Chen's narrative discourse they have hitherto viewed as mere fictitious documentary collections of the past.

6

Chinese immigrants often come to realize over time that their cultural background and beliefs become a cross to bear for however long they are unable to distinguish these subtleties.[7] Consequently, before they "cross over" these gaps which encompass a wide spectrum of perceptions and values, they will be duly tormented by conflicts within their own conscience as well as ostracized by both their old and new cultures in various ways.

The Polemic "Crossroads" Syndrome: The story "The Crossroads" (*Lukou*, 1980), from which the title of this collection was drawn, suggests its kinship with this multifaceted displacement and fragmentation faced by overseas Chinese and their families. It is a delightful satire on their shifting patterns of political allegiance and conflicting pledges of ideological commitment.

Indeed, this "crossroads" theme extends throughout the entire collection. Now, more than ever, Chinese-Americans are suffering the burden of living within the triangle of America, China, and Taiwan. Chen Ruoxi uses her protagonists as symbols of these identity crises, and the events that take place in each story represent ideological and social fluctuations that occur as a result of current Chinese political situations and divisions. Confronted with innumerable changes, her characters must somehow endure the confusing maze of situations that arise, and resist the urge to change their political allegiances as the moment dictates; thus, remaining faithful to that in which they believe.

By all accounts, Chen Ruoxi's own life is entwined with this polemic "crossroads" syndrome. Her keen insights into the relationships between character and culture stem directly from her own background. She was born

---

[7] See "On the Other Side of the Pacific" (Xiangzhe Taipingyang bi'an) by Chen Ruoxi, in Li Li, ed., *Haiwai huajen zuojia xiaoshuo xuan, ibid.*, p. 241. The entire story has been translated into English for this collection.

in rural Taiwan, and her family was working class. Excelling in school, she studied for her B.A. in English literature at National Taiwan University and continued in the United States where she eventually obtained her M.A. degree in creative writing in 1965. Now a naturalized American citizen, she has lived and experienced intimately the merging of two distinctive but often conflicting cultures within her own psycho-physical makeup. Motivated by political fervor, she and her husband emigrated to the People's Republic of China in 1966 where she personally witnessed the painful upheavals of the Great Proletarian Cultural Revolution. Completely disillusioned, they expatriated to the West again in 1974. The multiple dimensions of her East-West experiences connect Taiwan, the United States, the People's Republic of China, and Canada, and validate her status as an overseas Chinese-American writer. Her experiences also present us convincing and poignant perspectives on the unique drama of the Chinese-American dilemma.

In a recent interview,[8] Chen explained why she ceased her preoccupation with the painful attestations of "wounded literature" and now concentrates her energy on creating Chinese characters who are affected by the society in which they reside. She stated:

> I am very much interested in writing about Chinese living in American society. I want to write about how they think and live, their attitudes toward their split Motherland, and their problems of readjustment in America in the wake of the traumatic consequences of political chaos. I also intend to write about the scars of survival, the nuance and feeling of personal identity, and the vulnerability and ordinariness of being a Chinese-American.[9]

---

[8]See Yan Huo, *Haiwai huaren zuojia lueying*, ibid., pp. 54-71. Yan Huo's book is one of a series published by the Joint Publishing Company of Hong Kong which has continuously released overseas Chinese writers anthologies during the eighties. They publish books by authors such as Cao Youfang, Chen Ruoxi, Guo Songfen, Li Li, Nie Hualing, Shi Shuqing, Shui Jing, Wang Yu, Yi Li, Yu Lihua, Zhang Cuo, Zhao Shuxia, Zheng Chouyu, and others.

[9] Yan Huo, *ibid.*, p. 69.

Using her writing to act as the conscience of her people, she encourages them to play an effective role, and helps them become aware of the prevalence of their isolation, loneliness, and struggles. Her stories are written in response to the widespread impact of materialism, hypocrisy, and discrimination. In them, Chen illuminates and discusses the ills of society, and suggests alternative scales of value for survival and readjustment to life in America.

Along the same line, Chen also feels strongly about a writer's moral responsibilities. During the First International Chinese-American Women Writers Conference in July of 1989, she urged other writers to pride themselves on a moral depth, beyond the duplicities of sociopolitical realities in writing, since she believes a literary writer is the only voice of moral insurance a society has. It is this notion of "moral insurance" that leads her to write about what is considered some of the most difficult problems her newly immigrated countrymen and women are confronting: the superimposition of an alien culture and the consequent erosion of the indigenous personality; the ambiguous oscillation between the need to leap out and away from their Chinese Motherland: and, what is the reasonable price to pay for the marginality and isolation of living in a foreign land.[10]

It is in this sense that **the ten short stories translated in this collection** assume a high degree of uniqueness, imparting her wisdom in a way that is unforgettable. "The Prologue", a translation of Chen Ruoxi's discussion of "Homeland and New Land" both sets the tone for the following stories translated in this collection, and helps build the conceptual framework within which the nature of her thematic stresses can be comprehended. "The

---

[10]   There are various on-going discussions on overseas Chinese writers and their relationships with the Motherland. For the latest reference, see the special issue, entitled, "Zuixiang de quanyuan--tudi de liange" (The Most Endearing Origin: Romantic Songs of the Native Soil), in *Unitas*, vol. 7, no.3 (January, 1991): 10-61.

Crossroads" and "On the Other Side of the Pacific" were chosen as the opening stories, simply because they serve as the mouthpiece for Chen Ruoxi's own convictions. They exhibit her deep moral and political concerns, her feel for the lives of Chinese-Americans, and the moving, evocative language she uses to convey the existential nature of displacement. The succeeding eight stories focus on different thematic variations such as uprootedness, estrangement, fragmentation and frustration, the search for identity, cultural awareness, liberation, rejection, and assimilation.

Using these stories as the framework, Chen Ruoxi engages us fully as human beings, extending to us through her fiction the conviction and strength she feels as an individual and as an artist. She is a living example that, if we act from within ourselves on what we believe in, the world will progress in a fair and just manner, mending the disjointed lurking within us, and freeing the oppressed without.

PROLOGUE

Chen Ruoxi on "Homeland and New Land"

Editor's Notes:

The following essay appeared in the December 17, 1985 issue of "Dongxifeng" (East-West Wind), a supplement of the Zhongbao (China News), as part of a symposium sponsored by that publication. The topic of the symposium was "The Nativism of Chinese Overseas Writers." The symposium was held at New York City College on December 16, 1985. The participants included: Chen Ruoxi, Zhang Cuo, Yang Mu, Zhang Xiguo, Hong Mingshui, Cong Shu, Li Yu, and Tang Degang. The love and concern displayed by these writers during this symposium, and the sincerity and pertinence of the views they presented, were unforgettable. The following transcript by Chen Ruoxi was part of the proceedings released and published in Chinese by "Dongxifeng." Here it is translated into English for the first time by Hsin-sheng C. Kao.

Homeland and New Land

Writers, like artists, should not be limited by region or nationality. Artistic works are utterly internationalist in content, because they encompass subjects of basic human significance, such as birth and aging, sickness and death, delight and abhorrence, grief and joy; all of which differ but little throughout the world. What literature expresses through language does not fall outside of this universality.

On the other hand, different authors each have their own special characteristics. The most prominent among these is the way a work reflects the social environment in which an author lives or has been brought up. This is what makes for regional color and a sense of locale, that is, for what we are calling "nativism."

As I see it, no work eludes the two attributes of universality and provinciality. Even if it is a space-time leaping science fiction novel, it is no exception. The ratio of universality to provinciality is just greater. Most widespread, however, is the lurking mentality that one ought to "write with Chinese people in mind, for Chinese readers." Many authors hold this to be their sacred duty, and see it as a way of paying homage to their homeland. This sort of peculiarly Chinese sentiment, I believe, is the greatest source of nativism among writers.

Overseas writers are not a national product unique to China, but China is their largest exporter. The unfortunate circumstance of China's long political fragmentation has led a great many writers to take leave of their homeland and take up residence overseas. Most of them have gone to developed countries, and of these, the majority have settled in the United States. Today, in this Symposium on "The Nativism of Chinese Overseas Writers," both subjective and objective aspects of the question can only be considered with certain conditions attached.

Very few overseas writers left China to escape oppression. Most left of their own free will, leaving their homeland and choosing a new land in search of freedom and prosperity. This is the most distinguishing characteristic of Chinese overseas writers.

Whether they left of their own free will or not, these writers deeply miss their homeland and sometimes even feel a sense of guilt. Many writers confess that if it were not to assuage their homesick misgivings, they would never have felt the need to lift a pen to write. In the urge to excavate deeper and deeper, writing for the sake of one's longing for home is perhaps a kind of consolation for the psyche.

There are some writers who settled in the United States in their youth, yet like other middle aged and elderly Chinese-American writers, they harbor that same sense of being a transient visitor there. They have never once tried to break into the English-reading market, never tried to stake out a single spot in the field of American literature. This, of course, is due to various reasons, such as limitations of language.

Certainly to write of familiar scenes, to which one can easily relate, is only natural. Precisely in connection with subject matter, nativism takes on an entirely new layer of meaning. The adopted lands of overseas writers, where they settle down for long periods of time, also become environments of long attachment and gradual familiarity. To use one's present surroundings as the basic material for one's writing is also a logical way to develop a work. It is from this set of circumstances that nativism takes on a double meaning -- nativism for one's homeland on one hand, nativism for one's adopted land on the other. These two meanings constantly intertwine and meld into one another, until they become one. If we take the works of the writers in attendance today as examples, most of them focus on the lives of Chinese-Americans, or critique America from the standpoint of a Chinese emigre. Sometimes, experiences in the United States dominate the work, and experiences from mainland China or Taiwan only provide support; sometimes, it is the other way around.

Being an overseas writer has its advantages and disadvantages. Living abroad, one's field of vision is wider and one's experiences more diverse, but one also faces limitations that are difficult to cope with. The publication, layout and readership of a work form a bottleneck that is hard to break through. The vast majority of publishing firms are located in the homeland, yet a writer who leaves that homeland far behind cannot help but feel cut off from it. No matter how diligently one reads or how often one returns there, the goal of reattachment is beyond reach. The predicament of estrangement may be, I fear, that "It is hard to escape when you are already under siege."

The Crossroads

Editor's Notes:

According to Chen Ruoxi's note in the first draft of "The Crossroads", she completed this novelette in early November of 1979. However, the following month, she received news from Taiwan that many opponents of the Guomindang Party had been arrested and among them were Wang Tuo and Yang Qingshu, native Taiwanese writers. Saddened by this, Chen Ruoxi dedicated this story to these imprisoned writers to show her solidarity. Subsequently, the story was published in the February and March issues of 1980, in Hong Kong's Zhongbao yuekan (Zhongbao Monthly).

Befittingly situated in life's "crossroads," the heroine, Yu Wenxiu personifies the "average" Chinese person, bearing on her shoulders not only the whole of Chinese heritage, but also the burden of many Chinese-Americans who are caught between their loyalty to China, Taiwan, and America. Exploring the divisions that exist between China and Taiwan and the resulting two-pronged obsession with unification and independence, Chen creates a dynamic state of tension and conflict between the individual and political dogma. Mirroring the varied perspectives exploited and politicized by many overseas Chinese during the seventies and eighties, the characters in this story are confronted with the choice of coming to terms with his or her own conscience and taking a stand for what they believe in, or yielding themselves to an apathetic life of hypocrisy and ineffectuality.

16

THE CROSSROADS[1]

Shortly before five, Yu Wenxiu had already changed into an evening dress and put on a pair of stockings; only her shoes remained. She had always loved to go barefoot, even as a little girl. The only time she would wear shoes was when she was going out or receiving guests at home. She arranged her purse, high heels and sweater on the bed. Pulling a chair up to the window, she sat down and looked at the traffic below, taking note of every gray sedan driving toward the crossroads.

Her Auntie's house was situated close to the intersection of a main street and a small road. Wenxiu's bedroom was upstairs facing the southwest corner. Looking out from the bedroom, she had a perfect view of where the roads met.

In this tiny area of the crossroads, the busiest spot was the mailbox. Frequently, cars would stop abruptly, drop off some mail and continue on their way. The "Not A Through Street" sign did nothing to keep the traffic away -- often times cars would mistakenly enter, make a U-turn in the narrow lane, and then speed off impatiently. These hurried, careless drivers never

---

[1] "The Crossroads" (*Lukou*, 1980) was translated by Hsin-sheng C. Kao with the permission of the author and publisher, and is published here in English for the first time. This translation is based on the story in *Chengli chengwai* (Taibei: Shibao wenhua, 1983), pp. 85-146.

gave the lane a lonely appearance.

No matter how often she looked at them, Wenxiu was always fascinated by the lush trees surrounding their house. There were evergreen pines and waxy-looking magnolias, but the prettiest trees were a few dogwoods planted by her neighbor across the street. Their leaves, soaked by the frost, appeared in hues of red and yellow, making the trees look as if they were covered with an abundance of brilliant flowers. No other trees could compare with them. Both sides of the main street were lined with birch trees, so that when one looked down the row, a spectacular panorama of colorful leaves unfolded before the eye.

During the late afternoon rush hour, residents of Silver Springs poured in steadily from their offices in Washington, D.C. The cars moved swiftly, like wind and lighting. Even with the bedroom windows tightly shut, one could still constantly hear the loud noise from the passing cars.

However, the noise of the cars could not surpass the sound of disco music; its nerve racking beat gave Wenxiu an awful headache. Her room was connected to her daughter Ading's room, and although Ading had closed her door to do homework, the volume of the music was still deafeningly loud. How could she do her homework listening to such loud music? Wenxiu was disgusted, but didn't quite know how to deal with her daughter.

Several times Ading had argued defensively, "American teenagers always listen to music while they do their homework!"

She was indeed doing very well in school. Although Ading had only been in the United States for three years, her English had already reached the level of an average English-speaking person. So, Wenxiu really couldn't complain. The only worry she had was the careless way her daughter spoke. Her mouth was always full of chewing gum, and she constantly shook and twisted her body, trying to make herself look more and more like her American peers. This caused Wenxiu some anxiety. She thought that

Taiwanese girls should not be like the others. They should be better.

The golden, resplendent October sunset shone through the glass window onto Wenxiu's face--the rays of the sun were warm, but not burning. They felt as soft as the touch of a baby's finger. After a while, the sunset gradually disappeared, but the warmth lingered on Wenxiu's face.

It reminded her of when she was young. She had snuggled against her mother's bosom on winter afternoons, leisurely watching the cauliflower begin to turn yellow. The feeling of the sun on her face now gave her this same kind of sweet, warm feeling. The only difference was the place. In Taiwan, East Harbor was the kingdom of sunshine. There, both the sky and the earth were even brighter and more splendid than here in Silver Springs.

Her Auntie had warned Wenxiu that winter in the District of Columbia was cold. She and her daughter had just moved here from Houston. When they arrived, spring was so charmingly splendid, and now the autumn scenery was so captivating that it was impossible for Wenxiu to imagine the taste of a bitter cold winter.

After completing her divorce proceedings that summer, she had received a rash letter from her mother urging her to return to Taiwan. Yet, Ading eagerly awaited a white Christmas and Wenxiu herself wanted to see what heavy snow fall looked like. Aside from that, she had met Fang Hao, thus further postponing her departure date.

A silver-gray car drove swiftly in her direction. When it reached the intersection, it suddenly slowed down and made a right turn signal.

As soon as she saw it, Wenxiu stood up in excitement. Putting her face close to the window, she watched the car's every move.

Just as she had expected, the car turned on to her street. Fang Hao was driving. Instead of watching him back the car into the driveway, Wenxiu hurriedly put on her sweater and shoes, and grabbed her purse. When she stood in front of the mirror to examine herself, she realized just how nervous she was.

Almost thirty-five years old...how is it that I still can't restrain my own emotions? Thinking about it, she could not help but feel ridiculous.

She went to see her daughter.

As she pushed the door open, the loud music was suddenly transformed into a dreamy murmur. She had thought that Ading was busy doing her homework, but now, she could not believe what she was seeing. There was Ading, standing in front of the stereo, waving her head, twisting her hips, and shaking her entire body, as if both her heart and soul were submerged in that dreamy, trance-like melody.

Seeing her mother come in, Ading's almond-shaped eyes opened up widely.

"Mommy! Your new dress looks so pretty!"

Still moving, her body twisted right and left with the rhythm of the music. Her headful of long hair swung back and forth to the beat, falling in a scatter over her growing breasts.

Watching her dance so wildly, Wenxiu couldn't help but perceive the stark contrast between now and what she had been like three years ago. Her daughter had worn a China-doll hair style and was bashfully innocent, blushing whenever she met people. Wenxiu suddenly felt her heart sink. Knitting her brows she frowned unhappily.

Mother was right, she sighed, *I should have taken my child back to Taiwan sooner.*

"Ading, can't you lower the volume...."

Remembering that she wasn't taking her daughter with her tonight, Wenxiu felt a stab of guilt. Promptly changing the subject, she said, "Well, alright...leave it on if you want. Have you finished your homework yet?"

Ading nodded, tactfully turning off the stereo. Then, tilting her head, she acted as if she was a fashion expert and appraised her mother's new dress.

It was a blue floor-length dress with white flowers. Its low-cut neck line revealed the lotus-like beauty of her neck. She wore a string of pearls and had combed her headful of long hair into an aristocratic coiffure.

This was very appealing to Ading. In her mind, the ideal noble woman always wore a cloud-like coiffure. "Mommy, is this the dress that Grandma had made for you? Why haven't you worn it before? It's very pretty."

Wenxiu was unable to respond, feeling both pleased and self-conscious with the praise from her daughter.

Before coming to the United States, Ading's father had constantly told her that she should have a few more glamorous evening gowns, so that she could wear them to parties in America. Therefore, she had several gowns tailor-made. Unfortunately, as soon as she arrived, she and her husband began to quarrel for no apparent reason, eventually leading to their divorce. She never had a chance to wear a single one of them.

The night before, Fang Hao had phoned and invited her out for dinner, hinting that he had some good news to tell her. She had thought about it all night, but could not figure out what the good news could be; she finally decided to wear a formal gown as a pleasant surprise for him.

"I'm going to dinner with Fang Hao and will be back soon," Wenxiu said.

Not wanting to disappoint her daughter, she immediately placated her by saying, "Grand Auntie made some fried rice especially for you. You love it, don't you!"

"Oh...," Ading said, making a funny face, "I'd rather have a hamburger."

Looking at her daughter, she could feel a sense of disappointment surge inside her. Swallowing her feelings, she reminded Ading, "Don't forget, we are guests in your Grand Auntie's home. She spent quite a long time cooking, you should feel grateful to her. Don't be too picky tonight, understand?"

As if wanting to get rid of her mother, Ading raised her hands and waved them vigorously, urging her mother out the door, "All right, just go out with your boyfriend and don't worry about me. Have a good time tonight!"

Hearing the word "boyfriend" irritated Wenxiu.

Ading reassured her mother, adding, "Don't worry about me, Mom. It doesn't matter how late you stay out, I don't mind. I'll go to bed early, cross my heart."

"I won't be out too late," Wenxiu repeated and left. Upon returning to her own room, she realized that in her irritation her cheeks had become warm and flushed.

Ding Dong!

The doorbell rang downstairs--*it must be Fang Hao.*

Moving at a more leisurely pace, she went back to her dresser, found a bottle of Parisian perfume, and dabbed some behind her ears, chest and under her arms. Wearing a sweater over her evening gown made Wenxiu feel somewhat like a country bumpkin, so she wrapped a shawl around her shoulders instead. Again, she examined herself carefully in front of the mirror. After making sure that her hair, gown, and jewelry were all in the right position, she turned off the light. Quietly closing the door behind her, she slowly walked down the stairs.

Fang Hao stood at the foot of the staircase, greeting her Auntie.

Seeing her, Fang Hao was indeed pleasantly surprised. His eyes blinked unevenly behind his glasses and his mouth fell open in awe. He obviously wanted to compliment her, but after several attempts, all he could manage to say was "Hi!"

"Fang Hao, how are you?" Wenxiu greeted him with a smile.

She immediately noticed that he too was wearing something out of the ordinary. He was wearing a bluish-gray suit with razor sharp creases; it looked as if it had just come from the cleaners. His sparse gray hair was carefully parted in the middle of his head, but under the pressure of the oil and comb, it drooped down on both sides. His face was red, unlike his usual pale complexion. Wenxiu couldn't tell whether it was because of the wind that whipped around inside his car as he had driven to their house, or if it was simply excitement and happiness.

"Would you like to sit down for a minute?" Wenxiu invited him into the living room.

He glanced at his watch. Then looking at Wenxiu's Auntie, he said, "I'm afraid that the traffic into the city will be horrible."

"You should go early so you won't have to wait in line at the restaurant," Auntie politely urged them to leave.

Fang Hao graciously asked Wenxiu, "Shall we bring Ading with us?"

A feeling of awkwardness immediately washed over Wenxiu. *I thought you only invited me! How can you change your mind like this at the very last minute?*

"Oh, that's not necessary! Why take Ading along to disturb you two! Let her stay home and keep me company," Auntie quickly replied on Wenxiu's behalf.

Fang Hao was a friend of Wu Weixiong, Auntie's daughter Wenjuan's fiance. Last March, Wu Weixiong went to the Beijing Science Institute in China to do research for a year. Before he left, the family members gave him a *bon voyage* party. It was then that Fang Hao and Wenxiu had become acquainted with each other. On one hand, Auntie had always considered herself a good matchmaker, but on the other hand, her age was about the same as Fang Hao's--both of them were over fifty. Therefore, she had never been serious about matching up Wenxiu and Fang Hao, so she still poked fun at him from time to time. However, when she tried to tease him, Fang Hao only gave her a foolish smile, and never dared to talk back.

"Look here," Auntie said, grasping this opportunity to complain to Fang Hao. "Wenjuan went to Beijing and her father went to Taibei. They enjoyed themselves so much that neither of them want to return. I feel like I have such bad luck! It seems as if I'm only fit for house-sitting. And the house is so big, it's frightening during the day, not to mention the evening!"

"I'll come home early, Auntie," Wenxiu immediately injected, trying to comfort her.

"No need, no need!" Auntie objected repeatedly. "You go out so rarely, just relax and have a good time. But, you ought to take a heavier coat with you. It's a lot cooler in the evening and mornings now that it's autumn."

Without paying attention to what Wenxiu was going to say, Auntie insistently stuffed a heavy coat into Fang Hao's arms. Sending them out the door, she examined her niece up and down and silently nodded her head in approval, as if appraising a piece of art work.

Wenxiu was short in height, yet her face was large and round. Imitating Auntie's style, her thick, black hair was combed into a coiffure with a topknot, nesting on her head like a phoenix. By doing so, she had increased her height a few inches. Her willow shaped brows were painted into arched crescents. She wore no other makeup or lipstick. Though slightly pale, her face revealed a kind of dignified elegance.

When she moved in with her Auntie half a year ago, Wenxiu was extremely discouraged by her divorce. She had given up hopes on her appearance and looked despondent, wearing little or no make-up. But thanks to Auntie's advice and guidance, she began to take better care of herself, looking better with each day.

"Divorce is not a novelty nowadays," she continually encouraged Wenxiu. "As long as you keep your eyes open, you can still find a good husband."

According to Auntie, Fang Hao was a good candidate for a husband.

He was sixteen years older than Wenxiu--that could probably be considered a weakness--but he was a professor of economics at the University of Maryland and was a good scholar. Not only that, he was a favorite of the Chinese Embassy and received invitations to go there every two or three days. His social prestige was more than enough to compensate for his seniority. He was also divorced, just like Wenxiu. Although Fang Hao had no children of his own, it seemed that he was quite fond of Ading. Could anyone find a more suitable candidate than he?

Lately, Fang Hao called Wenxiu frequently, and tonight, they were going out again. Auntie looked like an artist enjoying one's own masterpiece, full of pride and self-satisfaction.

It was apparent that Fang Hao was stunned by Wenxiu's appearance. While driving on the highway, his eyes could not concentrate on the steering wheel. They were constantly drawn to Wenxiu's bare neck.

"The dress you're wearing tonight is especially beautiful and the fragrance of your perfume is especially appealing, too," he said admiringly.

His double emphasis on the words "especially" embarrassed Wenxiu. She couldn't believe that her minor tactics could produce such an enormous effect. Wenxiu felt very pleased with herself. She mumbled words of thanks and deliberately looked out the window. Staring blankly, she focused on the thick, dark night that was falling gradually.

"When is your cousin coming back?" Fang Hao asked, quickly changing the subject.

"The day after tomorrow," she replied.

Without invitation, Wenxiu continued, explaining her Auntie's parting complaints, "My Uncle went to Taiwan for the Double Ten Day celebration[2] and was supposed to be back today. But yesterday we received a telegram

---

[2] A national holiday in Taiwan, commemorating the founding of the Republic of China by Dr. Sun Yatsen on October 10, 1911.

saying that he postponed his return until the end of this month. My Auntie has to take care of the hotel herself, but, of course, it's been far too much for her to handle. Recently, I've been helping her with the bookkeeping and banking."

"Great! It's nice that you have an opportunity to use your skills. How's your mother? Has she written to you lately?" Fang Hao asked politely.

Quickly reviving Wenxiu's recent worries, she was reminded of the express letter she had received from her mother. Even now, she still did not know how to respond to it.

"My mother is fine. Lately, all she thinks about is retiring. Her eel-breeding farm has expanded, and she's hoping that I'll go back to take it over," Wenxiu answered.

It was no longer news to Fang Hao that Wenxiu's mother wanted her to return to Taiwan. Yet when she mentioned it this time, she intended to elicit some response from him.

Indeed, this time Fang Hao was different. Knitting his brows seriously, he asked, "Couldn't your mother train a few managers to help her? With such an arrangement, all she would have to do herself is supervise."

"Yes, we already have our Manager Lin's assistance. When I'm not around, he takes care of the supervising and accounting functions. Right now, he's away on a business trip in Japan."

"Oh, so there's no problem," he said conclusively, as if any problems that the Yu family had were already resolved.

It was not the right time to tell Fang Hao that her mother was deeply troubled by their relationship. A while back, her mother was only concerned about her boyfriend's age, insofar as he was a bit too old, and she advised Wenxiu to give their relationship some thought. She also said that Wenxiu should especially take Ading into consideration. When Uncle returned to

Taiwan, he probably described Fang Hao's political background in detail. This must have really scared her mother. Immediately, she sent a letter to Wenxiu and warned her not to get involved in any political entanglements.

"You can't afford to forget the pain even when a wound has healed." Mother repeatedly cautioned her in the letter.

Wenxiu did not want to forget either. As much as she knew that some things were more sensible than others, nine times out of ten practicality didn't change anything; the heart has a mind of its own, too often prevailing over the mind's sensibilities. Take mother and herself for example. From the beginning, neither of them had wanted to get involved with politics and were afraid of their inability to escape from it. Unfortunately, for years, they had both suffered from these kinds of troubles anyway. In this regard, her mother's determination was extremely strong. Wenxiu's father disappeared during a political coup after the restoration of Taiwan from the Japanese. Her mother had resigned from her elementary school teaching post without a second thought and opened an eel breeding farm. She underwent all sorts of hardships and deprivation in order to bring up Wenxiu. She had guided her daughter's studies in accounting in the hope that one day Wenxiu would not only be self-supporting, but could manage her business as well.

Growing up, Wenxiu had relied upon her mother for everything and was determined to devote her life to her. Yet, when she fell in love for the first time, her boyfriend was enthusiastically involved in politics. After their marriage, the dark cloud of politics once again cast a shadow over the Yu family. Her husband went to the United States, and Wenxiu was categorized as a family member of a Taiwanese independence activist. Her situation became very difficult.

For more than ten years, her mother made no complaints whatsoever. However, looking at her mother's gradually acquired deep, knife-like wrinkles, Wenxiu could see the scars of her mother's inner struggles. Even through

Wenxiu's divorce, her mother had not raised a fuss, she only offered her understanding and comfort. She was forever her daughter's solid backbone, an emotional sanctuary.

Because her mother was so kind, Wenxiu now felt especially hesitant when it came to replying to her letter. Sometimes she wondered whether her stubbornness was the cause of her divorce. For Ading, for herself, and especially for her mother, she hoped that in her second marriage--if she still had a chance--she would not repeat the same mistakes. Now, it seemed to Wenxiu that fate was really playing a joke on her, for Fang Hao's passion for politics was no less than that of Ading's father.

"No one is able to exist apart from politics," Fang Hao had tried to persuade her on several occasions. "A lot of people say, 'We don't talk about politics; we don't get involved with politics.' But as a matter of fact, our every word and action has some kind of political implication, the only difference being the degree of that implication."

One thing that perplexed her the most was that in spite of Fang Hao's unattractive, aging appearance, whenever he talked about politics or speculated on China's future, he became a completely different person, both high-spirited and majestic. He attracted her like a magnet. She didn't know if her feelings for him were out of admiration or love. The fine line between the two puzzled her endlessly.

Years ago, Ading's father had also attracted her in the same way.

Unfortunately, she did not understand politics then, and was, for the most part, frightened by it. It was truly ironic that the people she most admired were those involved in politics, people who dedicated themselves to it with ardent devotion. Although she did not agree with the idealogy advocated by Ading's father, she herself still had the same passionate obsession for Taiwan's future and concern for the well being of the people. When she was a college student, she had witnessed the eloquent speeches he delivered from the platform, and more than once she was moved to tears.

Sometimes, she asked herself whether she had fallen in love with him out of some kind of heroic worship. She disagreed with many of his political beliefs, and felt that their own personal habits were not compatible. Nevertheless, she had willingly adorned herself with bridal gown and bouquet, and walked with him down the red carpet. During the six or seven years he had been in exile in the United States, she had suffered because of him, yet she had never complained.

I've made some mistakes too, Wenxiu noted through self-examination. She herself had intensified the glorified image of him within which she had entrapped herself, to the point where she could not escape. It was for this very same reason that when she joined him in America, she could not overcome her surprise and disillusionment, despite many attempts. She found that her "hero" had given up his "ideals" and gone into the real estate business, now motivated by the profits he made from his business transactions. She thought of him as a fallen hero with a tarnished reputation, like a fine singer who was replaced by an unknown in the middle of a song. She was very disheartened.

Her ex-husband once argued fearfully, "You used to be against the Taiwanese Independence Movement. Now that I've given it up, why are you still unsatisfied?"

She stared at him, but did not know what to say.

"A car, a house, a savings account...I have given you everything! Wenxiu, why can't you be satisfied?"

Again, she could not respond.

"We've been separated too long, Wenxiu. I've become a stranger to you."

A stranger....He was correct indeed!

*　　　　*　　　　*

"Wenxiu, what are you thinking about?"

Fang Hao removed his right hand from the steering wheel and lightly placed his arm around her shoulder.

"Oh...nothing," she smiled tenderly, trying to hide her distraction.

"Here we are," he said, withdrawing his arm.

He carefully parked his car alongside the restaurant. The name of the restaurant, "Shimizu Restaurant," was handwritten on a sign in Chinese calligraphy.

"I didn't know you like Japanese food!" Wenxiu stated with some surprise.

"I don't eat it very often," Fang Hao confessed honestly. "I don't know anything about Japanese food. I asked some of my friends, and they recommended this restaurant as one of the best."

He helped Wenxiu out of the car, took her arm in his, and they walked into the restaurant.

"I thought you must enjoy Japanese food. So, as long as you like it, I could eat anything," he continued.

Wenxiu appreciated his thoughtfulness, but didn't have the heart to tell him that she hated Japanese food more than anything. However, she did enjoy the refined decor of the restaurant. With comfortable seats and calligraphy hanging on the wall, it appeared quite refreshing and elegant. Fang Hao had reserved a private room, and a smiling American woman wearing a kimono led them into an area separated by a paper door. Inside the room, a low tea table was on top of a tatami mat; on it, the bowls, chopsticks, and tea cups were neatly arranged. They took off their shoes and jackets, and kneeled down opposite each other across the table.

The waitress brought in some tea, presented them the menu, and left the room, sliding the paper door closed behind her. The tiny room became their private domain.

Wenxiu glanced over the room. There was a painted paper lantern hanging low, illuminating the room with a subtle yellow glow. The picture on the wall depicted a riverside sunrise, its color so transparent that it gave one a feeling of other-worldliness. She felt a strong sense of *deja vu*, and for a moment, she felt as if she were in a sushi restaurant in Taibei.

"Wenxiu, what are you going to have? Why don't you decide for both of us, since you're the expert. I only know that they have good Saki--let's have a bottle!"

Wenxiu could not refuse, and forced herself to order sashimi, some sizzling sukiyaki, and a hot teriyaki dish.

"Please don't blame me if you don't like the dishes I ordered," she warned him ahead of time. "I'm a layman as far as Japanese food is concerned."

Fang Hao flattered her once again by saying, "You're much better at this than I am! After all, I was born in Hubei!"

Wenxiu shook her head, smiling, but did not contradict him.

A lot of people believed that Taiwanese were fond of eating Japanese food, speaking Japanese, and enjoyed Japanese songs and tatami mats. They believed that during fifty years of Japanese occupation, the Taiwanese most certainly must have assimilated Japanese culture. Wenxiu was strongly displeased with these preconceptions. And now it seemed that Fang Hao was no exception, making her feel as if it was impossible to find someone who really understood her.

Yet, could she blame him for it? Some Taiwanese indeed gave others such an impression.

Even now, Ading's father retained some Japanese customs. He believed that cucumbers soaked in licorice were more delicious than salted cucumbers made in the native Taiwanese fashion. He thought that the tight, airless kimonos, which hindered a woman's movement, revealed much more of a woman's femininity than the traditional Chinese *qipao*.[3] Whenever he spoke Taiwanese, he always liked to sandwich in a few Japanese phrases, and if he was in good spirits, he loved to hum Japanese tunes. This "Japanization" was also revealed in the arrangement of his home; a Japanese tea set was positioned in the most elegant manner, and a few tasteful cloth-made banners hung on the kitchen door. Even before the birth of their child, Japanese names had already been chosen--a boy would be named Ken'ichi, and a girl, Machiko.[4] However, all of this was nothing compared to his deep-rooted machismo. This so-called Japanese masculinity had not manifested itself outwardly, that is, not until after they were married.

To her disappointment, she found that several Taiwanese independence activists, with whom she had personal contact, had various degrees of affinity for the Japanese. They intentionally, or maybe unintentionally, embraced their supposed superiority for having assimilated Japanese culture. They even acted superior to those who worshipped popular American fads.

"What are you worrying about?" Ading's father had said without batting an eye, "Culture is a selective process, an assimilation of the good and sometimes a compensation for the bad. Taiwanese culture is regional and needs to be reformed!"

In his view, those who neither spoke Japanese nor appreciated the significance of Japanese products were nothing more than country bumpkins. During the first two years of their marriage, Wenxiu had suspected herself of being too provincial, and she could not help but feel inferior to others. However, over the past few years, Taiwanese regional literature and folk arts had gradually gained prominence. More and more, Wenxiu identified herself

---

[3] *Qipao* is a tight fitting long gown worn by women in China, designed to flatter the female figure. The gown was initially introduced by the Manchus and is considered the national gown.

[4] Ken'ichi and Machiko are typical Japanese names for males and females, respectively. In this story, Yu Wenxiu's daughter's name, Ading, is written using the same characters in Chinese as in the Japanese counterpart, Machiko.

with native pride and felt proud of its growing importance; it gave her a new found sense of comfort.

"Come, Wenxiu, let me make a toast to you!"

The waitress brought in hot Saki and a plate of fruit. Fang Hao quickly poured the wine. He gave Wenxiu a cup, and with both hands he held his own, just like the Japanese do to show the highest respect.

"Following the incident with Chen Yingzhen, you helped me a lot, and I still haven't had a chance to thank you. Let this first toast show you my gratitude."

"That's not necessary, I did what I had to do," Wenxiu responded modestly. Since she was not much for drinking, she only took a sip from her tiny cup.

Fang Hao, definitely more of a drinker, quickly downed his cup of Saki. She immediately poured him another.

"I learned a lot from Chen Yingzhen's case. I have more the reason to thank you," she said.

With sincerity, Wenxiu raised her cup to Fang Hao and drank a mouthful of the wine.

*　　　　*　　　　*

After meeting Fang Hao, their relationship had progressed quickly, especially as of late. During the summer, they started to date here and there, and Ading tagged along on half of the occasions. Fang Hao was very fond of Ading, almost to the point of spoiling her; yet, his attitude toward Wenxiu seemed to be very casual. Wenxiu did not know whether he was acting cautiously or with deliberation. For a while, it felt as if she was suspended in mid-air, giving her surrealistic feelings of anxiety and displacement.

In October, the relationship between Fang Hao and Yu Wenxiu underwent a tremendous change. The main reason was the arrest of an alleged criminal, a Taiwanese writer named Chen Yingzhen.

The night Chen's arrest was announced, she and Fang Hao were having dinner at the Beijing Restaurant. He had put down his chopsticks and immediately called several people long distance to discuss ways to save Chen. At the same time, he notified Amnesty International as well as the Chinese Human Rights Society, and appealed to each of them for help. Wenxiu remembered that when they left the restaurant, he had not eaten a thing.

In less than two days, Chen Yingzhen was released on bail. Since the charge against him was serious and the case still pending, people said business at Chen Yingzhen's advertisement agency had experienced a drastic decline. Because of this, Fang Hao continued to offer his assistance, helping Chen stay secure financially.

Wenxiu knew nothing about literature, nor did she personally know Chen Yingzhen. Although she hadn't read any of his works, she vaguely remembered that he was noted as a very gifted native Taiwanese writer. It so happened that one of her elementary school classmates had recently become a famous writer as well. Through a roundabout course, she obtained her ex-classmate's telephone number and implored him to contact all of the established writers in Taiwan to jointly appeal to President Jiang Jingguo on Chen Yingzhen's behalf.

During this time, she and Fang Hao had contacted each other everyday on the phone. At first they only talked about business, then they discussed some personal matters, and eventually, they talked about almost everything. She had learned more about Fang Hao during the past two weeks than she had in the whole time she'd known him. Fang Hao called her every night before she went to bed. If he called late, she would feel disappointed and lost.

Last night, after they had decided to go out, just a few seconds before she hung up the phone, his low, yet clear voice suddenly said in English, "I love you, Wenxiu."

It was because of these three words that she was unable to sleep well. During the night she dreamed about herself standing at the crossroads, lost, not knowing which road to take. When she woke up, she still had not decided in which direction she should turn....

"Wenxiu, why aren't you talking tonight?"

Fang Hao's tender, concerned query woke her from her brooding. Turning her eyes to him, she quick-wittedly responded, "I'm waiting to hear your good news!"

Fang Hao acted as if he deliberately wanted to create suspense, "There's no hurry, let's eat first! Then I'll tell you."

The waitress brought in the various dishes, one after another. Besides the main courses, each of them had their own salad, rice, and tofu soup. Consequently, the table was entirely covered with dishes and bowls.

Fang Hao was not used to sitting on a tatami mat and was tired of kneeling, but he felt that pulling his legs up was not proper. Wenxiu noticed his uneasiness and asked the waitress to bring him a cushion.

Of all Japanese food, Wenxiu liked sashimi the most, especially at the moment when the scent of the ginger filled her nostrils, giving her a fleeting aroma of pepper and spice. Noticing her eating vigorously, her eyes closed enjoying the hot aroma, Fang Hao moved the sashimi in front of her.

"Having lived in America for twelve years, I have no problem with salad, but as far as Japanese food is concerned, I still can't eat raw fish or raw meat."

"In that case, you should eat the sizzling sukiyaki." Following his example, Wenxiu moved the beef dish in front of him.

Halfway through dinner, Fang Hao finally announced the good news.

"I received a letter from the Chinese Science Institute asking me to do research in China for six months."

"That's wonderful! This is something to really celebrate," Wenxiu exclaimed. She raised her cup feeling sincerely happy for him and again bravely downed a mouthful of Saki.

Naturally, Fang Hao happily drained his cup.

"What kind of research will you be doing?" Wenxiu asked. Not waiting for his answer, she burst out, knowingly, "Does it concern oil exploration?"

Fang Hao proudly nodded his head.

"Now that China is pursuing the Four Modernizations, this field is one of the most popular. The benefits given by the Science Institute are really very good. Besides round-trip airfares and living expenses, various excursions to oil exploration projects in the countryside are also included. I think the best part are these trips to the exploration projects."

Forgetting to eat her dinner, Wenxiu concentrated entirely on his words, her face revealing her awe and admiration.

As far as she knew, this would be his third trip to China within the past five years. During the last two, he had visited the northeastern and southeastern provinces, but had not had a chance to visit the vast areas in the northwest. This time, Fang Hao would have ample time to stay there. Since the Institution was paying for all his expenses, he most certainly would plan on and visit every corner of the region.

Wenxiu was born in Taiwan and had never had a chance to visit mainland China. Taking advantage of this, Fang Hao spent time describing to her the grand and spectacular views of western China: the snow-covered Tianshan Mountain; the raging Nu River; the winding, meandering herds of camels across the vast desert....She had only read about these things in her geography books, yet none of them sounded as attractive and appealing as when described by Fang Hao. She was so enchanted by his descriptive recollections that she felt as if her spirit had unconsciously flown outside to the Hangu Pass. The warm, yellow glow from the paper lantern above her transformed the room into a sandy desert, and the clanking sound of toasting glasses in the next room reminded her of bells on a camel's neck.

It took her a few moments to pull herself back to reality. "When do you plan to go?" she asked.

"Probably the end of November, or early December. The sooner I finish my students' grades, the earlier I'll go. With my six months sabbatical leave plus summer vacation, I could spend nine months in China," he answered.

Wenxiu never thought he would leave so soon, and for a moment she was dumbfounded. To hide her disappointment, she immediately stuffed a piece of sashimi into her mouth; but, except for its coldness, it had suddenly become tasteless.

I've only known him for six months, and soon we'll be separated for nine....

Her regretful sentiment now could only be swallowed along with the cold sashimi.

I can only blame it on my ill fate, she thought. Through the beginning years of her first marriage she had lived a separate life in Taiwan, away from her ex-husband; during the past two years, she had suffered through her divorce. Only now had her broken heart finally been healed. She was just congratulating herself on the fact that she had met Fang Hao, a good teacher and friend whom she could really trust. Who would have known that he would go so far away? Recalling him describing the scenery outside the Hangu Pass, she couldn't help but notice his overjoyed spirit. He was so excited that he could not even keep his glasses on, he had taken them off and thrown them aside onto the tatami. His heart probably had already flown to that far-away land--an entirely strange place for her, a place where she could probably never go.

Suddenly, the surrounding objects in the room were whirling around her, and the tiny room became barren and desolate.

Abruptly, Fang Hao stopped talking and stared at her intensely. Her incapacity to drink was quickly revealed by the few sips of Saki she had drunk. Her face was red and flushed. When she realized that she was being observed so closely, the redness spread to her ears.

"Wenxiu, you look exactly like a Japanese painting of a beautiful woman. Your face is like a full moon and your brows like spring water...."

"Rubbish!" Wenxiu broke out in laughter upon hearing his words.

Excited by her smile, Fang Hao reached out and grasped her hand. Gently, he asked, "Do you want to go to China with me?"

To China? Again, she was stunned.

"How could I go to China?"

"As my better-half," he answered in English.

She felt that he was teasing her and could not help but cast a charming glance at him. Yet the look on his face was not vague at all, but that of passionate expectation and composed self-confidence. She was baffled--*is this a marriage proposal*? The hand he was holding was warm and sweaty; Wenxiu could hear her own heart beating, and felt a nagging feeling of disappointment well up inside her.

"I've never been to the mainland...nor have I thought of going," she whispered kindly, not wanting to deliberately avoid giving him a direct response, the mainland just seemed too foreign to her.

The tenderness with which she spoke gave Fang Hao encouragement. He coaxed her, "You just come with me, there will be no problem whatsoever. Take my word for it!"

Before he completed the sentence, he had anxiously moved his body next to Wenxiu's, surrounding her waist with his arm. Wenxiu did not resist, instead, she moved closer to him and tenderly rested her head on his shoulder.

"If you like, we could get married in Beijing," he said.

His sweet words, mixed with the strong smell of alcohol, wafted into her ear.

Marriage? Oh, how unexpected! Wenxiu almost could not catch up with her thoughts--it felt as if her thinking machine had gone awry and momentarily refused to function. She thought of her mother and daughter, but was so confused that at the moment she didn't know what anything meant to her anymore.

"You need not answer me now, Wenxiu. I can wait for you until December."

His consideration and tenderness was irresistible. Wenxiu voluntarily withdrew her defenses and threw herself completely into his arms. Amidst the kisses, she lovingly closed her eyes. Without thinking, without resistance, she allowed her body to float up and down, like a piece of seaweed buffeted by the rise and fall of cascading foamy waves.

Suddenly, the paper door slid open. The intrusion of the waitress startled them both. Wenxiu struggled out of Fang Hao's embrace and was too embarrassed to raise her head. Although it appeared that Fang Hao did not mind, for a moment he could not find his glasses and groped around for them clumsily.

The waitress, seemingly used to this kind of scene, smiled and asked her patrons, "Do you have enough food? Is there anything else I can get you?"

"The food was delicious! May we have the check please?"

Wenxiu fixed her hair, and after Fang Hao paid the bill, they put their shoes on and left the restaurant.

"We're in Bethesda, near my house. How about stopping by my place?"

Sounding as if he were afraid of rejection, he immediately pleaded in a pleasant voice, "Let's go there, I'll make you a good cup of coffee."

"Alright," she answered.

Although she was somewhat hesitant, she responded in a straightforward manner. She remembered her promise to Ading, and now, she wondered when she would be able to get home once she went to his place. Yet she did not want to ruin Fang Hao's high spirits. It was such a lovely night that she could not bring herself to leave him.

In the car, Fang Hao indulged in conversation about his trip to China. He planned on the assumption that they would go together and talked about plans for their honeymoon. Wenxiu was light-headed, and told herself more than once: *The mainland! I'm going to mainland China, too!*

"Please don't go back to Taiwan," he said.

Having finished his imaginary tour of the mainland, Fan Hao suddenly turned his head around to advise Wenxiu, "Right now, Taiwan isn't even as democratic as China. Take the Xidan Democracy Wall, for example, big-character posters[5] cover everything and an abundance of private magazines can be found everywhere. Democracy, law, and even the socialist system all are coming together to be discussed publicly."

For many years, Wenxiu had listened to the accusations against the Taiwanese government and almost believed that they were true. However, the last few years, her understanding of the mainland had also increased. She could not help but compare the two, "I've heard that many people died because of the Cultural Revolution, isn't that right?"

"That's a dead issue now," Fang Hao said, summing up the issue in one short sentence. He continued, "The Communist Party has the courage to recognize its mistakes. If they wrongly condemned someone, they'll clear the

---

[5] *Dazibao*, a term referring to posters or articles written with a Chinese brush in large characters, at least three inches or more, on newspaper or colored paper. They are posted on the wall for the purposes of public criticism, attacking the government, and criticizing the ills of society.

person from the wrong accusation publicly. They have the guts to do that."

Wenxiu could not rebuke him. After all, Fang Hao had lived in Taiwan for more than ten years. He had even written articles for the *Free China* magazine. Moreover, he had been back to the mainland twice recently. He was a famous scholar! His analysis and comparison couldn't be wrong, could it?

She was quiet the rest of the way to his house. It was not until they arrived that she modestly expressed her attitude, "The reason I want to go back to Taiwan is not because it's better or worse than the mainland. If I go back, it's because it's Taiwan, my native country."

"Of course, of course," Fang Hao agreed, his tone mixed with admiration.

His two-bedroom apartment was the most Chinese-looking apartment Wenxiu had ever seen in America. Chinese paintings hung on the wall in his study and living room; imitations of porcelains and enamels from the Tang and Qing dynasties were spread out all over his coffee table and bookshelves. A scarlet oriental rug from Tianjing and several delicately carved ivory objects were a few of the many gifts he had brought back from his visits to China. There were newspapers and magazines that had been published in China laying everywhere, overwhelming the eyes, surely enough to form a small library.

"Is the decor O.K.?" Fang Hao seemed proud of himself. "Jenny...during the time right after my divorce from Jenny, I only had a toothbrush and a few pieces of clothing. These are things I have accumulated over the past few years."

"It's marvelous! The place looks like a museum!"

Wenxiu intended to compliment and comfort him at the same time. This was the first time she had ever heard him mention his ex-wife. According to her cousin, his ex-wife was a white woman who fell in love with one of his students, then cruelly kicked him out. Comparing her heart to his, Wenxiu believed that he certainly must have been deeply hurt, thus she dared not reopen his wound.

"Are you hot? Do you want to take off your sweater? I'll turn up the heater for you."

Listening to his contradictory words, Wenxiu just smiled forgivingly, her lips sealed. She took off her sweater and high heels, and walked back and forth over the thick, soft rug. Its warmth was soothing to her feet and even to her heart.

Fang Hao turned up the heater and took off his jacket and tie. Then, pulling her into his arms, he kissed her with the force of a raging storm. His roughness and the heavy smell of alcohol pressed on her so intensely that she could hardly breathe, and his angular glasses jabbed her neck.

"Please, can we wait a while?" she whispered in his ear. "Let me make some coffee for you first."

"O.K." he agreed, holding her for a moment longer before unwillingly letting her go.

"Do you mind if I browse through your newspapers?" she asked

"No, go right ahead," Fang Hao responded immediately.

She knew that both coffee and newspapers were important aspects of his life, and that he could not go for a day without them. She also knew that, most of all, he preferred honey in his coffee. Out of curiosity, she started to inspect his kitchen while she waited for the water to boil. She opened the cabinet above the oven and found five or six different brands of honey there, just as she had expected. Inside another cabinet were a dozen or so bottles of vitamins, Chinese-made honey jelly, kidney supplements, and other miscellaneous items. She never knew Fang Hao was such a health nut.

"How could that be? Fifteen years!" she heard Fang Hao say to himself in English as she brought the coffee into the living room.

"What's the matter?" she asked.

Holding the *Washington Post*, he kept shaking his head, and said, "Wei Jingsheng[6] was tried in the Beijing Court and was sentenced to fifteen years! It's crazy!"

"Isn't he the one who edited an underground magazine?"

"Right, he was the editor of *Explore*."

Wenxiu sat on the sofa side by side with Fang Hao, drinking coffee and listening to him describe the entire affair.

It was said that Wei Jingsheng had come from a cadre family. He was a Red Guard during the Cultural Revolution and went to the countryside. Afterwards, he became a member of the People's Liberation Army, and most recently, he was an electrical worker at the Beijing Zoo. He had edited magazines, written big-character posters, appealed for social reform, and publicly advocated the "Five Modernizations," of which he listed democratic freedom as the fifth and most important. Last March, his public criticism of Premier Deng Xiaoping's suppression of freedom of speech resulted in his arrest. For about half a year, no one heard anything about him. Now, all of a sudden, he was being sentenced to fifteen years in prison for the crimes of counter-revolutionary activity and secret collaboration with foreign countries.

Wenxiu did not understand, "What is this 'collaboration with foreign countries'?"

"It was said that he sold military secrets to foreign countries. He was accused of discussing the Sino-Vietnamese War with foreign news reporters, and listing the names of the commanders and the number of casualties. Actually, these things are not military secrets. The Chinese government itself had publicly talked about them."

---

[6] He is the most well-known Chinese dissent-worker who advocated democracy in China during the 1970s. He was arrested in 1979, and his edited underground magazine *Explore (Tansuo)* was prohibited from publication around the same time. Subsequently, he was sentenced to fifteen years of imprisonment.

Fang Hao's expression was indignant at the thought of this injustice, and Wenxiu was surprised.

"Are these false accusations? Fang Hao, I thought you said that China is undergoing the 'Four Modernizations' and widely advocates the freedom of speech?"

Fang Hao looked dejected, he had high hopes for the Democracy Wall, and now he felt it difficult to justify his previous statement. It was as if someone had thrown a bucket of cold water in his face. Embarrassed, he scratched his head. The carefully combed hair had already lost its shape throughout the course of the evening. Now his hair was as topsy-turvy as a pile of hemp.

"A sentence like this is really bad," he sighed regretfully. "The impact will be self-defeating. During this past year, civilian-sponsored magazines and big-character posters became the banners for a China marching towards democracy. At first they arrested Fu Yuehua, now they've sentenced Wei Jingsheng. If they don't act properly, they're going to kill the very root of democracy!"

"Who is this Fu Yuehua?"

Fang Hao did not want to say anything about her at first. Forcefully, he shook his head, and said, "That girl's guts have really driven her to the point of acting recklessly."

Fu Yuehua was a young intellectual who had been sent to labor in the countryside. Because of her sympathy toward the people who were suffering from extreme poverty, she went to Beijing to appeal to the authorities. She acted and wrote on their behalf, hung big-character posters to demand basic human rights, and, consequently, was arrested.

"That's terrible! Fang Hao, people are being arrested, right and left!" Wenxiu exclaimed, her crescent shaped brows arched into the shape of a half-moon.

44

From the bottom of her heart, she sympathized with these two suffering compatriots, especially Wei Jingsheng, who was sentenced to prison.

"You should rescue him, Fang Hao. Can't you protest to the Chinese government?"

"Em...." he said, looking troubled. "First, I have to exchange ideas with everyone. You should know that the mainland does not care about public opinion as much as Taiwan does. Taiwan talks about democracy and freedom, but mainland China is a dictatorship of the proletariat, clearly a dictatorship!"

Feeling somewhat depressed, Wenxiu suddenly remembered that Fang Hao admired Premier Deng Xiaoping the most. She shouted out as if she had found a light at the end of the tunnel, "That's what you can do--you can protest to Deng Xiaoping!"

"Protest to Deng Xiaoping?!" he repeated, stunned by her words. Then his frowning brows clouded, his expression was completely beyond her comprehension.

"How about appeal...," she immediately changed her wording.

According to her own simple, logical analysis, appeals by the leftists seemed like they would be the most effective. "Fang Hao, you know quite a few well-known leftists, don't you?" she asked eagerly, providing him with suggestions. "There are the Nobel Laureate scholars and famous writers. A handful of you could jointly send a telegram or letter to him. I'm sure Deng would read it!"

Fang Hao nodded with extreme difficulty, "Oh, I could try it...though I don't know everyone that well. How about this, let me contact them by phone first."

"Wonderful!" Wenxiu applauded in her excitement. "How about calling them now?!"

"Now?" Fang Hao looked straight at her, somewhat hesitantly.

"Oh, I forgot about the time....What time is it?" Wenxiu privately regretted acting so impatiently. Trying to compensate for her hastiness, she deliberately took his wrist in her hand and looked at his watch. *Ten thirty. Actually it's getting late, its still quite a distance from here to home. It wouldn't be wise if my daughter stayed up waiting for me.*

"Take your time calling. Fang Hao, I think I should be going now."

Even though she was holding his hand, and speaking softly and tenderly, she still could not dissolve the disillusioned expression on Fang Hao's face. He was silent; the silence itself was probably a form of complaint, protesting a warm and beautiful evening that had now been spoiled.

On the way home, neither of them wanted to talk. Just as they were parting, Fang Hao reminded her again, "I'll be waiting for your answer."

Climbing up the stairs, she heard the television from her Auntie's room. Holding her shoes, she quietly entered her bedroom.

Before turning on her light, she caught a glimpse of light coming from under Ading's door. *That girl hasn't gone to bed yet!* Being her mother, she felt a stab of guilt. For an instant, she thought of going in to say something, but the light was suddenly extinguished. She stood numbly in the dark for a moment, and then turned on the light in her room.

*   *   *

Two days later, Wenjuan came back from Beijing. She had left carrying only one small suitcase, but returned with a number of large and small ones. When she saw her mother and cousin, Wenxiu, she started to complain about how difficult it was to travel with all these suitcases, and that she wished she had two extra hands to carry them.

"These are all gifts! In the airport, Wu Weixiong bought more bags of dried Beijing dates. I had to grip them in my teeth to carry them!"

Helping her carry a heavy pigskin suitcase, Wenxiu could not help but ask, "Wenjuan, what kind of things did they give you?"

"Well, various local products. Some are souvenirs, not too practical in America," Wenjuan replied.

"How's Wu Weixiong?" Wenxiu asked her.

"What are his plans?" Auntie pressed her daughter. "He doesn't intend to stay there long, does he?"

Wenjuan scowled and shrugged her shoulders.

"Talk about Wu Weixiong! He's really successful there! People treat him like a guest, so his life is very comfortable. As for myself, the mainland's a nice place to visit, but I wouldn't want to live there! Oh no, not me! Nor does Wu Weixiong have such a plan. Next year, he'll be able to apply for an American citizenship; he'll never forego such a chance," she said dramatically, trying to give the impression she was acting according to her own whims.

As a member of the Taiwanese Athletic Delegation, Wenjuan went to Beijing in September to attend the Fourth National Sports Meeting. Though she knew nothing about sports, the Chinese Propaganda Bureau still welcomed her because her fiance was considered patriotic. Because of this, Wenjuan was able to see her fiance and visit many famous sights. The delegation had also been granted an audience and a reception by high-ranking officials of the Chinese Communist Party. Wenjuan never before had such an honor. Talking about this, she appeared extremely proud and satisfied, beaming with happiness.

"Mom, if there's a chance, you and Dad should visit the mainland. Wenxiu, you should also go there!"

Wenxiu opened her mouth in joy, but refrained from saying anything. She did not want to carelessly reveal her secret before she made up her mind. Since she was still hesitant about Fang Hao's marriage proposal, she spoke ambiguously about visiting China, "Of course, I'll consider it, if it's a free trip."

Auntie beamed, all smiles, and agreed immediately. The only worry she had was that once she visited the mainland, she was afraid she'd never be allowed to go back to Taiwan.

"I constantly think of returning to Taiwan to see my sister and offer incense to the Goddess of Mercy. I'd really like to chat with my relatives and old neighbors. All these things are far more important than seeing famous sights," she said.

"Then you don't have to worry," Wenxiu told her Auntie. "Fang Hao said that mainland China is very cooperative in this respect. They won't stamp your passport. Instead, they will attach another form to it."

"Really?" Auntie was really becoming excited now. "How about this? Why don't we have your father go there first and then we'll see what happens."

"What a coincidence!" Wenjuan said to her mother enthusiastically. "I heard that next spring, they're going to organize a basketball team to tour China. I'll call right away to register Dad. Most importantly, we need to have Wu Weixiong write a recommendation letter, his references are most effective!"

"Let my uncle join...a basketball team?" Wenxiu asked incredulously.

She felt it was improper. It was already quite absurd for her cousin to have visited China as an athlete and it would be very out of line for a businessman over sixty years old to pretend to be a ball player.

"My goodness, who would care about that! He would be just a name on a list. Do you think he's really going to play basketball? Don't be such a square, Wenxiu!" explained Wenjuan.

"Then you should write a letter soon," said Auntie, suddenly impatient, hoping that her daughter would write the letter immediately.

"Let me get some rest first. I still have jet-lag. Right now, I can't tell night from day."

Wenjuan slept the whole day.

The next morning, after sending Ading to school, and while Auntie went out to take care of some hotel business, Wenxiu brought a coffee pot and some crackers to Wenjuan's room. Her cousin was still lying down, completely covered by her quilt. Seeing Wenxiu come in, she struggled to sit up, yawning at the same time.

Wenjuan had a beautiful set of French furniture--a pink wooden bed with four posts holding up a charming, sensual canopy, and a dresser and vanity ensemble, all the same color. The floor was covered with soft cushions made of down. Whenever Wenxiu walked in, she could faintly smell a warm and lustrous fragrance so enthralling that it made her intoxicated to the point of feeling bloated.

She handed the tray to her cousin and opened the curtains and window. Afterwards, she found a cushion and sat by the head of the bed.

Wenjuan sat up, drinking coffee and eating. She must have been very hungry, because she completely devoured all of crackers in a very short time.

"Why don't you let me make you a couple slices of toast?" Wenxiu asked.

"Please don't," Wenjuan waved her hands to stop her. "I have to go on a diet. I ate too much in Beijing and gained four pounds."

Wenxiu teased her, "Why do you want to slim down? After all, Wu Weixiong isn't here, so don't be too hard on yourself. When are you going to see your sweetie again?"

"We can't talk about this openly, but as soon as he comes back next February, we're going to get married. This is our secret, Wenxiu; I haven't even mentioned it to Mom."

Deeply touched by Wenjuan's trust in her, Wenxiu nodded her head. Her cousin had searched for a husband for several years, yet none of the men she met were satisfactory. Finally, she was engaged to Wu Weixiong, but sometimes she still flew off the handle at him. Wenxiu never thought that Wenjuan would become so determined after her return.

"Have you and Weixiong already decided?"

"If we don't decide now, who knows what is going to happen?"

Wenjuan tilted her headful of messy hair, and shrugged her half-bare shoulders in resignation.

"After all, people's feelings are always like this. When he was here, I always criticized him; now that he's away, I miss him--missing him is a good sign. Besides, if I don't marry him, what am I going to do? Rather than be satisfied as a typist for the rest of my life, it's better for me to grab this chance to become a professor's wife. Don't you agree?"

Wenxiu could not respond.

Wenjuan did not wait for her opinion. Straightening her hair, she continued, "It isn't good to be separated for too long, because your feelings would certainly be affected. I'm sure your divorce was caused by the prolonged separation between you two. As far as men are concerned, a woman has to grab one and not let go. Wenxiu, let me tell you something in all honesty. Beijing women are not as bashful as Taibei's--they'll break their necks trying to marry any student who's returned from studying in the United States."

"Really? As far as that goes, it's the same situation in Taiwan. Women in Taiwan aren't that bashful anymore either, and ultimately quite a few marriages are broken up because of it."

"Just wait and see," Wenjuan predicted. "Everything that Taiwan has, eventually, the mainland will have too! Good things and bad things, just the same."

Wenxiu sighed slightly. She did not know whether this trend would be good or bad for the Chinese people. She wanted to know more about the mainlanders' thoughts and feelings, yet Wenjuan could not offer her the insight she wanted.

"Our schedules were so tightly arranged, how could I find time to visit others!" Wenjuan told her. In the middle of her complaint, her eyes suddenly sparkled, "There was only one exception. Wu Weixiong took me to dinner at the home of a friend from his hometown. We ate fried rice noodles, turnips and pickled vegetable soup. It wasn't bad at all."

"What did they talk about most of the time?"

Without a second thought, her cousin immediately replied, "Xidan's Democracy Wall."

"Did they read any privately printed articles, or talk about a case involving someone named Yuehua?"

"You mean Fu Yuehua, a woman?"

"That's her!"

As soon as Fu Yuehua's name was mentioned, Wenjuan enthusiastically told some stories that she had heard. It was said that when Fu Yuehua was arrested, the most serious and embarrassing charge against her was that she had slept with foreigners, and, consequently, she had been suspected of conspiring with foreign countries. After hearing of the charges, foreign specialists were very angry, and together they wrote to the Department of Public Security in protest, demanding that they name the person who had slept with her. After receiving the threatening letter, the Department of Public Security immediately withdrew the allegations against Fu Yuehua.

Wenxiu frowned in disbelief.

"Here comes the juicy part!" Wenjuan continued. "When they tried her for falsely accusing a high-ranking official of raping her, this same official went to court to be a witness. Fu Yuehua said that if they didn't believe her story, they should just check the scars on the official's back. He was really taken aback and even the judge lost his composure. The trial could not be continued. Finally, the court was adjourned and her sentencing postponed. This woman isn't naive, is she?"

"That's strange! She was arrested because of her petitions on behalf of the farmers and workers. How could she be charged with anything concerning her private life?"

"Who knows? After all, a woman's lot is hard!" Wenjuan said, making a gesture of disgust with her hand. She told Wenxiu matter-of-factly, "When I was in Beijing, I also heard people talking about Madame Mao's decadent private life. They said she had kept several men for herself. Evidently, this old lady was a tigress in bed! It's up to you, you can believe whatever you want!"

Wenxiu shook her head and forced a smile onto her face.

A few moments later, she asked Wenjuan, "Did anyone mention anything about Wei Jingsheng?"

"Of course. I can vaguely remember that he advocated 'Five Modernizations' and made the criticism that the 'Four Modernizations' were not enough, or not good....I don't understand. You know, whenever I hear people talking about politics, I always feel like I'm getting a headache! Anyway, I did hear Wu Weixiong and his friends say that they also believe that China needs five modernizations. As far as I know, they all agree with the idea. Yet their agreement has nothing to do with Wei Jingsheng, for he was already arrested."

"He was sentenced to fifteen years."

"That's too severe!" Wenjuan gasped sympathetically. Using her own logic, she continued, "He was also charged with collaboration with foreigners, wasn't he?"

"How did you know that?"

"Fu Yuehua was accused of the same thing. My goodness, there are so many foreigners! Each and every person has an opportunity to get involved with a foreigner. One can easily round up a dozen people who have been arrested on the same charge"

"That can really cause harm to people!" Wenxiu sighed deeply, and felt her heart sinking.

Smiling, Wenjuan suddenly asked, "Wenxiu, let me ask you something. Why are you so interested in mainland China all of a sudden?" Watching Wenxiu blush, she broke out in laughter.

"I know! Fang Hao has already converted you into a devoted leftist!"

"Nonsense!" Wenxiu replied, giving her a dirty look. "What are you talking about, leftist or rightist?"

Wenjuan was not willing to let the topic go easily. She quickly climbed down from her bed and sat beside Wenxiu, giving her an affectionate hug.

"What's up? I bet Fang Hao has been pursuing you energetically!"

Wenxiu smiled, but did not deny it. Since her cousin insisted on hearing about things in more detail, she responded evasively, "He hasn't used many of Wu Weixiong's tactics, such as sending you flowers and taking you out dancing all night."

Wenjuan's smile was sweeter than honey. She comforted Wenxiu, "Don't worry about that. Fang Hao is not twenty years old. Of course he has to act in a more mature manner. I think he matches you quite well, even though he is seventeen years older than you..."

"Sixteen," Wenxiu immediately corrected Wenjuan.

"Oh, I'm sorry, it's sixteen years," Wenjuan apologized, hugging her again.

"He's relatively well-known in China, did you know that? Wu Weixiong told me that the last time Fang Hao visited China, they reprinted his article 'Current Research,' which he had written after his return to the States. If you marry him, I'm ninety percent sure you could visit China for free!"

Several times, Wenxiu wanted to tell her about Fang Hao's proposal; yet, when the words were on the tip of her tongue, she restrained herself. Instead, she insisted that because of her recent divorce, she preferred to act cautiously, so that she didn't repeat the same mistakes.

"Did you know that Fang Hao is going to China again?"

She told Wenjuan about the invitation from the Chinese Science Institute.

"Wonderful! Wu Weixiong gave me something to give him. Let's have him over for dinner to congratulate him. Maybe later we'll be able to squeeze an expensive meal out of him! I'm going to ask Mom."

Auntie loved guests and was happy to have Fang Hao over. After some discussion, the three of them decided to serve crab as the main dish. It was Fang Hao's favorite.

* * *

After learning about Wei Jingsheng's sentence, Wenxiu started to read the English-language newspapers carefully. Considering that the daily *Post* was not enough, she asked Ading to buy the *Evening Star* on her way home after school. That day, she read an article, stating that the Soviet scientist, Andrew Sakharov, had already sent a telegram to the Chinese Communist leaders on Wei Jingsheng's behalf, and that the International Humane Organization had also issued a protest to the Chinese government. She felt a great sense of relief. Now that foreigners were publicly expressing their concerns, Chinese descendants would certainly not fall too far behind.

That night, Fang Hao called again. She told him of Auntie's invitation. Fang Hao accepted with great relish, assuring her that he would be able to come on Saturday.

"Fang Hao, how's Wei Jingsheng's case coming along? Is everything progressing smoothly?"

Her questions evoked a sigh.

"I'm afraid this matter is too difficult to deal with. I called one professor twice, and both times he wasn't there. Later, his assistant informed me that he definitely wouldn't appeal to the Chinese leaders, not to mention issue a protest."

"Oh...." Wenxiu gasped in astonishment, sounding completely rejected.

"Another one also didn't want to get involved. He said he didn't care about politics."

"Then what does he care about?" she asked bluntly.

"Wenxiu, you shouldn't blame them," Fang Hao said defensively. "These people all care about the 'Four Modernizations,' and they often go to China to give lectures. Needless to say, they have worked hard on helping China speed up its modernizations in science and technology!"

Wenxiu continued earnestly, "But, if the Chinese people don't have democracy and freedom, will science alone be sufficient?"

"Please, Wenxiu, don't be so pessimistic! We can't demand too much from the scientists."

She was about to protest when Fang Hao's deep voice came through the receiver again, calming her with his words, "Don't be discouraged Wenxiu, I'll contact some other people. I'll look for some writers, they're more passionate. There shouldn't be any problem for them to write a joint letter of appeal. However, you've got to give me some time because I have to find their phone numbers. As soon as I have any news, I'll let you know."

Again, he said a few kind parting remarks and then hung up the phone.

At that time, Ading, already in her pajamas, came to say good-night to her mother.

"Mommy, wasn't that Fang Hao who just called?"

"Yes."

"He talks like a Communist."

"Nonsense!"

Though Wenxiu frowned in an effort to scold her daughter, she was inwardly amused.

"Ading, do you know what a Communist is?"

The girl shrugged her shoulders and made a face.

"He likes China, he's Chinese."

"Not every Chinese is a Communist. For example, I'm Chinese, but I'm not a Communist. Your Daddy isn't either," Wenxiu explained patiently.

"We're not Chinese," Ading countered, looking quite seriously at her mother. "We're Taiwanese. Daddy said so!"

Wenxiu stared at her daughter, not knowing how to react to her daughter's statement. She almost wanted to say out loud, "Yes, but your Daddy doesn't want to be Taiwanese any more! Now all he does is concentrate on being an American--an American businessman!"

Looking at her daughter's naive, innocent face, she controlled her temper. Instead, she said, "Ading, it doesn't matter whether we're Chinese or Taiwanese. The most important thing is to be a good person. Our ancestors came from China, isn't that correct?"

"So what! Who cares whether they came from China," Ading seemed unmoved.

"Don't you want to visit China? China is huge--there is the Great Wall, the Palace Museum...."

"Maybe I'll go there later, but now I'd rather go back to Taiwan and visit Grandma."

Helpless, Wenxiu knew that she could not sway her daughter's opinion in such a short period of time. Yet Ading's love for her Grandmother always aroused Wenxiu's mutual feelings of love for her mother. She held Ading in her arms and kissed her little face again and again.

"Certainly we'll go back to Taiwan. Now go to sleep, my darling."

          *   *   *

The next Saturday Fang Hao arrived at six o'clock sharp.

He brought two bottles of champagne for Auntie, and a box of Ading's favorite chocolates. Looking at the chocolate, Wenxiu was worried. Ading was already getting a little chubby. What's going to happen if she keeps on eating chocolates? She hinted at this several times, yet Fang Hao did not pay any attention and continued to spoil Ading.

Wenjuan bought two dozen Chesapeake Bay crabs. Auntie prepared several dishes and a thin oyster noodle soup. Before the main dishes were brought out, they ate crab meat and drank champagne.

Fang Hao raised his glass to toast Auntie, "Thank you for this wonderful crab dinner!"

"Congratulations on your invitation to Beijing," Auntie returned his toast.

"Fang Hao, this is great news, you should celebrate!" Wenjuan urged, hoping to use this opportunity to get him to take them out later.

"I certainly will, I certainly will!" Fang Hao promised Wenjuan, while at the same time staring unwaveringly at Wenxiu. Tilting his head back, he emptied his glass.

"A toast to the far-away Wu Weixiong!" exclaimed Wenjuan, thinking of her fiance, and everyone followed her example, making a toast to him.

"Bottoms up for Wei Jingsheng!"

Since everyone knew Wei Jingsheng's name by now, all of them responded enthusiastically after Wenxiu announced her toast. Even Ading raised her glass of Coca-Cola.

Eating crab was a very messy business with all the hammers, tongs and various other devices needed to perform the task. Wenxiu was too busy helping Ading strip her crab shell to talk with others. Wenjuan was talkative by nature, so she talked non-stop as she ate. She spoke of many things she had experienced and learned during her stay in Beijing, and also mentioned the Democracy Wall. Fang Hao listened attentively, making no response.

"Professor Fang," Wenjuan suddenly changed the subject, focusing directly on him, "I heard that you're going to write a letter to Premier Deng, is that right?"

"Uh...," with a mouthful of crab meat, Fang Hao could not speak. Instead, he just shook his head lightly.

Wenxiu immediately answered for him, "It's not only him writing the letter, he is organizing several other writers to write it jointly."

Finally, Fang Hao swallowed his food, but he was still shaking his head.

"Forget that," he told Wenxiu, not daring to look at her directly.

"What happened?" Wenxiu's surprise was greater than her disappointment. "Are they afraid?"

"They all said they didn't know the real circumstances, so they didn't want to write too hastily. To sum it up briefly, they didn't want to get politically involved."

"I hate politics, too!" Wenjuan exclaimed loathingly, tossing aside an empty crab leg at the same time.

"If someone really wrote to Deng, do you think he actually would get the letter?" Auntie asked, her question directed at no one in particular. None of them responded; except for the empty cracking sound of metal tongs squeezing the crab legs, the room was silent.

Wenxiu noticed that Fang Hao had lowered his head and was concentrating on prying the crab meat out of its shell. His face was gentle and content, as if the whole thing had nothing to do with him anymore. When Chen Yingzhen was arrested, not too long ago, this same face had been filled with enormous rage. She could not understand why he responded so differently to these same types of incidents. Thinking of this, her temper reached its boiling point.

"I never did like politics," she said angrily. Speaking her peace of mind once and for all, she continued, "Here is someone who was thrown into jail because he spoke out on behalf of others. What does it have to do with politics if you say a few words on this man's behalf? If this is politics, then what about the scholars who were received by the chairman or the premier when they visited mainland China. Their pictures were printed in the newspapers--isn't that more political? And, when they returned to the States, they lectured everywhere, giving reports and writing articles praising the accomplishments of China. Now, can't this be considered political as well?"

No one disputed her. Ading, who only half understood, asked innocently, "Mommy, why are you so excited?"

Auntie noticed that Wenxiu's speech was directly aimed at Fang Hao, who was quietly drinking his champagne, not saying a word, and she felt uneasy. She followed Ading and criticized her niece, "That's right, Wenxiu, just look at yourself! Really, you're just like your father! He was always so stubborn. Like father, like daughter! Like I've said before, your Yu family will always be involved in politics."

Wenjuan also tried to save Fang Hao from embarrassment, "What's the hurry? The foreigners' help is good enough. Today's newspapers mentioned that the U.S. State Department was already expressing its concern--this is much more effective than writing letters!"

"That's right!" Auntie echoed her daughter. "One sentence from a foreigner is worth ten times more than that from a Chinese! A few words from a respectable person would be more effective than the endless pursuit of the common people."

This time, it was Wenxiu's turn to shake her head. She did not like involving foreigners. When Ading's father had been involved in the Taiwanese Independence Movement, he had often brought in his American and Japanese connections. At that time, she had felt it was not suitable. Assistance from foreigners was welcome of course, but Chinese affairs should be handled by the Chinese themselves.

Now, looking at Fang Hao's neatly tied tie and his champagne-tinted red cheeks, Wenxiu was suddenly inspired with another idea.

"Fang Hao, there's no need to find others to write at all. You can write a letter yourself!"

"Me?" He shook his head modestly and said, "I'm not well-known."

"Who says that?" Wenjuan flattered him. "You are a renowned patriotic scholar in Beijing!"

Fang Hao tried to object, but Wenxiu ignored his protest, and continued, "Don't be so modest, Fang Hao. Though you haven't met the first or second high-ranking officials, you still get to see officials from the Propaganda Bureau. Write to them, and ask them to convey your sincere concerns to Hua Guofeng and Deng Xiaoping. It will bring you the same result!"

Wenxiu spoke of this so zealously, Fang Hao noncommittally promised that he would consider it.

"Al...alright....Let me think it over."

Ading, who sat next to him, spoke up impatiently, "Why is it such a big deal to write a letter? At our school, there are students who wrote to President Carter and state senators. No one ever said it's impossible to write a letter--they even received replies!"

The child's innocence clearly amused the grown-ups.

"Ading, this is America," Auntie tried to explain to her. "In America, of course, everything is possible."

"That's correct," Ading said with confidence. "Aren't we now in America?"

No one paid any attention to her but her mother, who looked at her appreciatively.

Auntie stood up and said, "Take your time eating, I'll cook some Chinese vegetables to go with the noodles."

That night, no one mentioned the subject of writing a letter again.

Wenxiu regretted the differences between Fang Hao's thinking and her own. She felt she could only blame herself for her lack of knowledge about

China's current situation, especially the issues surrounding Wei Jingsheng's case. The very next day, she went to the Library of Congress to read, and she checked out newspapers and magazines. In addition, a Chinese student of Fang Hao's gave her two articles written by Wei Jingsheng on jails for political prisoners and read them thoroughly. The dark side of the Chinese judicial system revealed by the articles made her blood boil.

One day, she finally called Fang Hao and asked him about the authenticity of these stories.

He replied, "Wei Jingsheng certainly exaggerated some. During the 'Gang of Four' era, these things probably existed. Now, certainly nothing like this would happen. Peng Zhen got involved and personally drew up a whole set of legal documents. I believe China will step onto the right judicial path. During the Cultural Revolution, Peng suffered from the anarchy as well and had some painful experiences of his own. So, let him take charge of the law, he can be trusted. Take it easy on everything, Wenxiu, nothing can be done in such haste. China has been a feudal society for several thousand years, you can't expect it to be transformed into a country of law and order so quickly. They are really making a big effort to change. You'll understand that if you go there and see it for yourself."

In the middle of talking about going to the mainland, Fang Hao paused for a moment, then gently queried, "Wenxiu, you will be going, won't you?!"

She stared at the receiver, unable to explain her inner conflicts to herself, let alone someone else. Even the thought of telling her mother made her somewhat hesitant. For something so important, she felt she should let her mother know and get her approval. Yet how could she explain it to her?

"Fang Hao, it would be wonderful if you could see my mother! Is it possible for you to visit Taiwan?"

"Absolutely impossible--unless it's the day of reunification!"

At first, his voice sounded slightly regretful. Then it changed into a firm tone, "Even if the Taiwanese government grants me a visa, I wouldn't be able to go!"

Though the answer was what she had expected, it still made her feel sad. *When would these man-made adversities be overcome?* She sighed.

"Wenxiu, why don't you invite your mother here? She hasn't been to America yet, how about inviting her for Thanksgiving?"

"I received a letter from her today. She asked me to return home to Taiwan."

Mother's letter also mentioned that Manager Lin, whom she had sent to Japan on business, had disappeared. Her mother suspected that he embezzled some money and fled abroad. She had already contacted her lawyer to investigate it. Trying not to alarm her daughter, she described the incident rather briefly, as if it didn't deserve any special attention. Yet, at the end of the letter she mentioned her plan for retirement again, stating that she hoped Wenxiu would not stay abroad too much longer and would come back soon to take over her business.

"How about persuading your mother to sell her eel farm?" Fang Hao suggested. "Nowadays, bankruptcy has become epidemic. These so-called economic crimes are very serious and it's too difficult to run a business. It would be simple for her to run a business here. It wouldn't be bad running a hotel in the United States, you know, like your Uncle."

"No, you don't know my mother. It would be impossible!"

Wenxiu had already told Fang Hao that her mother was widowed at a very young age. She had resisted pressure from all her relatives, and refused to remarry, under any condition. Mother started her business in a small pond near the seashore. She went to the sea to catch baby eels with a net, beginning her day early, when it was still dark outside. She had worked diligently everyday for the past twenty-odd-years, and finally expanded her business to the scale it was now, employing more than forty people. She was very proud of both herself and her self-made enterprise.

"Don't just make empty talk about politics," she once advised her daughter, "only industry can save Taiwan."

During the peak period of the eel farm business, she indeed made a lot of hard cash. Over the past few years though, the export business had drastically declined, but Wenxiu never heard her mother complain. All she knew was that her mother worked even more diligently. Fish farming was her mother's lifelong pride, how could one ask her to give it up? Not only that, Wenxiu had also worked hard, contributing to the business. That made her reluctant to give it up as well.

"Wenxiu, why don't you try it anyway. After the setback with Manager Lin, your mother may be easier to persuade."

"Alright," she promised him reticently, although she had no intention of mentioning it to her mother. Instead, their telephone conversation had aroused her homesickness. She recalled the year-round summer-like scenery, and thought about how her native land would look now, so busy with everyone getting ready for the upcoming festivities. This year, they would welcome the native God. Were the musical bands going to be more splendid than last year's? Last year, the Yu family had made a generous pledge to the northern and southern string bands. What kind of contribution would they make this year?

Her homesickness was too strong to dissolve. The entire night Wenxiu tossed and turned, unable to sleep. The next day, she calculated the time-zone difference and waited impatiently until midnight when she finally made a call home to Taiwan.

Her mother answered the phone, and was pleasantly surprised to hear Wenxiu's voice. When Wenxiu asked about Manager Lin's disappearance, her mother acted as if things had changed with the passage of time and did not seem overly concerned.

"No one knows where he is now. Several Japanese companies sent telegrams here, mentioning that they had already paid both the I.O.U. and money order and urged us to speed up our shipment of the eels."

"Doesn't Manager Lin's family know of his whereabouts?"

"I really don't like to talk about this, it makes me too upset! Apparently, when he disappeared, his wife already had a green card. She secretly left for America a few days earlier than he. To think that I've always valued him so highly, you just can't trust people so much anymore!"

The grief she felt from being swindled and cheated drifted over the oceans and seas, permeating Wenxiu's mind, making her feel very angry and tormented.

"Please try not to worry about it anymore, Mom. Did you lose a lot of money?"

"Of course there's some loss, but in comparison to the embezzlement at Yang-yang Department Store, a fortune worth several millions, our loss is too small to be mentioned. How true it is, our proverb that says the human heart is covered by belly skin! It's hard to see through it! For such a small amount of money, he traded his trust and moral integrity...it saddens me just to think about it!"

Even though she had somewhat succeeded in getting over it, the importance of the monetary loss did not seem to worry her as much as the prospect of her daughter getting married.

"Wenxiu, you and Fang Hao...what is happening between the two of you?"

"We are...still friends."

Wenxiu could not immediately explain her hesitation and self-conflict. Yet, in a spurt of emotional hastiness, she revealed the information she was most concerned about, "Mom, this December, Fang Hao is going...going over there. He's going to do six months of research."

"Oh....Fine!" her mother sighed in relief, immediately sounding as if she had shed her heaviest worries.

"Then when do you plan to come back?" she asked quickly.

Without waiting for an answer, her mother urged her, overjoyed, "How about coming home for New Year, Wenxiu? Bring Ading back with you. Tell her Grandma misses her to the point of craziness!"

"All right....let me see...," Wenxiu vaguely promised. "I'll write you a letter explaining everything."

"Recently, exports to Japan have shown some signs of improvement! I hope you'll come back soon. Together, we can discuss how to improve the business, maybe we can even expand our export market. Hopefully, next year, we'll be able to avoid losing money."

Wenxiu asked her mother about the upcoming festivities, and as soon as she mentioned the deity, her non-superstitious mother talked with great relish. She said that this year the deity's parade would be headed by the marching of eight generals, with a folk-hero Song Jiang-style layout of troops. In celebration of the abundant fishing harvest, the ceremony and entertainment would be much more lavish than before.

"How wonderful it would be if you were back here in East Harbor! Our Yu family has contributed the deity's boat. Your Uncle is leaving the day after tomorrow, he's worried about his hotel business. It's a real shame for him to miss this big festivity."

Wenxiu also felt much regret, for this would be the largest annual celebration. In a foreign country on this desolate autumn night, she imagined East Harbor with sunshine everywhere, everyone turning out to watch the deity's welcoming parade--her eyes became blurred with tears.

"Come back early, don't forget!" her mother lovingly reminded Wenxiu before she hung up the phone.

*   *   *

Auntie, just like Fang Hao, firmly insisted on handing the ownership of the Yu family's eel farm to someone else and bringing Mrs. Yu to the States for her retirement.

The quick-mouthed Wenjuan suggested trying action before persuasion, "Wenxiu, just don't listen to her. Apply for her immigration visa first."

Her Auntie also placed her bets and said, "My sister has only you as her daughter. If you don't go back, I don't believe she'd want to stay in Taiwan until she dies!"

"But, I'm afraid to stay in America till my death!" Wenxiu responded.

Wenjuan half-jokingly warned her, "You'd better be careful. Fang Hao is sympathetic toward China. If you get involved with him, I'm afraid your name will soon be on the Taiwanese government's 'Black List.' You're still constantly thinking of going back to Taiwan, just be careful. You could go to the mainland and then not be allowed to return to Taiwan!"

"Now the regulations are much more relaxed. Would it be so serious?" Wenxiu asked in a tone of half-belief.

Wenjuan strongly disagreed with her.

Auntie also repeated her old theory, "The Yu family has always entangled itself in politics, stubborn and totally insensitive to the overall situation! Don't tempt fate by going back. If you do, at least wait until you get your American citizenship!"

Two days later, Uncle came back from Taiwan.

He had joined a delegation that visited Taiwan in celebration of Double Ten. They had visited ten big construction sites and toured the entire island. He returned with his face darkly tanned, even a little red. Uncle highly praised his native country's prosperity and progress, but when it came to the subject of the Yu family, he thought that selling the eel farm was the best solution. He felt that the earlier the money was transferred to America for reinvestment, the better off they would be.

"Wenjuan's Auntie is too stubborn," he said. "Several times, people wanted to buy it at a high price, but she refused to accept any of the offers. She doesn't have a son or son-in-law to help her. This will obviously be a temptation to the covetous desires of crooks and swindlers. Doesn't she already have problems now? In Taiwan, many rich people want to go abroad. So before leaving, they grab any chance to embezzle money. That's why bad debts and accounts have become such an epidemic problem. I was there for only a month, and I personally heard that seven or eight companies went bankrupt!"

"Then what would she do?" Auntie asked, worried about her sister. She urged her niece, "Wenxiu, try to get your mother to sell it! Bring the money to America, and we'll put our money together and invest in a hotel."

Wenxiu became nervous being advised in so many different directions by them. Consequently, she wrote a letter home, asking how difficult it was to run a business as of late, and how great the risk was. She did not mention immigration, knowing it would be to no avail.

*　　　　*　　　　*

One morning, tired of reading, Wenxiu stood by the window looking at the crossroads in front of her house. There was a strong wind that day. The leaves on the dogwoods had fallen off almost completely, leaving only a few to struggle and twist against the wind. It looked tragically beautiful and yet so stubborn. The tall birch trees could not stand up to the billowing gusts of air, their yellowish leaves floating downward one by one. The falling leaves, blown by the wind, suddenly drifted to the east and then the west, appearing to be wandering and forlorn.

Wenxiu realized it was already late autumn.

Suddenly the phone rang, it was Fang Hao.

"Wenxiu, can you get away and have lunch with me? I'm in the city."

"Which city?" she asked, momentarily confused.

"Oh, pardon me, Washington D.C. I went to the Chinese Embassy for a visa. How about this, I'll meet you at the Beijing Restaurant at 12:30. Catch a cab, and I'll drive you home afterwards."

She accepted his invitation. Realizing that she did not have much time, she hurriedly changed her clothes and rushed over in a taxi.

Upon her arrival at Beijing Restaurant, she was introduced to another guest, who was about Fang Hao's age, Consul Gao. Fang Hao treated the Consul with great respect, lighting his cigarettes and pouring his tea.

Subconsciously, Wenxiu also felt a great sense of respect rising in her heart. This was the first time she had ever met anyone from China, and by coincidence he happened to be a government official. She was confused as to how to conduct herself properly in his presence. However, Consul Gao was very amicable, gentle and polite. His slightly plump face was always smiling, and he frequently nodded his head, giving the impression of a willingness to listen and accept other's opinions. Except for the fact that his wool uniform looked different from other respectable elderly Chinese-American's, Wenxiu's nervousness was immediately calmed.

While they were eating, the Consul asked about Wenxiu's background. He again and again expressed his respect for her mother and her establishing an enterprise on her own. He was also interested in the lives of Taiwanese fishermen. When Wenxiu talked about their customs and habits, he seemed completely absorbed. She thought the official had a very human touch, leaving her with a good impression.

Unintentionally, Fang Hao revealed that Consul Gao had just come from Beijing. Wenxiu then asked him about the trial of Wei Jingsheng.

"At that time, I had already left Beijing, so I don't know many details," the Consul said, completely brushing the issue aside.

Wenxiu's eyes begged Fang Hao for help, but he busied himself with the sweet-and-sour fish steaks and did not express any opinion. She felt she had only one alternative. She mustered up all her courage and said, "We all feel that the sentence of fifteen years is too severe."

"Oh...," the Consul's face suddenly sunk, and his smile was replaced by a look of surprise.

Fang Hao slightly lowered his brows, furtively trying to send eye signals to Wenxiu. But having already started on the subject, she continued without worrying about the consequences, "Big-character posters have been publicly approved by your government. Wei's criticism of the government was fair and frank. How could he be charged as an Counter-revolutionist? It doesn't seem possible for a zoo worker to obtain any military secrets, and if they really were military secrets, then the person who provided him with the information should be punished. Isn't that right? Many of us here believe that this kind of accusation is out of line. Perhaps his speech was too critical, or his method wasn't proper, maybe he shouldn't have discussed the Vietnam War with foreigners, but for a twenty-nine-year-old man, a fifteen-year sentence is just too harsh. In Taiwan...."

As if being choked by a fish bone, Fang Hao suddenly started coughing loudly. He finally succeeded in interrupted Wenxiu.

The Consul was a bit embarrassed, yet he nodded toward Wenxiu gracefully, "All right, I will certainly relay your opinion back to our government."

"Thank you, Mr. Gao," Wenxiu thanked him gratefully. She continued sincerely, "We hope you'll relay this to your government as soon as possible. We hope to see China march toward democracy. The Democracy Wall is a symbol of the freedom of speech, so Wei Jingsheng's heavy sentence will make people feel discouraged and disappointed."

She looked at Fang Hao for approval, but again he was only occupying himself with his food. He had polished off almost the entire plate of fish.

"Does mainland China have sincere intentions of bringing democracy into practice?" she added curiously.

"Miss Yu, China's intent to practice democratic politics is sincere," the Consul reassured her. "After many years, this was the first time a political case was fairly tried. Moreover, since each person is responsible for their own actions, we only tried Wei Jingsheng and no one else. It was all very fair and reasonable."

Then, the Consul nodded his head and added quietly, "Fifteen years, uh...is indeed too severe."

It did not matter that this was merely verbal sympathy; it made Wenxiu so happy that she wanted to extend her hand to thank him. Chinese diplomats were not as stiff and cold as she had previously imagined. This conclusion suddenly made her spirits soar.

After lunch, she and Fang Hao escorted the Consul back to the consulate. Before leaving, the Consul earnestly invited Wenxiu to the mainland, "Miss Yu, I hope you can come to our country for a visit very soon."

"Thank you. Someday I'll be able to go," Wenxiu replied congenially.

The traffic out of the city was very heavy. They were stuck in a traffic jam, and Fang Hao had a tough time going anywhere, with all the stop and go. Though he uttered no complaints, he looked remorseful. Wenxiu knew that he was administering final exams to his students, and had to be back before three o'clock. She thought he was worried about whether or not he would be late.

Finally, the car was on the highway. After accelerating, Fang Hao opened his tightly clenched mouth and said, "I thought it was understood that you wouldn't mention Wei Jingsheng's case to the Consul."

His tone sounded like a reprimand.

Wenxiu felt very dejected, like an elementary-school student being wrongly scolded by her teacher.

"Why not?" she asked, not wanting to yield.

"There is no need for you to appeal so enthusiastically on behalf of a convicted counter-revolutionist."

He said this so calmly and with so much composure that Wenxiu wondered if she had misunderstood him. She turned to look at him. He was looking straight ahead, gazing steadily forward, and exuded an air of confidence.

"Aren't you also sympathetic toward him?" she asked, wondering why Fang Hao had changed his tone. It was as if he had become a completely different person.

"Sympathy is one thing. Whether or not you should've spoken out like that under these circumstances is another!"

The image of Ading's father unexpectedly popped into her mind like a dark cloud. She stared at Fang Hao, trying to convince herself, *No, they're not the same! The two of them aren't the same.*

Perhaps sensing that he was too harsh with Wenxiu, Fang Hao explained to her softly, "China has a population of nine hundred million people. One person is like a grain of salt in a boundless sea. Sentencing one person is hardly worth talking about. If it had happened while the Gang of Four was in power, Wei Jingsheng would have either been sentenced to death or condemned to a life sentence of hard-labor. Now, he's only sentenced to fifteen years. From the Chinese government's point of view, they've already been very lenient! With regard to the Xidan Democracy Wall, I believe that it will soon be destroyed. The Chinese people, to tell you the truth, are very greedy! Give them some freedom and they'll ignorantly abuse these privileges. This results in a no-win situation! Really, they have more capacity for disaster than success!"

The more he talked, the more distressed he became. He kept shaking his head, and his voice grew louder and more angry by the moment.

Since Wenxiu was used to him criticizing the government harshly and treating people leniently, she could not accept Fang Hao's severe reproach toward the Chinese people.

"How could one expect the democratic movement to sail smoothly?" Wenxiu confronted him. "Communist China might as well admit to acting iron-handedly to the end, otherwise if they talk about democracy on one hand, but then refuse to grant people freedom of speech on the other, aren't they being self-contradictory? If they want to demolish the Democracy Wall and forbid people from posting big-character posters, then they should let people print magazines. After all, those nine hundred million people ought to have an opportunity to speak out!"

Fang Hao seemed to cool down a little, yet he was still frowning disapprovingly.

"Let them proceed slowly. These complicated Chinese affairs have many ramifications and just can't be rushed," he told her.

Wenxiu changed her tone of voice, pleading with him, "You should at least write a letter for Wei Jingsheng."

"I'm leaving for China soon, so I just can't be involved with this case."

"If you don't care, who else will?" Wenxiu persisted trying to change his mind. "Fang Hao, this is not Wei Jingsheng on trial, this is the future of Chinese democracy on trial!"

Fang Hao was quiet. He signaled a right-turn and put his foot on the gas. He swiftly caught up with the car on his right and cut in, rushing over to the right lane. Never having seen him drive so fiercely, Wenxiu held her breath in fright. As soon as the car left the expressway, she immediately lowered the window a few inches, turned her face outside, and breathed some fresh air.

"Wenxiu, can I give you a piece of advice?"

Just as the car had slowed down, so, too, did Fang Hao's face become warm and soft.

"Go ahead, Fang Hao."

"I know you're a righteous and kind person, but...if we go to China together, I hope you won't mention Wei Jingsheng's case again! Anything we see, we should just observe and not criticize. That's the best way to go about it. Chinese politics are so complicated that it's hard for anyone to figure out. The simplest and safest way is to proceed according to the official tone. I can guarantee you won't be at a disadvantage."

Wenxiu listened attentively to his advice. Now, having heard it, her heart sank low. She did not know how to respond.

Near the crossroads of her Auntie's home, she glanced at her watch and reminded him, "Fang Hao, you don't have much time. Why don't you just drop me off at the intersection, so you won't have to turn onto the side street. You need to hurry back and give the exam."

He looked at his watch and found there was only half an hour left.

"All right! I'm sorry that I can't drive you to your door this time."

"Don't worry about it, I need to walk a little."

When the car stopped, she offered her hand to him.

"Many thanks for the lunch."

Fang Hao took her hand and kissed it, then released it unwillingly.

"Good-bye, Wenxiu. As soon as the exam is over, I'll call you."

"Good-bye, Fang Hao. I'll give you a call, too."

She stood on the sidewalk at the intersection and watched his car moving away until it was hidden from sight by other cars.

The wind had ceased blowing. The sun was shining everywhere with brightness and warmth; a few patches of white clouds decorated the blue sky, the autumn air so clear and crisp. This morning, the strong winds had blown away many leaves: birch leaves, magnolia leaves, and nameless others--yellow, red, dark and light. The fallen leaves laid at the sides of the road, gathered in clumps, all were competing in their uniqueness and beauty amidst the glory of the autumn sun.

This splendid autumn scenery could not arouse even the slightest bit of interest from Wenxiu. Although she stood in the street, she was totally absorbed by her brooding mind. She stood there for a while. When a car turned into the lane, it was as if she had just awakened from a dream, and she started home.

*   *   *

That night, Wenxiu took out a pen and paper. After tossing a few thoughts around, she forced herself to write a brief letter:

October 30, 1979

Dear Premier Deng:

Xidan's big-character posters and Wei Jingsheng's magazine greatly stirred the Chinese, and are publicly recognized symbols of China's march toward democracy. Now, Wei Jingsheng has been sentenced to fifteen years in prison, and we feel much regret. This charge of Counter-revolutionary activity, according to our standard of judgment, is unfair. I feel deeply sympathetic toward him, as I believe other Taiwanese do. You have been hailed as "The Fairest Judge Deng," and have publicly supported big-character posters. For this, you have been praised both inside China and abroad. We sincerely hope that you will keep your promises. If you would reconsider Wei Jingsheng's sentence, we will be deeply grateful.

Wishing you excellent health, we remain,

Sincerely,

Yu Wenxiu
East Harbor, Taiwan

Having finished, she wrote a letter to Fang Hao. This letter was even more difficult to write. She made several attempts, each time scratching and changing words. After using several sheets of paper, she still could not convey her intentions. Late into the night, and after prolonged suffering, Wenxiu finally wrote him a short letter, telling him she was very sorry that she would not be able to go to Beijing with him this year. She had to go back to Taiwan.

She sealed the letter, taking a deep breath. After she completing this grand task, she was extremely exhausted. It was as if her entire body and soul had collapsed. Lying sleeplessly in bed, her tumultuous train of thoughts overwhelmed her mind like a spring flood.

She felt proud and relieved by her action, yet, at the same time, she also felt tormented. *Am I being fair to Fang Hao?* she asked herself time and time again. She was, on one hand, worrying about losing a good friend, and on the other, worrying about making the same mistake twice. She tossed around in bed, still unable to resolve her dilemma.

Am I stupid to do this?... she thought, *How good it would be if mother was here next to me!*

Family love and homesickness were like fated spring silkworms weaving a continuous, unending web of silk threads. She had never been so homesick as she was at this very moment. How much she yearned to rush back to East Harbor! In the darkness, she hoped for it with every ounce of her being, her eyes wide open until dawn.

The next morning, she waited until Auntie's family members had gone to work and Ading to school. Wrapped in a scarf, Wenxiu left the house. She walked to the mailbox at the street corner and threw in her letters. Afterwards, she leaned against the mailbox for a while.

Another clear, crisp autumn day. The sky was crystalline like water, so blue and profound, yet so near as well. Wenxiu looked up at the blue sky, her eyes moistening. She did not feel sad, but wished that she could hold on to someone and have a good cry.

On her way home, she walked on the fallen leaves, humming a Taiwanese folk song:

Thinking...Oh...Thinking of....

On The Other Side of the Pacific

Editor's Notes:

Similar to "The Crossroads," this story's protagonist is also an heroine, Lin Yizhen. The backbone of the story is simple, yet through Lin Yizhen and the other characters, we stumble unto vast cross-cultural issues and glimpse a dizzying array of Chinese political problems. Her husband, for example, serves as an ironic understatement for the author. His ill health delineates the gradual decomposition of his strong belief in the future of China, while his untimely death a year later inevitably yokes the death of his patriotic idealism to silence and disappearance. However, amidst tragedies such as these that occur in her life, Lin Yizhen still optimistically looks forward to the day when Taiwan and China peacefully co-exist, reunited under democratic rule.

In this novelette, three salient characteristics need to be cited. First, we can read this work as a piece of "testimonial literature." Fragmented bits and pieces of Lin Yizhen's family members serve as a collective document, representing the common struggles of the Chinese people. Thus, collectively, the characters can be read as a challenge to the function and textual presence of the author herself. This is specifically referring to Chen Ruoxi's description of the explosive "Gaoxiong Incident" of 1979. In the story, she outlines the real-life political assassination of the former Taiwanese senator Lin Yixiong's family. To this day, this novelette is still banned in Taiwan due to Chen's critical discussion of the incident.

Secondly, this work is written in narrative discourse, figuratively resembling the "crossroads" between history and fiction. By giving a voice to her characters and then inserting stories with historical validity, Chen's writing and her characters' actions enable unknown people, such as Lin Yizhen, to "write" history. Fictional history is different from the official one as it often unmasks hidden truths and uncovers rhetorical "make-up" used by historiographers. In this case, Guomindang historiographers negate that the actual Gaoxiong Incident ever took place.

Lastly, on a sociopolitical level, the end of this novelette reflects the China-pride optimism generated throughout the Chinese-American community in the late seventies and early eighties. Lin Yizhen's final words to law professor, Qiao Jianguang, "See you in Beijing!" signifies the author's own hopes for China. In essence, Qiao embodies a new breed of Chinese intellectuals who have broken out of the narrow perspectives of their own privileged class and developed a social awareness that enables them to arrive at a better understanding of Chinese needs and problems.

ON THE OTHER SIDE OF THE PACIFIC[1]

From the moment she turned the calendar to the month of February, Lin Yizhen had become more and more excited as each day went by. It was almost time for the lunar New Year. This would be the first time she and her two sons spent the holidays together alone, and she pondered over how to celebrate it.

"The first Chinese New Year of the 1980s," she said to herself. This called for a special celebration, one which was rich in tradition but also included something new. Maybe the New Year would bring her good luck.

She borrowed a two-tiered steamer from Mrs. Wu, a fellow Taiwanese who lived in the same apartment building, found some recipes, and planned to make New Year's cake and radish cake. She even asked her niece Lina to drive her to San Francisco's Chinatown to purchase the necessary ingredients. Since she had never steamed any of those cakes before, she wanted to do a little experimenting, in the hope she'd get the hang of it before New Year's. After supper, she often tinkered with the measuring cups

---

[1] "On the Other Side of the Pacific" (*Xiangzhe Taipingyang bi'an*) was translated by Shiao-ling Yu with the permission of the author and publisher, and is published here in English for the first time. This translation is based on the story's first appearance, in four installments of the *Mingbao yuekan* (*Mingbao Monthly*) -- no. 9 (1980): 393-397, no. 10 (1980): 109-115, no. 11 (1980): 100-104, and, no. 12 (1980): 109-115.

and tried her recipes several times.

The first batch that came out of the steamer was a plateful of a sticky, lumpy dough. Yizhen shook her head. "Ah, too much water. Next time, I must use less."

But she was not discouraged. Two days later, she was bustling about mixing another batch of rice flour.

Her two sons were too preoccupied with their studies to offer her any assistance. Seeing their mother work so hard at making the cakes, they both tried to persuade her to give up making them.

"Mom, we don't really care for those cakes," said her older son Su Tai. "Now that we're in America, we should act like Americans. As for the Chinese New Year, just a little something will do."

Su Tai would be twenty-one this year. He had spent three years learning English and taking American high school courses he needed before entering San Jose State University last fall as an electrical engineering student. As the oldest student in his class, he was anxious to do well and worked especially hard for his grades. Normally he lived near the university; even when he came home on weekends, he was never without a book in his hand. Even so, he always spared some time to help his mother when she was busy. Ever since his father passed away, he had been very solicitous toward his mother, ready to lend her a hand whenever necessary. Shy and taciturn by nature, he was mature beyond his age.

Her younger son, Su Zhong, spoke up seconding his older brother, "Why don't we make some dumplings to celebrate as we used to do in Beijing? That should be enough!"

Su Zhong was two years younger than Su Tai. Quick and energetic, he had always been a good student. Since he was now a senior at San Mateo High School, he had been busy lately filing college entrance applications.

"Of course we'll have dumplings. It's the Beijing custom."

Yizhen knew what her sons had in mind, but she was not to be deterred. On the contrary, it made her even more ambitious.

"I also want to learn to make radish cake. It's our hometown specialty and is very delicious. Besides, it's your Grandma's favorite."

The mention of their Grandma immediately silenced the two boys.

In the Su family, Grandma was the person of authority. Now more than seventy years old, she had spent most of her life in the countryside in Taizhong. Occasionally she would come to America for a visit, but she always complained that life here was not as congenial as that in Taiwan, and she wanted everybody to go back. Widowed at a young age, she had worked hard to bring up her two sons. The eldest, Deming, had become a businessman; and the younger son, Yizhen's husband, Deqing, studied medicine in Great Britain before going back to China to practice. Appreciative of what she had done for the family, the Su clan treated her with affection and respect.

Deqing and his family left China in the spring of 1976 to visit his brother and sister-in-law in America. The old lady made a special trip to America to meet her younger son, whom she had not seen for more than thirty years. When she saw him, Deqing was already terminally ill. He passed away the following year. The old lady was especially fond of her grandsons and could not bear to be separated from them. So, thereafter, she never again mentioned anything about going back to Taiwan.

In the past, they had always spent the New Year at Deming's house, with three generations gathered together for a lively celebration. Now, Yizhen and her sons were living separately. The old lady seemed to want Yizhen to be more independent. Knowing her mother-in-law's wishes, Yizhen was determined to cook a few hometown dishes to please her.

"This year I'm going to learn how to make these cakes, so that next year we can invite Grandma to celebrate the New Year with us!" Having said that, Yizhen picked up her measuring cups, studied her recipes, and was ready to start all over again. Over ten years of teaching soil analysis in China had helped her cultivate a lot of patience.

"Mom, let's invite Uncle Qiao, too," her older son suggested.

"All right. I'll ask him tomorrow."

She had wanted to invite Qiao Jianguang to spend the New Year with them for quite some time. She was moved that her son had thought to bring up the subject himself.

"Uncle Qiao is from Shandong. He likes steamed buns," the younger boy said, as he suddenly came up with a good idea. "Why don't we make some really tasty and chewy Shandong steamed buns? Uncle Qiao said he hates those soft and spongy cottonball-like things they serve in the restaurants."

As soon as he heard this, Su Tai immediately wanted to get into the act. "Mom, let me make the buns. During my two years in the Chinese countryside, I didn't learn anything except how to make good steamed buns!"

"I'll help you knead the dough," his younger brother chimed in excitedly. "Buns should be decorated with those large, red dates, and they should be as big as rice bowls."

"Oh, great! And how about Eight-Precious-Rice-Pudding for dessert? We could really surprise Uncle Qiao!"

Yizhen was delighted to see her sons so anxious to please Uncle Qiao and wanting to show him their gratitude.

Qiao Jianguang was their best friend in America. He was a professor of law at Golden Gate University, and the legal consultant for Deming's import and export company. In the early 1970s, he went back to China for a visit, and, at the request of Deming, located Deqing and his family. It was Qiao who assisted them in getting out of China and applying for immigrant status in the United States. After Deqing passed away, Qiao was very concerned about the welfare of the two boys and treated them like his own children. Last summer, when he took his son skiing in Canada, he also took the two Su brothers along. The brothers had great respect for his knowledge and opinions, and they often sought his advice on matters concerning college choices and future career plans. If Uncle Qiao pointed his finger to the east, they would not think of going west.

"Isn't his son coming home for the New Year?" Su Zhong suddenly asked.

"Probably not," Yizhen said. "He's in Chicago. It's too far to come back. Besides, he grew up in America and is completely Americanized. Maybe he doesn't even celebrate the Chinese New Year."

"He celebrates Christmas," Su Tai said. "It's the same as our Spring Festival."

"That's right. It's just as important, and it's also rich in tradition," Yizhen replied. She did not dare to mention that their Uncle Qiao had spent last Christmas with an American family. He had been divorced for many years, and his son had been alternating his holidays between his parents. Last year, it was his mother's turn to have him over for Christmas, and his father only received a phone call from him. Yizhen was not accustomed to such a high frequency of divorce and separation, and the general lack of affection in American families. She did not want to talk about it for fear that her boys might be affected in a negative way.

Yizhen's enthusiasm for the holidays finally rubbed off on her sons. They, too, made themselves busy preparing for the New Year's celebrations. The day before New Year's Eve, the steamed buns, and the salty and sweet New Year's cakes were made. They were actually quite successful. Yizhen chose one of each kind and took them over to Mrs. Wu, after making sure that Mr. Wu was away at work.

"You're so talented, Mrs. Su!" Mrs. Wu was full of praise for her, and repeatedly invited Yizhen to come in to the house.

"I've got some other affairs to attend to. I can't stay today, but if it's okay I'll return your steamer after New Year's Day."

"There's no hurry. I won't be using it. But...," Mrs. Wu paused momentarily and seemed to be embarrassed to bring up her request. "The faucet in our washroom is leaking, and the shower in the bathroom is also dripping from morning till night. Could you get someone to fix it?"

"Sure, I'll have Su Zhong take a look at it first. If he can't fix it, we'll get a plumber."

The apartment building belonged to Deming. Yizhen and her two sons lived in a three-bedroom unit. Feeling obligated toward Deming for his kindness, she had taken it upon herself to look after the eight-unit building. She always kept the walkway clean, mowed and watered the lawn, and changed the light bulbs. She was like a manager, only she did not collect the rent.

With the exception of the Wu family, all the other tenants were white. Though there had been little occupant turnover, the tenants never had anything to do with one another. Yizhen's family had lived in this building ever since the day they arrived America, almost four years ago. For some reason, Chinese neighborly friendliness did not seem to have any place here. When neighbors came face to face with one another, they just smiled and said, "Hi!" This "Hi" seemed to be a summation of all human relationships in America.

The Sus were friendly to the Wu family the moment they first arrived. Being Taiwanese, they were naturally drawn together by their common dialect. But after a while, Mr. Wu's political prejudice cast a dark shadow over their friendship. He believed that the Taiwanese had long been oppressed by the mainlanders, and only when Taiwan finally became independent could they escape such oppression for good. Since Deming supported the current regime in Taiwan, Mr. Wu sarcastically referred to him as a "rightist" behind his back. Yizhen and her sons came from the mainland, but they were not as anti-Communist as he had expected, so he openly called them "leftists." In Mr. Wu's eyes, leftist Taiwanese were even more hopeless than the rightist Taiwanese. Yizhen was not sure whether or not she was oversensitive, but every time she met him, she thought she could see a mixture of anger, pity and contempt in his eyes. Her sons resented being treated this way, and they often argued with him. As for herself, she simply preferred to avoid him.

Because the Wu's were their tenants, Yizhen immediately responded to Mrs. Wu's request. She sent Su Zhong over that very night to take care of the problems. He changed the washer in the faucet, which ceased the leakage, but the problem with the shower head was too complicated for him to fix. The next day, Yizhen called a plumber, and notified her sister-in-law, Zhao E, who always handled the rent and repair expenses.

"I'll bring you some New Year's cakes," Yizhen told her.

"Oh, are the vegetable cakes all done? You don't need to make a special trip, Yizhen, I'll come pick them up myself. I'm going out anyway."

Before long, Zhao E arrived at the apartment in her Mercedes. Yizhen lived in a downstairs apartment. From her window, she could see her sister-in-law getting out of her car, her hands full of packages, big and small. She rushed out to greet her.

"You went out shopping this morning?" Yizhen took one package from her hands.

"I bought them some time ago--New Year's presents for your boys."

"But you always give them presents. You really have spoiled them!" Yizhen protested sincerely, feeling embarrassed.

"It's New Year's. According to Taiwanese customs, we should all wear new clothes. If the sizes aren't right, you can exchange them," Zhao E insisted.

It was only a short distance from the driveway to the living room, but Zhao E was already panting. She was short, but chubby. Today, she was wearing a moss-green silk dress that was so tight it cut her body into two rounded segments, very much like the gourds sold at Beijing markets in the summertime. Her patent leather four-inch high heels made walking difficult for her. As soon as she was near the sofa, she immediately collapsed onto it.

Yizhen made some tea and poured her a cup, then sat down across from her. "How is mother-in-law?"

"She's just the same! Always making a big fuss when the New Year approaches. It's a good thing that you made these cakes this year. You saved me a trip to Chinatown. Actually, no one really wants to eat them. Even she hardly takes a bite herself. Nonetheless, she must have them all, otherwise she feels mistreated. In my opinion, if she is really so particular about it, she should go back to Taiwan and spend the New Year there!"

"Older people tend to be nostalgic about old customs--especially when they live abroad," Yizhen sympathized with both of them. It reminded her of her own mother. "My mother used to be like that, too. There were many Taiwanese people in Tokyo then. During New Year's or other festivals, each family would make many cakes and exchange them with one another. My family always received a bunch of them, all different kinds. We wouldn't think of making so many varieties for ourselves."

"During my first two years in America, I missed Taiwanese snacks so much!" Zhao E exclaimed. "At first, I just couldn't get through the week without making a trip to Chinatown. Now, after being here for sixteen years, I don't care for them any more. If I really want anything badly enough, I can always take a trip to Taiwan. It's easy enough!"

Yizhen smiled without saying anything, only envious of her sister-in-law's good fortune. She had been wanting to visit her homeland so much the last couple years that she often dreamed about visiting there; sometimes, she even dreamed about walking on her ancestors' graves. But in reality, she had not been able to go. First, she was waiting for her green card; then, Deming went back to Taiwan and looked into the government's possible reaction to her visiting Taiwan. It was not until last year that she finally received a positive response. She immediately applied for an entry visa last November and was preparing to accompany her mother-in-law to Taizhong. They were planning to stay there until after New Year's. Then, unexpectedly, the

Gaoxiong Incident[2] occurred on December 10, followed by the arrest of many people active in Taiwan's democracy movement. The atmosphere on the island was very tense after that, and she had to postpone her trip.

Zhao E could tell what Yizhen was thinking and tried to comfort her, "There shouldn't be any problem with you going back to Taiwan. Deming just came back from Taibei last week. He said the situation there is still unclear, so it would be better for you to wait until the investigations have been completed. Once peace is restored, you can go anywhere you want. Right now, it's not a good time to go. They're still arresting people over there! My nephew was detained and questioned for three days. Luckily, he was released, but the whole family had been worried to death about him!"

"Why did they arrest him? Did he take part in the demonstration in Gaoxiong?"

"It was some really rotten luck! Some acquaintance persuaded him to attend a public lecture sponsored by *Beautiful Island* in Nantou. This happened long before the Gaoxiong Incident. He was extremely cautious when he went there. He purposely parked his car far away and walked half an hour to get to the place. Still, somebody took down his license plate number, and the police wanted to know what his relationship was with *Beautiful Island*. What relationship? You tell me. A business man went to a public lecture out of simple curiosity, but was questioned for three days!"

Zhao E's face was round and flat, with small eyes and thin eyebrows. She wore her hair high on top of her head in a style that reminded Yizhen of a steamed bun. To disguise her dark complexion, she covered her face with a thick layer of white powder, making it look like a mask in a Japanese opera. Only in moments of agitation like this did her face become animated. With

---

[2] This refers to the very explosive and brutal confrontation between the Nationalist government and native Taiwanese in the southwest city of Gaoxiong in 1979. Many outspoken, anti-Nationalist people were arrested, tried, and imprisoned. This incident further sharpened and divided the delicate relationship between these two parties.

her thin eyebrows raised high and her small eyes open wide, her wrinkles cracked through the barrier of facial powder, spreading out like a fish net.

This was the first time Yizhen had seen her sister-in-law so upset. She had never been interested in politics before. Although she regretted that most of the people arrested were Taiwanese, she thought it was their own fault for not obeying the law. But now that her own nephew was implicated, she began to feel the personal impact of this incident and was angered by it.

Yizhen had similar concerns. She thought about her own nephew whom she had never seen. Would he and his mother be safe?

When Yizhen was eleven years old, she had gone to Japan with her parents, who had business there. Her older brother, Yiwei, and younger brother, Yilie, had remained in Taiwan, living with their grandmother. Later on, when she had went Beijing to go to college, her parents had passed away in Japan, and she lost contact with her brothers. When she finally saw Yilie in America, she learned that Yiwei had once run for the position of a municipal representative in Taiwan, but lost. He was later put in jail for eight years because of his "seditious actions," and died shortly after he was released. Yiwei's wife and her only son were still living, but they did not want to correspond with Yizhen, a fact that saddened her a great deal. The reason Yizhen was anxious to return to Taiwan was to see her sister-in-law's family.

"Don't be upset," Yizhen comforted Zhao E. "Your nephew was lucky enough to be released without a scratch. I just hope that nephew of mine is safe and sound."

"When Deming goes back to Taiwan next time, we can ask him to find out for you," Zhao E replied.

"Is Deming very busy with his work? I haven't seen him for quite some time now."

"When is he ever not busy? He is out every day attending this function or that function. It seems our house has become a hotel to him!"

Yizhen smiled sympathetically, knowing full well that Zhao E complained only behind her husband's back; when she was with him, she was as gentle as a lamb.

"You don't have to worry about him here in America!" Yizhen tried to boost her sister-in-law's spirit. "We don't have that kind of Taiwanese 'noontime wife' you told me about. No seducer, no one seduced. You've been married for thirty years now and still get so jealous. You must be very much in love with your husband!"

Zhao E laughed out loud, seeming pleased with herself, but almost instantly she started to complain again, "You have no idea how addicted men are to that wild night life of wine, women and song in Taibei! Deming just came back, right? But he says he has to go there again this summer to sign some contract!"

Judging by the way she talked, one would think that Zhao E wanted to tie her husband up with a leash. Yizhen felt that Zhao E was unduly nervous. Perhaps Deming had a "previous record" in Taiwan, but she was too embarrassed to ask. Every time he wanted to go to Taiwan, Zhao E became extremely worried.

"If you're so worried about this, why don't you go with him this time?"

"I hardly had a chance to speak up! I was only able to ask him a few questions before he became angry. Mother-in-law was also on his side. She said, 'If you go with him, who's going to look after the house?' Just listen to that. It seems that all I'm expected to do is to wait on the old and the young of the Su family my entire life!"

"Be patient. Once Lina is married, you can follow Deming everywhere he goes. Who will say no then?"

"Don't mention Lina, she only makes me mad! I just fixed her up with someone, but she broke up with him after only going out with him twice!"

"What? Was it Paul?"

"That's right, Paul Wan. Lina said that he is uncultured and filthy rich....Just listen to that. She just graduated from Stanford, but already thinks of herself as high and mighty. Raising daughters in America is a thankless job. You eat your heart out for nothing!"

Yizhen remembered meeting Paul Wan once. He was not bad-looking, but very arrogant. He had the air of someone who was really rolling in the dough. Even Yizhen did not like him. No wonder Lina found him vulgar. She heard he was the only son of Deming's Cantonese friend, a wealthy businessman in San Francisco. He was Deming's choice for Lina. Yizhen did not think it was right for herself to express any opinion.

"Lina just graduated from college. She's still young, and there are many eligible Chinese bachelors here. She can take her time."

"It's not me who's worried, it's the old woman. The reason that she wanted to stay here these past few years is to guard Lina from being snatched away by someone who isn't Chinese. Every time Lina goes out with a white boy, mother-in-law pouts her lips, and her face darkens as if someone owes her money."

Yizhen knew that her brother-in-law's entire family was concerned about finding a good match for Lina. Even though Zhao E was annoyed with her daughter's unappreciativeness, she was actually very fond of her and always let her have her way. Ever since their eldest daughter had married an American and moved to the East Coast, they hardly saw her anymore. Mother-in-law and Deming were afraid that Lina might follow the same footsteps. That was why they all tried very hard to fix her up with Chinese men.

In the beginning, they limited their search to young Taiwanese men. After Lina broke up with several of them, they were forced to break the geographic barrier and asked only that the young man be from a cultural background similar to theirs, and could speak at least a little bit of their dialect. This Paul Wan, Yizhen recalled, could only speak a few sentences in broken Mandarin. He conversed with Lina entirely in English.

"Oh, Ah Zhen, you've been in America just four years. Your sons are still busy with their studies, so you don't have to worry about them yet. Wait till they have girlfriends, then you'll worry endlessly!"

The two sisters-in-law chatted some more before Zhao E got up to leave. Yizhen wrapped up a few New Year's cakes for her to take home. She also selected two steamed buns decorated with red dates for her mother-in-law.

Before Zhao E drove away, she loudly reminded Yizhen, "Do come on New Year's Day. We'll be expecting you for dinner."

Zhao E said that Yizhen did not have to worry about her sons' marriages yet, but Zhao E's words caused Yizhen to reflect on the matter. If they continued to live in America, how could there be any guarantee that the next generation would not marry someone of another race? Lina's older sister was a good example. If the same thing happened to her sons, what would she do? Not only would the living members of the Su family be disappointed, wouldn't Deqing's spirit be saddened by it as well?

Deqing loved China and had always been proud of being Chinese. In the early 1950s, as soon as he had completed his studies in England, he rushed back to China to take part in the country's reconstruction program. He had never dreamed of settling down in a foreign country. The excesses perpetrated during the ten years of the Cultural Revolution had saddened him; they also destroyed his health. For the sake of the children, he decided to leave the country just when he had become seriously ill. Even so, he did not forget China when he died.

"Give our children the best education possible," he had told Yizhen. "Tell them not to forget that they are Chinese."

If they were both to marry someone who wasn't Chinese, how would she explain it to Deqing? This question lingered on in her mind for a long time until the boys returned home from school in the afternoon. She made herself very busy with preparations for the New Year's Eve dinner and gradually forgot about the whole thing.

"Celebrating the New Year in California just doesn't feel the same as it did in China," Su Tai commented with regret while straightening up the living room.

"Why?" his mother asked, popping her head out of the kitchen.

"Well," Su Tai continued, "the weather's not even right! It's always sunny here. Without winter, you just can't appreciate the loveliness of spring. I remember when we were little, New Year's in Beijing was so cold, and the wind blew very hard. The entire family sat around the fireplace, roasting New Year's cakes. It was so warm and so happy inside the house. When we felt like it, we would go outside to light the firecrackers or drop in at the neighbors' houses. It was really great fun!"

Su Zhong abruptly stopped mixing the filling for the dumplings and said regretfully, "Chinese New Year's here just means eating. There's not much to it. Grandma said that New Year's in Taiwan is really something! People start preparations three days before New Year's Day. There are sacrifices to be made to the Heavenly God, the Earth God, and the Kitchen God. Besides that there are many other ceremonies! The celebration lasts fifteen days, and there's something to do every day. The women go to the temples and burn incense. Married daughters go home to visit. Grandma said that next year we'll all go to Taiwan to spend the New Year there!"

"That's right. We'll all go back to Taiwan to see your cousin!" Yizhen encouraged her son's enthusiasm; at the same time, she secretly prayed that the day of reunion would come soon.

*   *   *

Uncle Qiao arrived promptly at six thirty.

Yizhen took off her apron, changed into a plain dress, and slipped on a black Chinese-style jacket with purple flowers. She combed her short, straight hair one more time. When Deqing was still alive, he liked her hair short, and it had become a habit for her to wear it that way. Her sister-in-law had tried several times to persuade her to perm her hair, but she did not want to change her hair style. Now, looking at herself in the mirror, she discovered that her face looked a little pale. Her straight hair made her face appear very dull and uninteresting. "It's New Year's Eve today," she said to herself. "I should look merrier." While she was pondering over what to do, she heard the doorbell ring. As her son went to answer the door, she quickly dabbed a little rouge on her cheeks, and rubbed them evenly until they turned to the same color as her naturally red lips. She then put on a pair of medium-heeled shoes and rushed out to greet the guest.

"I'm not much good at anything else, but when it comes to making dumplings, I'm an expert at rolling out the wrappers!" Qiao Jianguang said enthusiastically, volunteering to help the boys. He then took off his jacket, rolled up his sleeves, and was ready to go to work.

After Yizhen exchanged greetings with him, she noticed there were three beautifully wrapped packages on the sofa. She protested in a soft voice, "Lao Qiao,[3] You're too polite. Every time you come, you bring presents. There's no end to your gift-giving!"

"It's New Year's!" he exclaimed, suddenly remembering something. He quickly took out an envelope from the pocket of his jacket and gave it to Su Tai. "This is good-luck money for you two. Sorry, I didn't have time to go to Chinatown to buy a red envelope to put it in."

Su Tai blushed, refusing to take it, "We're all grown up now, Uncle Qiao. We can't accept good-luck money anymore."

"You're not married yet, so you're still a kid in our eyes."

Qiao Jianguang had a gentle manner about him. He did not say much, but whatever he did say, he meant whole-heartedly. That was why, when he insisted, neither Yizhen nor her sons felt right refusing him. Yizhen respectfully put the envelope and the presents on the television, "Please have a seat, Lao Qiao. I'll go make some tea."

---

[3] "Lao," literally meaning "old," is a familiar way of addressing a senior male.

"Please, don't bother. I just had some tea with my students before I came. Let's see here, the dumpling filling is ready. I can start rolling the wrappers. Who's going to mix the dough?"

"I will," Su Tai said.

The dining room was an extension of the living room, and it was connected to the kitchen. Lao Qiao's eagerness to get into the act was contagious. He raised everyone's spirits, and they all moved to the dining table.

The top of the dining table was formica, so Yizhen placed a wooden board on the table with a towel underneath it. Lao Qiao could use the board to roll out the wrappers when the dough was ready, and her sons would make the dumplings as she moved in and out, taking care of things in the kitchen.

"Su Tai, how is school? Is it hard?"

"It's all right."

Lao Qiao was happy to know that Su Tai was doing well in school. It was his strong recommendation that secured Su Tai's admission to college.

"As long as you can keep up with your studies, that's good enough. In your spare time, you ought to ask some girls out."

Su Tai smiled bashfully, lowering his head to concentrate on the dumplings, not saying anything.

Lao Qiao said this, half encouragingly and half teasingly, while casting a sidelong glance toward the young man's mother.

"Ask Uncle Qiao to introduce you to a girl," Yizhen answered for her son.

Lao Qiao readily agreed, smiling broadly.

Yizhen noticed that Lao Qiao was especially talkative today. He looked very excited and his eyes sparkled behind his gold-rimmed glasses. Did he have some good news? Could it be that he had been given a promotion and a raise by his university? Out of respect for him, she kept her questions to herself, tightly sealed in her heart.

Qiao Jianguang was fifty-five years old. He was rather tall, and his ample frame was further augmented by his middle-age spread. He played tennis to keep his weight down. His oblong face was very suntanned, making his wrinkles appear even more deeply etched. Either being a lawyer was too mentally exhausting, or he was exhibiting the effects that his troubled marriage had had on him. Whatever the reason, he appeared older than his age. His temples had already turned gray and his hairline receded into the shape of a horseshoe. When he scowled and pressed his lips into a thin line, he looked absolutely forbidding.

But today, he was encouraging Su Tai to go out with girls. This really surprised Yizhen. He had been divorced for more than ten years. Even though Deming and his wife had tried several times to play matchmakers, they never succeeded.

"It's all Qiao Jianguang's fault," Zhao E once complained to Yizhen. "The ladies were interested in him, but he beat a hasty retreat every time! I think he must have had a rotten relationship with his ex-wife. Now he seems afraid of marriage and will probably remain single for the rest of his life!"

Lao Qiao's ex-wife was an American-born Chinese. People say that she was very pretty, but by nature suspicious and easily jealous. She used to throw temper tantrums over nothing and even attempted committing suicide several times. Hospitalization and therapy had failed to cure her. Strangely, she calmed down after the divorce. She was able to hold down a job and raise her son properly. Two years ago, she married a retired white professor.

"They were not suited for each other by fate," was Zhao E's conclusion.

"Uncle Qiao, do you have many female students in your class?" Su Zhong asked, extending his hand to catch the wrappers thrown to him. The two brothers worked very fast with the dumplings; Lao Qiao could not keep up with them.

"Eh, very few! American girls just don't go into law, it's hard to find a job after they graduate. The legal profession still discriminates against women."

"What about in Taiwan?"

"About the same. There are more female law students there than in America, but their chances of employment are not very good."

"It's better on the mainland," Su Zhong said. "I received a letter from my former classmate several days ago. Last year, she was admitted to the People's University law school. I'm sure she's going to be a judge."

Lao Qiao was very interested to hear this, and he inquired about the girl in detail.

Yizhen placed a big pot of water on the stove, ready to put the dumplings in once the water was boiling. She sat next to Lao Qiao, helping him cut the dough into small pieces and roll them into balls.

"I have something to tell you all," Lao Qiao suddenly stopped rolling and began rubbing the rolling-pin with flour. He announced calmly, "I've decided to go back to China to teach."

Yizhen and her sons were stunned. Three pairs of eyes stared at him, unable to comprehend what he had just said.

Qiao Jianguang had been to China twice before. The first time he went, the Sus were still in Beijing. That was in 1974. Last year he went again with a delegation of lawyers and law professors from the West Coast. He had more criticism than praise for China, but he never expressed his views in print or in public lectures.

After he came back last year, he had said, "In some ways, such as in self-confidence and public morality, China is worse off now than during the days of the Gang of Four! When I first visited, the slogan was, 'The whole country learns from the Liberation Army.' Now it's 'The whole country learns from America!'"

Why did he, seemingly out of the blue, decide to go there and teach? The news hit Yizhen like a clap of thunder. She became very confused, but tried to compose herself and asked him, "Is it for a short term?"

"Not too short, one year."

They all felt relieved.

Su Zhong said frankly, "Thank God it's only for one year. For a moment, I thought you weren't coming back!"

A smile spread across Lao Qiao's face. Looking at the rolling-pin in his hand, he said carefully, "If everything goes smoothly and the work is interesting, I might stay longer. I'll just have to wait and see."

Yizhen's heart skipped a beat. It seemed that Lao Qiao intended to go back for good. It was strange that she had not the slightest notion about it before.

"I never thought you'd go back to China," she confessed. "I thought that if you ever wanted to go anywhere, it would be Taiwan."

Lao Qiao made frequent trips to Taiwan. He still had many classmates and friends there. He always had more praise than criticism for Taiwan's economic prosperity and democratic movement. During the past thirty years, Taiwan's achievements surpassed those of the mainland. On this point, he and Deming were in agreement.

When he heard Yizhen bring up the subject of Taiwan, Lao Qiao shook his head slightly and continued to roll the wrappers. "Taiwan does not need legal experts. There are plenty of them there, and they are of the highest calibre," he commented matter-of-factly, as if giving a lecture in the classroom. "The problem with Taiwan is whether the government has the determination and sincerity to implement democratic reforms and rule the country according to law. The situation in the mainland is quite different. Thirty years of self-imposed isolation and self-destruction have created a wasteland in the legal field. Not only are they in urgent need of general legal knowledge, they also need to fully understand and develop the concept of ruling by law. Last year, when we visited Beijing University, the People's University, and the Institute of Law, we talked with the schools' administrators and exchanged views with their faculties. I was deeply impressed by their sincere desire to attract legal experts to work for them. After I returned to the States, I thought about it a lot. Only recently did I make up my mind."

"Uncle Qiao," Su Zhong said, "I bet after one year, you can't wait to come back to America!"

"You think so?" Lao Qiao smiled and turned to Su Tai. "What do you think?"

Su Tai, who had said nothing the entire time, answered truthfully, "I don't know."

"A year is very short. I'll certainly come back to tell you my impressions," Lao Qiao said, determined to be cheerful.

A year was certainly not a long time. Yizhen agreed with him, but she felt an unspeakable sense of regret, even loss. Since reaching middle age, she understood the meaning of the passage of time, and was even more keenly aware of the transiency of life. Lao Qiao was their best friend. They had always relied on him for everything big or small--from the boys' choice of college to her taking English lessons. Now he was leaving. Would he really come back in a year?

She, too, had gone back home when she was young. Even now that kind of bravery seemed very idealistic and romantic. Although she had experienced many ups and downs afterwards, she never regretted her actions; she could only feel a lingering sadness. Perhaps it was like a girl's first love, which never loses its sweetness in one's memory.

"A year is very short. Besides, you'll certainly enjoy your stay and accomplish a great deal," Yizhen predicted. As she was saying this, she blurted out, "Even *I* would like to go back and see how things are now."

"Really?" Lao Qiao, who was bending over rolling the wrappers, immediately stopped, turned around, and asked her seriously.

To the small and thin Yizhen, his massive form loomed like a big mountain before her. Under his steady gaze, she felt as if she was being cross-examined by a judge in the court room. She was at loss for words. Instead of answering him, she addressed her children, trying to avoid the intensity of his blazing eyes, "Do you want to go back to China?"

The older boy was concentrating on making dumplings. With lips slightly apart, he had a serious expression on his face, like he was deep in thought.

This boy is becoming more and more like his late father, Yizhen thought. He rarely showed his emotions.

The younger boy answered loudly, "Of course not! It was so much trouble to get out, why would we want to go back? Living in America is better than in China, no matter how you look at it. Mom, you must be joking!"

Yizhen smiled evasively. She did not look up, but judging from Lao Qiao's silence in rolling the wrappers, she could tell that he was a little disappointed.

After a long pause, Su Tai finally spoke up. His voice was low and his words came out slowly, sounding as if they were the result of much careful consideration. "Life in America is free, but we could be truly happy if we enjoyed this freedom on Chinese soil. I think if there's an opportunity, it would be better to go back to China. But, there's no point in going back now, you have to have special skills to work for the Four Modernizations."

The younger boy stubbornly declared, "Even if I had special skills, I wouldn't go back!" He stopped making dumplings altogether, looked around at everybody, ready to carry his argument to the end. "Didn't father have special skills when he went back?" he asked his older brother. "He was a lung specialist of the highest calibre. He saved so many people! But as soon as the Cultural Revolution started, he was sent to the countryside to wield a hoe. They only remembered him when they needed him to butcher hogs and sheep for their New Year's feasts."

"Ah Zhong, there is no need to drag out the past," Yizhen interrupted her son gently. It was New Year's Eve. Why mention all the sadness of the past?

All the wrappers were finally made. Lao Qiao put down his rolling pin, dusted the flour off his hands, and sat down.

"A Chinese person should always want to do something for China," he tried to reason with Su Zhong. "But of course, it would also depend on the circumstances. You can't force anything."

Su Zhong shook his head and continued to insist on his views, "Our family has done enough for China, and has also suffered enough! Father was denounced as a British spy; Mother was a Japanese spy. What about my brother and I? We were branded 'educatable children.' That was just a slogan. What it really meant was that we were hopeless! Our whole family worked in the field. Father got out only when he became terminally ill. Even at death, he had to die outside of China, so he could save the government some medical expenses. To tell you the truth, we do not owe China anything, but China owes us a lot!"

He went on and on without being interrupted or challenged. Finally, his mother calmed him, "The relationship between the country and the individual is just like that between parents and children. It's hard to say who owes whom. Ah Zhong, no one is forcing you to go back. You don't have to be so defensive."

"It's time to cook the dumplings," Lao Qiao reminded his hostess.

The steam from the pot was already coming out of the kitchen door, so Yizhen and her sons went to work on their separate tasks. Su Tai was responsible for cooking the dumplings and steaming the buns; his mother was to cut the meat and cook the dishes; Su Zhong stayed in the living room with Uncle Qiao, discussing his applications to various colleges. He had applied to eight or nine colleges but had not heard from any of them yet. Being young and impatient, he was getting very anxious. Every time he saw Uncle Qiao, their conversation invariably turned to the merits of these colleges.

Qiao Jianguang had the reputation of a gourmet, because he had sampled many delicacies on his frequent visits to various places in the world. He rarely praised other people's cooking but seemed to make an exception for Yizhen. On the occasions he dined with them, he always had a few good words for her. Today he was especially generous with his compliments. Yizhen and the boys really felt flattered.

"I haven't had these steamed buns with red dates for many years. They're really good! You boys really know how to make buns!"

"Uncle Qiao, if you like them, just let us know. We can make more for you anytime."

"There are still lots of them left. Why don't you take some home?" Yizhen suggested. "When you want to eat them, just steam them in your rice cooker."

Qiao Jianguang gladly accepted them.

After dinner, they chatted in the dining room. Around ten o'clock, Qiao was just getting up to leave when the telephone rang.

Su Zhong answered the phone, exchanged a few words with the caller, then called his mother to the phone. "It's Uncle Yilie," he announced.

Yizhen apologized to Qiao, "Excuse me, I'll be right back, after I talk with Yilie for a moment."

Lao Qiao waved his hands and sat down again."

"Hi, Yizhen, how are you all?"

Yilie's baritone Taiwanese made his sister feel like she was back home.

"We're fine. What about you? Where are you spending the New Year?"

"We're having firepot[4] at a friend's house. And you?"

"We're having dumplings."

"Ha, they must be Chinese dumplings."

---

[4] In Chinese, firepot is called *huoguo*, similar to a Western-style winter stew, except that it is prepared and eaten as people sit around a table with a firepot in the center.

Not to be outdone, Yizhen retorted, "You must be having Japanese firepot, right?" Her brother's chuckle reverberated in the receiver. She continued, "Ah Lie, how is your work at the company?"

"Pretty good. I haven't been fired yet."

"When can you come see us? You said you would come, it's been two years...."

"How about March? I have a one-week vacation, and I also have some business to attend to in San Francisco."

Yizhen bit her lip, suppressing the urge to ask him what business he had in San Francisco.

"Hey, do you leftists have any news?" her brother asked.

"No. What about your Taiwan Independence Movement?"

"We're still protesting and demonstrating, carrying on our lonely struggle. The more setbacks we suffer, the more determined we are to fight on."

"You know what? That's a quotation from Chairman Mao!"

He chuckled again. It was hard to tell whether it was a forced laugh or a bitter one.

"How's that 'clique of Jiang Jieshi' doing?" Yilie asked.

This was a nickname Yilie gave to Su Deming because Deming was politically conservative and had befriended several prominent political figures in Taiwan during his frequent business trips to the island. Yilie used to include the adjective "reactionary" with the nickname, but dropped it only after his sister had pleaded several times on behalf of her brother-in-law.

Not waiting for her reply, Yilie continued, "Those involved in the Gaoxiong Incident will be tried under martial law soon, and the leaders of Taiwan's democracy movement will all be wiped out. The Jiang cliques must be very happy."

"You're wrong. No one is taking pleasure in this misfortune. Yilie, you can't just lump everybody together. You should be objective about things.

This very afternoon our sister-in-law, Zhao E, was here complaining to me about her nephew getting arrested."

After Yizhen told him the story of Zhao E's nephew, Yilie sneered, "How does this differ from your political campaigns on the mainland? Track down everybody on some kind of trumped-up charge. The Guomindang has learned well. The Chinese Communists must be praised for their good pupils!"

"How do you know?" Yizhen asked.

"The Guomindang said that those people who advocate democracy are plotting an overthrow of the government in order to achieve Taiwan's independence, and that this alone justified their bloody suppression. The Chinese Communists haven't said a thing about this matter. This means that they approve of it. Damn it! If we Taiwanese still entertain any illusion about the mainland, we must be blind!"

"Yilie, please don't be such an extremist, you're so pessimistic, too...."

"On the contrary, we, the oppressed people, have no right to be pessimistic, only the right to struggle!"

Yizhen shook her head and sighed. She changed the topic of conversation by asking him questions about his everyday life until finally they hung up. Not wanting to reveal her sorrow, she forced a smile when she faced Lao Qiao.

Lao Qiao got up again and asked her sympathetically, "Lin Yilie is becoming a radical, isn't he? Did he join the Taiwan Independence Alliance?"

Yizhen nodded, not knowing what to say.

"When my uncle came to see us last time, he had given up his insistence on Taiwan's independence. This Gaoxiong Incident must have forced him into taking action again," Su Tai remarked, feeling sorry for his uncle, his young face looking grim.

Su Zhong took exception to his brother's comment, "Uncle is really foolish. He always wants to do the impossible."

Yizhen did not have the heart to reproach her own brother. Instead, she gently corrected her son, "He is not foolish. China has disappointed him too much."

Lao Qiao wanted to change the tense atmosphere. He said in a tone of admiration, "No matter what, Lin Yilie's persistence is very heroic!"

Yizhen nodded, smiling sadly, "We Taiwanese have always been heroic and tragic."

After Lao Qiao left, her sons helped her clean up, then went to bed.

*   *   *

Yizhen sat alone in the living room. Supporting her chin on the palm of her hand, her eyes stared straight ahead into the empty television screen. Sitting there, she resembled an old monk in a trance, keeping her body still, not making the slightest movement.

She had never made a habit of staying up all night on New Year's Eve, but this New Year's Eve she did not feel sleepy at all. All the events that took place during the day and evening now reappeared in her mind, as if she was playing back a reel of film. Of these scenes, the news about Lao Qiao's return to China was the most poignant, recreated in close-up shots. In the stillness of the night, Yizhen began to realize the full impact of what all this meant to her.

The news alone was enough to revive many memories. Memory is like an old trunk: once it is opened, all its contents must be emptied. Forty-five years is not a short time. Recalling the vicissitudes of all those years filled Yizhen's heart with sadness. She remembered leaving Taiwan to go to Japan, then leaving Japan to go to China. She recalled her marriage, having her children, and how her family was shattered by the Cultural Revolution, then sunk into despair. She also remembered how Qiao Jianguang had found them, and all of a sudden, they had come to live in America; and, even more sharp was the memory of her husband's unexpected death. If life is like a journey, then, where would her next stop be?

The night was as cool as water. She sat there until her hands and feet turned icy cold and her body started to shiver; then she went into her room. She flung herself onto the big double bed and laid awake until dawn.

The next morning, Su Tai took the bus to go to school. After Su Zhong had also gone to school, Yizhen called Lucky Supermarket to say that she was unable to go to work. Not having slept a wink the previous night, she felt dizzy and unsteady on her feet. She did not feel like standing for four hours at the cash register. Actually, her being "unable to work" was just an excuse. The fact was, she did not want to work that day. Three days a week, she worked as a cashier at a supermarket for four hours a day to earn some extra income, as well as to idle away her time. Her mother-in-law and Deming did not really want her to work. Like Qiao Jianguang, they urged her to improve her English skills and then look for a more suitable job. For someone who was used to labor, Yizhen just could not stay at home. Besides, having some income of her own helped to alleviate the oppressive feeling of living under someone else's roof. Having been tempered in the May Seventh Cadre School,[5] she did not mind the change from being a university lecturer to a supermarket cashier in America, but she could not bring herself to tell her brother-in-law and mother-in-law how she felt.

There was something good about reform through labor, she thought. In some ways, it was similar to the American concept of the dignity of labor. But, of course, to use it as a means to persecute the intellectuals was something else. In some ways she felt that her sons had benefitted from having been sent to the countryside. Now, they especially appreciated the opportunity to go to college, and they knew the meaning of self reliance. Su

---

[5] The May Seventh Cadre School (*Wuqi ganxiao*) derived its name from the directive issued on that day in 1966 by Mao Zedong, in which he called for the re-education of the intellectuals by sending them down to the countryside to engage in physical labor. These "schools" were established throughout the country during the decade of the Cultural Revolution.

Tai was applying for a research assistantship for the next school year; Su Zhong also planned to find a job after he began college. Their uncle was willing to offer them financial support for their studies, but they both hoped to be self-supporting as soon as possible.

However, today, Yizhen had absolutely no interest in going to work. This lack of interest turned into feelings of guilt and confusion after reading a letter from Beijing.

The postman had arrived at about ten o'clock, as usual. Yizhen was sweeping the driveway. Seeing her, he picked out a letter and handed it to her.

"Mrs. Su, you have a letter from China. The stamp is really pretty."

"Thank you. I'll save the stamp for you."

She knew it was from her old classmate Yao Ping. Putting down her broom, she went inside to read the letter.

Yao Ping was a colleague at the College of Agriculture who continued to correspond with her, keeping her informed of recent developments at the college and news in Beijing. Her letters had become Yizhen's only contact with China.

When Yizhen and her family left China, the reason they gave was that Deqing was coming to America to visit his relatives and get medical treatment. All the people at the college speculated that Yizhen would not return; however, the school administrators still considered her request as a leave of absence, not a resignation.

The old Party Secretary who had just returned from the cadre school said to her, "You're one of our own graduates and an outstanding teacher at our college. Now you're leaving. It is our fault and our loss. But your *alma mater* will always welcome you back. Your position will remain open, and we will keep your name on the payroll. If you ever need us for anything, please feel free to contact us."

After they left China, Deqing's illness proved to be incurable. Amidst her sorrow, Yizhen did not have time to think about anything else. She had also put the college out of her mind. After Deqing's death, she wrote to Yao Ping and mentioned the unfortunate event in her family. Little did she expect that this letter would result in an avalanche of condolences from Yao Ping, her other colleagues and the leading cadres of the department. They expressed sorrow and regret at Deqing's death, some even blamed the "Gang of Four"[6] for his illness. From that time onward, Yao Ping and Yizhen corresponded regularly.

"We're critically short of teachers!" Yao Ping told her in the letter. "Of those who returned from overseas, more than half have left, and the other half are not sure whether they'll stay or not. People continue to apply to go abroad. The Party Secretary of our college said that we may have to hire people from foreign countries. Many of our faculty members have died, some are sick, and the rest are overworked. Do you remember the first two classes of worker-peasant-soldier students who stayed on to become lecturers? Now they all must take remedial courses before they can be sent into the classrooms to face the students. So, by a strange combination of circumstances, people of our generation have become the pillars of our college. Because the Four Modernizations have become a rallying point in recent years, all sorts of programs and research projects have mushroomed. Our teaching load is very heavy. I practically split myself in half trying to do all the work that needs to be done! Now, I have to give direction to graduate students. For fear that I'm not up to the task, I am doing some advanced studies on my own. Fortunately, I managed to learn some English during the Cultural Revolution, when I was 'pushed to the sideline.' English comes in handy now. Yizhen, could you send me some American books pertaining to

---

[6] The "Gang of Four" (*Sirenbang*) refers to the four radical leaders of the Cultural Revolution, headed by Mao's wife Jiang Qing. The other three high-ranking members were Zhang Chunqiao, Yao Wenyuan, and Wang Hongwen. Along with Jiang, they were all ousted in October, 1976.

my field?"

Yizhen read her friend's letter several times, feeling very guilty, as if the work she left behind was now pressuring her friend, Yao Ping. They were the best of friends in their student days. They had shared a bunk bed in the dorm and dreamed about carrying out a green revolution in China to revitalize its impoverished soil. But now, one was still at her job, while the other was drifting in a foreign land.

Yizhen was ashamed that she had let her professional training slip since leaving China. What were the newest reference works available in her field? She did not have the slightest idea.

She quickly made a sandwich, and took it with her to the library, intending to bury herself in books again for the first time in years.

Toward the evening, when Yizhen came home with several books, Lina had already arrived and Su Zhong was waiting impatiently.

"Auntie, where have you been?"

"Sorry, I was in the library reading and forgot the time."

Her son took her books and was a little surprised, "Mom, do you want to start working in your field again?"

"Aunt Yao asked me to send her some reference books. I need to familiarize myself with recent publications before I know what to send her."

Because of his mother's influence, Su Zhong had wanted to study agriculture since he was a little boy. He was happy to see his mother picking up her old trade. "Mom, do you want to take a course?"

"That's right, Auntie. If you take some courses, it will help you find a job," Lina chimed in.

"I'll wait and see. I'm afraid my English is not good enough."

Lina reminded them that Grandma must be getting anxious and asked them to hurry. They still had to pick up Su Tai from school.

"Ah Zhong, do you want to drive?" Lina asked her cousin. She had taught both brothers to drive.

"Lina, you better drive," Yizhen said. She did not quite trust her son's driving.

"Let me!" Su Zhong took the car keys and drove, his cousin sitting beside him. He first drove to his brother's school, then headed toward his uncle's house. Yizhen sat in the back seat, feeling uneasy the entire time. Cars and highways represented modern civilization to her, all of which she found a little threatening.

"Ah Zhong, drive slowly."

"Alright."

"Auntie, don't worry. It's the evening rush hour, he couldn't drive fast even if he wanted to."

Lina was always quick-witted, poised, and had an easy manner. She was not particularly pretty, but she had delicate features and beautiful jet black hair that fell to her waist. Her clothing showed discriminating taste, although she never looked flashy. She was the kind of girl who had style, and was well worth a second look. Since she graduated from college last year, she had been working as a newspaper reporter, and often drove around the Bay Area as part of her job. Zhao E felt that it was inappropriate for a girl to work in public all the time, and had been nagging her to work for her father in his import-export business. But, Lina had no interest in business.

Yizhen liked her niece very much, and they always had a lot to talk about when they saw each other.

"Lina, how is a reporter's work suiting you?"

"Not very well, I always get to go to city hall and the airport, but I never get to work on the big stories. I'm thinking of quitting."

Yizhen was about to advise her to be patient when Su Zhong suggested, "Why don't you go to graduate school?"

"I'm thinking about that, too, but both Mother and Grandma want me to get married first."

She was telling the truth. Yizhen thought about Paul Wan.

"Paul....How is Paul?" she asked intentionally; she wanted to know what her niece thought about him.

"We have nothing in common. He is an expert when it comes to having a good time. He's also interested in stocks. Other than that, he doesn't know anything."

"There are many boys from Taiwan," Yizhen comforted her. "You'll meet others."

Lina gave a snort of disapproval, "People from Taiwan are very hardworking, but they do not seem to know what they want, and they feel insecure. So, they only talk about green cards and job opportunities. They complain about America and they complain about Taiwan. I don't know, but I identify with America, and I don't have the kind of complaints they have." Lina was frank about her identification with America, and she felt right about being here. There was nothing that anyone could say against it.

Yizhen did not believe that Lina would go without having problems. She knew that she herself was troubled by many problems right now. Since she could not even sort out her own, she did not know what to say to Lina.

The two brothers did not have anything to say either. Luckily, the silence was broken when they arrived at their uncle's house.

Grandma was already waiting by the door. She was both happy to see them and annoyed that they had arrived so late.

"Ah Zhong did the driving," Lina laughingly reported. "How else could we get here so fast?"

"My goodness! But he just got his driver's license, how could you let him drive?" the old lady asked, her worry and concern clearly visible on her face.

"Didn't we all arrive safely?"

The old lady was still muttering, but she broke out with a smile anyway, displaying her neat white dentures.

Yizhen used to think that those dentures were her mother-in-law's only concession to the modern age. Today, for instance, her hair was combed into a big bun behind her head. She was dressed in a dark-colored, Chinese-style jacket with buttons down the front, and on her feet, she had on a pair of round-toed, flat-heeled shoes. This style was no different from what the wealthy old ladies used to wear in Yizhen's hometown when she was a little girl. Except for her white hair and many layers of wrinkles, time had stood still for her mother-in-law.

Deming had not come home yet. Zhao E was busy in the kitchen, so everyone went in and said hello to her.

"Everybody first drink a cup of red-date tea. We should all drink red-date tea on New Year's day," the old lady pointed to a pot of red-date and green tea on the table, directing Lina to pour it out for the assembled people.

"Let me do it," Yizhen volunteered. Knowing that Lina was afraid to gain weight and never touched anything sweet, she only poured a small cup for her as a symbolic gesture.

The Su family's house was big. The living room was spacious and tastefully furnished, and there was beautiful rosewood dinettes set imported from Taiwan in the formal dining room. But Yizhen's favorite room was the kitchen. It was about the same size as the living room, its walls were lined with cabinets, and it was equipped with all kinds of electric appliances. Besides a bar-style counter, there was enough room for a dining table and four chairs. Glass sliding doors led directly to the swimming pool in the backyard, and let in an abundance of sunlight, giving the room a bright and airy feeling.

Every time she saw this kitchen, Yizhen thought about the four-foot square kitchen she had in Beijing, and she thought about the pitiful sight of families cooking their meals in the hallway. She couldn't help but feel remorse about China's poverty and backwardness as opposed to America's affluence and wastefulness.

"Tonight we're going to have a vegetarian meal," Zhao E announced in a tone suggesting a slight warning while casting a glance toward her mother-in-law.

"We are not supposed to eat meat for breakfast or lunch on New Year's day, only at dinner can we eat meat," the old lady took great pains to explain.

"Since our entire family did not get to eat breakfast and lunch together, we have to make up for it by having a vegetarian meal for dinner. We're going to have twelve courses."

Mother-in-law pointed to the dishes on the counter. They were all the foods symbolizing good wishes, such as happiness, wealth and longevity, each according to its shape or name. For instance, noodles represented long life, and in the Taiwanese dialect, the word for "beans" sounded like the word for "old," so eating beans meant one would have nice things to eat during one's life. Yizhen was never very particular about the New Year's observations even when she was in China. She had been even more careless during the last several years in America. She did not expect the old lady to be so insistent on these old customs this year, and she could not help but sympathize with her sister-in-law. Serving such a mother-in-law really was no easy job.

"You're living in America now. Why do you still stick to Taiwanese customs?" Lina asked bluntly, taking exception to her grandmother's views.

"For Taiwanese living in America, if we don't keep our own traditions, then how are we different from the Americans?" the old lady forcefully refuted her granddaughter. Then, she turned to her second daughter-in-law, "Don't you agree, Ah Zhen?"

"Yes," Yizhen dared not disagree. Besides, she could not think of any reason for not doing so. She had heard that the Jewish people in America were very conservative about keeping their own traditions; their unity and outstanding achievements were a well-known fact.

A big pot of water was boiling on the stove. Her sister-in-law began cooking the noodles and remarked in a lukewarm voice, "If we want to stick to the old ways one hundred percent, it can only be done if we go back to Taiwan."

"That's not necessarily true. It depends on our efforts," the old lady immediately retorted, the muscles on her face tautly stretched. She did not have the slightest intention of compromising.

She turned to lecture Yizhen and her two grandsons, "How can we give up our traditions? As long as I'm alive, I'll keep reminding younger generations not to forget where they came from. Being in America is all the more reason not to forget Taiwan. If we forget Taiwan, we've forgotten our roots. Then we'll be just like a falling leaf driven by the wind, unable to ever reach the shore. What will we be then? Next year, you'll all have to go back with me to Taiwan for the New Year."

Zhao E winked at Yizhen behind the old lady's back, indicating her readiness to send her off.

From the front yard came the sound of a car door closing. Deming was home. In the kitchen the war of words immediately ceased.

Deming was a jovial fellow with a round face and ruddy complexion; only his piercing eyes revealed his intelligence and ability. His hair was thinning but carefully dyed black and neatly combed. He was putting on weight and had the confident look of someone who was successful in his career.

The old lady had a great deal of respect for her son, and her son was also filial toward his mother. So, the friction between mother-in-law and daughter-in-law was never mentioned in front of him.

After he arrived home, he first shot a round of pool with the Su brothers, then it was time for dinner.

"What's the matter? I heard that Qiao Jianguang is going to the mainland?" Deming lifted up a bowl of noodles and sought confirmation from Yizhen.

"He's going to the People's University to teach international law for a year."

Everyone was shocked to hear this news.

"Life is so hard on the mainland. Why does he want to look for trouble for himself? Will he be able to leave China after a year?" Zhao E could not conceal her astonishment and disbelief. In her way of thinking, Lao Qiao was taking too great of a risk.

"The Chinese government is welcoming people who go there to teach. They wouldn't dare detain anyone!" Deming said rationally. "Life in Beijing must have improved somewhat by now."

"Is he going to stay in a hotel?" the old lady asked, concerned about Qiao's welfare. "I heard that you can only find good things to eat in the hotels."

"During the last several years, they have treated those returning from abroad very well," Yizhen explained to her mother-in-law. "There won't be any problems with living conditions. I only worry about the possibility of political struggles starting up all over again."

"Deng Xiaoping and company should be able to keep the lid on everything for several years," Deming expressed his cautious optimism. Then, in a moment of sudden inspiration, he smiled and said, "Hey, one of these days I'm going there, too. I want to see if there are any opportunities for doing business with them. The way it is now the Japanese are pocketing all the profits from the sales of Taiwanese goods to the mainland!"

"You're going to the mainland!" Zhao E stared at her husband so hard that her small eyeballs bulged. She returned the spinach to her bowl that she was about to eat, too stunned to want to know the taste of food.

The old lady frowned and looked at her son, not knowing whether or not he was joking.

"Well, what's there to be afraid of?" Deming seemed nonchalant. "It would just be for the purpose of doing business. Even the Taiwanese government keeps one eye open and the other eye closed."

"Why not?" Lina supported her father. "Trade is mutually beneficial. It's good for both sides."

Zhao E was still dead set against her husband going to China. She was afraid that her entire family would be unable to return to Taiwan as a result.

"Deming," the old lady spoke up, "you'd better wait till Ah Zhen has visited Taiwan before you consider going to the mainland."

"All right, all right, I'm not going anyway! I was just kidding," Deming tried to calm everybody down, and they all ceased talking about going to the mainland.

After dinner, Yizhen had just put the plates in the dishwasher when the doorbell rang.

"Who could that be?" Zhao E was a little surprised.

"It must be my friend!" Lina jumped up.

"What, you have a date?" Zhao E followed her daughter out, questioning her, displeased that she was planning to go out on a day meant for family reunions.

"Johnny asked me to see a movie," Lina explained a little apologetically and gave her mother a quick hug. Then she hurried to the door. A few moments later, she returned with a young tall blond American man. He was impeccably dressed in a suit and tie.

"Dad, this is Johnny. He's a graduate student at Stanford. Johnny, this is my father, that is my grandmother...."

Lina introduced Johnny to everyone as he nodded and said "Hi" to each of them. He was very polite, even though he could not disguise his surprise at seeing so many people assembled in the living room.

"Today is Chinese New Year. So all the members of our Su family are gathered here," Lina told him.

"I see! Happy New Year!" he exclaimed, wishing everyone well in a friendly manner.

"Please wait a minute. I'll be right back," Lina said as she went upstairs.

Deming asked Johnny to sit down, as Lina's grandmother brought out the candy tray. She did not approve of her granddaughter having an "American" boyfriend, but she would never be caught lacking in etiquette. She treated him with the same courtesy as she extended to all of her guests.

"What are you studying?" Deming passed a cigarette to Johnny.

"No thank you, I don't smoke. I'm studying sociology."

"Sociology? Ah, that's good."

They chatted for a little before Lina came down with her purse. She had changed into high-heels, put on some lipstick and a pink wool jacket. She looked very lovely in the light, her shining black hair flattering her pretty face.

"We'll be back right after the movie," Lina told her parents.

"Come home early!" Zhao E added.

Amidst good-byes, they watched Lina leave holding onto Johnny's arm. "Sociology!" Deming spit out the syllables, took a deep puff off his cigarette, then fell silent.

Zhao E collapsed into the sofa, her small eyes staring fixedly ahead, her powdered face was ashen.

Her mother-in-law sat between Yizhen's sons, pressing herself tightly against them as if she was afraid that they might also run away.

Lina took with her the happy mood of the New Year's celebration, her family's lively conversation was silenced. After making small talk with her mother-in-law about New Year's customs in Taiwan, Yizhen got up to leave, unable to bear the depressing atmosphere any longer.

Zhao E drove them home. On the way, she said to the two brothers half seriously, half jokingly, "Ah Tai, Ah Zhong, you must both go back to Taiwan to get married. This way you will not hurt your Grandma's feelings."

They all laughed in embarrassment.

"It's too early for them to worry about that!" Yizhen said as she burst out laughing. Her own laughter startled her, it was so dry and hollow.

*   *   *

The most surprising development was yet to come. Several days later, a terribly agitated Zhao E paid an unexpected visit to Yizhen. She informed Yizhen that Lina had moved out.

"Why? Did she have a fight with the family?" Yizhen knew that her niece had a mind of her own and was quite Americanized. Her way of thinking was very different from that of her family.

"I wouldn't call it a fight. But she wanted to marry Johnny, and we did not approve. That was all."

"Get married!" Yizhen was startled. "Their relationship has gone as far as that?"

Feeling depressed, Zhao E shook her head and sighed repeatedly. She was not wearing much make-up, and her face looked sallow. She had lost several pounds in just a few days. The wrinkles on her face were now clearly visible, making her look much older than before.

"We're as confused as you are. How could she become so involved with that American student so fast? Her father doesn't even dare openly oppose her. He just says that since the young man is not financially independent yet, she should wait a couple of years. In the meantime, she should make more friends and keep her eyes open."

"What he says is right. She's still young. What's her hurry?"

"I agree! This child...her father blames me for spoiling her, she even accused us of racial discrimination! She said we're always prejudiced against Americans! She said that her sister married an American, why can't she do the same? And she said...," Zhao E was too angry to repeat what her daughter had said.

Yizhen patted her sister-in-law's trembling shoulders, trying to comfort her, "Well now, don't be so upset, don't take the matter so seriously. Lina is a sensible girl after all. What did mother-in-law say about it?"

In their emotional state, they had forgotten the reaction of the most important member in the family.

"She wouldn't say a single word to me," Zhao E replied. "She just shuts herself up in her room all day long. Deming is all gloom and doom as well. I didn't have a fight with Lina! But, now that she has moved out, they blame everything on me. Can you see what a fix I'm in?"

"Don't be upset. I'll have a talk with Lina. Do you know where she moved to?"

"It's better not to talk about it. It's really a disgrace!" she said, not realizing that she had lowered her voice. "She just called me. She said...she's living with Johnny for the time being."

Yizhen could not conceal her shock. She never expected that Lina would be as liberal as that. She said, "Deming and mother-in-law...do they know?"

Zhao E shook her head in despair, "What are we going to do?"

Her eyes were red and swollen from crying. She looked so miserable and vulnerable that she reminded Yizhen of a little lamb who had lost its way in the mountains.

"Don't tell them yet. I'll find Lina immediately and tell her to move out and find a place of her own. Everything else we can discuss later."

Zhao E left a check with Yizhen and asked her to give it to her daughter. Having done this, she seemed to be a little relieved and drove back home.

Yizhen did not tell her sons about this matter. That same night, she called Lina and asked her to come over for lunch the next day. Guessing Yizhen's intentions, Lina hesitated somewhat before accepting the invitation.

Yizhen cooked a potful of rice noodles and made Lina's favorite hot and sour soup. Although Lina was Americanized, her taste in food was still Chinese, and she especially liked the dishes from certain provinces.

"How long have you been in love with Johnny?" Yizhen asked her niece point-blank.

"I don't know exactly when I fell in love with him, but we have known each other for almost a year."

Yizhen did not dare say that their acquaintance was too short; she only nodded understandingly, "If you really love each other, your father and mother will surely agree to your marriage. Your Grandma will also."

Yizhen took the liberty of making this promise and then proceeded to reason with her. She explained to Lina that, given her father's social status both in Taiwan and in America, and his prestige among the Taiwanese circles here, it would be very hard for him to accept the fact that his daughter was living with a man out of wedlock. She urged Lina to go back to her family or rent an apartment on her own. At the very least, she should not disgrace her parents.

"They really love you. You don't doubt that do you?"

Lina nodded.

"Then, you must make some symbolic sacrifice for them. Is that too much to ask?"

"I always thought that one's actions should be consistent with one's beliefs. Everyone should be honest to him or herself. Johnny loves me, and I love Johnny. There's no reason why we shouldn't live together. But as you say, in order to prove that I also love my father and mother, I will move out of Johnny's place."

"Why don't you move back in with your family? You are the only daughter your parents have now."

Lina firmly shook her head.

"I never wanted to date the Chinese boys they introduced to me!"

Lina's irritable and somewhat contemptuous answer displeased Yizhen, but she suppressed her annoyance and forced a smile. When she thought about Paul Wan, she could not blame her niece. "It's up to you," she said, "but please find somewhere else to stay as soon as possible. Your mother and

I will come to see you."

She took out the check Zhao E gave her, but Lina refused to take it.

"I can support myself. Whether I get a fellowship or not, I'm going back to graduate school this fall. I won't ask my parents for money. Johnny and I can help each other."

Yizhen did not have a very high impression of that American boy, but now she felt some respect for him.

Two days later, Lina called to say that she had found a small apartment in Palo Alto.

"When I get my telephone and put my apartment in order, I'll invite you and Mother to come to see me."

"Great! We'll certainly come. But, Lina, if you have time now, why don't you go home and see Grandma. She misses you tremendously!"

"Oh, I can do that. But if I go, I want to take Johnny with me."

Yizhen sighed, but after thinking it over, she cheerfully agreed, "Of course, you go ahead and bring him along."

After some persistence, the trouble in Deming's household was finally resolved.

*   *   *

In the middle of March, Lin Yilie came to San Francisco to participate in political activities, and he took some time off from his work to stay at his sister's house for two nights.

"Yilie, why don't you get married? If you do, at least you'll have someone to look after you," Yizhen tried to advise her brother who was already forty years old and still single.

The last time she saw him, at Deqing's funeral, Yilie had not looked so exhausted and emotional. Although he was far from being fat then, he was not as skinny as he was now. He had lost so much weight that he could hardly hold up his pants with a belt. The lack of sleep had caused his eyes to sink in; his gaze burned like a torch, as if he could incinerate anything around him with a mere glance. His disheveled hair looked like it had not been washed for years. Judging from his appearance, people might easily think that he had just been released from prison.

"There's no hurry. If I want a wife, I'll go back to Taiwan to get one," Yilie answered nonchalantly.

"Now that you've joined the Taiwan Independence Alliance, and your name appears on the blacklist, how can you return to Taiwan?"

"I'll go back some day," Yilie shrugged his bamboo-stick-like shoulders and bared his white teeth. His expression was both stubborn and naive.

Seeing this, Yizhen could not help but feel sad.

Political passion was truly a mystery to Yizhen . It was something which Yizhen could not understand. For the sake of Taiwan's democracy, the two Lin brothers had paid a heavy price: one had been imprisoned and died, the other was on Taiwan's wanted list.

"Please don't regard all the people who want Taiwan's independence as dangerous," Yilie tried to lure his sister to his side. He continued, trying to explain to her the situation in Taiwan, "After the Gaoxiong Incident, all Taiwanese who want reform are suspects in the eyes of the government. Those who show some regional sentiment are considered to be promoting Taiwan's independence! As for the mainlanders, if they want reform, they are Communist sympathizers. You are a Taiwanese who has been to the mainland. If you go back to Taiwan, you must play the role of a so-called anti-Communist warrior, otherwise, political labels will be pinned on you--an advocate for Taiwan's independence, or a Communist sympathizer. These ready-made labels will be bestowed upon you by some magazine, in complete disregard of reason and logic. Yizhen, you definitely cannot go back now!"

Yizhen knew that she could not go back right now, but she still held on to her hopes for Taiwan.

"I don't want to get involved in politics. Having been through the Cultural Revolution, I believe in peaceful reform. If you really want to do something for our people, you should go back to Taiwan and work for your cause. Now, when you're thousands of miles away from our homeland, can you really expect to establish an independent country by smashing the windows of government agencies and bombing empty houses that belong to the children of government officials? I think you'd better withdraw from the Taiwan Independence Alliance."

Yilie forced a smile, "There's no turning back for me."

Yizhen could detect bitterness and despair in his otherwise calm tone. She saw his sad smile of determination. His mood also affected hers.

When she thought about the recent murder of Lin Yixiong's family, on the anniversary of the February Twenty-eighth Incident,[7] she quivered. The price for political activism was to have one's own mother and young daughter murdered! This tragedy really elicited her sympathy for Lin Yixiong; it also made her more concerned about her brother.

So full of her own self-contradiction, she revised her own way of thinking and pleaded, "Yilie, you definitely should not go back to Taiwan now. Just think about it, our Lin family has only you and our nephew left!"

"Elder Sister, don't worry! A righteous family will always have heirs," Yilie laughed out loud, hoping to dispel his sister's fears.

Yizhen was perplexed as she watched her brother pace back and forth across the living room, not knowing how to help him. She hoped that the political chill in Taiwan would only be temporary, and that the situation would soon take a turn for the better so that no harm would come to her brother.

"The future of Taiwan will be bright. I believe that economic development, advances in science and technology, the spread of education and

---

[7] Or *Taiwan Ererba shibian*. This refers to an incident that occured on February 28, 1947 in Taibei, Taiwan, between a female Taiwanese cigarette peddler, Lin Jiangmai, and some official inspectors--Sheng Tiefu, Zhong Yanzhou, Zhao Zijian, Fu Xuetong, and Ye Degen. The inspectors' brutal assault on this woman ignited a chaotic riot throughout the province, resulting in the loss of many innocent lives and the distrust of Taiwanese people toward the Nationalist government.

literacy, and most important of all, the people's desire for political participation will make the Nationalist government more open and democratic. The current situation cannot last long. We shouldn't lose hope," she said, not only comforting her brother, but also consoling herself.

She noticed Yilie was standing in front of the window, gazing at the mountains to the west. Following his line of vision, she saw a horizontal band of white clouds covering the mountain top, and she understood how her brother felt at this moment. In the past, when he was seriously ill, Deqing often asked her to draw open the curtain of the westward window to let him see the scenery that was so similar to today's. She knew that the clouds were formed by water vapors as they rose from the ocean. She also knew that the Pacific Ocean lay some where beyond this green mountain and these white clouds. And on the other side of the ocean was her home and country, the land that constantly filled her thoughts.

At this moment, the look in Yilie's eyes was unusually gentle and calm, as if he was flying over the Pacific Ocean to his homeland, giving him an air of peacefulness. Yizhen understood how her brother felt. She herself left Taiwan when she was eleven years old, yet she still cherished the memory of the people and the scenery there. How much more this must be true for her brother who had devoted his whole life to his native land. She recalled a line from "Ascending a Tower," a rhymed-prose by the Han dynasty writer, Wang Can: "It is human nature to be attached to one's homeland, a nature not changed by adversity or prosperity."[8] While living in Tokyo with her parents, she had first read this line as a child; later, when she was in Beijing with Deqing, they had savored this line together. Now, at middle age, after traveling such a long road and becoming separated farther and farther from home, she appreciated the meaning of this sentence even more.

---

[8] Wang Can (177-217), a famous rhymed-prose (*fu*) writer, wrote "Ascending a Tower" (*Denglou fu*) to register his nostalgia, homesickness, and loneliness over his hometown, north of Changan, the Western Capital of the Han empire.

It was quiet in the living room. Brother and sister stood side by side in front of the window, gazing at the white clouds and green mountains to the west, dreaming about their homeland on the other side of the Pacific Ocean.

When Deming heard about Yilie's arrival, he called and insisted on giving a dinner party in his honor. He said, "Zhao E has a cold, so she and Mother would rather stay home. We'll go to a restaurant. I'll pick you up at six o'clock this evening. If Lao Qiao is free, I'll ask him to join us."

Yilie had no intention of troubling Deming with a dinner invitation, but he accepted for the sake of his sister.

Deming made a reservation at the Yipinxiang Restaurant. When he arrived at the restaurant with Yizhen and her family, Qiao Jianguang was already there.

"I haven't seen you for several years, Yilie. How have you been?" Lao Qiao shook hands with him warmly.

"I'm still alive, thank you. How are you, Professor Qiao?" Yilie grinned broadly, very much his lively and humorous self.

"Just call him Lao Qiao," Deming suggested. "We're good friends. Please don't be so formal."

Business was brisk at Yipinxiang; every table was occupied. Service was good and fast. As soon as the four *hors d'oeuvres* were taken away, a piping hot firepot was brought to the table.

"What do you think, Lao Qiao? The food here is pretty good. Isn't it?" Deming was anxious to hear Lao Qiao's approval.

Lao Qiao just smiled, not saying yes or no.

"He is a gourmet," the host explained to Yilie. "Any restaurant he approves is guaranteed to be good. You can walk in with your eyes closed."

"Stop," Lao Qiao protested. "Your lavish praise makes me look like a glutton. Actually, any food that I don't have to take the time to cook myself is good food in my book."

"I agree!" Yilie raised his glass to him.

Everybody agreed with this philosophy, so they all drank to it.

The dishes were well prepared and the conversation was congenial. Deming liked to entertain in restaurants. Without his mother and wife at his side, he was particularly talkative. After a couple of drinks, he suddenly asked Yilie in a friendly tone, "Yilie, what do you think of the recent murder of the Lin family?"

When Yizhen heard this question, her heart sank. *Men are such strange animals*, she thought to herself, *why must they always talk about politics?*

Everyone present looked at Yilie.

"It was obviously a terrorist act intended to frame someone," Yilie replied.

When he talked about politics, Yilie's long, skinny face suddenly took on a very sharp and serious expression, as if his entire face had been chiseled by knives. "The newspapers hinted over and over again that it must be the work of the opposition party or the Taiwan Independence Movement. As a matter of fact, the more the government tries to cover up, the more they expose their own dirty work."

Becoming very agitated, Yilie continued, "The two accused parties wouldn't be so stupid as to hurt their own people. Even if they contemplated such an action, they wouldn't have the ability to carry it out! The Taiwanese people don't have a tradition of political assassinations, especially murdering an entire family. They really overestimated our capabilities!" Anger flashed in Yilie's eyes, which protruded like those of a goldfish--looking as if at any moment they would pop out of their sockets.

"I'm sure the government didn't do it," Deming hastened to defend the government. "Now that all the people involved with *Beautiful Island* magazine have been arrested, the government has scored a major victory. There's no point in resorting to such stupid tactics and bringing trouble upon themselves. Wouldn't you agree? President Jiang Jingguo is promoting a 'Love Campaign.' He certainly would not let his subordinates carry out such a despicable act."

"It's too horrible!" Yizhen instinctively lowered her voice as if by doing so, she could reduce the terror of this incident. "No matter how guilty Lin Yixiong is, this blood bath should have cleansed him."

"He never did actually take part in the Gaoxiong Incident. Now, because of this tragedy, the government will most probably declare him innocent of all charges," Deming replied. He did not approve of the extremist actions taken by those associated with *Beautiful Island*, but he was sympathetic toward Lin Yixiong.

"I met Lin Yixiong once," Lao Qiao expressed his opinion. "He is a very frank and straightforward person, a conscientious lawyer and provincial representative. For a person of his caliber to be drawn into a political storm and bloody murder, it is a great loss, both for him and for the country."

As they talked, the mood at the table became more and more depressing. Yizhen never before had such an upset stomach. She was about to change the subject of the conversation when Deming abruptly struck the table top and came up with a startling new idea.

"Since neither the opposition party nor the Nationalist Party did it, it must be the work of the Chinese Communists!"

Before Yizhen could say anything, her two sons already protested in unison, "Impossible! Absolutely impossible!"

"It's hard to say," Deming's shining face was now shrouded in a dark shadow, "Didn't they kill a lot of people during the Cultural Revolution? In order to stir up trouble, they might have taken advantage of the situation in Taiwan and killed a few people. It's not impossible!"

Lao Qiao shook his head, "I think at present, China would prefer a stable Taiwan."

Yilie nodded, then added with a touch of contempt, "Moreover, the Communists' ability to engage in political activities is ten thousand times below that of Taiwan's own opposition party!"

"This is not a matter of ability," Su Zhong came forward with his explanation. "The Communists do not engage in assassinations. What Lin Biao's gang did during the Cultural Revolution was an exception."

Lao Qiao pointed out to Deming, "As you know, public security organizations in Taiwan are very efficient. If this case has really involved the Communists, wouldn't they know about it?"

"Please, I beg you, don't talk about this anymore, all right?" Yizhen's face was ashen white. She added, "I think a mad man did it!"

"I'm sorry, Ah Zhen," Deming quickly apologized, "we won't talk about it anymore."

All the courses were now on the table. Deming urged everybody to eat.

"Believe it or not," he said to Yilie, "Lao Qiao is going to the mainland to teach law for a year."

"What?"

Yilie looked at Lao Qiao in astonishment, as if he was an alien from another planet, an object of curiosity.

"That's right. I'm selling my house."

Yizhen was stunned by Lao Qiao's latest announcement. *Doesn't he plan to come back to America?*

"Why sell the house?" Deming also found it hard to believe, he continued, "You'll be gone for only one year. You can rent it out. I'll manage it for you."

"Thank you, Deming. To tell you the truth, I've been tired of living in a house for quite a while; it takes too much of my time to take care of it. If I lived in an apartment, it'd save me a lot of work."

Except for Yilie, they had all been to Lao Qiao's house. It was a huge house with a large lawn. It really did need a lot of work to maintain.

"Then you should buy a condo. Because of high interest rates and the recession, home prices have dropped. If you buy one and sell one, you can

128

still break even," Deming advised. When it came to the subject of doing business, Deming's interest was immediately aroused.

Lao Qiao nodded, "I might consider that."

His answer was rather evasive--an evasiveness only noticed by Yizhen and she was troubled by it. Consequently, she was unable to pay attention to what was said the rest of the evening.

The next day, early in the morning, Yilie drove away from his sister's house. He headed south. He did not divulge where his next stop would be, and Yizhen did not feel it was appropriate to ask.

"Ah Lie, you must be careful, very careful!"

All her anxiety and concern were fully contained in this one piece of advice.

"Don't be afraid, Yizhen."

Yilie tried hard to keep his composure. As he waved good-bye, a faint smile appeared on his face; it looked so sad, yet so heroic.

Yizhen stood at the street corner watching him drive away. Even after he turned the corner and his car disappeared from view, she remained standing there, frozen. She was seized by a sense of aimlessness. The sun had just come out, its rays blurring her vision. She had to squint to make out the street scene at the crossroads. The commuters' cars drove by, one after another, some going from this side to the other side, some coming from the other side to this side. They were all in a great hurry, yet they moved in an orderly fashion, each having its own sense of direction. Only she stood there alone at the crossroads, watching from the sidelines. Transfixed, she was overcome by feelings of loss and confusion, suddenly so keenly aware of the onset middle age.

"Mom, I'm going," her son said, quickly walking past her, his backpack bulging with books. Still chewing the last bite of toast in his mouth, he was on his way to catch the bus to school.

His backpack reminded her of the stack of books she had left on the windowsill in her bedroom. Her reading had been progressing slowly, because she had to stop frequently to consult the dictionary. She had finished reading only a small portion of her books.

"At least, let me finish reading those books," she thought to herself. When it came to her work, Yizhen had always been enthusiastic. She turned around and ran back into the house.

* * *

Yizhen resigned from her part-time cashier job and immersed herself in reading. Because of her training and interest in the field, she was unable to put the books down once she picked them up. She busied herself with looking up words in the dictionary and taking notes. Sometimes she worked until past midnight. She worked even harder than Su Zhong.

"Mom is really working hard!"

Her sons praised her, but they were also concerned about her health. At times, when she removed her reading glasses and rubbed her strained eyes, they would say to her, "Mom, you're not going to take a test. There's no need to be so serious!"

"I've been out of practice for so long. If I don't work hard, how can I catch up?"

Yizhen buried herself completely in her studies as time sped by. One day, as she was turning over the calendar, she discovered that it was almost time for the Qingming Festival.[9]

According to the precedent set during the last two years, Yizhen and her mother-in-law would go to sweep Deqing's grave on this day. This year's Qingming Festival fell on a Saturday. Su Tai had to help his professor work on a research project, so he could not come home. Su Zhong was on his school's basketball team, and he had to attend practice and go play in a game over the weekend. So her mother-in-law decided that they would go on

[9] The Qingming Festival is the traditional Chinese festival to honor the dead.

Sunday instead.

Yizhen woke up very early on the morning of April fifth. Unable to resist the sound of the birds chirping outside, she got up, pushed the window open and looked out. The streets and the houses in the neighborhood were very quiet, as if they had not woken up from last night's sleep.

The house across the street had a row of jasmine flowers planted around it, their sweet fragrance assailing one's nostrils and even penetrating one's heart. Deqing's cemetery was surrounded by a fence of jasmine bushes. *It must be permeated with the fragrance of jasmine by now*, Yizhen thought. *I'm going to see him alone*, she told herself. *I want to have a heart-to-heart talk with him.*

She and Ah Zhong had breakfast. After sending him off, she changed into a plain-looking dress and left home. She bought a bouquet of yellow chrysanthemums, Deqing's favorite flowers. He had worked on a state farm in China and experienced the scenery described by the poet Tao Qian [A.D.365-427], "plucking chrysanthemums under the eastern hedge, gazing leisurely at the southern mountains." From that time on, he was in love with chrysanthemums.

After changing buses, she walked for about fifteen minutes before arriving at the cemetery. The jasmine flowers were in buds, but their faint fragrance could already be detected. The delicate scent wafted throughout the cemetery. It had been a year since she visited this place, and now the row where Deqing's tombstone stood was almost completely filled. With all these new companions, he should not feel so lonesome. On her first visit, her heart had jumped when she discovered a new tombstone beside his, but now she was more calm about things.

She laid down the flowers before the tombstone and stood facing east, her palms drawn together, her head bowed, and her eyes closed. Whenever she came here, she always felt that Deqing was beside her. When the breeze touched her dress, she even imagined that it was Deqing's caress. Her husband had been a man of few words, but his heart had always been very close to hers. She had understood his every glance and gesture.

As she stood there with her eyes closed, she mentally reviewed her life and her sons' lives during the past year. She told Deqing that their sons were both striving to make progress. Ah Tai was catching up with his studies as a college freshman. He even received an A in one subject. He was honest and hard-working. His professors were very fond of him and were willing to assist him outside class. The chances that he would get a scholarship this fall were very good.

Ah Zhong was very bright and he also knew how to apply himself to his studies. During the past year in high school, he excelled in both academics and athletics. He had been selected for the school's basketball team. That made him busier than ever, but it was also an honor to have been chosen. He had applied to several colleges, and half of them were out of state. This fall, he probably would leave home to go to college.

As for myself...suddenly she faltered, not knowing what to say next. It seemed to her that reaching middle age was like coming to a crossroad; abruptly, life's course seemed so uncertain.

"What am I to do?" she entreated her dead husband.

"It was for the sake of our children's future that we backtracked from our original goal," Deqing had said to her right before he died. "If appropriate arrangements are made for their education and you no longer need to worry about them, then you should consider your own future."

"If you leave me, what future will I have?" she had choked, sobbing.

"Don't be so foolish, Ah Zhen, listen to me. You're still young. If you meet a good reliable person, you should remarry. The children will have one more person to look after them. This is my wish."

The thoughtful Deqing had even thought out other possible arrangements for her. "If you do not like America, you can go back to the mainland or Taiwan. Choose a place where you can live and work in dignity.

Taiwan, I will never see Taiwan again, but you can go. You must go there and see it for me."

Yizhen opened her eyes, turned around, and looked in the direction of the tombstone. High above the jasmine bushes was a clear blue sky. And she knew that under that blue sky was the Pacific Ocean, and on the other side of the ocean was her homeland.

When Deqing had realized that he was not going to recover, he left instructions that his tombstone must face the Pacific Ocean. He also asked to be cremated.

"For the time being, I'll keep all of you company. But one day, when you are all independent, please let my ashes rest on the soil of my native country."

Thinking about her husband's love for his native land, how he died before he could realize his ambitions, and about herself drifting alone in a strange country, Yizhen's eyes began to moisten.

The spring sun in California was unusually fierce around noontime. Yizhen did not know how long she had been there; she only knew that she felt dizzy and feverish and that she could not stand there any longer. She took one more look at the tombstone then walked toward the cemetery gate.

"Yizhen!"

She looked up and saw Qiao Jianguang walking toward her with a bouquet of carnations in his arms.

"Why are you here...," she stammered, too surprised to complete her sentence.

Lao Qiao probably had walked too fast, for drops of perspiration appeared on his forehead and he was breathing heavily. As soon as he stopped in front of Yizhen, he took out his handkerchief to wipe away his sweat.

"You came by yourself? Why didn't you tell me? I could've given you a ride."

"Both of my kids are busy today; they'll come tomorrow."

"I was talking to a Cantonese friend this morning and found out the Qingming Festival is today. I'm leaving soon, so I thought this would be a good chance to say good-bye to Lao Su."

"It was very nice of you to be so thoughtful." Yizhen expressed her gratitude on behalf of her dead husband, then accompanied Lao Qiao to the grave site. They laid down the flowers and bowed their heads in prayer.

By this time, there were other mourners in the cemetery, but everything was still quiet and peaceful. The jasmine flowers, basking in the sunlight, gave off a rich perfume. The entire cemetery was enveloped in a warm and sweet fragrance.

Lao Qiao and Yizhen left the cemetery and walked toward the parking lot.

"Do you need to be home by noon?"

Yizhen shook her head. Her sons were not at home. No matter where she was, she was always alone.

"That's good. Let's have lunch first, then I'll take you home."

They found a Chinese restaurant in San Mateo and decided on what to order. The waiter brought them two glasses of ice water. Lao Qiao was so thirsty he gulped his down instantly.

"I signed the contract this morning. My house is sold!" he said, sounding very cheerful and relaxed, as if he had just completed an important task.

"So fast! Did you sell it too cheaply?"

Lao Qiao was very evasive, and he smiled but did not answer her question. It was obvious that the deal was closed with great haste.

Yizhen felt sorry for him. It was very difficult to sell a house these days because of the high interest rates. Deming said that there were absolutely no buyers for houses and, unless one was willing to sell below market cost, there would be no chance for a sale.

"I hope you can buy a condo just as smoothly," Yizhen tried to comfort him, at the same time regretting his loss.

Lao Qiao leaned back against his chair, thus putting more distance between himself and Yizhen, but his gaze never left her face.

"I'm not going to buy a condo. I've decided to invest the money in government bonds to earn long-term interest."

This unexpected development and the intensity of Lao Qiao's steady gaze were too much for Yizhen to bear. She lowered her eyes, stuttered and stammered, not knowing what to say.

"Then you'll come back...not come back...stay in China permanently?"

He did not answer but kept looking at her, as if not wanting to miss any change in her facial expression. He finally asked her, "Do you think I'm taking too great a risk?"

At this moment, she raised her head bravely and looked straight at him. *Risk or no risk, was there any need to ask? Didn't our Su family's experience happen during the past quarter of a century right in front of your very own eyes?*

She did not speak her thoughts. Time was marching forward. But China, with its land and people, with its heavy burden of history, would forever be waiting for change.

She moistened her lips with her tongue, keeping her agitation under control, and said calmly, "Now is the best time to go back to live and work. China really needs talented people."

This kind of reply was a cliche right from the newspapers and magazines, but Lao Qiao was greatly encouraged. He let out a long sigh, his gaze softened. He was so moved that tears welled up in his eyes.

Yizhen believed that with his knowledge and experience, he certainly could not be asking her for advice. On the other hand, he was going through a fierce struggle in his own mind at this moment, and it seemed that he wanted reassurance to support his decision.

"Going back at my age is not heroic at all--not like when you and your husband returned out of patriotism. I'm going back for myself, for my own salvation." In a deep and slow voice, he bared his feelings of isolation from having lived in a foreign country for so long. "I've taught law in America for more than twenty years. Every day I look at the same people's faces--faces that chase after money. It gets really boring after a while. If I continue to live this way, I'm afraid I'll become insane some day. I had lofty ideals before, but I lacked the courage to realize them. No matter what I wanted to do, I always had to consider raising and educating my son first. Now that he has graduated from college and left home, I have no more worries. So you see, my motives for going back are quite selfish."

Yizhen did not agree.

"I think you want to go back because you love China and want to do something for your country."

Lao Qiao raised his eyebrows and smiled, the wrinkles on his face and forehead extended to his graying temples. He was the very image of wisdom and humility.

The waiter first brought a dish of Double Crisp. Lao Qiao spread out his napkin and tucked it under his chin. At the same time, he urged Yizhen to eat.

"I never gamble, but this time I'm willing to bet ten years of my life. Whether or not China is going to have law and a government by law, we'll know in ten years." After saying this, he leaned forward, his searching eyes still fixed on her face. "You suffered a great deal during the Cultural Revolution. Did that experience leave a permanent fear in your heart?"

Yizhen smiled gently, and replied, "It did leave a scar, but it has not become a permanent one. I think the Cultural Revolution was an aberration, not at all the norm. With the wisdom of the Chinese people, we should be able to prevent such things from happening again."

The waiter brought a plate of stir-fried shrimp to the table. Lao Qiao helped Yizhen to a spoonful of the shrimp, but he did not take a bite himself.

"I do not entertain great hopes," Lao Qiao said, revealing his plan to her. "If the political situation remains stable for ten years, I'll be able to teach several thousand students before I retire. I'll be satisfied with that!"

Enviously, Yizhen exclaimed, "That would be a great accomplishment!"

"I'll give it a try. When they don't need me anymore, I can always pack up my bags and come back to America." Lao Qiao was in high spirits now, and he picked up a shrimp to put into his mouth. When the meal was half way over, he put down his chopsticks abruptly and asked her, "Yizhen, I hope you'll come for a visit, to see for yourself what new developments are taking place in China in the 1980s." His facial expression was very sincere. His eyes were open wide and looking right into hers.

This was the first time Yizhen had ever seen such an earnest expression on Lao Qiao's face. This expression was familiar to her, but it had been buried in her memory for so long. Seeing it again so unexpectedly, she felt confused, surprised, and very nervous.

"Yes...yes...I think I will...."

At this moment, she could not sort out her thoughts. When she left China several years ago, she never thought about returning. It had never occurred to her to go to China as a tourist. Tourism seemed very remote from her homeland and the people who toiled on it. In her way of thinking, when you stood on Chinese soil, there was no alternative but to be completely involved with it--with love, hate, and perhaps with a mixture of both, but never with indifference.

"You must come back, Yizhen, come back to see me."

For the first time he diverted his gaze from her face, lowered his head, and pleaded with her in a husky and almost inaudible voice.

At this instant, Yizhen noticed his usual composure and reserve had disappeared from his face. What was left was a look of humble and earnest longing.

The decision to go back was never an easy one, she knew from her own experience. On no account would she disappoint him. "Of course, we'll come to see you." She readily agreed with him, complimenting with a smile, "Deming will probably be the first to see you in Beijing."

Lao Qiao was moved but quickly added, "But, my greatest hope is that you will come."

The waiter came up to their table and asked, "Do you want more tea?"

"No more, thank you. Would you please bring us the check."

On the way home, Lao Qiao mentioned his plan for packing and disposing of his furniture and household belongings. He planned to leave many things for her.

Based on her experience in this matter, she said to him, "You're going to ship your books anyway, why don't you have your furniture and refrigerator shipped, too? These things will come in handy, and they are quite common in Beijing now. Maybe you'll get...."

She forced herself to swallow the word "married," which was already on the tip of her tongue. Most women on the mainland wanted very much to marry scholars who had returned from overseas. The chances of Lao Qiao's getting married were great. She was not sure when this thought had first occurred to her, but she was troubled by it. She could not suppress the idea nor could she accept it. In the end, it became a secret worry in her heart.

"All these things will be useful," she finally corrected herself. "Don't give them away so quickly. I'll help you take care of everything."

When she said that she had not realized how much work it was to move in America. She recalled when her own family had left Beijing. Their move was really simple and fast. Their one desk and two chairs belonged to the government, so did their three beds. All she had to do was to give their pots and pans to their neighbors and pack their meager personal belongings.

She had not expected that an old bachelor like Lao Qiao would have so many possessions. The memorabilia he had collected on his many trips, and those given to him by his friends and students filled an entire room. He wanted to take with him only a small portion of these. The rest he would leave to his son or distribute to members of the Su family. Su Tai loved music, so Lao Qiao gave him his stereo.

The house had to be ready for the new owner by the end of May. Since Lao Qiao was too busy teaching and giving exams, the women of the Su family insisted on helping him pack and clean up. Even Yizhen's mother-in-law pitched in to help.

"If we knew he would sell his house so cheap, we would have bought it," Zhao E said remorsefully. "With just a coat of paint, we could've made a profit of thirty to forty thousand dollars by reselling it! Lao Qiao was really foolish. He'll never be able to buy another house like this when he returns."

"Maybe he's not coming back," Yizhen hinted, since Lao Qiao did not ask her to reveal his intention of staying in China permanently.

"I bet he'll be back in two or three years!" Zhao E was particularly confident. "When you're used to the good life in America, how could you stand the hard life on the mainland? There was a program about China on television last night. They looked so pitiful, those old people and children on the mainland I mean. Their clothes were patches upon patches; even the beggars in Taiwan dress better than they do!"

"China has always been poor," Yizhen admitted, not wanting to deny this fact.

"So, if he wants to go back, he should go back to Taiwan! We have a relative named Wu Chunfa, who will be going back to Taiwan next month. Nowadays, going to the mainland is a fad. I think Lao Qiao's return is also a passing fad."

This remark brought an unexpected rebuttal from her mother-in-law, although it was never the old lady's practice to talk about politics. "Either going back to the mainland or going back to Taiwan is the right thing to do. How can you call it a passing fad?" She looked at her elder daughter-in-law harshly and continued, "We Chinese all have this concept about returning to our roots some day. The desire to return is very natural. No matter how good America is, it belongs to other people. If we live here forever, our children will all marry Americans and our Chinese identity will vanish completely!"

The old lady's speech really hit Zhao E on a sore spot. She fell silent instantly.

Yizhen thought about Lina and her sister. Since Lina left home, her sister-in-law had been distraught, and she clearly regretted having driven her out. Yizhen believed that Lina would eventually follow her elder sister's footsteps and marry an American.

"If Professor Qiao really does settle down on the mainland," the old lady came up with another idea, "wouldn't his son go visit him sooner or later? Didn't you all say that he is very Americanized? If he visits China more often, he is bound to have some Chinese characteristics rub off on him!"

Her mother-in-law's compelling words left a deep impression on Yizhen.

Since the middle of May, notices of admission had begun to arrive for Su Zhong. Several colleges admitted him, some of which were out-of-state, and he ruled them out because they were too far from home. In the end, he had narrowed down his choice to two schools: one was the School of Agriculture at the University of California at Davis; and the other was electrical engineering at the same college his brother was attending.

Making a decision was no less difficult for Yizhen than it was for her son, if not more so. For the sake of family togetherness, it would be ideal if the two brothers attended the same college, and their mother moved there to be with them. This way, the three of them could look after one another and not be lonely. They could also cut down on expenses. On the other hand, agriculture was Yizhen's major in college, and now, Su Zhong was also interested in the same field, even though he was confident of doing well in electrical engineering. To be able to pass down her expertise to her son would be immensely gratifying. But since Davis was such a long distance to commute, Su Zhong would have to live on campus. This meant the three of them could no longer live together. Yizhen was vexed by this prospect.

"I heard that the agriculture department of UC Davis is one of the best in the country," Su Zhong explained to his mother.

His uncle had promised long ago to pay for his college expenses. Being an independently minded young man, he would not object to living at school. But he loved his mother and knew she did not want him to go far away. Thus, he did not insist on going to Davis.

"Ah Tai, what do you say?"

The elder son replied, "There are advantages and disadvantages in either choice. You'd better decide for yourself, Mom. Or, we can ask Uncle Qiao."

Yizhen quickly stopped him, "He's busy getting ready to leave. We better not bother him. Anyway, we don't have to decide just yet. We can take some time to think about it."

She said Lao Qiao was busy, but it was only an excuse. No matter how busy he was, he would be willing to advise them on this matter. The fact was that she was afraid to hear his opinion. During the last several years, Lao Qiao had time and time again given his counsel to her family, and his advice was always sensible and reasonable. He enjoyed such high prestige in the minds of herself and her sons that if she failed to follow his advice this time, she would indeed feel very guilty.

Yizhen could now truly understand and sympathize with her sister-in-law. She worried about her daughter marrying an American and her husband having an affair. These things revealed her fear of being left alone. Yizhen realized that this fear had descended upon her as well. Her son was not getting married yet; however, he was prepared to cast his mother aside so he could attend the college of his choice. *I'll be left alone in this house, how am*

I going to pass my time? She was afraid to think about it. *After Lao Qiao leaves, I'll take more time to think about myself.* She suddenly felt as if she had become an ostrich with her head in the sand, unable to face reality, much less make a timely decision.

Lao Qiao decided to leave in early June to give himself time to prepare for his classes in Beijing. Yizhen helped him pack the odds and ends in his house and put everything in order. On the day he turned over his house key, his baggage was ready for shipment, and his house was spic-and-span, inside and out. For the three days prior to his scheduled departure, Lao Qiao stayed at Deming's house at Deming's insistence.

It so happened that Wu Chunfa arrived in San Francisco at this time, and he also stayed at Deming's house. Wu had just completed his master's degree in architecture at Yale and was on his way back to Taiwan.

On the eve of Lao Qiao's departure, Deming threw a big party in honor of his two guests. Yizhen and her sons arrived early to help. Even Lina came home, without her boyfriend. On an occasion like this, it would be very awkward for a "foreigner" who did not know the Chinese language. The Su family breathed a collective sigh of relief over Lina's clever and considerate action.

Zhao E was so overjoyed by her daughter's return that her small eyes followed her everywhere. How she wished to clasp her daughter to her bosom and give her a big hug!

Seizing an opportunity in the kitchen, Zhao E whispered to Yizhen, "Oh, it would be so good to have Lina come back to live in the house. Auntie, you go talk to her."

"All right."

Knowing her niece's stubborn disposition, Yizhen was not at all sure about the success of her mission, but she could not turn down her sister-in-law's request.

Zhao E confided to Yizhen, "Deming misses her too, but he wouldn't admit it. Without her presence, this big house is as quiet as a tomb sometimes!"

Yizhen placed her hands on her sister-in-law's shoulders, offering her sympathy and consolation.

"Ah Zhen, I have an idea. But don't tell mother-in-law or Deming about it yet, O.K.?"

Yizhen agreed.

Zhao E again whispered into her ear. "Let Lina and Johnny get engaged first, so she can move back in with us. If she wants to go to graduate school, she can do so as she pleases. After a year or two, if they're still in love with each other, they can get married."

"All right. I can tell Lina that. She's a sensible girl," Yizhen said. Feeling more confident about this proposition, she readily agreed to take on the assignment. "Do you think mother-in-law and Deming will agree to their marriage?"

Zhao E sighed, "What if they don't agree? There's not much they can do about it!"

At this moment, their mother-in-law stepped into the kitchen, putting an end to their conversation.

She was very good at making Taiwanese dishes, especially when it came to preparing a banquet, she was a real pro. Today, Yizhen and Zhao E both became her assistants. The two sisters-in-law devoted the entire afternoon to peeling cucumbers, slicing salted vegetables, and chopping meat. This was the first time Yizhen seriously learned to cook the dishes of her native land, and she worked with the concentration of a pupil learning a trade. The ten dishes were carefully placed in large bowls like flower arrangements and were kept warm in a steamer. Then, all one needed to do was to turn them over onto plates and add some soup stock before they were ready to serve.

Lina and her two cousins had taken Chunfa to the city for sightseeing.

After they came back, they soaked themselves in the swimming pool. The four of them were close in age and had a lot to talk about.

Chunfa was an outgoing person who liked to travel. Two years ago, before he came to America to study, he had backpacked all over Japan. He had also been to Korea, Thailand and Malaysia. His wide-range of knowledge made his conversation very captivating. The Su brothers listened raptly until their ears nearly dropped off.

"In Southeast Asia, which country do you think is the best?" Su Zhong asked him.

"Our Taiwan!" he said, holding up his thumb, full of pride. "You come to Taiwan, and I'll take you on a round-the-island tour. It's all on me!"

Wu Chunfa's love for his homeland was like that of a woman's first love, unrequited. He not only gained the Su brothers' respect and envy, but also made a deep impression on Yizhen at the dinner table.

Wu Chunfa had been awarded a fellowship to study for his doctorate, but had consented to participate in the design of an American-style shopping mall in the suburb of Taizhong instead. This was why he was in such a hurry to return to Taiwan.

"Ah Chun, won't you regret giving up a Ph.D. degree?" Deming said, feeling regretful for the young man.

"That's right," Zhao E echoed her husband. "Wouldn't it be easier to finish your Ph.D. first? Who knows when you'll be able to come back again? The situation in Taiwan is changing!"

"It is precisely because of the unstable situation that I'm anxious to go back. If everyone loves Taiwan, then the country will be at peace." Having said this, he laughed heartily as if there were nothing to fear.

Chunfa had a large mouth and thin lips. When he laughed, his teeth, gums, and even the tip of his tongue were all exposed. Like his laughter, he was the kind of person who revealed his thoughts for everyone to see.

"You must be an exception," Lina scowled, expressing a different opinion. "I know some people who would fight to get out of Taiwan. Many of them asked my father to take their money out and deposit it in American banks. Some of them have even bought foreign passports from some small countries. They regard Taiwan as a sinking ship, and they are ready to grab their toothbrush and leave the moment there's any disturbance. Isn't that so?"

"It's not as bad as that. Those deserters are a minority, and they are despised by everyone!" he replied, shaking his head, his mouth twitching, as if his gesture could shake that handful of people out of his mind. "There are many people in Taiwan, just like myself, who sincerely want to do something for Taiwan. We grew up in the sixties when our society was opening up and becoming prosperous. Although we've seen some injustice, we've also seen the progressive and prosperous side of Taiwan. What's more important, this progress and prosperity is closely linked to our own participation!"

As he talked, he turned to his host, "Uncle Ah Ming, you've lived in America for more than ten years now, right? Do you feel you have a sense of participation in American society?"

The question made Deming hesitate for several moments, then he said, "How should I put it? I'm a businessman. I pay taxes but I don't get involved in politics. I think, to tell you the truth, I haven't really taken part in American society."

Deming looked at Lao Qiao, seeking his opinion. Slowly, but seriously, Lao Qiao nodded in agreement.

Chunfa said, "I've lived in America for two years. I don't have the slightest sense of being a part of it. But in Taiwan it's very different!" When he mentioned Taiwan, the young man's voice became nostalgic. It sounded like he was reading poetry. "Every time I leave Taiwan, I feel the excitement of seeing the outside world. But after a while, I miss it very much and can't wait to go back. I work twice as hard to make up for the time I was away. Taiwan has given me so much; I have always wanted to repay my country in some way. It's not the best place in the world, but it is our home. So, we all work hard for it. Who does not love Taiwan?"

The room fell in a hush.

As Yizhen had listened to him speak, a warm current ran through her heart. It had been a long time since she heard such a manifestation of love for one's homeland.

Lao Qiao apparently liked Chunfa, too, but with the concern of an older person, he gently reminded him, "Enthusiasm and idealism are both precious qualities and you certainly have plenty of both. However, now, especially since the people involved in the Gaoxiong Incident were tried under martial law, conservatism has gained an upper hand in Taiwan. The gap between the Taiwanese and mainlanders has widened. You must be very careful in whatever you do."

Chunfa acknowledged his advice, smiling, "The current situation is an abnormal phenomenon, it will soon pass. Professor Qiao, I think the risk I'm taking by going back to Taiwan will not be any greater than the risk you're taking by going back to the mainland."

Lao Qiao cocked his head and smiled, "Perhaps."

At this moment, Deming laughed aloud. "Splendid!" he exclaimed. "You two sides can hold a contest! We Taiwanese are not against reuniting with China one day, but we should have a fair contest. Only this can be called a peaceful reunification!"

Chunfa immediately raised his glass.

The conversation became so lively that they almost forgot about the food. The hostess urged them, "Eat, eat, let's not talk about politics."

But the quick-witted Lina would not let any chance slip by to express her opinion. "Why can't the Chinese put down roots in America?" she asked. "Their divided loyalty can only lead to frustration for themselves. Since we live in America, we should identify ourselves with this society and become Americans. This is my attitude."

Her father sighed, "That is the right way to be, but it is difficult for my generation to do that!"

As everyone present pondered about this question, Su Zhong suddenly asked, "What about the Jewish Americans?"

Everyone at the table had a lot to say about the Jewish people. Some praised them, some criticized them. There was no consensus, but the majority had a great deal of respect for them.

Lao Qiao remarked, "The sense of unity among the Jewish people is worthy of our emulation. Overseas Chinese are as divided as loose sand."

Lina suggested, "Chinese should learn everything from Jewish people. They thrive and prosper in America, but at the same time they remain one-hundred-percent Jewish. Isn't this what the Chinese people of your generation wanted to achieve?"

Grandma was prejudiced against the Jews. She pouted and said, "Jewish people are so stingy. I think we'd better not learn from them. Come on, let's eat. Taiwanese cooking has a lot of gravy and broth, but it's not greasy. Professor Qiao, please eat some more. When you go to Beijing, you probably won't be able to find this kind of food."

"These Taiwanese dishes are delicious, so light and tasty. Auntie, you're an excellent cook!" Lao Qiao's praise made the old lady grin from ear to ear. She hardly ate anything herself; she was too busy serving others the food. The more the guests ate, the happier she was. She smiled broadly until the end of the banquet.

After dinner, the guests moved to the living room. Zhao E served tea and Lina brought out the dessert. Only Yizhen and her mother-in-law were left in the kitchen to do the dishes.

"Which college is Ah Zhong going to?"

"We haven't decided yet."

Yizhen informed her mother-in-law of the reasons behind their indecision.

Swiftly cutting through the tangle of problems, her mother-in-law pointed out the crux of the matter. "Didn't you leave China for the sake of your children's education? Once the children are grown up, they leave home. There's no way you can make them stay, sooner or later they will go away. If Ah Zhong wants to attend a good college, you should let him. As for the expenses, you don't have to worry about that. It's an uncle's duty to help in the education of his nephews. Besides, I've also saved some money for them. I have a house in Taizhong and I'll leave it to you and your boys. These two boys are the hope of the Su family and they are also my hope. I've made appropriate arrangements for you all. You just set your mind at ease, Ah Zhen."

Yizhen dared not say no, nor could she actually find any reason to object to her mother-in-law's arrangements. She could only agree respectfully.

"Come and have some refreshments with us," Zhao E asked, coming into the kitchen.

The old lady always had respect for Qiao Jianguang. As soon as she went into the living room, she asked his opinion about which college Su Zhong should attend.

"UC Davis is of course the best choice. Its School of Agriculture, especially the nutrition program, is among the top five in the nation," Lao Qiao pointed out. As soon as he finished speaking, everybody congratulated Su Zhong on being accepted by Davis.

When Yizhen realized that indeed her son would be going to a very fine college, she burst into a smile. But almost immediately she thought about the imminent family separation, and felt an inexpressible sense of regret. Seeing Yizhen's silence, Lao Qiao took out two keys from the pocket of his jacket and said, "I never planned to sell my car. Now I'm giving it to Ah Zhong. If you have a car, you can go home to see your mother every weekend. How is that?"

Yizhen was about to decline the offer, when her younger son over-zealously accepted, "Oh, great! Thank you, Uncle Qiao!"

"How can we accept...," Yizhen's modesty seemed superfluous. *This child is also Americanized,* she thought to herself, *he doesn't know how to be modest anymore.*

Deming also approved of Lao Qiao's generosity. "Thanks a lot, Lao Qiao. I'll take responsibility for the car insurance and maintenance costs."

"I'll have the title transferred to Ah Zhong immediately. You can drive the car home tonight."

Yizhen felt very embarrassed. She thought they ought to at least wait until Lao Qiao left before taking his car from him.

"I really dread saying our good-byes at the airport," Lao Qiao said. "Tomorrow I beg all of you not to come. I just need Deming to take me to the airport."

After some discussion, it was decided that Deming and Yizhen would be their representatives to see him off.

That evening, Su Tai drove Lao Qiao's car home. Not only was he interested in electrical engineering, he was also interested in mechanics. He had already fixed the car for their neighbor, Mrs. Wu, several times.

After that, Yizhen had suddenly changed her mind about buying cars. In the past, she had always regarded having a car as a luxury. When they went grocery shopping, the boys would carry back the bags.

She had remarked, "Ah Tai, if you see a good used car, I'll buy it for you. It'd be more convenient when we have to go somewhere or buy groceries."

"Mom, I can take the bus to school. I don't really need a car. As for grocery shopping, we can wait until the weekend when Ah Zhong comes home."

He was always considerate of his mother.

"No, I must buy a car for you. I want to learn to drive myself."

Actually, both boys were crazy about cars. As soon as they got home, they took out all kinds of road maps to look for a shortcut to Davis. They then located various parks in the vicinity. Talking and gesturing, they were extremely excited. Seeing them so involved in the maps, Yizhen did not want to dampen their enthusiasm. She quietly went into her room and went to bed. Even then she could still hear them jabbering and chattering away in the dining room. They were now so close to her, yet she knew they would soon be far away. Her sister-in-law's fear was again troubling her.

But I should not end up like this, she tried to argue with herself. *I used to be as enthusiastic and idealistic as Wu Chunfa, and I also loved my career of teaching. But now, what is my work?* she asked herself.

From the front hall came the voices of her sons talking about cars and travels. Yizhen could almost foresee their future: study engineering and agriculture, get Ph.D.s, work for some big companies, and become the first generation of Chinese-Americans. Then intermarry with Americans and produce a half-Chinese, half-American second generation. After that would come the third generation, which probably would lose its Chinese identity altogether.

Su Tai was right. No matter how free and comfortable life might be in America, one always felt that something was missing. There was no sense of participation. Wu Chunfa's words were truly to the point!

In order to live in dignity as Chinese, her whole family had come here from the other side of the ocean. If, after so much struggle, they lost their Chinese identity, wouldn't that defeat their original purpose of coming here?

Yizhen tossed and turned in bed, the soft mattress of her queen-size bed shaking under her body. Her head felt heavy and dizzy, her entire body seemed to be floating in an ocean. *Am I seaweed helplessly being tossed about in the waves?* That night she thought very hard.

The following afternoon, Deming drove Lao Qiao to Yizhen's place to pick her up at the appointed hour. Her children bid Uncle Qiao good-bye.

"You must all come to Beijing!" Lao Qiao implored them.

"We will. Have a pleasant journey, Uncle Qiao!"

Yizhen noticed that Lao Qiao looked very serious today. He frequently adjusted the position of his eyeglasses even though they were perfectly straight. Deep wrinkles appeared at the corners of his mouth. The look in his eyes betrayed a feeling of restlessness. His thinning hair was so heavily greased that the neatly combed rows of furrows and ridges were stiff and lifeless. His face looked tired from over-excitement and nervousness.

From Lao's appearance, Yizhen surmised that her face must also look frightful. She wished she had put on some make-up before leaving the house. Feeling ashamed, she lowered her head.

Many of Lao Qiao's colleagues from Golden Gate University came to the airport to see him off. Lao Qiao shook hands with them one by one before he entered the gate.

"Lao Qiao, *bon voyage!*"

"Deming, see you in Beijing!"

The two old friends embraced.

"Lao Qiao, when you come back, I'll take you to all the Chinese restaurants in San Francisco!"

"If you come to Beijing, I'll treat you to Beijing duck at Quanjude Restaurant!"

"Well, the Beijing duck in Taibei is even better. If you don't believe it, let's compare. You be my guest!"

These two would not miss one chance of bantering with one another before parting. They made all of those present laugh.

Lao Qiao shook hands last with Yizhen, "Ah Zhen, take care of yourself."

"I'll come to see you soon," she told him calmly but with determination.

"Really?"

The surprise flickered happily in his eyes, sweeping away the anxiety and restlessness of just a short while ago. His eyes shone brightly. His fleshy palm squeezed her hand harder and harder as if he wanted to concentrate all his strength into this one handshake.

"Really."

Yizhen had never experienced such a powerful handshake before. The pain made her blink.

"Then, see you in Beijing!"

She clenched her teeth, raised her still-hurting hand to wave good-bye to him, and watched him disappear into the cabin of the plane.

On their way home, Deming asked her, "Ah Zhen, why are you going to Beijing? I thought you were going to Taiwan."

"I will go to both places."

She was full of confidence. Her hand still hurt a little, but the feeling of numbness turned into a feeling of warmth and hope in her heart.

Suyue's New Year's Eve

Editor's Notes:

In 1979, the United States established a diplomatic relationship with China and severed its official ties with Taiwan. For the Taiwanese government, this was a traumatic political blow. Many Taiwanese people viewed it as a possible threat to the Nationalist government of Taiwan and have since left their homeland to come live in the United States on a permanent basis. Among them, a staggering number of teens have been sent by their parents to study in American schools. As a literary observer, Chen sees in this immigration phenomenon not only the breakdown of the formative bonds between parents and children, but also the abyss that separates the older immigrant generation from its younger "Americanized" offspring.

In "Suyue's New Year's Eve," Chen depicts the uncertain future of one such family. With the prevailing belief being that one must endure in spite of hardships, the Chinese-American family, especially the newly immigrated ones, becomes the embodiment of the quintessential modern marginal man: alienated from Chinese culture, uprooted from one's heritage, and cut off from one's children and American society. A symbol of the burial of one's past and the welcoming of the new, New Year's Eve is representative of Chinese ethnic heritage and identity; however, as Suyue and her sons begin to assimilate American culture, they instead face the realities of cultural erosion and family separation. Caught between symbols of the old and new, Suyue is left to find her own equilibrium without sacrificing her identity, as must other immigrants living in American society today.

SUYUE'S NEW YEAR'S EVE[1]

At not quite four o'clock on a Sunday afternoon, Suyue rounded up her two boys and brought them over to the telephone.

"Each of you say a few words to Daddy. Afterwards, don't forget to wish Daddy a happy New Year. Understand?"

As she instructed them she unfolded the paper on which she had copied down the long telephone number.

"We understand."

It wasn't often that they could make a phone call across the ocean. The brothers' anxious faces were tight like skin stretched taut over a drum.

"Now, Dabao, you read the number while I dial."

The first try didn't go through. Only a buzzing sound came on the line.

She quickly replaced the receiver, her heart beating like a busy signal.

Is he not home? Or is he also using the phone?

Amidst Suyue's uncertainty was a thread of fear. Gui Wuqi wasn't one to make a lot of phone calls. Besides that, she had sent a letter to Taiwan the

---

[1]"Suyue's New Year's Eve" *(Suyue de chuxi)* was translated by Shu-mei Shih and Adam Schorr with the permission of the author and publisher, and is published here in English for the first time. This translation is based on the story's first appearance in *Wenxuejie* (Literary Circle) (Summer, 1985): 66-80.

week before saying she would call today. He ought to be waiting by the phone, unless, by chance, the letter hadn't arrived. . . .

She quickly dismissed these conjectures. She hadn't heard of any big political controversies in Taiwan recently, so the mail shouldn't have been delayed for inspection. Last year, in October, members of the Bamboo Gang flew to San Francisco and killed a Chinese writer. After that, it took at least three extra days for a letter from Los Angeles to get to Miaoli.

Apprehensive, she dialed the number again.

This time it took only one ring before that familiar, rapid Shandong accent came on the line.

"Hello, who is this?"

"Wuqi, it's Suyue!"

A smile parted her lips. She turned her head to the boys, nodding vigorously, signaling that she had reached their father.

"Oh my, Suyue. I've been up since two this morning, waiting for your call the whole time! Are the children alright?"

"Fine. They're right here beside me. Do you want to. . . ."

"No hurry, no hurry! Today's New Year's Eve and we're finally having our reunion on the phone, uh. . . hey. . . ."

The last sound was drawn out and indistinct, not clearly a laugh or a cry.

The mention of the word reunion made Suyue think about home and her mother.

"Go over to Sanyi today for New Year's, alright Wuqi? Brother's letter said that Mama invited you over. The whole family is going to sit around a table and have a firepot style dinner."

"Don't worry I'll go for a New Year's visit first thing tomorrow morning. This evening I promised our old commanding officer, Commander

Sun, that we'd go to the Veteran's Home[2] and get together with a few of the old bachelors. . . ."

He suddenly fell silent.

She knew what her husband meant. He had always sympathized with those old soldiers who retired with him, those poor men alone in Taiwan with no family. And now, he too was left alone, without his family. He must feel really bad.

"When you go to Sanyi tomorrow," she changed the subject, "remember to buy Mama a box of those cookies from Yimei's."

"Yes, yes, I won't forget. The three of you will spend New Year's at my cousin's, I suppose."

She responded vaguely, not wanting to say straight out that she hadn't even received an invitation.

"Over here they don't do much for Chinese New Year."

"How can that be? Everyone says the place where you live is called Little Taibei.[3] New Year's there, in Monterey Park, that should be really exciting!"

She immediately told her husband that there was a party that night at Mrs. Hong's house, with four mothers from Taiwan and their six children, and that she had been busy all morning steaming vegetable cakes and red date buns.

"That's good! You've really got to celebrate New Year's. Can't let the kids forget Chinese ways. When I was young. . . ."

At this point his voice became hoarse, followed by coughing.

"Are you feeling alright? You should take some medicine for that cough!"

---

[2] Veteran's Home, *Rongmin zhi jia*, refers to the institution which houses retired Guomindang soldiers whose original homes were left behind on the mainland.

[3] Monterey Park near Los Angeles is called "Little Taibei" because of the large number of Taiwanese immigrants living there.

She wondered if her husband's ailment had erupted again. When he was a teenager, he was drafted into the army and contracted a serious bronchial infection. After coming to Taiwan, the infection didn't resurface until a year after he retired from the military. Then, unexpectedly, a bout of flu brought it on again. Ever since then, particularly during the wintertime, it would come and go with no apparent pattern. He often complained that perhaps fate was telling him he should have stayed in the army, because then he had no ailments.

"The weather's been rotten recently. If it's not overcast, it's raining. It makes my hands and feet numb, and. . . well, I've been having a bit of trouble breathing."

There it is. He admits his old illness has flared up again.

She glanced out the living room window at the bright sunlight and freshly scrubbed blue sky. The past six months, the weather in Southern California had been like that popular song in Taiwan, "Every Day a Blue Sky." She suddenly felt ashamed, as if she had stolen the sun from Miaoli.

"Remember to take your medicine, Wuqi, and don't be too thrifty, eat well. . . ."

A fifty-four-year-old man alone in Taiwan, how could he eat well? She heard her own voice choke and felt her nose stuff up. She couldn't continue.

Luckily he asked to speak with the children, inadvertently relieving her of her awkwardness.

Dabao took the receiver first. He talked a while about things at school, and then nodded over and over again, saying, "OK." Afterwards he wished his father "Happy New Year," and handed the phone to his little brother.

As soon as Xiaobao got on the line he asked, "When are you coming to America?"

She was not quick enough to stop the child's question and only tugged powerlessly at his sleeve.

Apparently, his father's answer was disappointing. Xiaobao petulantly warned his father, "Daddy, if you don't come here soon, Mommy'll want to go back to Miaoli. She misses home."

Suddenly, his mouth dropped open. His eyeballs became big and round, like glass marbles, staring motionlessly ahead of him.

"What is it?" she gasped, grabbing the receiver.

Her son stood aside, stuttering, "Daddy sounds like he's crying."

"Wuqi, are you. . . ."

"I miss you all," he said pitifully, sounding as if he had a steamed bun stuck to the roof of his mouth.

A man crying is the saddest sound of all, she thought. In a moment, her eyes were moist and burning. She also missed him. She missed the whole family, her mother, her brother. She especially worried about him, his everyday needs, his meals. Even though he had been a soldier for thirty years and proudly proclaimed time and again that he could take care of himself, he hadn't washed a single dish since their wedding. Could he now really cook and care for himself? His dormitory was a seven or eight minute walk from the restaurant that served baked cakes and deep-fried bread. Did he skip breakfast because the distance made it too much trouble? And, what about rainy days? It was bothersome to carry an umbrella. He had always hated them.

"Wuqi, I'm coming back in the summer!" she announced involuntarily, gritting her teeth in dismay.

"No, don't. I'm fine, really," he said haltingly.

Suyue could picture him anxiously fumbling for his handkerchief to blow his nose.

"You and the children stay there and don't worry. Really, Suyue, I'm alright on my own," he reassured her confidently, his voice quickly regaining its strong clear tone. He continued, asking her to push the boys to study hard and to remind them that their wish for Daddy to come to America rested completely on their shoulders.

"Tell them to write. A letter a week isn't too much, is it? I just nailed up a good sturdy mailbox. Every day I look forward to your letters. Right after work, I rush home to check the mail. . . . Write to me, phone calls are expensive. . . ."

Then, abruptly, his throat acted up again, and he had to hang up.

She massaged the place where the receiver had pressed painfully against her earlobe, but she couldn't massage away the sound of his final sob.

. Dabao had already sneaked off and was watching television in the bedroom, the volume turned low, like a lover's whisper.

Xiaobao sat silently beside her, his face expressionless. Surprisingly, when he heard his father cry he hadn't shed a tear. The child had grown up quite a bit in the last half year. She wondered if he remembered his cries at Taoyuan airport, "Daddy, I don't want to go to America!"

In sixteen years of marriage, that was the first time she had seen her husband cry. It came unexpectedly, his tears flowing like a mountain flood out of control. He held one child by each hand, eyes brimming, lips parted and trembling, his Adam's apple protruding so much it looked like it would tear his new tie. Usually resembling a dried red date, his tear-soaked face became the bloated fiery visage of Judge Guangong.[4]

The two boys cried along with their father, especially Xiaobao, usually his father's favorite. He clutched his father's waist, weeping and hollering, mournfully protesting against whomever would separate father and son. It looked like something out of the movies, the excruciating parting of two people whose destinies will separate them forever.

The whole time, she regretted that she didn't carry a handkerchief. Mama wiped her tears on her sleeves. Her brother, frowning, stood to one

---

[4] Guangong is a legendary warrior from *Romance of the Three Kingdoms*, famous for his valor in battle.

side shaking his head and sighing.

The airport personnel cast sidelong glances. Some people even pointed their fingers at them, probably never having seen such a woeful departure.

Thinking back on it now, Suyue thought that Wuqi's pitiful crying must have been some kind of self-fulfilling prophecy.

Originally, the plan had been for Suyue to accompany the boys to California so they could go to an American high school. She would live with them for a year at Wuqi's cousin's home where she could help out with the housework. After the children were settled, she would return to Taiwan. Once back home, Suyue and Wuqi would struggle together, regularly sending money to reimburse Wuqi's cousin and his wife. They both worked, but didn't have any children of their own and had expressed willingness to help the boys come to California. Since high school was free in America, the only costs to worry about would be living expenses. Wuqi figured that with both of them working in Taiwan they would just scrimp a little on food and clothing, and they could make it.

Once she arrived in America she found that the situation wasn't that simple.

Wuqi's cousin's wife had her paralyzed mother staying at their home. She needed a cane to walk. The old woman was somewhat feeble-minded, often mumbling to herself or crying and laughing for no reason. His cousin's wife made a show of complete devotion to her mother, but actually preferred to go to work each day and hire someone else to care for the old woman. Naturally this wasn't so easy with the cost of hired help in America. From the beginning they encouraged Suyue and the children to come live with them, probably with the intention of hiring Suyue as a domestic. They merely failed to mention these details in any of the letters they had sent. So, Suyue didn't know a thing about the old woman until after her arrival in America.

Suyue had started working at a young age, so she was accustomed to the idea. Being the maid and nurse at Wuqi's cousin's house didn't bother her, but the boys couldn't get used to it. Whenever the old woman came near, the boys would run in fright. As soon as she opened her mouth, Xiaobao would become so agitated he couldn't study. At night, he would have nightmares, shouting out loud, "The crazy woman is coming!"

Suyue realized that the children couldn't stay at Wuqi's cousin's house for long and considered taking them back to Taiwan. But she hesitated, fearing it would disappoint her husband. Luckily, the first day she took the boys to school, she met Mrs. Hong and they became friends.

Mrs. Hong also had two children studying here. Her husband owned a soy sauce factory in Taiwan. Since she had an alien residence card, she could freely enter and exit the country and often travelled back and forth. She was a capable woman who knew her way around and soon introduced Suyue to a number of other mothers in similar situations.

With Mrs. Hong's help and encouragement, Suyue moved out of Wuqi's cousin's house. She found a job as a maid for an elderly American woman twenty hours a week. In return, the woman gave her two rooms rent-free. Three evenings a week, she also took care of a sick elderly lady who lived in an apartment. Surprisingly, her earnings were enough to feed the three of them. She saved the money Wuqi borrowed through the loan association, using it sparingly to supplement their needs. The problem of their livelihood had been solved, even if it was barely satisfactory.

Since changing their living arrangements, she had postponed the date of her return home. How could she leave her thirteen- and fifteen-year-old boys in America without adult supervision? It was impossible to do without worrying, especially in Southern California. She heard there had been a rush of immigrants the past few years, and because of that, a rise in gang activity. The crime rate was increasing dramatically. Violent incidents had even been occurring in high schools, some motivated by racial antagonism.

One day, Dabao had returned home from school sullen and silent with a big lump on his forehead, most likely from a blow. But, no matter how much she prodded him he wouldn't say one word about it. In Taiwan, Dabao was so busy with school and tutoring he never had time to get into fights. He had always been of the best sort, receiving praise from his teachers. Why did he start fighting after coming to America? She couldn't figure it out what was wrong.

Mrs. Hong also said that one couldn't just go off and leave children alone in America. In the high schools, drug peddlers were intimidating. If her children were to get mixed up with drugs, Suyue knew she would regret it forever. Mrs. Hong suggested Suyue join their "Mommies' Club." The "Mommies" took turns returning to Taiwan to be with their husbands, and while one was away, the other mothers would take care of her children.

Suyue didn't dare take the risk. Buying the plane ticket wasn't a problem. A few night's extra work would pay for the round-trip fare. She was only afraid that once she left she would be unable to return. Tourist visas were valid for six months. She had just renewed hers, but this coming July would make it a full year and after that it couldn't be renewed again. Continuing to live here meant being an illegal alien, and if she was discovered by the Immigration and Naturalization Service she could be deported immediately. The prospect of her illegal status made her feel so nervous she couldn't eat sometimes.

She couldn't go back and Wuqi, naturally, couldn't get out. With his wife and children stuck in America, he simply didn't have the courage to apply for a tourist visa. Not only that, he wasn't sure he was willing to risk losing his job in the government tax office knowing he would spend an enormous sum visiting America. So when he missed his family, he could only send letter after letter urging them to write.

In all his letters he never forgot to console and encourage Suyue, "For the sake of a wonderful future, you'll just have to endure it for a few years." Yes, just endure. She was only thirty-six. The future was far away. How else but to endure? She felt deep sense of yearning that she couldn't shake. It followed her like a shadow. She couldn't speak to the children about it, and the people in the "Mommies' Club" didn't seem to comprehend or share her anxiety. They even made fun of her, calling her "the frightened mouse."

At the outset, when she enthusiastically accompanied her sons to America, she had been so excited. Who could have foreseen the trepidation and anxiety with which she would have to serve this interminable sentence? When she thought about her plight, she had no choice, she could only grieve inwardly.

"Hey, Suyue, you're fretting only because you don't understand American law!"

Whatever Mrs. Hong said she accepted with a smile. She had never gone to college herself and really did feel that she lacked the knowledge she needed.

Mrs. Hong told her, "There are too many illegal aliens. There's no way the INS is going to handle them all--they can't. You just go right on living here. Even if you aren't legally granted amnesty, after five years they can't deport you anyway. There are all kinds of loopholes and stalling tactics. So, what are you afraid of?"

Suyue couldn't explain what she was afraid of, much less explain what this whole immigration mess was about in the first place.

The phone rang.

She stared blankly at the phone for some time. The phone suddenly rang louder, as if angry.

She hurriedly picked it up.

It was Mrs. Hong asking her to go to her house a little early and help prepare for the get-together.

"I'll be ready soon, Mrs. Hong. All I have to do is to fry the vegetable cakes," Suyue answered.

"Alright then, I'll pick you up at quarter past five. Be ready and waiting out in front." Mrs. Hong instructed and quickly hung up.

Suyue looked for Xiaobao. For some time, the brothers had been planted in front of the television like a pair of coconut trees, eyes unblinking, watching a football game.

"Dabao, you've watched television all afternoon. Are you sure you don't have any homework?" she asked, walking over to urge them to change their clothes.

"No, I don't. Really, if I'm lying turn me into a ghost! I finished my math assignment in class, and one of my friends took it home to copy. I could do my algebra assignment with my eyes closed!" Dabao replied.

"I finished my homework, too!" Xiaobao voluntarily echoed, his eyes never wavering from the television.

No wonder those two don't want to leave America. Going to an American school is like having a half-day vacation every day, very little homework and no pressure. Back in Taiwan, Dabao started taking tutorial classes after school in the fourth grade. He reported to school at six-thirty in the morning. By the time he came home, it was seven in the evening. With dinner still warm in his belly, he would hunch over his books and bury his head in his homework. He was never able to go to bed before eleven.

By the time Xiaobao entered school, it was even more severe. Tutorial classes started in the first grade. Carrying that bookbag, wider than his shoulders, with his head craned forward to balance the weight, made him look like a thin old man from afar. It really pained his mother's heart.

Every time Suyue took Dabao to be examined for his near-sightedness and watched the lenses get thicker with the passing years, how she wished she could exchange her eyes for his.

Mothers were destined to worry. The boys studied and she worried. Now they didn't have to study and she still worried.

"If you don't have any homework," she entreated, "you can still read on your own. You want to go to college, you know. . . ."

"Mom, getting into college is no sweat," Dabao retorted self-confidently. He then added, "In America, going to college is no big deal. It's making big money that you don't see every day. Lots of Americans don't even want to go to college."

"How can you think like that!" she scolded him, her face hardening.

Actually, she felt that wasn't entirely unreasonable. In Sanyi, people didn't pay so much attention to a college diploma. In recent years, there were a couple of people who earned foreign doctorates, but the person everyone always recalled was the sculptor, Zhu Ming. He did his apprenticeship in Sanyi, carving religious figures. He never went to college, but nevertheless, he had made a name for himself. After high school her own brother failed the college entrance exam. He started a business in town and made a lot of money over the past few years. There wasn't one of his friends or relatives who didn't praise him.

But Wuqi didn't think that way. He became a soldier before finishing high school. He had always had his heart set on going to college. According to him, his lateness in both retiring from the army and starting a family were to blame for his lack of a college diploma. My children, he swore pounding on his chest, are going to get that diploma no matter what!

Moreover, to him, a diploma from Taiwan was not good enough. Every now and then, Wuqi would comment on Commander Sun's five kids. Which one of them didn't go abroad? If they didn't win a scholarship, they provided the special one-time tuition deposit that was required to study overseas themselves. Sometimes they were able to get help from old friends and colleagues to cover other tuition costs. The youngest, and least able, flunked the college entrance exam three years in a row. Finally, he ended up using a tourist visa to get overseas.

"In what way is Dabao inferior to them?" his father would ask. Dabao's teachers said he wouldn't have any problem getting into college. He even had a chance at Taiwan University. If you can get into Taiwan

University, then you most definitely have a chance of going abroad.

After the United States broke diplomatic relations with Taiwan, Wuqi's hope became his resolution.[5] He inquired everywhere for his cousin's address in America. Wuqi sent him several letters asking for his help. For the sake of the children's education he was willing to endure anything, including splitting up the family.

"What's a temporary separation?" he persuaded Suyue, saying that it was at any rate better than letting the family be killed when the communists came to Taiwan. She was young, and he still had a few years before retiring at the age of sixty. They could pool their energy and work hard for a few years, until the kids were grown. Once Dabao received his diploma, they could go to America and all live together!

Were the communists really that terrible? Since she'd been in America, Suyue had met quite a few people from mainland China. Except for their clothes being somewhat unstylish, they really weren't any different from people in Taiwan.

Perhaps they weren't real communists. Wuqi fought the communists, so naturally it must be a difficult experience to forget. If they made him relinquish what he calls the happiest and most comfortable life there ever was, then the communists must indeed be terrible.

Suyue felt that because of the difference in their ages and background, she did not fully understand Wuqi. Nonetheless, he was a good husband and father, and her mother's family was saying more and more good things about him. She always respected his decisions and wanted to help him realize his dreams. But this separation, and the harsh reality of a broken family, made her increasingly depressed, even irritated. That's what it was, a nameless irritation, not knowing where to direct itself--the communists, her husband, or

---

[5] The U.S. cut off diplomatic relations with Taiwan and formally established its relationship with Beijing on January 1, 1979.

herself.

Maybe it was just her mood. This carefree attitude the children had toward their studies vexed her.

"Daddy's having a difficult time alone in Taiwan. He works extra hours at night and the two of you sit here and don't even study hard. How are you going to face him?" she asked, standing by the bedroom door.

"Your math is better than the American students. I believe that, but, your English is not as good as the others. . . ," she scolded them.

"Mom, we're watching TV," Dabao cut her off in an irritating tone of voice. Adjusting his glasses, he exclaimed, "This _is_ studying English!"

"Our teacher said we could watch TV," the younger one imitated his brother, "like channel nine."

This silenced her. It was just what Mrs. Hong had suggested to her. She told her that when she had the time she should watch television, and that way her English would improve quicker.

She had nothing more to say to the boys, it would be best to drop it.

"OK, let's not argue. Auntie Hong is coming to pick us up a little after five. Both of you go change your clothes and put on new shirts."

Xiaobao was just standing up when his older brother firmly held him back, "Mom, you go ahead. We won't go."

"What?" she asked, shocked. "Today's New Year's Day! In Taiwan, didn't you love Chinese New Year the best?"

"This is America. Why do we have to be bothered with Chinese New Year?" Dabao smugly replied. Perhaps in order to avoid further arousing his mother's ire, he immediately softened his tone a bit, "Well, you take little brother and I'll watch the house."

Saying this, he let go of his brother. Making this concession, he revealed more clearly his own determination. Xiaobao, encouraged, set his bottom back down on the floor.

Suyue couldn't help but become angry. Her child had changed so rapidly! Not only did he talk back at every turn, but now he's completely forgotten his place. If six months in America made him unwilling to celebrate Chinese New Year, what's going to happen in the future? And, now, Xiaobao was imitating his brother. He's spoiling him. Her first impulse was to charge over and drag him up to change his clothes. In the past, when he didn't want to visit his grandparents for the holidays, she would always force his clothes on him and drag him with her anyway.

Even though she felt this way, it seemed as if her feet were nailed to the ground, unable to move one step forward.

After all, Dabao was too big to be treated like a baby any more. Looking at him reclined on the floor, his two arms propped behind him, his legs splayed on the floor like a fan, she wondered if she would be able to move him at all. He had not only grown taller, but a lot heavier, his shining red face an explosion of pimples. Lit up like a lantern, his face warned her that the days of mother leading her child around were over.

After turning these thoughts over in her mind, she softened her voice and tried to entice him, "The whole meal today is going to be treats from Taiwan, like Zhanghua dumplings, Xinzhu meatballs, sweet rice cakes, and the vegetable cakes I'm going to fry. So many delicious things, it would really be a shame not to go and eat them!"

"You can get all that stuff in Monterey Park, like at 'Dinghao' or 'Yimei' or 'Guxiang.' All those stores sell them. I can have New Year's every day. What do I have to go to Auntie Hong's place for?"

"If you don't go I'm afraid I won't have time to cook your dinner," she said, threateningly.

Unconcerned, he replied, "I'll open a can of something for myself."

She was taken back for a moment, but then remembered Mrs. Hong's son, "Aren't you in the same English class as Hong Mingxiong? If you don't go. . . ."

"That doesn't matter to me," he said, sitting up and adjusting his glassses. Suddenly, he frowned, his pouting face an expression of distaste.

"Humph! He's always bragging about his rich dad. . . . What's so great about that? A Taiwanese Independence Activist!"[6] he snorted indignantly.

"Nonsense!" Suyue scolded loudly. "The man makes a good living in Taiwan running a soy sauce factory. Don't you go bad-mouthing him!"

Dabao chuckled as he explained, "When a man lives alone in Taiwan and the rest of his family lives abroad, he's humorously referred to as an 'independent Taiwanese activist', that's all."

She laughed involuntarily.

"Mommy, Daddy's not a separatist," Xiaobao ingeniously comforted her. "He's from the Shandong Province."

"No more loose talk," she warned, her face hardening. "Advocating Taiwan separatism is against the law. There's a chance that what you say will be reported and get someone into serious trouble. People really do report these things. The man in San Francisco who was killed by the Bamboo Gang was an informer. It's true. Remember, at school you are not allowed to say that word. You hear?"

Dabao shrugged his reply. Xiaobao answered whole-heartedly, "We understand."

"Dabao, if you're not going, that's fine. Come along Xiaobao. If neither of you go, Mrs. Hong will get suspicious. Get moving, Xiaobao, hurry and change your clothes."

As Suyue finished speaking, she turned and went into the kitchen.

She plucked an apron off the wall, tied it around her waist, and wandered over to the sink. Dirty dishes from lunch were stacked in the sink. On one plate was a baked drumstick, evidently left there to be thrown away. As soon as she saw it, the anger she had just repressed welled up again inside

---

[6] This term normally refers to those who claim that Taiwan should be independent from the Republic of China government.

her breast.

Returning home from work this morning, the first thing Suyue had to do was to start preparing the New Year's cakes and steamed buns. She was too busy to eat a meal herself, but she still spent time looking at the recipe book and took pains to make the boys drumsticks in tomato sauce. Who would have imagined that it'd end up ruined like this? They've become so spoiled. They were not this way in Taiwan!

As far back as Suyue could remember, the Taiwanese government had promoted the policy of "land for every tiller" in Sanyi, and everybody was basically clothed and fed. She had never known the pain of hunger. Nevertheless, everyone had frugal habits and did not lightly throw away food. Her parents taught her that being frugal was an essential virtue. Such a virtue had to be instilled when young. She couldn't see any reason that moral principles should be discarded as soon as one arrived in America.

"Hey, listen here. . . . "

Too angry to continue, she reached out and grabbed the drumstick, and like a charging bull rushed toward the bedroom.

"Who was so wasteful? You think drumsticks don't cost money?" she accused angrily.

Dabao, seeing his mother's red face, realized the seriousness of the situation and jumped up to turn off the television. "It wasn't me," he said defensively, his voice even and his face guiltless.

"Xiaobao, what do you have to say!"

Like a tiger eyeing its prey, she glared at the younger one who was changing his clothes. Xiaobao's shirt was unbuttoned and his trousers were undone. He guiltily lowered his head, both hands holding up his trousers.

"I don't like tomato sauce. . . . I wasn't hungry!" he mumbled in self-defense.

"If you're not hungry, then leave it. Why did you throw it away? What did your father say? Be thrifty. Don't be wasteful. Now that life is comfortable we should be even more frugal. Don't forget, when your daddy was fleeing for his life, he didn't have anything to eat. . . ."

"We know," Dabao cut her off, exasperated. "When Daddy was fleeing for his life he ate roots and tree bark and Goddess of Mercy clay. We've never even seen Goddess of Mercy clay. Eating roots and tree bark here is probably against the law, and you'd get arrested by the police. . . . Daddy sent us to America to study, not to flee for our lives. Why do you have to bring up that stuff?"

What nerve! He isn't in law school yet, but he's already arguing with his mother. If he thinks he's so capable, he can go use his words on his American classmates. And then he could tell his mother how he got a swollen lump on his forehead.

"I'm talking to your little brother Dabao. Who asked you to interfere? Wasting is just not right. Do you still have some smart argument?"

Hearing the sharpness of her rebuke, Dabao didn't dare answer back.

Getting no further response, the momentum of her anger quickly subsided. She turned to Xiaobao, the drumstick raised in her hand, "Tomorrow this drumstick will be your lunch!"

Without waiting to see her son's reaction, she turned and walked heavily into the kitchen. Her heart felt like a deflated plastic cushion, soft and empty.

Taiwan separatist, New Year's, fleeing for one's life. . . . These words were like New Year's Eve firecrackers exploding one after another in her head. She seemed to understand them, but couldn't hold on to them. She only felt confused and empty.

The vegetable cakes were still laying on the chopping board, waiting for her to cut them into pieces and fry them golden brown. Her child's words echoed in her ears, *Why do we have to bother with Chinese New Year. . . .*

Her eyes moved to the sink. The dishes were in a messy pile, like scattered ruins.

Clenching her teeth, she threw the drumstick behind her.

Outside the window, the sky was still a freshly-scrubbed blue, so blue, almost as if dusk had not already fallen.

The Woman from Guizhou

Editor's Notes:

Representative of Chen Ruoxi's recent thematic shift, "The Woman from Guizhou" illustrates some of the problems confronted by elderly Chinese-Americans. Chen artfully details the lack of balance between the old society, China, associated with the emotive world of one's roots, parental lineage and historical continuity; and, the new society, America, a world where reason, science and technology is forcefully connected with one's adopted identity, career, and self-worth. Through the deliberate isolation of the main character, Weng Dehe, Chen condenses the story setting into a microcosm that furnishes the immediacy of the isolation and alienation felt by many elderly Chinese in America.

Without attempting to pass judgement on the integrity and morality of the characters, one must scrutinize several aspects of the story. One of these aspects, perhaps the most important, is the special significance of the protagonist's wife's name, Shuiyue. Literally meaning "Moon in the Water", her name connotes illusion and insubstantiality in the world of reality. Thus, when Weng attempts to use his marriage as a means to strike that elusive balance between the old and new (China and his life in America), the adversities he encounters should not be unexpected.

Furthermore, while one may consider that Weng is the victim in this story, we should hesitate and ask ourselves if that is really true. If it is not, then who is the real victim and what has victimized that person? Where we live in a society that is full of quick and easy answers and solutions, it is the less obvious that sometimes portends the most meaningful implications.

THE WOMAN FROM GUIZHOU[1]

When he bid good-bye to Abing, Weng Dehe's mind was muddled and confused. He did not know what to do.

He stood in front of the restaurant for a while watching Abing walk away, his large steps heading east. His thick, strong arms swung in rhythm like the paddling feet of a swimming duck. Dehe could only turn around and drag his feet in the opposite direction.

This part of Eighth Street is a populated section of Oakland's Chinatown. There were rows upon rows of shops on both sides of the street, with vegetable peddlers occupying portions of the sidewalk. This normally congested quarter of the town seemed even more crowded on weekend afternoons. Actually, Dehe liked this kind of crowded atmosphere. People gave him a sense of security. If he had not come here once every few days for that secure feeling, it would have made him feel like he had lost something. For twenty years he had been working and living here, watching the streets become more and more prosperous each day was a comfort to him. He knew how to drift into the crowd, shrinking his shoulders, lowering his

---

[1] "The Woman from Guizhou" (*Guizhou nuren*) was translated by Tammy C. Peng with the permission of the author and publisher, and is published here in English for the first time. This translation is based on the original that appeared in *Guizhou nuren* (Taibei: Yuanlin Publishing Co., 1989), pp. 141-148.

head, moving horizontally like a crab. Thanks to this, he could momentarily forget the confusion still lingering in his mind, and simply concentrate on not getting knocked over by other pedestrians.

People become rather fragile when they get older. It was a risky business even to turn their bodies around. One time, a lady let go of a shopping cart, and when he dodged quickly to avoid being hit by it, he twisted the muscles around his waist. Quack medicine, hot baths, massage, electro-therapy...had all been applied for months until he finally felt that he had recovered half of his midriff. Now, whenever he saw a cart or something of that sort, he stayed as far away from it as possible.

Finally, he made it across the street. The crowd pushed him to the Maochang Fish and Meat Store, in front of a glass fish tank. Inside the fish tank there were all sizes of fish swimming back and forth, seemingly enjoying themselves. Among them were relaxed steel-heads and ink-black catfish. The catfish, with their fins flapping around in the water, resembled gentlemen dressed in tuxedos, so handsome they made people envious.

"Old Weng, have you eaten yet?" asked the salesperson at the fish stand. "Buying any fish or shrimp? We have jumbo prawns that just arrived from Tianjin. There are five pounds to a box."

Abing isn't coming for dinner, should I still get seafood? The old man pondered.

"Brother Dehe, did you bring Mrs. Weng along for a walk today? Look at you, you're looking better and better each day!"

The old, husky voice of the shopkeeper came from behind him.

"I'm doing alright," Dehe turned to answer, but he could only see the white cap and thick eyebrows of the shopkeeper.

"Old Weng, not only do you have good fortune, but you know how to take care of yourself!" the salesperson agreed with his boss as he cut open a fish. He continued, "The catfish are fresh, and the price is good today, too."

The old man was tempted, besides, his wife liked to eat fish, so he decided to purchase a live one.

"Good! Give me a catfish, not too big and not too small, about one-and-a-half pounds would be just right!"

The salesperson knew Dehe's temperament well. Taking care of his old patron, he picked his fish first without having him take a number and wait. The salesperson cut open the fish's stomach, cleaned out the intestines thoroughly, and gave him a free piece of ginger and some scallions before wrapping the fish in a bag.

Enjoying his shopping, he went ahead and bought some beef, roasted duck, and fresh vegetables. He also did not forget to buy some of the preserved plums and dried peaches that his wife had become so fond of lately. It wasn't until his arms began to feel sore that he stopped shopping and slowly strolled back to the parking lot.

His house was nearby. It was only five minutes by car. As soon as he parked the car by the curb, Shuiyue came out of the house to greet him.

She was wearing a dressy outfit. Her full, moon-shaped face was lightly touched up with makeup, and a smile curved around the corners of her mouth. She looked even more glamorous than she did in the morning when they parted. As she moved, the hem of her one-piece apple-green dress rippled into waves of green light and shadows, bringing out the flaming redness of the camellias by the flight of stairs. Hurrying down the steps, her newly done curls swung between her ears and cheeks, and her full, snow-white thighs moved about under her dress, reminding him of a dancing ballerina.

Still sitting in the driver's seat, he stared at her coming toward him, a vision in green. Enchanted by what he saw, his chin dropped.

It was hard to believe that this was the same elementary school teacher that he had met from the mountains of Guiyang[2] some years ago. Her face

---

[2] Guiyang is the provincial capital of Guishou Province in Southeast China

was so skinny that it looked like an olive kernel, and her hair was burned yellow from a perm. She had been wearing a long, blue dress that hung limply on her body, giving her a weightless appearance. She did not look like the thirty-year-old spinster that the matchmaker had said she was. So short and dry, she looked more like a little girl yet to be fully developed.

He could not help but sigh. *Time sure flies!* It had been years since he last recalled the way she looked when they were first engaged.

"You bought so much food again!"

Shuiyue feigned astonishment, though her voice remained deep, low and husky. To show her modesty and appreciation, she blinked her dark, almond-shaped eyes as if she was surprised.

"Well...whether or not we have house guests, we...we can still eat it."

Although he drank so much soup and tea during lunch, his words were fragmented and his throat still felt dry, as if it might crack at any moment.

She did not seem to detect anything unusual in her husband's tone of voice. Instead, she picked up all the plastic bags in one hand, and helped her husband walk up the stairs with the other.

"I baked some cupcakes so you can take some to little Tom."

He had just sat down next to the dining table when he noticed the finely wrapped package. He extended his hands to touch the package. It was still warm, making him aware that his hands were cold and his heart was shuddering. He licked his lips a few times, still, he could not figure out a way to tell his wife about Abing.

Shuiyue was busy pouring tea for him. The door leading downstairs was open, and he could hear the sound of the laundry dryer turning. The noise of the machine reminded him of an electric fan.

Here, in Oakland, Dehe had difficulties finding an electric fan during any season of the year. The last time he saw one was in his hotel room in Guiyang. The temperature had been very high, and he was soaked in sweat while he waited to meet Shuiyue.

"You look tired. Do you want to lie down for a while before you go out?"

His wife's kindness pulled him back to reality.

"Go out? I'm not going out today," he answered her, taking the opportunity to divulge his secret.

Now it was her turn to be shocked. The light smile she'd had on her face froze and became twisted. She held the tea in her hand with no intention of passing it to him.

"Abing...is not coming."

The old man finally spit it out all at once. He then used what remained of his valor to move his eyes away from his wife to the window above the sink.

The scenery outside looked especially bright through the glass. The apple tree was full of flowers, light, pink, and delicate. Like clouds descending from heaven, they filled a good part of the window. In the corner of the yard was a wild bunch of camellias blossoming in a profusion of color. Their full, crimson petals pushed against the window, as if they were ready to break their heads to peek inside the room.

"Abing? Did something happen to him?"

Shuiyue's voice was unusually high pitched.

"He's getting married."

Having said that, he felt relieved from a heavy burden. Suddenly, he heard a loud "*pa*", and his heart jumped. He turned his head around and saw Shuiyue still standing there; the teacup was shattered into pieces, and the tea spilt all over the floor and her feet.

The look on her face was a scary one, her face was pale--no, it was green, as green as her dress. Her almond-shaped eyes protruded and looked cold, like two columns of ice piercing through her husband.

The old man dropped his head guiltily. He felt as if his body had become paralyzed, especially the lower part, numb and unconscious like a bundle of cotton swabs.

After a few moments of silence, Shuiyue finally bent down to pick up the glass.

"Be careful, don't cut yourself."

He wanted to help, but when he struggled to get up, he could not move.

Shuiyue quietly and quickly cleaned up the mess. She washed her hands and wiped them dry with a towel. Gradually, color returned to her plump face, yet the coldness in her eyes remained. Her chest heaved up and down nervously, as if her rounded breasts would burst from her dress any minute.

His late wife was a woman of bad temper, he could still remember the mean looks she had given him when they had an argument. But, from the moment Shuiyue had entered his door, he had not ever seen her this angry. Now, he felt the gravity of her rage. He secretly blamed Abing for not telling him earlier. Abing must have been afraid of scene like this too, so he intentionally left the mess for Dehe to clean up. Abing repeatedly told him at the restaurant, "Old Weng, you said I could pull out any time."

Of course. He could not blame Abing for not keeping his word, he could only blame himself for being so incompetent. The good life he had been leading had made him forget to prepare for a rainy day.

Now, he searched to find the right words to say to his wife, though he felt there was really nothing meaningful he could say.

"I don't want to drink any tea," he ventured. "If I do, I won't be able to sleep tonight."

His wife did not respond. She simply put away the towel, leaned against the snow-white refrigerator, and stared into her husband's eyes. Her serious expression reminded him of a judge examining a criminal case.

"Who's Abing marrying?" she asked.

"He said they were introduced by the owner of the meat shop. She's a nurse in some hospital and was widowed the year before last. They went out several times and are getting married next month," he replied, beginning to feel angry with himself. "That Abing, he didn't even mention anything to me earlier."

"He only told you, and everything else...just forget about it? What does he take me for?"

Listening to his angry wife biting and grinding her teeth, and questioning him in such a high-pitched tone made him feel very guilty. He lifted his eyes to peek at her and was shocked by the look on her face. How could that poor little woman from Guizhou suddenly turn into such a monster, her hands on her hips and her eyes glaring so fiercely?

He should have anticipated that this would happen one day. He blamed himself for not having prepared for it. The more he thought about it, the more guilty he felt.

"He said...it's best not to see you any more. He really wants to get married...."

The old man had always felt confident about his communication skills, but right now, he could not even describe to Shuiyue the conversation he had with Abing over lunch. Like glue, his guilt tightly sealed off his lips. He did not dare look his wife straight in the eyes. Instead he dropped his eyes to her waist. It had been a long time since he last paid any attention to her waist line, he realized that she had put on some weight. The willow-like waist she had just a year ago now looked round. Following the heaves of her bosom, her waist floated like a ball in the green ocean of her dress.

"I'll go see him!"

Her scream was as sharp as a knife, shocking the old man so much that it numbed his arms and legs.

She then stepped forward, her hands on her waist, and dashed furiously between the sink and the dining table. Her wild ferocity made her look like a beast that had fallen into a trap.

"Don't do this...," the old man waved his hand and pleaded. "Abing said he's moved, and he didn't give me his new address."

"Huh, I'll find out where he moved to!"

With such threats slipping out between her teeth, she lifted up one of her legs and stomped it on the ground with full force. The sound of her heel knocking on the ground felt like an iron stick thrust into his heart; it hurt so much that he drew his hand to his chest protectively.

"Don't mess things up,...you can't, Shuiyue...I'm sorry, I'll think of a way...I'll make it up to you."

The angry woman finally noticed the old man's pain, she stared at him coldly for a moment and suppressed her own temper. She then walked over to comfort him and rubbed his chest.

"Oh, look at you. It's nothing, don't be so mad, alright?" Like pacifying an infant, she blew into his ear, as soft as caramel candy, "Our affair...has nothing to do with you now."

The old man believed her, so he thankfully held the hands that were rubbing his chest and moved them to his lips and kissed them. Receiving no rejection, he extended his arms around her waist and buried his head in it like a child. This waist of hers was strong and elastic like a ball, but a very soft one. In the midst of this gentle confusion, he could feel her heart beat as clearly as if it was right next to his ears, except he was not sure for whom the heart beat.

Shuiyue quickly pulled her body away, but he held on to one of her hands and would not let go.

"I won't go out today, O.K.?" he pleaded like a spoiled child. "I'll stay home with you."

But his wife would not allow it, "Wanfen will be suspicious if you don't go. Let me drive you to the bus stop now."

·"You'll be too lonely here at home. I'll be worried."

Actually, he simply did not want to leave. In the past three years, aside from the times when Abing came to their house, the couple had never been separated, for even one day.

"A grown-up like me won't get stolen by a cat, what's there to worry about?"

The tone of her voice was cold and calm. It was difficult to tell whether she was trying to persuade him or being sarcastic. He was indeed a bit scared. Normally, he was afraid of loneliness, of being left out by others, but now, at this very moment, the only thing he was frightened of was her eyes. They suddenly seemed empty as they looked at him, piercing through him and sinking into somewhere far, far away.

He was discouraged when he saw this look in her eyes. During the first couple of years of their marriage, she often displayed this kind of soulless mood, not saying a word. It confused him. He had not seen this look for a few years and hadn't thought it would ever come back again. He must try to dissolve it quickly.

"Or," he tried both persuading and begging, "you come with me. My daughter has invited you to go a few times already."

"No, I'd like to stay home by myself for some peace and quiet. You better go soon so you won't miss the bus."

Nothing he said was any use. His wife seemed to have become rather stubborn. The past few years had gone by so smoothly that he had failed to recognize that she was no longer that good-tempered, obedient woman from Guizhou.

He felt himself become a puppet under her manipulation: *Wash your hands, change your clothes, wear a hat, change your shoes, go out, get in the car, wait for the bus, get off it....* When he woke up, he was already sitting on a large bus speeding down the highway. The bus driver was black, and the passengers surrounding him were either black or elderly. Despite his gloominess, he felt a sense of security.

Outside the windows was a hot, beautiful sun. However, the heat of the sunshine was filtered by the tinted windows and the air conditioning inside the bus, so it actually was very comfortable to ride. On weekends, the highway always looked like a stream full of automobiles, flowing with cars of all shapes and sizes, occupying the entire five lanes. Each car vied for speed, impatiently rushing to reach its destination. He used to view this situation as part of the scenery; now he envied those drivers. He only wished that he too had a known destination.

What's going to happen now that Abing is not going to come any more? The problem had become so urgent now that, alone on the bus, he could no longer avoid thinking about it. He tossed the question around in his head over and over again, until it gradually became clear. The moment Abing announced his engagement, he was actually announcing the end of their triangular relationship.

It was agreed that it would be "temporary" anyway, and that Abing could "stop at any time." Could he blame Abing for anything?

Abing had refused to comply with him in the beginning. If it weren't for him, Abing would not have done it. He had once saved Abing's life by allowing him to stay and work at the restaurant when he first arrived in America, at the same time helping him apply for a work permit and green card. Abing was so grateful to him that he reluctantly agreed to the deal, not only because he felt he had to do it as a gesture of friendship to Dehe. For three years, they had gotten along rather well. Abing really had been a true friend--he had never done anything obtrusive aside from coming over for dinner on weekends and staying over night.

Shuiyue, herself, had never mentioned a word about Abing--it had become an implicit agreement between husband and wife. The only difference was just that whenever the old man returned home from his daughter's place, he found Shuiyue in a merry mood, humming while she was cooking, obviously pleased with the arrangement.

How could a human being not have any feelings? It has been three years, and everything ended in such a flash. No wonder Shuiyue was so upset. Even the old man started to blame himself for choosing the wrong man in the first place.

It was his initial impression that Abing did not like women. In the restaurant, he had worked as a waiter and an assistant to the chef. He always had a smile for the waitresses and female customers, spoke with a gentle tone, and was liked by many people. But, whenever a woman tried to flirt with him, he would pretend not to hear or see anything. If a new young man came to work in the kitchen, he would quickly become intimate friends with him, as if they were two brothers wearing the same pair of pants.

"Why haven't you ever been married?" Dehe had asked him many times.

"Marriage is too troublesome," Abing once replied with a strange expression and sighed, "women are too hard to please nowadays! The Chinese women here are even worse because they're neither fully Chinese, nor American."

Now, he is about to please a widow, this chap!

It must have been Shuiyue who changed his mind, and now he realized the advantages of having a woman. Or perhaps it was fear of the recent AIDS epidemic that caused him to reject his old ways of living.

The old man felt dizzy even though he had only been reminiscing for a short while. At his age, he warned himself, it was not good for him to overexert his brain too much. Quickly, he tried to drive away all his worries. There was a moment for everything; he had seen it all in his life time. Years ago, when he had left Liuzhou on a boat, alone without any money, he would have never dreamed of ending up in America. Then, while he was struggling to make a living in Chinatown, didn't he conquer all of his obstacles and end up alright?

Shuiyue's outburst at Abing's sudden departure was forgivable. He would just have to comfort her, to treat her twice as well, surely then she would readjust to her old life. *Shuiyue is a genial person and should be easy to persuade. Besides, she's not the type of person who would forget about the good things she's received from other people.* Three years ago, when she wanted to leave him, didn't he talk her out of it? When he met her in Guiyang, he had not misjudged her.

The old saying was right: Things will take care of themselves when the time comes. Having argued and fought, things should be easier to handle. On the way to the station she did not say a word. He believed that this storm would pass in no time.

From noon that day, he had been bombarded with surprises. Once he relaxed, letting down his guard, a feeling of fatigue quickly crept up on him. The noise coming from the engine of the bus hypnotized the old man, and he soon fell asleep.

"We're in Stockton!"

The voice of the bus driver woke him up. Dehe rubbed his eyes to look outside the window, and saw Wanfen and her oldest daughter waving their hands at him.

He was glad that he arrived on time. When he reached Wanfen's house, he was told that his daughter and son-in-law had a social engagement that night and would be playing *mahjongg* afterwards. If he had not come here today, they would not have been able to go to dinner or play *mahjongg*, and he would have definitely been scolded.

As soon as they arrived home, Wanfen rushed to prepare dinner for her father and children. There was the children's favorite, fried chicken, and pea congee for the old father.

His son-in-law, Xiluo, was especially friendly to him today. He started chatting with the old man immediately; he even asked about Shuiyue.

"Why didn't Shuiyue come with you to visit? Is she still studying English at the language school?"

"She's graduating this summer."

"That's good. It'll be easier for her to find a job then," Xiluo responded.

The old man quietly shook his head, then glanced at his daughter. She and Shuiyue were the same age. *Wanfen doesn't have to work, of course Shuiyue shouldn't have to either.*

"Life would be more meaningful with a job," Wanfen said. "I want to go out and work when Tom is older."

Dehe agreed half-heartedly and changed the subject. He already had to drive Shuiyue to class every time, not to mention if she worked.

Before the couple left, Wanfen asked her father with complete sincerity, "Father, when will you bring Shuiyue here for a weekend?"

His son-in-law concurred, "Seriously, how about a weekend in mid April? I have to go to New York for a meeting, around the Easter holiday, I think. Wanfen can come with me for a few days. When Shuiyue comes, we'll turn the kids and the house over to you completely."

"Okay, okay, I'll tell her when I go back."

The old man nodded in agreement. This was the first time they formally extended their invitation to Shuiyue, not just saying it to try and be nice. He was quite touched. That feeling stayed with him until his daughter left the house, and he started watching television with his grandchildren.

Then he thought, *Would Shuiyue be happy to come?* He was not so sure. She would notice the change in Wanfen's attitude.

He remembered when he first announced his decision to get married again. His daughter was not too pleased. She suggested him moving in with them, as if all that the old man needed was someone to take care of his three meals. She had expressed her disapproval even before she met Shuiyue, and belittled all the people in Guizhou. One time, he overheard the young couple gossiping about Guizhou people, saying that over there "the sky's never clear more than three days, the road's never smooth more than three miles,"[3] and that it was so poor in Guizhou even the people had lost the will to fight. He overheard them whispering other derogatory comments making Guizhou sou2nd like such an undesirable place to live that it had no redeeming value whatsoever.

But his son, who lived far away in Boston, had the exact opposite reaction. He welcomed the news of his father remarrying--then, it would free him from the responsibility of flying back and forth to visit his father on the West Coast every year. Of course, he was genuinely happy about the news. However, he and his wife reminded him that a woman from Guizhou, especially with an age difference of thirty seven years, marrying someone thousands of miles away, really just wanted American citizenship and money. They cautioned their father not to fall into her trap.

So, Dehe found a lawyer to help him write up a will, naming his daughter and son as the heirs to all of his real estate properties and stocks, and thereby solved a family crisis. Even then, when he gave a huge wedding banquet in Chinatown, only presents came, but not his children.

Dehe's son came back to visit him the year before last. When he noticed the healthy red glow on his father's cheeks, he finally expressed some appreciation, "You've really taken good care of my father," he said to Shuiyue.

---

[3] Referring to the poor weather and deprived economic conditions in Guizhou province.

"He looks at least ten years younger now!"

Shuiyue's good points were discovered by Wanfen even earlier than by his son; and so, Wanfen's attitude towards her had softened as well.

After they were married, Shuiyue solely took over the job of taking care of the old man and freed his daughter from her worries. From then on, Wanfen no longer felt obliged to drive five hours each month to visit the old man. When she did come to Oakland, it was to go shopping in Chinatown. Then she would leave her two kids with Shuiyue, who had proven to be a fine babysitter.

The old man was especially fond of his grandchildren, and they got along very well. Every time grandpa came to visit them, Shuiyue would prepare bags and bags of presents. Little Tom was the tamer one of the two children. He was the first to obey his grandfather and call Shuiyue "grandma." Now, whatever he wanted to eat, all he needed to do was to call "grandma," and she would send grandpa to deliver the food. His mother, Wanfen, no longer referred to Shuiyue as "the woman from Guizhou," but followed the American custom of kindly addressing her by name, adding that Shuiyue's name sounded beautiful and out of the ordinary.

The real extraordinary qualities of this woman from Guizhou were her honesty and sincerity. She never tried to conceal the fact that coming to America was a way out for her. Back in her poor home town, she could envision no future; she had experienced a difficult relationship once already, and her family was heavily in debt. She had no choice but to place all her hopes on this marriage. As for their relationship, she never tried any phony sweet talk on the old man. He remembered his first meeting with her in Guizhou--she did not say much then, except repeating the same line, *I'll take good care of you.*

And she did. She always followed his wishes and gave the old man gentle loving care in his everyday life. The entire first year of their marriage passed without him ever seeing her laugh out loud, or him ever hearing her complain about anything; she acted as if she was working quietly to carry out her duties on a contractual basis, to complete a fair deal.

In the San Francisco Bay area, there were a few other old men like Dehe who married young women from mainland China. Dehe had met those women before and gradually discovered that Shuiyue resembled them less and less.

When she first arrived in America, she went crazy shopping for clothes and jewelry; as long as her husband did not object, she would buy them all. She learned to put on makeup, and used expensive, brand name cosmetics. She dressed nicely and fashionably, looking almost too gaudy at times.

In the beginning, he liked to walk with her, hand in hand, on the streets, introducing her to his friends everywhere. Weng Dehe, a man who never even graduated from elementary school in China, had now brought home a young and beautiful elementary school teacher, his wife. How lucky he was! Then, when he received too many astonished looks from people, he began to avoid showing her off so much.

Shuiyue also enjoyed eating out and going to movies. Every time the Chinese theaters in San Francisco's Chinatown showed a new film, she would drag her husband to see it with her. At first, he tried wholeheartedly to accommodate her, but soon he became worn out. Many times, he would fall asleep in the middle of a film.

Luckily, her enthusiasm died down quickly. She became lethargic, and sometimes, she refused to go out for an entire week. If her husband did not force her, she would not even go grocery shopping. Nobody had ever said anything to her about her clothes, but soon, she changed her wardrobe from flashy outfits to dark colored ones. Her cosmetics remained in boxes unopened, her facial expressions resembled still water.

The new world obviously did not turn out to be the paradise she had in mind. People from Guizhou wrote to her and asked her to be their matchmaker. They wanted to be married to an American, no matter what it cost. Shuiyue, however, began to loath her life in America and even missed the poverty of her home town. Writing letters and waiting to receive them became her major tasks each day. Dehe soon discovered that Shuiyue really enjoyed children. However, the couple had agreed before the marriage that she would not have any. He would provide her with a lifetime of fine clothing and good food, even her birth control pills were all arranged for her. Her life was peaceful and calm, but she was not happy.

It had been the exact opposite for the old man. He was not expecting much from the second marriage, but simply to satisfy his everyday and sexual needs. Before this marriage, in order to avoid any unnecessary gossip, he commissioned a matchmaker to go outside of his home town, to Guizhou, and find a wife for him. He only wanted to find a middle-age widow, but unexpectedly, the matchmaker found him a young woman. Adding more excitement to his joy was the fact that the first time he touched a woman since his wife died ten years ago, he could actually feel some passion. This little woman from Guizhou had brought him comfort and joy, and he quickly fell in love with her.

His second marriage--his second spring--had genuinely blessed him with the fountain of youth.

People became strange when they aged. He loved Shuiyue, yet was afraid that she would one day leave him. Amidst his happiness there was also some degree of fear.

Perhaps it was because of this fear that one year after they were married, he became sexually impotent. He could not remember the panic he had felt then, but he did remember the embarrassing experience of frantically running in and out of the doctor's office and the Chinese pharmacy to buy all sorts of dietary supplements. He bought almost everything on the shelves of the Chinatown stores. One time, an overdose of ginseng caused pimples to break out all over his face, and he was harshly scolded by the salesman at the pharmacy!

He could not help but laugh when he thought of this incident.

"Why are you laughing, grandpa, because the man's dying?"

His eight-year-old granddaughter pointed her finger at the television screen and interrogated him like a young adult.

He gathered his attention and stared at the bloody dying scene displayed on the television.

"This is too pathetic, let's not watch it," he said to her. Then pointing at the wall clock, he added, "Time to go to sleep, it's nine o'clock. Grandpa is tired today, let's all go to bed early."

She pouted in protest, "Tomorrow is Sunday, we don't need to get up early!"

However, the usually kind grandpa rushed her to the bedroom, then took her younger brother's hand and walked him to his.

"Grandma is coming. When is grandma coming?"

Even his grandson remembered the adults' conversation.

As his grandson said the word "grandma," a slight warmth filled the old man's heart. He quickly kissed Tom a few times on his little cheeks. Shuiyue held a certain attraction for children, and they could not forget her.

"Soon. Grandma will come for sure and she'll bring you lots of goodies to eat."

"I like sweet egg rolls. Tell grandma to make me egg rolls."

Grandpa nodded in agreement. Seeing the child close his eyes pleased him; he turned off the light and left his room.

Would Shuiyue come as a house guest? He continued to ponder this question as he walked toward the guest room. They had been living together for five years. Now, all of a sudden, he had lost confidence in his wife over such a trivial matter.

If only his daughter's invitation was more sincere. Wanfen and her husband would be away for the weekend, obviously leaving the two kids for them to babysit. For the past three years, he had been coming here every weekend to babysit. He did that out of his own free will and out of necessity. *Now that she's been given an inch, Wanfen seemed to be asking for a yard. The first time she has invited Shuiyue to her house, and she's employed such a tactic! Wouldn't Shuiyue be displeased with her because of it?*

Shuiyue was kind and talked little, but she was not without her own thoughts and opinions. In fact, once she had made up her mind, she could be very stubborn! But she was intrinsically kind and did not want to hurt other people, and thus appeared easy going on the outside.

Dehe recalled that one time, about half a year after he became impotent, Shuiyue asked him for a divorce. She wanted to return to Guizhou. He was not too surprised about her asking for a divorce, but for her to go back to Guizhou, back to the place where "no road is smooth within three miles," would have been a loss of face for him. None of the old men who married a Chinese woman had gotten a divorce within three years, Weng Dehe did not want to be the first one. Besides, he was used to having Shuiyue around to take care of him, he could not let her go. No matter how he begged her to stay, it was of no use. Finally, he was forced to play his last card.

"Shuiyue if you leave now, you won't be able to get your green card. Isn't that a pity?"

She shook her head and replied, "I've been to America and I've seen America. That's enough."

"If you return to Guizhou, what will you do?"

"I can still teach at the elementary school."

Shuiyue finally gave in after the old man broke down in tears, threatening her with suicide and high blood pressure. However, she continued to live unhappily for several months, always displaying that horrible empty look in her eyes. The few pounds she had managed to gain since coming here gradually disappeared. The old man lost his taste for food and soon his belt shrunk two more notches. He realized that he loved her so much that he could no longer live without her smile and happiness. It was for that reason that he thought of Abing.

Now that Abing won't be coming here any more, it will probably take a while for Shuiyue to calm down. Initially Shuiyue had not agreed to the arrangement of having Abing replace him. She insisted that was not the reason behind her wanting a divorce. Doing his best, the old man had tried to persuade her with using sincere words and dramatic acts of kneeling down. Finally, she agreed.

Shuiyue would not be so hard to convince. From now on he would have to treat her much better, so would his children. Together they would most definitely change her mind about leaving. For life to be fun and fulfilling, *"that"* should not be the only thing that's needed to keep it going. A man of his age had seen it all, he knew. He had to persuade her slowly, step by step.

Anyway, an invitation from his daughter and son-in-law could not have come at a better time. I must tell Shuiyue right away.

Thinking about it, he went back to the family room and dialed his home phone number.

Shuiyue picked it up as soon as the phone rang, as if she were sitting right next to it.

"Hello....Who's this?" she answered frantically, the shrillness of her voice piercing his ear. "Is this Abing?"

"It's me...," he replied. Dehe seldom called his wife at home. Now it made him feel rather nervous.

"Oh, it's you," she said flatly. Her voice suddenly calmed down.

"What are you doing, Shuiyue?"

The old man regretted his question as soon as he asked. After all, he did not call to check up on her, he had always trusted her.

"Nothing....I was just writing to my mother."

He detected a sob in Shuiyue's voice. It sounded as if she had been crying. This time, he would not ask anything, nor would he comfort her. He would act as if nothing had ever happened. He then told her about the invitation from his daughter and son-in-law. Carefully he avoided mentioning the fact that they planned to go away to New York.

For what seemed like hours, there wasn't a sound from the other side of the receiver. He anxiously asked, "Will you come, Shuiyue? They've wanted to invite you over for a long time now. Really, it's the first thing Xiluo said to me today."

"Thank them for me. We'll discuss it when you come back. It's still a long time away, there's no hurry."

"Yes, yes. It's still a long time off," he responded quickly, nodding his head at the receiver. He continued gently, "You're all alone, you should go to bed early. I'll be back after breakfast tomorrow."

"But, why? I'm fine, don't you worry about me. Just come back in the evening as you planned."

"No, no, I'll come back in the morning."

He insisted, so Shuiyue did not argue further and ended the phone conversation.

He could feel the warmth in his wife's voice during the latter part of the conversation. Obviously, her emotions had been calmed. He was glad he made that call. Now, he felt as if a huge rock had been removed from his chest, and that his entire body was free. He was so light-footed, he felt like he had just had a couple of glasses of *Maotai* wine. He was not worried about being unable to sleep tonight, but just to make sure, he swallowed two sleeping pills.

As soon as he hit the bed, he fell into a deep slumber.

The next morning, he awoke to the sound of dogs barking and pigs squealing. Lying in bed, in the guest room, he could hear little Tom watching cartoons in the family room. The old man closed his eyes and laid there, listening. Suddenly he remembered a scene from his childhood of him chasing ducks by the river of Liuzhou.

The flock of ducks slipped into the water and fled, leaving one female behind, yapping alone. Her heavy, dull lower body pressured her feet wide open. Her awkward movements had resembled that of a pregnant woman.

The ducks reminded him of many other things. Things he had all but forgotten, for nearly half a century, were now surfacing out of the still water. Wave after wave of memories flooded his mind. Shuiyue, Abing, the broken tea cup...the decision he had made last night, all exhibited in front of his eyes.

A day's planning starts in the morning. Once his eyes were open, ideas began to pop up one after another.

First of all, he wanted to take Shuiyue on a trip. She liked Guizhou, so first they would go back to Guizhou. He must spare some five thousand dollars for her to prepare for an impressive homecoming. He also needed to get away. Strangely enough, but after he became impotent, he started to gain weight. Being overweight was dangerous for men of his age; he had better not to be too careless.

Most importantly, he had to change his will and reassign his possessions. He wanted to leave Shuiyue the house they now lived in and all his stocks, so she would not have to worry about making a living. Then, she would know that her husband loved her, appreciated her, and would never mistreat her.

Upon finishing a rough draft of his plans in his mind, the old man got out of bed to write them down. He could not find any paper in the guest room except some white napkins. So he wrote two new wills on the napkins, one in Chinese and one in English.

. Putting the wills inside his suit pocket, he waltzed a little in the room. He thought of himself as a generous man and was deeply touched by his own deeds. He decided that as soon as he got home, he would let Shuiyue look over the will, and take her to see his attorney on Monday so she could witness the procedure of him changing the will.

His desire to return home as soon as possible was so great that he was unhappy about his daughter not being awake. He fed the children breakfast and played Monopoly with them. Finally, at ten-thirty, Wanfen came out of her room in her bathrobe and entered the family room yawning continuously. The tired look on her face, the leftover makeup, and her disheveled hair made her look like a witch.

Secretly, Dehe was glad that Shuiyue, who was the same age as Wanfen, never looked like such a mess.

"Wanfen, take me to the bus station, quickly, I want to go home."

"Now?" his daughter exclaimed, rubbing her eyes. She glanced at the clock on the wall and said slowly, "We didn't end *mahjongg* until two this morning. Xiluo was still snoring when I woke up. We'll take you to a new Cantonese restaurant in a while. Dim sum doesn't start until eleven-thirty. There's nothing good to eat if you go too early."

He tried to explain patiently, "I already ate, I'm not hungry at all. I just want to go home as soon as possible."

"What's the hurry?" his daughter asked, wondering aloud. "Did something happen to Shuiyue?"

"Oh, no, no!" he immediately denied. Feeling pressure from Wanfen, he told her a lie, "I promised Shuiyue...I told her I'd help her trim the camellias this afternoon."

"I thought it was something urgent! Father, I think you should stay until this evening. Xiluo and I are going to see some houses, we've already made an appointment with the real estate agent. With two kids...."

He tried to suppress his annoyance and interrupted, "I must go back early today. And I'm not coming here next week."

"Why not?"

Now, his daughter's eyes were wide open, her alarmed expression made her look like an owl.

"Xiluo's boss has invited us to dinner next Saturday! Father, if you don't come, where will I find a babysitter?"

"You must figure that out yourself!" he snapped. Again, he tried hard to suppress his anger and announced in a nicer tone of voice, "From now on, I don't think I will come here alone on the weekends."

His daughter misinterpreted the old man. She quickly explained, "We've been wanting to invite Shuiyue for a long time, really. If you don't believe me, I can call her myself today!"

"Go ahead and call her. You must call her often from now on."

"I promise I will. She's been so good to you, we all know that."

The old man's heart softened. He ended up going to dim sum with the family before catching the bus home.

The town was dead silent on Sunday afternoons, except in Chinatown, where businesses were open as usual. He got off the bus nearby there, found a familiar flower shop and picked out a half-dozen white roses. He asked the salesperson to wrap the flowers in a green sheet of paper, and tie it with a red ribbon. Then he went to catch another bus home.

This Sunday, he was the only passenger on the entire bus, it was as if he owned the bus. Senior citizens paid almost nothing to ride it; he enjoyed this privilege. Before coming back, Wanfen wanted to call Shuiyue so she could pick him up, but Dehe turned down the offer. The bus stop was right in front of his neighbor's house, it could not be more convenient.

As he descended from the bus, he felt pain in his leg muscles. He had walked too much after all. He saw his car parked on the side of the street and felt relieved. No matter how close he was to the children, their house was incomparable to his own. Besides, Shuiyue was here. The weather seemed particularly nice today. Though nearly sunset, rays of sunlight fell on the grass, the buildings, the trees and flowers, like a thin layer of gold--bright but warm, especially pleasing to the eyes. He held the roses in his hands and walked up the stairs. Welcoming the old man were the camellias on both sides of the steps, bright red like a burning flame. He was proud of the present in his hands. There were already too many red flowers in the house, these white ones would mellow the scenery a little. Shuiyue would be impressed by them, too.

He rang the door bell twice, but there was not a sound inside. *What's Shuiyue busy doing in the kitchen?* He was curious. He had never been greeted by an empty house, yet he was not at all surprised. *Women....They always have their own little business to take care of.* He searched around, found the house key and opened the front door for himself.

"Shuiyue, Shuiyue!"

From the living room to the kitchen, he shouted and heard no reply. The stove was empty, the cutting board was clean, and there was not one sign of cooking. *She must be in the bedroom.* So he walked in with the flowers. The door was open. The two single beds were nicely made, next to one another. The bathroom was also empty. He carefully searched the room again with his eyes. Everything was in its usual place, except the purse that Shuiyue usually placed on the dresser. *Then, she's gone out.*

As he was thinking, a sudden suffocating feeling struck his chest. Holding the flowers close to his body, he struggled back to the kitchen. He sat down at the table, laid the roses down, put his hands on his chest and began rubbing it.

He glanced out the window. The setting sunset reflected on the apple tree, forming bundles of red clouds, dyeing the camellias bloody red.

When his chest pain faded away, he continued the search for his wife. He got up from the chair, walked over and pushed open the door leading downstairs. The stairs looked dark and endlessly long, a mass of cold air struck his face; he felt a chill.

He walked back to the chair and waited. The entire house was quiet. *Shuiyue went to look for Abing.*

This thought unconsciously crept inside his head. When the setting sun took away the last beam of light, the thin curtain was filled with darkness. Weng Dehe knew that it was no illusion.

I'm not getting a divorce, he mumbled to himself. *I'll wait for her to come back.*

He continued to sit there, his eyes staring out the window. In the misty dusk, the redness of the camellias appeared even more intense, like blood stains splattered on the window.

Guest from the Homeland

Editor's Notes:

Interacting between documentary, ideological, and critical dimensions, "Guest from the Homeland" is a story rich with sociopolitical details. Correlating to three decades of Chinese politics and history, spanning from 1960 to 1980, Chen Ruoxi takes great pains to insure that each passage is relevant to some aspect of her main characters. These characters, each representative of current ideological perspectives held by overseas Chinese, play the role of witness of their age. They are the embodiment of the mentality, problems, and issues of Chinese who immigrated to America during the sixties and seventies. However, amongst these old friends, there is a measure of outsidership imperceptibly linked to the transitions that have taken place in their lives as well as individual ideologies. Where once their youthful dreams and ideas bound them together, now change, time, and lack of communication has pulled them apart. Thus, when they attempt to meet physically and mentally on a neutral ground, the characters reach an inevitable crossroad, figuratively paralleling the irresolute division between China and Taiwan.

GUEST FROM THE HOMELAND[1]

By the time Luo Shaoyong drove home, it was already twilight. Sometime earlier the wind had begun to blow, and it made his small VW bug swing back and forth and its windows whistle. Before he turned the car from Interstate 80 to the Bay Bridge, he slowed down. He tried to look sideways as he drove. The sky and ocean joined to become a part of the sunset, and the entire city of San Francisco was illuminated to transparency by lights. It was like a glamorous phoenix rising from the burning ashes, resplendent but innocent.

He had been living in San Francisco for four years. He loved to see the city at night, especially when viewing it from the other side of the Bay. The scene was almost sacred to him. Whenever he had a chance to go to the East Bay, he tried to stay there until dark so he could enjoy this feast for the eyes.

Tonight, he had been the first to bid farewell to his host. The houseful of guests had been entertained by many good conversations, so the host was surprised to hear that he was already leaving.

---

[1] "Guest from the Homeland" (*Ke zi guxiang lai*) was translated by Feng-ying Ming with the permission of the author and publisher, and is published here in English for the first time. This translation is based on the story's appearance in *Chengli chengwai* (Taibei: Shibao, 1983), pp. 162-194.

"Mingming is home by himself and I'm worried. I should leave now."
He told a lie.

The guest of honor, Wang Zhi, had been busy answering questions
about living on the mainland. Shaoyong wanted to sneak out without
interrupting the other guests' enthusiastic conversations. But Wang Zhi, who
watched every movement in the house, rushed to the door to shake hands
with Shaoyong.

"Old Luo, you went back fifteen years too early, the time was not right-
everything is all right now! Because of the "Four Modernizations" there is a
need for all kinds of talents, even artists like you are indispensable. Why
don't you go and see for yourself? Give me a call when you get to Beijing...."

Fifteen years too early. Could that be true?

Shaoyong smiled in silence. He shook his head before realizing what
he was doing and stepped on the brake.

Ahead of him were several lines of cars waiting to pass the bridge toll
booths. While searching inside his pocket for cash, he wondered why it was
so crowded at this time of the day. He suddenly realized that it was Friday,
the beginning of the weekend. People had just finished dinner and were
coming into town for fun.

Upon passing the toll booth, he rolled up the window, stepped on the
accelerator, and shifted gears. His car quickly merged with other cars in the
lane and followed the line of traffic to the bridge. The ocean wind blew
vehemently. Shaoyong's small car was sandwiched between cars that were
seemingly chasing one another in a reckless fashion, all involuntarily following
the leading car. At moments like this, Shaoyong always felt a sort of
unspeakable nervousness and uneasiness. It was a feeling similar to the
political climate he experienced in mainland China, forced, worrisome, and
unspeakably suffocating.

"You went back fifteen years too early, the time was not right--everything

is all right now!"

Wang Zhi's words resounded in his ears.

This year Shaoyong had met quite a few people from the mainland; some had just emigrated here, some were sent to study or to do research at American universities, and others were like himself, who had once "returned to the homeland" and left again. Wang Zhi was the first person he had met that had returned to the mainland for only half a year before being sent back to the States again.

Before he left, Wang Zhi taught at the University of San Francisco. It was only last year that Shaoyong heard from another friend that Wang Zhi and his family were going back to the homeland permanently. They had met twice before, both times at the house of tonight's host. Wang Zhi had not been as eloquent and humorous a speaker as he was now. Instead, he had been very serious, even nervous, like a martyr who was about to go into battle. His wife, on the other hand, tried to act cheerful, despite the insecurity revealed between her brows. Shaoyong had reassured them over and over again that the living conditions on the mainland had improved, that there was also a new policy for returning intellectuals, and it should not be too difficult to cope with life there.

"We have prepared for the worst anyway."

Mrs. Wang talked as if she was determined to make a noble sacrifice.

The Chinese Communists were treating overseas students with great courtesy now, and they had arranged a position that met Wang Zhi's requirements. Though Mrs. Wang had not worked for many years, she was assigned to the same department where her husband worked. Aside from a regular salary, they received a subsidized allowance. Their monthly salary amounted to 460 Chinese *yuan*, which equals that of a general in the

Liberation Army.[2] No wonder Wang Zhi repeatedly said that they could not use all the money up no matter how they spent it.

What surprised Shaoyong was the special treatment they received on housing. He heard that the new housing policy had designated a unit of six rooms with kitchen and bathroom as the ideal housing arrangement for returning overseas students. However, in the city where Wang Zhi stayed, the best residence was a unit of only four rooms. In order to comply with the new policy, the city government forced some families to move out of the building so the Wang family could have a total of six rooms. The two extra rooms were not on the same floor as the other four rooms. In fact, the rooms were so inconvenient to use that they became their storage rooms.

"Couldn't you possibly give up these rooms?" Shaoyong asked.

"I have thought about it, but my co-worker told me how serious the housing shortage is in China. If I give them up now, I'm afraid I'll never be able to get them back again. Many husbands and wives even live apart so that they can keep some rooms for their children when they get married. Four rooms are enough for us at this time, but the children are growing up so fast. We have to plan ahead."

He was right. All parents shared these feelings for their children. Didn't he leave China for the same reason, for the welfare of his children? He had been condemned as "the Stinky Ninth",[3] "Stooge of the American Imperialists",[4] and "the Suspected Secret Agent"....He was forced to leave China and went into exile because he was afraid that there would always be

---

[2] This refers to the Chinese People's Liberation Army, *Jiefang jun,* or PLA.

[3] Or *Choulaojiu,* a term referring to the intellectuals as the lowest of nine categories during the Chinese Cultural Revolution period. A similar phrase, "The Ninth Confucianists and the Tenth Beggars" (*Jiuru shigai*), was used in the Yuan dynasty of the 13th century when Confucian scholars were degraded as the second lowest class in the social hierarchy.

[4] It also can be translated as "the lackeys of American Imperialism," *Meidi zougou,* which is a phrase referring to the people who are on good terms with the Americans.

discrimination against his children.

"This Lane for Broadway Exit Only"....When did he choose this exit? Since he was already there, why bother worrying about anything else? He followed the traffic and drove into a nightless portion of the city where the many colored lights endlessly illuminated the streets.

Broadway was a world made of neon signs, a swamp of cars, and a human market for pleasure seekers. The strip show signs were dazzling, and the chaotic pop music was deafening. "Speed" was a meaningless term in this world. Shaoyong's car moved at a snail's pace at first, and finally became immobile. While he was lowering his car window to get some fresh air, he heard the passionate greetings outside of a night club: "Come on in, take a look for free!"

"While Meiyu is away," he thought, "I should spend one evening over here. Maybe I'll get some inspiration." Two years ago, he had drawn a portrait of a stripper. It was a charcoal sketch of a girl who had just finished dancing and was bending down to pick up her dress. The drawing was placed on display for only one day before it was sold. He was not particularly interested in portraiture, though it could be a profitable way of living.

His car entered the tunnel. All of a sudden the noise was left behind. He sucked in a deep breath of relief and realized how suffocating the clamor had been.

Parking his car on the street, he walked a short distance to his apartment. He opened the mailbox only to find it empty, and then recalled that he had already collected the mail earlier in the afternoon.

He walked upstairs and started to open the door. Even before he turned the key, he could hear disco music coming out of the room. *I'll have to keep my son in line, he reminded himself.* The volume is too high for this time of the day, and he certainly didn't want to get an eviction notice from the landlord.

Mingming was lying on the sofa reading a copy of *Scientific American*, with his foot on the floor beating to the rhythm of the music.

"Dad, someone called you twice. He sounded like he's from China. I took his phone number down."

"Yeah? I just met someone from China. Turn down the volume a little bit, Mingming."

His son's room was the farthest one away from the living room. But with the door open, the sound of music flowed like a flood from there to every corner of the house. It could be tolerated on most days, but he was feeling low tonight, and this uproar made him rather uncomfortable.

"What did you eat for dinner?"

"Campbell's soup and a sandwich."

"Still hungry?"

"No."

He felt relieved and went to the phone. Reading the telephone number, Shaoyong noted it had an East Bay prefix. Does this have something to do with Wang Zhi? Out of courtesy, he went ahead and dialed the number. A voice came on the line, "Holiday Inn." He gave the extension and waited.

Mingming was an understanding child after all. He had turned off the music.

"Hello, who is this?"

The voice that answered was a low familiar voice of a male.

Shaoyong stated his name. The person on the other end of the line responded in a high pitched squeak, "Hey, Old Luo, don't you recognize my voice any more? This is Guan Li!"

"Guan Li? God! It's you?"

Now was Shaoyong's turn to yell. After six years of separation, he had never dreamed that Guan Li would come to America.

"When did you get here? How long are you staying? I'll come over to see you right now...." he exclaimed, blurting out question upon question.

His friend responded calmly, "I came with the provincial cadre for business. Old Bai is here. I'll let him talk to you about getting together."

Old Bai? Another familiar name. It must be the bookstore owner from Chinatown. Everybody calls him "Old Bai". The three of them, Old Bai, Guan Li, and he were in the same group when they joined the Taiwan Reserve Officer Training Corp.

"Hey, Old Luo, where have you been all night? We've been trying to find you! Tell you what, Guan Li and his academic delegation will be in the United States for three weeks. They'll stay in New York for two weeks to negotiate and sign some project proposals. They're flying to the East Coast tomorrow, and they're leaving from Seattle. So, tonight...."

"I'll come over right now!" Shaoyong said immediately, so frustrated he almost stamped his feet. "If I had only known about this earlier! I just came back from Berkeley."

"What a coincidence! But you can't run back and forth like this....I'll tell you what, since I'm going into the city anyway, let me take him to your place, and then you will be responsible for getting him back."

"Do you remember my house? Actually, it's very easy for me to pick him up," Shaoyong replied, feeling rather concerned.

"Didn't I move some paintings for you the last time you had an exhibition? I can still remember a little."

Shaoyong did not put down the telephone until he had given more detailed directions and had spoken to Guan Li again.

"Mingming, Uncle Guan has come from China!" he told his son immediately. "Don't go to bed until you meet him."

"Which Uncle Guan?"

Looking at his uncomprehending face, Shaoyong was angry as well as anxious.

"The Uncle Guan who held you in his arms shortly after you were born! Some time after that their whole family went into exile....I mean, they moved away from Beijing. But when we left China, they came to see us off, don't you remember? The Uncle Guan who has twin sons, they're only one year younger than you?"

Mingming shrugged his shoulders. He could not remember. He was not interested either. He yawned and said reluctantly, "All right, I'll wait."

Having said that, he threw himself back on to the sofa indolently.

Shaoyong sighed helplessly. Maybe this was one kind of generation gap--not knowing how to appreciate the joy of having a guest coming from the homeland.

The problem of being in America for so long was that children gradually forget about their native country. Parents were so worried about this that whenever they had the opportunity, they sent their children to relatives in Taiwan for vacations. But this arrangement was like the delicate touch of a dragonfly upon the surface of water, only slightly better than nothing.

"Come on, help me tidy up the living room. It's so messy, how can we entertain our guest from China?"

The American-born Mingming seemed to recognize that this was a serious matter, so he jumped up right away.

Not long after the start of summer vacation, Meiyu took their second son to Taiwan to visit relatives. Without the supervision and management of his wife, their lives became undisciplined. They had not straightened up the house since she left. At first, they started leaving their clothes in the living room, and later their sneakers and soiled socks as well. Shaoyong's studio, facing west, was almost impossible for him to work in on summer afternoons, so he moved his easels, his paints, and brushes...all into the living room. His son also moved his violin and music stand there to enjoy the cool air. Of course they ate while watching television, so the salt and pepper shakers together with tubes of pigment occupied the entire coffee table top. It took them only ten days to transform the living room into what resembled a Jewish-style secondhand store.

Shaoyong quickly moved his easels and tools back to the studio and left everything else to his son. He then rushed to the kitchen to prepare something to eat.

Guan Li was capable of drinking. If it were not so late already, he would go to Chinatown to get two bottles of *Maotai* or *Luzhou Daqu*. How nice it would be to share some with old friends! Fortunately, they always kept some whiskey and Johnny Walker in the house. He checked the refrigerator and there were more than half a dozen beers left. Good. At least they could get a little drunk.

He opened all the kitchen cabinets to search for food that would go well with the drinks. Meiyu was very considerate. Before she left she had bought lots of canned goods for them, enough to fill the space on the shelves. After inspecting everything, he found canned lichee, phoenix-tailed fish, and grilled bamboo, as well as a big package of peanuts, and a can of roasted almonds. These should be enough, he thought.

It had been years since they last saw each other. They deserved to get really drunk. Shaoyong hoped the guests would arrive soon.

He still remembered the time, in 1975, when they were about to leave China, and Guan Li came to say good-bye to them. The two of them were drunk like mud. Their words became fewer and fewer, but they still drank more and more. According to Meiyu, Shaoyong had cried bitterly before he fell asleep. Guan Li, she said, had laughed like an idiot and then began to cry in a lunatic fashion.

How many times can one have worthwhile intoxication in a life time? he had asked himself. Afterwards, Shaoyong had many chances to drink, but he never got drunk again. In the past forty-five years of his life, that was the only time he had ever been so absolutely drunk. He had been totally unconscious, like a dead man. After that, whenever he felt that he was lacking artistic inspiration or was depressed, he would think of getting drunk again in order to experience the state of absolute purity that could never be attained from sleep. The more he drank, however, the more sober he became. He even threw up at times.

Drinking was like being in love, he thought. *You can encounter it, but can't force it.*

Just as Mingming turned off the vacuum cleaner, and Shaoyong was hastily setting the food and drink on the table, Old Bai arrived with his friend Guan Li.

"You haven't changed much, Old Luo!"

"You haven't either!"

The two old friends held each other's hands and remarked in excitement how the other did not change a bit. It seemed that their unchanged appearance was a consolation to them as much as their everlasting friendship.

However Shaoyong knew that he himself had changed a lot, or at least he felt he had. But Old Guan really had not changed much at all. His dark face still looked as vigorous as before, and his friendly grin, with its even white teeth, was confident and reassuring. Guan Li's back, which Shaoyong once thought would be broken under heavy shoulder poles, was still as straight as a corn stalk. When Shaoyong took a closer look though, he knew this old Guan was different from the Old Guan of six years ago. The eyes that he remembered as sad and perplexed were now confident and calm, and revealed a threatening power when they looked straight at you.

"Is this your eldest son? He's as tall as his Dad now!"

Old Guan shook hands with Mingming formally as if Mingming were a little adult.

Shaoyong immediately explained that Meiyu had gone back to Taiwan with their second son to visit relatives. Then he asked about Mrs. Guan and the twins.

Old Guan said they were all well.

"The children are both like their Mom, not too tall, dark and strong, with wide backs and broad shoulders. But we're always sorry that we don't have more time to spend with them."

He didn't explain why there wasn't time to be with their own children. Shaoyong didn't have time to press the matter either. He invited his two guests to sit down.

Mingming having said hello to the visitors, retreated back to his own room and closed his door.

Shaoyong passed cigarettes around and asked when his old friend had arrived in San Francisco.

"The day before yesterday."

"So soon?" he was surprised. "Why didn't you tell me right away? I've sent you a Christmas card every year, you should have my address."

Old Guan nodded without answering the question. Instead he said, "Yesterday, I spent the whole day visiting the University of California, and today I met with Old Bai. He gave me your phone number."

Shaoyong remembered that Old Guan and Old Bai knew each other in the Reserve Officer Training Corps, but they didn't keep in touch with each other afterwards. Why did Old Guan contact Old Bai as soon as he came to America? Shaoyong could not help feeling a little bit jealous, but he smiled without asking any more about it.

Shaoyong was not very close to Old Bai, but he knew Old Bai was quite popular in the Chinese community. He had very wide interests and was especially interested in public affairs and politics. His bookstore had become an important stop for Chinese visitors. Recalling this, Shaoyong felt better.

Old Bai didn't seem ready to leave, so Shaoyong graciously offered his guests some wine. Old Bai wanted straight whiskey, and he seemed to be capable of drinking. Old Guan just wanted beer. He was very controlled, sipping only once in a while. Shaoyong drank beer too, to keep him company.

"I said a long time ago, you were a talented painter," Old Guan said after viewing the painting hanging in the living room.

His words were rather dry. Shaoyong could not tell whether he was praising the painting or just saying that there was nothing special about it. Guan had graduated with a degree in Political Science and appreciated painting that was not abstract. Living in China for the past fifteen years had not changed his artistic preferences a bit.

"Old Luo paints very well!" Old Bai praised his painting, supporting his host. "He participated in the Art Exhibition our cultural center sponsored last year. His paintings were highly praised."

"I'm an old man with no ambition now," Shaoyong said casually. "I started late, and I'm just trying to survive."

He never felt comfortable talking about his paintings with others, but instead felt embarrassed, as if he was an ugly daughter-in-law meeting her parents-in-law for the first time. He tried to change the subject, asking his friend, "Are you still teaching English?"

"No, I haven't for a long time. I spent this quarter just dealing with administrative problems," Old Guan replied.

Shaoyong did not understand exactly what he meant by administrative work, but decided against asking. In his experience, living on the mainland, if someone did not give out details about their job, it meant it was confidential. Other people had better not ask. It would be smart not to ask.

But Old Guan explained candidly, "I am responsible for the

administration of my department now."

"Wow, you are department chairman now. Congratulations!"

He was really happy for his old friend. Who would have had such luck during the "Gang of Four" era?

"What about Liwen?" he asked, wondering about Old Guan's wife.

"She is the head of the English section. But she will be in charge of the entire department next fall."

"Good for you! The Foreign Languages department is becoming your own little kingdom."

"No. I won't be in the department then. I'm being transferred to the College Revolution Committee after this visit."

Shaoyong didn't know what kind of position Old Guan would be taking in the College Revolution Committee. Maybe he did not tell out of modesty or because it was a secret, but he was not that interested in finding out anyway.

The Chinese Communists had recently reinstituted the classified information policy of the fifties. Strictly speaking, under that policy, everything was considered secret except such matters as eating and sleeping. Wei Jingsheng was sentenced to fifteen years in jail merely for telling foreign reporters the name of the Chinese general who supervised during the Vietnam War. As a junior Communist official, Old Guan understood this.

"Cheers!" Shaoyong raised a toast, "Five years in the May Seventh Cadre School was worthwhile. Sweetness comes after the bitterness! It deserves a toast!"

Old Bai raised his glass too, "The new policy on intellectuals began two years ago. It's worth a celebration!"

Old Guan finished his beer, and put down his glass, saying regretfully to Shaoyong, "Everything would be fine if you had just stayed there for two more years. If you had waited until the "Gang of Four" stepped down, I'm sure you wouldn't have left."

Shaoyong thought about it for a moment, and then said carelessly, "Really?"

Who knows? Guan Li says two years later....Somebody else says fifteen years earlier....The Actualization Policy--six rooms, high salary--is it that simple?

Drinking beer left a bitterness and coolness in his throat that lingered for a long time. Shaoyong swallowed a mouthful of saliva, but it was still bitter. He shook his head and said with regret, "I feel the present Intellectuals Actualization Policy is just a bribe aimed at a small group of elites rather than to better the life of the mass of intellectuals."

He brought up Wang Zhi as an example and worried aloud that the policy would cultivate a new class of special privileges.

Old Guan explained that for the sake of the Four Modernizations, China needs talented people, and so treating intellectuals favorably should be one of their principles now. His strong statement seemed to say that to achieve this, even the creation of a new class was acceptable. For instance, later on, at the Teachers' College where he taught, they planned to adopt "the specialists govern the school" policy.

"Frankly speaking, we are not afraid of privilege, we're only worried about incompetent officials."

Old Guan's determination and resolution shocked Shaoyong. Compared to the old Guan who pursued the ideal of a proletarian society, this was a substantial change.

Old Bai also spoke up, "For these returning intellectuals, special favors are all right and necessary--they need time to adapt themselves to the new environment. But it can't be too different from the policy for the intellectuals at home or the effect will be detrimental...."

Right now there was too much of a difference between the way the two groups were treated. When Shaoyong closed his eyes, he could still see his old colleagues and friends' living quarters. A family of four, sometimes even three generations, packed together in one room. Clothes lines were crisscrossed overhead, and the beds were all jammed together on the floor. Several people competed for the only desk; and no matter how many there were in the family, only two chairs would be issued by house management.

Shaoyong still remembered when Guan Li was transferred from the country to the Teachers' College. Guan Li wrote that the school authorities had given him two small rooms, but they had to use a public kitchen and restroom. The kitchen was so far away that, according to Guan Li, "During the winter, a hot dish became frozen by the time we could get it back to the room."

"How many rooms do you have now?" Shaoyong asked curiously.

Old Guan answered with a clear conscience, "Still two, but they are larger than before, together with a private kitchen and restroom. It's a single unit with its own entrance."

Both Shaoyong and Old Bai nodded with admiration. They respected him for not being corrupted by fortune and power. But Shaoyong still could not help sighing. Though Old Guan got two rooms because of his office, most people might well live under the same crowded conditions for another thirty years.

"I'm not objecting to favorable treatment for returning intellectuals," Shaoyong said, afraid that his friend would misunderstand him. Continuing, he spoke from his heart, "But both of us experienced the Cultural Revolution. Remember why we supported it at the beginning? It was because the bureaucracy and privileged classes were what the masses were mobilizing to attack. Unrest is the result of unfair treatment. If the class gap is too wide now, the intellectuals will suffer later."

Old Bai agreed, frequently nodding his head.

Shaoyong took the opportunity to drive his point home, "The returning people return because of their love for the country. They aren't really concerned about the material life. Just think, when you returned, did you return for six rooms and the salary of a general?"

To Shaoyong's surprise, Guan Li wasn't moved at all, but just shook his head and sighed, "Old Luo, times have changed, it's different from when we went back."

The social status of the intellectuals had been rising higher and higher in the last two years. However, Guan Li said there were still a lot of people applying to go abroad, including those who had returned only three or four years ago. They claimed that they were unable to adapt to the environment or simply wanted to go abroad to study some more. The Chinese Communists tried their best to please them, but there were still returning scholars who quarreled with their supervisors over housing and promotions and finally left China in rage. After situations such as these began to occur, the government cut other departmental funding in order to offer the best living conditions to the scholars and specialists returning from abroad.

"Take our Teachers' College for example. We invited two Australians to teach English this spring. In addition to their travel expenses, we offered the best high-rise housing, five hundred a month salary, housekeepers, cars and drivers...."

Shaoyong was about to swallow a mouthful of beer when he heard the offer of cars and drivers. He was so surprised, he choked on his drink and coughed until his eyes were wet.

"They even offered a car and a driver? That's really too much!" Old Bai protested. Either because of the beer or the excitement, his face had turned red and his eyes blinked repeatedly. He was overwhelmed and emotional.

Old Guan however looked very solemn. He appeared dignified and confident as if he had prepared himself for a fight to the finish.

"If we don't offer them cars, do you want our distinguished guests to be squeezed in a bus among the common people?"

"What's wrong with taking a bus?" Shaoyong asked immediately, trying very hard to stop coughing.

Waving a hand, his friend indicated that it was out of the question. He frowned, as if he wondered why Shaoyong could not understand him.

"You've been to China before. Don't you remember how curious Chinese people are? Foreigners are treated almost like rare species in a zoo. People stare and follow them everywhere like a troop of soldiers....It's so embarrassing!"

Of course Shaoyong had witnessed such scenes. He still felt ashamed when thinking about it, but people can be educated. Now the administration was apparently concentrating on trivialities, thus forgetting the main purpose of the program. They kept the distinguished guests in a wire cage. Shaoyong sighed but did not say anything else.

"They can ride bicycles," Old Bai did not give up. He argued confidently, "I've been to Australia before. It's very common to ride bicycles there."

Guan Li did not argue any more. He explained patiently, "We have too many people. Our traffic system is crowded, too. If foreign guests get lost or if they are hurt in an accident, can you imagine what a bad impression that would give others!"

Having said that, Old Guan put away the American cigarette his host gave him and took a pack of "China Brand" from his shirt pocket, lit one up and smoked leisurely. He did not seem to care at all about Shaoyong and Old Bai's objections.

"Accidents, even murders, can be handled according to law, can't they? Westerners don't get such delicate treatment in Africa!"

Shaoyong heard his own shrill and anxious voice. He felt like he was about to cough again.

Old Bai tried to persuade Old Guan from another angle, "Lots of foreigners try to go to China by any means. They don't actually care about the pay, or at least they don't need such high compensation."

"Exactly!" Shaoyong joined him. "China is not a barren land. We don't have to degrade ourselves like this."

"Well, you don't understand the difficulties we administrators have encountered," Old Guan felt he had been misunderstood. "These two foreign specialists are the first we have ever invited there. As a pilot program, our responsibility is heavy and it has important consequences. For the purpose of the Four Modernizations, we can only succeed, we cannot fail!"

Shaoyong and Old Bai exchanged looks without further arguments.

"Frankly speaking, quite a few teachers raised the same objections you just did. We got them the car only because I insisted on it."

Shaoyong was stunned. How could this be Old Guan's idea? He put his glass down and rubbed his forehead.

"Just think about it! If they quit in the middle of the semester simply because they aren't satisfied with the living conditions, the result will be disastrous. Who would be willing to come to China then? It is easy to be one of the common people and complain. But to be a leader, one has to take on a lot of responsibilities. You cannot make any mistakes."

Guan Li's last sentence was said slowly and seriously. It sounded as if his every word was pulled out of his throat by iron pincers. Old Bai and Shaoyong were deeply affected by Guan Li's tone of voice and his solemn, hard face. They lowered their eyes, trying to feel the emotions of this purposeful, devoted official.

After a moment, Shaoyong raised his eyes and looked straight at Old Guan. He had just inhaled a mouthful of his "China Brand" cigarette and was slowly releasing the vapor from the side of his mouth. With the cigarette in his right hand, and his left arm holding his right arm, he leaned back on the long sofa and stared straight ahead. It was a pose that even thunder could not disturb. His shirt had been buttoned to the very top of his throat, but it was loosened now. Shaoyong could even see the corner of his undershirt. His well-creased light grey trousers fit him very well. They must have been newly made for this trip. His shoes were also brand new. His eyes showed an air of confidence that was very close to being imperious or arrogant.

Shaoyong was suddenly reminded of a book that both of them had loved to read, "How Steel Was Produced".

Old Bai looked at his watch, and said it was about midnight and that he had to go home. But his body was comfortably entrenched in the sofa and did not show any signs of moving.

"Aren't you hungry?" his host asked, "I'll cook some noodles."

Old Guan said he was not hungry and told Shaoyong not to bother. He pointed at all the food still sitting on the coffee table, most of it untouched.

"It appears that we all have a Chinese appetite. How about a pot of hot tea?" he suggested.

Shaoyong got up quickly to make tea. He put the tea kettle on the stove. When he returned to the living room, Guan and Bai were talking about the "peaceful reunification of China".

This Old Guan, Shaoyong thought, *was always exaggerating the importance of politics.*

"The party we will be dealing with is definitely the Guomindang."

"In Taiwan, from all the evidence of the past thirty years, the Guomindang can never be overthrown. They govern Taiwan efficiently, and have set records for economic growth. If we look forward to peaceful reunification, negotiation is the only way."

The Guomindang can never be overthrown.

These words were spoken by Guan Li! Shaoyong marvelled at how Guan Li had changed. In Guan's family, both Guan Li's grandfather and father were Guomindang members, but Guan Li had been a rebel. In the sixties, especially during the two years that Guan Li studied in the States, he became a well-known "Big Left." As long as Guan Li was present, any student gathering would turn into a political debate. Often times, with several bottles of beer in his stomach, he would start making comments on political issues. The more he talked, the more excited he got, and he always ended up pounding on the table and giving the same conclusion:

"The day that the old power dies in Taiwan is the day of Chinese reunification."

Now after twenty years, and a trip around the globe, Guan Li just sat there, easily overthrowing his own "Guan Theory" that was once so well known. Guan Li had changed, Shaoyong found.

"Old Guan, have you heard anything from your family?" Shaoyong asked enthusiastically.

Shaoyong had thought of making inquiries about Guan Li's parents for him when Shaoyong first left the mainland, but Guan Li had refused, exclaiming magnanimously, "I'll wait until the day when Taiwan is liberated."

"My father and mother are both fine. Some friends from the States visited me last year. They told me about my parents. They are very well."

Old Guan's face softened. His tone was softer, too. At this moment, Guan Li was no longer a browbeating official, but a human being.

Whoo...whoo....

The water was boiling. Shaoyong went to fix the tea. He still tried to listen to the conversation going on in the living room. Old Bai mentioned some concerns of Taiwan and the case of Wei Jingsheng.

This Old Bai! Shaoyong could not help but laugh. *He was just like the Guan Li of twenty years ago. Who says that history does not repeat itself?*

"Wei Jingsheng's sentence was too harsh. He was just a loyal worker who wanted to call attention to the need for reform. You should report our opinion to them when you return and try to reduce his prison term."

Old Bai was appealing on Wei Jingsheng's behalf when Shaoyong brought out the tea. He poured the first cup and handed it to Old Guan.

Old Guan took the tea and found it steaming hot. He blew on it a little and put it down. His eyebrows were raised high and his eyes wandered in disbelief as if he could not comprehend what he was hearing.

"Why do you people abroad all look upon Wei Jingsheng so highly. Last night at the University of California, the audience raised questions about Wei Jingsheng, too. In China, we don't even pay any attention to him. He sold information about our national security, and he attacked our national leaders; why, fifteen years is too generous a sentence for him."

Generous! Shaoyong was one of those who had experienced the Chinese Cultural Revolution. He understood what "generosity" meant. In contrast to the lawless, godless era of the "Gang of Four," he couldn't believe that they were wasting so many people's energy and time on one young man. *This was certainly much more generous treatment than before*, he thought sarcastically.

Old Bai could not agree at all. He defended Wei Jingsheng. He regretted the end of the democratic spirit that this case symbolized and struggled with the frustrations he felt regarding his own ideals and dreams. When he got to some exciting point, his eyes burned, and his forehead became wet with beads of sweat--his emotion and passion shining like crystals. Even though his throat was already hoarse, he was not even in the mood to try the fresh tea his host had prepared.

Shaoyong knew it was because of Old Bai's patriotism. It was not easy for a forty-year-old man to maintain his enthusiastic emotion. In the old days, his own idealism and passion were by no means less strong than Old Bai's.

As for Old Guan, he had been even more intense. But now the Old Guan in front of them, with his solemn face and icy stare, was twisting his lips in disdain.

Shaoyong's surprise and doubts were gradually transformed into righteous resentment.

"The Cultural Revolution generation is not worthy of sympathy," Guan Li told Old Bai. "They were illiterates and rascals. They knew nothing but destruction. They had no ability to do anything constructive. To tell you the truth, we've already given up on them."

Shaoyong was stunned.

Illiterates and rascal? When did Old Guan become such a harsh judge? He had admired the Red Guard before. He even wrote to the central government requesting permission to join the Red Guard and rove around the country. At the time though, the social status of overseas students who had studied in America was even lower than that of property owners, wealthy people, and other "Five Black Categories,"[5] therefore he was not qualified to join the revolutionary action. Yes, the Red Guard had a record of being destructive, and they had made serious mistwakes, but they charged ahead under the spell of idealism and the deceptions of Chairman Mao. They were not ringleaders, they were the victims! Others might not understand, but Old Guan himself had witnessed the bleeding and dying of that generation. Those people died with a smile only because they believed that they were martyrs of the people.

"Old Guan, how can you give up a whole generation of people so easily?" Shaoyong protested.

"Exactly!" Old Bai joined him. "The Party and the country are

---

[5] This is a term refers commonly to the five "bad" categories of people. They are: the former landlords, rich peasants, counter-revolutionaries, common criminals, and rightist. The former four types belong to "the conflict between enemy and the Party" category, and the latter, to "the conflict between the people."

responsible for them and their bad behavior. It has to be made up, not given up!"

Old Guan spread out his hands, indicating that he was helpless.

"Make up? In what way? We have so much to do now. But we are ready to feed that generation of people anyway."

He acted as if he had done everything he could in the spirit of benevolence and duty. They could only remain speechless.

Old Bai looked exhausted. He stood up to say goodbye.

"Keep in touch." Old Bai shook hands firmly with Old Guan. "I'll be sure to visit you when I go to China next year."

Shaoyong walked his guest out to his car. When he returned, he saw that Guan Li was looking at his paintings on the wall, standing with his hands clasped behind his back.

"Do you want to see my studio?"

He led his remaining guest back there. He had been in such a hurry to tidy up the living room that he had dumped everything into the studio. Now the messy room had no space left for anyone to set foot in. Guan Li could only look into the studio from the door. An oil painting entitled "Thoughts of Tiananmen Square" caught his eye. It covered the entire wall. Except for one corner of the city wall, the entire painting was filled with flowing red and black, symbols of the associations and imagery that had filled Shaoyong's mind. This painting was completed in one night in the spring of 1976. Afterwards, Shaoyong hung it on the wall facing west and never moved it again. It was not for exhibition or for sale.

Old Guan stared at it for a while, then returned to the living room silently.

"Can you make a living by painting?" he asked, with caring and concern in his voice.

Shaoyong shook his head with a bitter smile, "The whole family would starve if they depended on me."

He told him the truth frankly. It was Meiyu who took the responsibility for making ends meet by running a jewelry and souvenir stand at Fisherman's Wharf. The profits he earned from painting only served as supplementary income.

"Is your income stable then?" His old friend's concern turned into worry.

"It's OK. The rent is always paid on time, and we haven't been evicted yet," he said with a deliberate, casual smile.

He did not like to complain. It wasn't necessary to tell friends about his experiences in recent years. In order to make a living, he had tried all kinds of jobs, from selling hotdogs and scraping off fish scales to washing cars and guarding gas stations. It wasn't until a year ago that his paintings started to sell better, the souvenir stand business stabilized, and he began to paint regularly.

To reassure his friend and to indicate that he was not a complete loser, he told Guan he had bought a piece of land--four acres, near a mountain in northern California. He planned to build a cottage there in the forest for Meiyu and himself after the kids grew up.

Unexpectedly Old Guan burst out laughing. His laughter released the tension that had been building up all night.

"I didn't know you were so negative. You're thinking about retreating to the forest and becoming a hermit!"

He sat down on the easy chair that Old Bai had sat on a little while ago. He stretched out his legs and put his feet on the coffee table. He took out another "China Brand" cigarette and lit it.

Shaoyong followed his example by lying down on the long sofa. He used one end of the sofa as a pillow and the other as a foot rest. He asked old Guan for a "China Brand" cigarette. The two friends faced each other and smoked.

Aside from the fact that both of them were now fifteen years older, nothing had changed--the beer, the cigarettes, and their congenial talks.

"You can think about returning again."

Old Guan obviously meant well.

Shaoyong shook his head without saying anything. His friend continued trying to persuade him.

"We need people to help with the Four Modernizations. Really! We need all kinds of people. We need everything, including abstract painters. The most important thing is that our policies are all in the process of actualization, and both democracy and law are essential. Our future hasn't been so bright for thirty years. It's hard to believe, isn't it?"

Shaoyong narrowed his eyes and blew out several rings of smoke before he cautiously nodded his head.

When the warmth of the Democracy Wall had prevailed over the chill of Beijing in early 1979, his heart had been revived. But the dream of democracy was as short-lived as the life of the Democracy Wall. From that time on, his heart had not been touched.

"Come back and take a look for yourself when you get a chance."

"Yes," Shaoyong replied shortly.

His friend did not ask for any further details, and Shaoyong did not tell his friend how little that chance would be either. The soaring costs of traveling in China quoted by the travel agencies recently had been the subject of many complaints. With an artist's humble income, how could he ever have enough money to go? Besides, he had never thought about taking a trip back to China. He did not understand why his attitude toward China was so stubborn and extreme. He either embraced it whole-heartedly or exiled himself from it completely. There was no compromise. This was a painful and lonely feeling--he could not even explain it to Old Guan.

He asked about living conditions on the mainland and found it had improved a great deal. Salaries had doubled. Guan's family owned a black-and-white Taiwan-made television and even watched Hollywood movies sometimes. The only problem was that they all had too much to do, and they sometimes did not even have time to take care of their children. On occasion, when both parents had to go out of town, they sent the kids to the neighbors for meals and let them take care of themselves.

"Fortunately the social fabric on the mainland is quite good. The kids behave themselves, although they pretty much have grown up on their own. We still plan to hire a tutor for them after they get into junior high school. If they don't start preparing now, it will be too late for the college entrance exam. Nowadays, the competition is very intense."

*Tutor, competition...*reminded Shaoyong of his student life in Taiwan. His tutoring income helped him finish his college education.

"Old Guan, how do you feel about being an administrator? Tell me about it."

Shaoyong's curiosity brought out his friend's bitter complaints and frustrations.

He told Shaoyong that there were a lot of responsible officials, but the capable ones were few. Although the "Gang of Four" had collapsed, the old power was still there. Thus, they formed a group of people waiting to see what was going happen. The old cadres were restored to their positions, but they also brought with them their old habits. It became a stumbling block for the Four Modernizations. The middle-aged administrators took on the main responsibilities and had to deal with the old hands while training the young ones at the same time. They had to work twice as hard as anyone else.

Shaoyong could imagine how hard it was. He nodded sympathetically.

"Deng Xiaoping has set an example for the retirement policy now," he consoled his friend. "This is one way to transfer power from the old to the new generation."

Old Guan supported this policy passionately and confidently. But, he sighed again, "Our Party policy tries to take care of everything, from housing to clothing, from birth to death, including marriage and divorce, but it may not be a good method."

Upon hearing that, Shaoyong immediately raised his eyebrows.

"Wow, now you are an absolute revisionist! Good, you are back to the main stream of historical trends."

Old Guan just smiled, not defending himself. He grasped a handful of almonds and chewed on them happily. Shaoyong took two bottles of beer from the refrigerator. After opening them, they each drank from the bottle without using a glass. They talked about their old classmates. Shaoyong told him about so and so's divorce, someone who committed suicide, another who won an award for being one of the "Ten Outstanding Young Men", and someone else's new promotion as a government official. There had been so many changes within the past twenty years.

"Do you still remember the time we drove to Yellowstone?" Old Guan suddenly recalled. "We didn't sleep the whole night, and we talked about the Chinese revolution while we drank by the lake?"

Shaoyong nodded. It was there they had decided to go back to the mainland and join the great "Socialist construction" immediately after their graduation.

"Drinking American beer, smoking American cigarettes, talking about Chinese revolution...that was a romantic experience...."

Old Guan's voice gradually softened and eventually faded into a sigh. Holding the bottle of beer, his eyes searched and landed on the corner of the wall and ceiling. His brush-like eyelashes did not even blink. At that moment, he looked drawn into his own thoughts as if he had fallen back into the memories of when he debated political issues as a young student.

The younger Guan Li used to retreat to silence and indulge in his own hopes and dreams after he was done with his passionate and idealistic talks. Now he looked like a meditating old monk again. This is exactly the Guan Li Shaoyong remembered, the enduring, unchanging aspect of Guan Li that had not been vanquished by time.

Suddenly Guan Li sat up straight, withdrew his legs from the coffee table, and asked his host guiltily, "Hey, you won't laugh at my lingering in the past, will you?"

Shaoyong said with a smile, "I always think of the time at the May Seventh Cadre School. We, 'the Stinky Scholars,' cultivated the land together; we worked from daybreak till sunset; we did not think much but worked hard; sometimes we sang simple songs just to kill time. How much leisure time do we get in our life anyway?..."

Right away Old Guan waved his hand to interrupt him, "There is no May Seventh Cadre School now! We don't even have enough intellectuals, how can one have time to cultivate the land?"

He pulled back his sleeve to look at his watch.

Shaoyong also glanced at the clock on the wall. It was two o'clock.

"I have to go back to my hotel now."

"Why don't you sleep here tonight? I'll take you back early tomorrow morning."

"No, it's better to go back tonight, or else the others will be worried."

"They must be asleep by now, so they're not going to worry. You'll get back there early enough to have breakfast with them."

Old Guan still shook his head.

"Last May, there was an interpreter who committed high treason, and it made everybody nervous. I better go back tonight, so there won't be any misunderstanding."

Shaoyong didn't dare insist. He took out two coats from the closet and gave the flannel one to his guest.

"Put it on, Old Guan. It's cold here, both in the morning and at night. Keep this coat. You might find it useful later when you stop in Seattle."

His guest put on the coat obediently.

"Old Guan, do they treat you as one of them now?"

"Of course."

"Did you apply to be a party member?'

"I'm already a party member now."

This is really something worth celebrating, Shaoyong thought. To be a member of the Communist Party was their highest hope in the 1960's. After all the disillusionment and frustrations of the 70's, Guan Li finally realized his dream twenty years later. This definitely was worthy of a celebration.

Yet, Shaoyong could not utter the words. He nodded to show his congratulations, then he put his hand in his pocket and led his guest out the door.

On the way back, both of them were quiet. They had said all they needed to say. They had never talked just to make polite conversation. As they crossed the bridge, the lights on the east side of the bay shone brilliantly and seemed to go on forever.

"This night view reminds me of New York," Guan Li remarked. It was the only true confession he made of his feelings that night.

After crossing the bridge, they saw the "Holiday Inn" sign immediately. The old friends were about to say goodbye. After this separation, who knew when they would see each other again. Shaoyong felt a deep loss in his heart.

"Where will your next stop be?"

"New York first, and then we're going to Philadelphia to visit the chemist...."

Shaoyong had heard a lot about this chemist, and he could not help interrupting, "Old Guan, I've heard that this person is trying to get ahead in academia by cheating. There were many complaints from the Shanghai Biochemical Research Institute, didn't you hear about it? He isn't very outstanding in his field of biochemistry in America either, he took advantage of that award from China for his personal use. All the Chinese scholars with any integrity are ashamed of him. If you want to flatter a Chinese scientist, you should at least choose the right one to flatter."

"Don't worry. We were fooled once, but we won't be fooled any more," Guan Li said with confidence and ease.

"I went to Beijing for several days before I came here. Some scholarly friends there told me about the so called 'Four Overseas Shameless Persons', which consist of two men and two women. This person is one of them. There is another opportunist who once cheered Taiwan on to "Live ten thousand years," and later advocated "Let's learn from our Comrade Jiang Qing." We know their backgrounds very well, but we will still visit them out of courtesy. This is how we conduct the politics of unification."

Shaoyong could not agree with him. He frowned and said impulsively, "Your method for unification operates without any principle."

Guan Li did not seem to care, "What do you mean without principle? Our principle is, 'No discrimination on the subject of patriotism.' Do you understand?"

"Of course this is a matter with no discrimination. But it depends on whether the recipient is sincere or not. You have to make sure the person is not trying to take advantage of the country. Otherwise the bad and the good are all mixed up together. Finally, the sincere ones may have to withdraw."

"Of course we have our principles, Old Luo. China needs support now. These people are willing to say good things about China. We will, of course, show our appreciation and give them rewards."

Shaoyong felt he had nothing more to say. He parked the car in front

232

of the hotel. It was already very late, and everything was quiet outside the hotel entrance.

"All of us who come to America visit him, Old Luo. Everybody knows he is a leftist. He is safe for us."

Before getting out of the car, Old Guan patted his friend's shoulder and explained patiently and apologetically, "For example, I can't make it public that I have visited you, at least not at this time. But if we visit *them*, my leader will say we did a good job! It is an absolutely secure thing to do. Old Luo, all of this...I know you will understand."

But he didn't. He felt a pain in his heart. Nonetheless, he patted his friend's back heartily, indicating that he didn't mind. He accompanied Old Guan inside the hotel, asked for the key from the front desk, and went with him to the stairs.

"Let me know sooner, the next time you come. We'll have more time to spend together."

"Yes, I'll come again. I want to see all my other friends, too."

After shaking hands good-bye, Shaoyong drove home alone. On his way back, the traffic was very light, and the wind had all but stopped. It was a perfect time to speed up without worrying about the police giving him a ticket, but instead he drove extremely slow. There was a commotion in head, but his mind was a blank.

Democracy and law....

Illiteracy and rascals....

He shook his head resentfully and exhaled a puff of air from his nose. He rolled down the window. The wet morning breeze gently touched his face. It was cool, but not cold. He looked out the window and thought, *tomorrow, no, today, will be a fine day!*

Green Card

Editor's Notes:

In 1965, an amendment was made to the United States Immigration Nationality Act abolishing previous exclusionary immigration restrictions. Since that time, there has been a steady influx of Asian immigrants to the United States. Among the first groups were many Chinese professionals and intellectuals who left their homeland for America in the pursuit of freedom, a freedom that they envisioned would allow each individual to discover his or her own potential. Following the arrival and settlement of these immigrants, many of their aging or retiring parents followed suit, coming to live with their now grown-up and well-established children. However, in order to legally reside in the United States, a green card must first be secured.

"Green Card" is the simple story of an elderly Chinese couple, Lin Tungfu and his wife, who wish to keep their green card as a symbol of security. The statement of the theme, though, undercuts the pathetic complexity of such a desire and this complexity is precisely what Chen is trying to impress upon her readers. Though the green card undoubtedly holds a promise, the transitory lifestyle they must maintain in order to keep it has the capacity to tear them away from their roots and everything they worked and yearned for in their lifetime. In determining whether or not to make further sacrifices in their lives, they must decide if this plastic card is worth striving for; because, it would be an ironic twist of fate to become slaves to something that, to them, symbolizes America and freedom.

GREEN CARD[1]

It's hard to change your habits when you get old. Although soon it will have been a month since Lin Tongfu arrived in America, he had yet to overcome jet lag. And tonight, once again, he was wide awake shortly after midnight. Counting on his fingers, Tongfu knew that dusk had just fallen in Taibei. No wonder he felt so full of vigor, thinking of the lights and clamor permeating the night markets. If he was at home in Taibei, he would spring out of bed the instant he opened his eyes; but here, there was nothing for him to do. He couldn't even get out of bed without waking his wife. So, reluctantly he forced himself to stay in bed.

Finally, the color of dawn sifted through the cracks of the blinds, and the restless old man slid out of bed. His dear wife had the fortunate ability to sleep in the morning. Sensing that he was up, her eyelids stirred momentarily; then she clutched the fluffy quilt and continued her sound sleep.

After putting on his clothes and finishing his morning routine, he went into the living room and sat facing the window. Parted day and night, the curtains let in a bit of the blue sky, streaked with brushstrokes of morning

---

[1] "Green Card" (*Luka*) was translated by Zilan Debra Sang with the permission of the author and publisher, and is published here in English for the first time. This translation is based on the story's appearance in *Chengli chengwai* (Taibei: Shibao, 1983), pp. 195-222.

clouds, pale red and light purple. It was a most glamorous sight. Indeed, one had to credit Southern California for this early summer-like sunshine in the month of November. Every day the clear sky extended beyond sight. Relatives and friends in Taibei often asked him, "What's good about America?" To which he always replied, "The climate in California is beautiful." This he could swear by heaven and earth, but he lacked the courage to finish the second half of his sentence, "But, one doesn't live just for the climate, does one?"

Bored with sitting, he stood up to shift the eight or nine plants in the living room. He changed the arrangement of the pots, and then watered them with care. The one bedroom apartment, with its box-like living room, was cramped and sterile. No matter how he rearranged the plants, it still looked the same. Since moving into the apartment, Tongfu had been incredibly bored, suffering from the lack of activity and too many meals. Stirred by his boredom, he had already rearranged those same flowerpots seven or eight times over.

Before his retirement, he worked at the Office of Deployment in a department of the Taiwanese Provincial Government; he had been accustomed to a busy schedule, summoning and dispatching vehicles. Now, it seemed as though his hands could not sit still, always itching to fiddle with something. It was because of this industrious disposition of his that he had opened a fast-food restaurant in Shilin after his retirement.

Tongfu couldn't bear to be inactive. One reason was his strong constitution. After the Lunar New Year, he would be seventy, never once having suffered a serious ailment. But the main reason he couldn't sit still was that he simply loved to work. As long as he was working, he felt that life had substance, that days were spent honestly, and that he owed nothing to anyone. His conscience was at ease. When "Little Chengdu" was first opened, his son and daughter were unanimously against the idea. They cautioned him

236

to not look for trouble, and tried to persuade him instead to come to the United States, to receive their support and attention, and to enjoy pure leisure and bliss. After four years in business, he was all the more enthusiastic about the restaurant; but contrary to that, his visits to America were becoming more and more insipid.

With his hands crossed behind his back, he stood before the window, looking into the distance. There was a ten-story apartment building across the street. As far as he could see, every house had heavy curtains and tight blinds, shutting out the bright morning sun. Down below on the road, though, there were signs of life; cars drove by in twos and threes. But to his amazement, during the long span of time he spent gazing out the window, he didn't even see one pedestrian.

He began to pace between the window and the sofa. Every day around this time he usually went out to walk for an hour, but today he decided to change his usual morning practice. Feeling a little ashamed, he reasoned that at least a stroll in the cramped room was better than no walk at all.

*   *   *

Yesterday Tongfu had bought a copy of "World's Journal." The Los Angeles section included two reports of violence, and reading them had made the old man shudder. The first one reported that an elderly man walking in the street bumped into five teenagers. For some unknown reason, they beat him up and left, yelling victory. The police rushed the old man to the hospital, and when he regained consciousness, he told journalists that he had never met the culprits before, let alone had trouble with them. The other item of news said that an old Chinese lady was attacked by a criminal in the elevator of her apartment building and was robbed of her bag, wrist watch, ring, and so forth.

After reading the newspaper, Tongfu quietly hurried to throw away that page. His wife was very sensitive and would worry needlessly. He did not want to alarm her.

In Los Angeles, murders and muggings were no longer news to them, they were a part of everyday life. Nonetheless, learning of two cases in such a short period of time involving elderly people, especially one being Chinese, troubled him deeply.

"Tongfu, didn't you go out for a walk today?"

His wife had quietly gotten up and was passing through the living room on her way to the kitchen to boil water for tea.

"Er...I was working on the plants and forgot the time...."

He stopped walking and mumbled an excuse. Breaking his everyday regimen made him feel quite guilty, so he quickly added, "Right after breakfast I'll go out and take a walk."

"After breakfast we have to leave," his wife reminded him. "Did you forget? This morning Xiaomei[2] will come pick us up to see some apartments."

See some apartments? For a second he was dumbfounded; then he finally remembered. That's right, he almost forgot. To say that the old man was completely without problems was not precise. Tongfu did have a small problem, a selective memory. The things he disliked doing were the things most quickly forgotten.

"Why don't you choose an apartment you like. I'll go for a walk in the park."

"Tongfu, please!" his wife implored him with a smile.

"Tongfu, we're going to live in this apartment for half a year. If you don't like it, how could I possibly rent it?"

"If you ask me, the less we bother the better," he replied. "Apartments are expensive everywhere. Even if we do find a place, we probably won't save much. Why don't we just stay here!"

---

[2] This is a typical nickname for the youngest female child in the family. Literally, it means "little daughter," or "little sister."

He was the type that stuck to a place and didn't take moving lightly. During thirty-one years of living in Taiwan, he had only moved twice. It upset him to think that he had been in the United States for one short month and already needed to move.

"We're away from home. We should save whatever we can."

His wife was afraid that he'd be stubbornly pigheaded. Before entering the kitchen, she tried to sway him with her soft Sichuan dialect, the way she had always done the past few decades, as if coaxing a child.

"Tongfu, consider the green card. We have to be patient, all right?"

"Ah! The green card!"

Suddenly his bushy eyebrows lowered to a scowl. The furrow was deep enough to hang an oil bottle. He turned his head away and stared at the building opposite, glaring at the uniform windows. At the mention of the green card, an angry breath surged up inside him and lodged itself in his throat. He wanted to bring it out but couldn't. Dryly he kept his smoldering anger inside until his heart almost grew weary of it.

To him, the green card was nothing but a reminder of much grief and bitterness.

The idea had been his wife's. Of course he himself was also to blame for listening to her, but now he didn't feel he could back out even if he wanted to. To continue with it or to quit - it was like being caught between the devil and the deep blue sea!

*   *   *

Ever since his son and daughter had become permanent residents in the United States, his wife had begun hinting that the children ought to apply for a green card for them, too.

"Who can tell if the United States won't change its mind one of these days? Then, how much longer can Taiwan survive? It's better to complete the procedures for leaving beforehand. Should any crisis arise, it'll be more convenient to leave."

Tongfu had always heard that America was "a heaven for the young, a battlefield for the middle-aged, and a graveyard for the old." To come as a tourist and sightsee once in his lifetime appealed to him, but to live here and possibly even to die here was not his wish. Unfortunately, his wife's Communist-phobia was beyond any medical help. Without a green card in her pocket, she could not live in peace in Taiwan.

In early 1976, upon finalizing his retirement, he received his green card also. Tongfu prepared for the trip financially, and his children sent him money to cover part of the traveling expenses. The old couple flew to America. They stayed at their son's home in Wisconsin for two weeks. Accompanied by their son, they toured Chicago and New York. Finally, they flew to Los Angeles to stay at their daughter's house for another two weeks. What they wanted to see most was their son and daughter; after seeing them they were fully satisfied. They went to the ever popular Disneyland merely to fulfill their daughter's wishes, and after a day of accompanying their granddaughter, Cathy, they were left utterly exhausted.

"Papa, do you like life in America?" his daughter had asked.

"Ah, Taibei is much more comfortable!" responded Tongfu.

His wife agreed, "Speaking of living conditions, of course Taibei is more comfortable. We have all our friends to play mahjongg and socialize with, and all our favorite delicacies are easily available there. And there's no problem in getting where you want to go either. There are so many cars in America, but if you don't know how to drive, it's just like having no legs!"

"And in Taibei, there are more opportunities for running a business," Tongfu added cheerfully.

This was Tongfu's favorite topic. Having worked for the government all his life, he had long been anxious to try his hand at operating his own business. Two years before his retirement, he had started his plans to open a small restaurant with his wife, so as to make the most of her cooking expertise and his zest for management. Running a business would keep him busy and financially independent of his children. He also longed to visit his former home and family in Shandong, and he needed money for the trip.

So, after returning from their trip to the United States, they opened a restaurant called "Little Chengdu," in Shilin. They used their savings, Tongfu's pension, and money borrowed from friends. His wife had worked with flour all her life and was good at making many kinds of pastries and noodles. Her specialty was Sichuan snacks and beef; beef steamed with starch, hot peppered, red-stewed with soy sauce, or chilled in a salad--no matter how she prepared it, the beef was always delicate and delicious. She worked in the kitchen herself and at the same time supervised and trained the cook. With her patient instructions and some actual practice, the new cook soon mastered genuine *Hongyu-chaoshou*[3] and hot-spiced beef. Both became signboard delicacies. Their business was amateurish in spirit, so the shop hours were short; the place would open at dusk and close at ten p.m. They hired two assistants and a part-time worker. Tongfu supervised them in addition to handling the accounts. The days were busy, but manageable. In spite of the stress and hard work, they thoroughly enjoyed running the restaurant.

By the second year, their business had improved, and they started to show a profit. Then, their children had sent them a letter urging them to come for a visit, otherwise their permanent residency status was in danger of cancellation. So, having no other choice, they hired a manager and accountant to run the restaurant, collected some traveling funds, and flew to America again to live for a month.

Being with their children and grandchildren delighted the elderly couple. Nevertheless, the trip was expensive. After they returned to Taiwan, it took

---

[3] Sichuan style noodles, cooked with red hot oil.

them half-a-year's work in the restaurant to make up for all the money they had spent.

In 1978, they once again had to report to the United States. By this time Tongfu had begun to feel both mentally and physically tired. Their economic situation was weighing heavily on him.

Tongfu's son and daughter were dutiful children and often sent them money, but the money was too little to be of use in the cash-turnover of a business. His son expressed in every letter that if his father and mother needed money, they should feel free to tell him; but his father was proud and would never stoop to ask for his son's assistance.

The old man was a competitive person. With only a middle school degree, and a lifetime of diligence, thrift, and loyalty to his duties, he had raised and supported his children. Because of him they were able to go abroad, and both obtained their master's degrees. His accomplishments awed all of his relatives and friends. He felt that he should be more vigorous than ever in spite of his age, that he ought to scale new heights even from the top of the ladder where he already was. In his old age he wanted to be self-sufficient and do without his children's money, that would be his real glory. The gifts from his children could be taken only as unexpected extra income. No matter how cornered he felt, he would not open his mouth to ask for help.

Tongfu's wife had never kept books in her life. Sometimes when she saw her husband frowning at the account book, she would say kind-heartedly, "Is everything okay? Tell the children if we are short of money."

"No need for that," the old man had refused, without so much as even lifting his head.

Unfortunately, a restaurant run on a small amount of capital cannot withstand losses year after year. Every time the couple left and returned, they had to spend two or three times the effort and time to cover their deficit.

Without their supervision in the kitchen, the quality and quantity of the food declined, customers became dissatisfied and some did not return. When they were gone, the clerk neglected his job and the accounts fell into disarray. Tongfu did not even know where to begin to inspect them; it was all in a disarray. Eventually he was forced to give up investigating the matter.

After more than four years had passed, Tongfu found that despite their painstaking care, there was no money left. His friends who had opened stores during the same period when he went into business were all prospering. Take Old Shen for example, he ran a furniture store. He recently planned to open a branch store. And how about "Little Chengdu"? Last year Tongfu had to mortgage his own home to get a loan to pay for some renovations in the restaurant.

The old man was worried that if things continued like this, the money he needed to visit his old home in Shandong would disappear like a bubble into thin air. The older he became, the more homesick he grew; sometimes he could only sigh in despair.

"The money we earn is all eaten up by the green card!" he often complained to his wife.

Losing money was not the worst of it though. Every time they went to America, they had to refrain from talking about it with relatives and friends for fear that people would sneer at them for practicing "toothbrushism."[4] Their feeling guilty in spite of knowing they were being wrongly accused was what vexed the old man most.

Therefore, the mere thought of the green card brought him nothing but heartache and grief.

*   *   *

---

[4] Or *Yashua zhuyi*. It is an expression which satirizes the unhealthy mentality of certain emigrants from Taiwan. A person is said to be a practitioner of "toothbrushism" if he is more concerned about his own toothbrush than his country, and if an emergency should occur, he would run away rather than defend his country.

"Tongfu, I made scallion oil pancakes for you, come eat!"

The aroma of Taiwanese tea and oil pancakes soon superseded old Mr. Lin's worries and aroused his appetite. He sat down, ate two pancakes in one breath, and drained a bowl of rock sugar and snowcloud ears. There was still a stack of pancakes on the plate.

"Why did you make so many pancakes? They don't taste as good when they get cold."

"They're for Xiaomei to take home," said his wife. "She can just reheat them in the oven. She told me that John has come to like these pancakes, too."

At the thought of her son-in-law also admiring her pastries, the old woman's finely wrinkled face burst into a proud smile.

"That was delicious! Aren't you having any?" asked Tongfu.

"I've had enough. You eat as much as you like; I'll wrap up what's left and Xiaomei will take it home."

His wife enjoyed seeing her husband and children eat heartily, although she ate very little herself. She was thin and wiry, but fortunately her spirit was strong and she was quite energetic.

After his wife said she'd offer them to Xiaomei, the old man put down his chopsticks. "I've also had enough, you can wrap them up."

Their daughter was married to an American, and her every breakfast consisted of milk and bread. She had grown used to it, but her mother felt miserable for her. When she lived at home, her mother varied her breakfast every day. One day, soy-bean milk and deep-fried twisted dough sticks, the next day scallion oil cellophane noodles. She would not make the same meal twice in one week. Seeing how monotonous her daughter's meals had become made her heart ache, and she wished she could cook every meal for her.

After cleaning up, the old couple sat down to wait for Xiaomei. It wasn't until after nine that she arrived with her two year-old daughter, Helen, in tow.

"Where is Cathy?" Grandmother asked, holding her youngest granddaughter to her bosom affectionately.

"She's at day care. I'll start working part-time next month, and Helen will have to go there, too."

"Send both of them to a day care center? What a shame!"

Upon hearing that her granddaughters would both be sent to a day care center, she hugged Helen even tighter. Seeing her reluctance to part with the child, one would think that the girls were going to be sent to prison. Tongfu knew his son-in-law's temper and that he didn't want his in-laws to babysit for free. It would be no use talking to him, so he did not attempt to dissuade his daughter.

"Xiaomei, how many apartments will we see today?" he asked.

"I found three ads that sounded good; maybe we'll go see all of them."

The neighborhood in which the apartments were located was a suburb of Los Angeles, called Monterey Park.

"Papa, you'll definitely like this place," said Xiaomei, introducing the booming city to her parents on the way.

"There are many Chinese stores here, and the street names are written in both Chinese and English," she added. "It's as convenient and bustling as the Chinatown in Los Angeles, but the streets are much wider and not as crowded. Now, more and more Chinese people are moving here; people call it New Chinatown."

Xiaomei drove them around the city of Monterey Park for more than an hour; and indeed, the place lived up to its reputation. There were many Chinese faces, very wide streets, and no crowds or traffic jams--there was still much room for development.

"This place should be renamed Taiwan Town," Tongfu suggested to Xiaomei.

Here he felt as though he were back in Taiwan. He went to two shops at random, and immediately heard people speaking Mandarin and Taiwanese. It was unlike the Chinatown in Los Angeles, which was solely occupied by Cantonese. Even the shop signs, such as *Supreme Excellence* and *Nine Granted Wishes*, were names and patterns often seen in Taiwan. They made one feel that it was a genuine overall reflection of Chinese taste, not only Cantonese influence. On Good-Savor Street, Chinese newspaper offices were as numerous as trees in a forest. He saw *World Daily* and *Far Eastern Times;* at least five or six different buildings dazzled the eyes of the old man. It seemed more concentrated than Taibei, even busier.

Among the three landlord families in the neighborhood, two came from Taiwan; one was native Taiwanese and the other from the Zhejiang province. They spoke Mandarin, making them feel close to one another, like running into an old friend in a strange country. The third was an old Cantonese couple who had never lived in Taiwan and could not speak Mandarin. They only spoke English, and the two parties had to rely on Tongfu's daughter to interpret.

The living circumstances happened to be ideal at the Cantonese couple's place. They lived downstairs, where they also ran a sundry goods store. Upstairs, one room was filled with stock for their store; and, there was an apartment with a living room, bedroom, kitchen, and bath. The walls were freshly painted, and the furniture set was old, but complete. Including utilities, the rent was only three hundred dollars a month.

"This is very cheap, Mom and Dad, take it!" whispered Xiaomei.

His wife had no complaint at all. She whispered in the old man's ear, "Tongfu, it seems to be a terrific bargain...."

The Cantonese couple seemed to think the old Lins were very agreeable, and continued speaking and gesturing to Xiaomei for a long while.

After listening to the landlords, his daughter instantly tried to rush her parents' decision. "Papa, if you want it, decide now! They say there are people waiting to take the apartment! But they like the quiet, so they are waiting for the right people to rent it to. If you want it, you must answer by ten o'clock tonight; later than that and they'll rent it to someone else!"

"Tongfu...," his wife said anxiously, watching him, the look on her face urging him to pay a deposit at once.

"We'll decide this evening then."

Not having to decide on the spot, Tongfu heaved a sigh of relief.

On the way back to their daughter's house, however, his wife gave him an unreservedly long-winded lecture, "Tongfu, we should just rent it. Here it costs us four hundred fifty a month, plus electricity and odds and ends, almost five hundred total. There they ask only three hundred a month. On the rent alone, we can save one thousand dollars in half a year. One thousand dollars is no small sum!"

Hearing the joy in her voice at that thought, one would think that the $1,000 was already in her pocket.

Tongfu of course agreed that money was an important consideration. The United States immigration laws were getting tougher and tougher. Because they did not reside in America at all last year, this year they had to live here at least half a year. They had racked their brains trying to find enough money to pay for their expenses. Finally, they borrowed seven thousand dollars from a friend at a very high interest rate and made their departure. The airfare alone was over one thousand five hundred dollars, and they still had a long time to go. They could not afford to be wasteful.

"If you live in Monterey Park, it would be so convenient!" Xiaomei joined her mother, trying to persuade him. "Downstairs there is a grocery store; whatever you want, you need only go downstairs to get it. As for other things, you can get them within two blocks. You know the language, and the buses are convenient. Papa, you love reading the newspaper and the streets are full of Chinese newspapers. And if Mama feels like playing a few rounds of mahjongg, she need not worry about finding partners either."

"Most importantly, one can converse without any language barrier. That beats everything!" his wife chimed in, the wrinkles on her face beaming like a flower at the prospect of mixing the mahjongg pieces.

All the while Tongfu listened to them without reply. What his wife and daughter said was true. His daughter was going to start working; so, she would not be able to visit them very often or keep them company. Perhaps she was afraid they'd be lonely. Tongfu thought that must be why she suggested they move to Monterey Park. They had been coming to Los Angeles to visit their daughter almost every year; it was shameful enough that they could not lend her any assistance. How could they possibly justify adding to her worries? He was afraid that this time they had no choice but to move.

"Papa likes to run a business. Monterey Park is a terrific location!" his daughter said, fixing her eyes on the highway as she spoke. "Try it for a while and see what it's like to live there; if it's okay, you can consider transferring the restaurant in Shilin to here!"

Run a restaurant in America? "Hey, hey," Tongfu laughed dryly, but still did not say a word.

He had lived in Taibei for almost thirty years, longer than in his old home in Shandong, or any other place on the mainland. When he went out for a walk down the street, it was seldom that he didn't say hello to three or four people. In a familiar environment like that, his business was barely surviving; how could he dare come to America, where he didn't know the people, the places, and least of all the language, to try and run a business?

"A business is easier to run in Taiwan; at least there we know the people!" his wife replied sympathetically.

Hmm...the old man snorted lightly. If it were not for the green card, by now perhaps "Little Chengdu" would have opened a branch.

Finally, his daughter fetched Cathy and drove home.

"Mom! What are we having for lunch?" Xiaomei asked.

"You choose. I'll make whatever you'd like," her mother replied lovingly, letting her daughter order.

"How about *Dalu* noodles?"[5] Tongfu suggested, wanting to save time.

"No, I feel like eating *Dandan* noodles!"[6] Xiaomei demanded like a spoiled girl.

"Then we'll eat *Dandan* noodles, it's no big deal!" her mother gladly promised. Letting Xiaomei look after her two granddaughters, she went into the kitchen.

The moment Tongfu entered his daughter's house, he discovered a teddy bear blocking the hallway and a mess in the living room. His daughter invited him to sit down, but he could not sit still; he preferred to go to the backyard under the scorching sun and tend the plants for her.

His son-in-law was a teacher at the University of California, and for convenience he had bought a house close to campus. It was located in one of the golden districts, where housing costs were sky-high. They had three tiny bedrooms, and a backyard as big as the palm of your hand. Their mortgage payment was five hundred dollars a month. His daughter had not worked since getting married, so the young couple depended solely on her husband's salary, and they were barely getting by. When relatives and friends heard that the young lady of the Lin family was married to a foreigner, they all thought it meant honor and wealth, and they envied her. But her old papa, having visited her several times, knew the real situation thoroughly in his heart and stomach; he never dared boast in front of others.

His son-in-law was not selfish, he had invited his in-laws to move in with

---

[5] A kind of noodle soup with egg, pieces of bok choy and meat.

[6] They are noodles cooked with a ground meat sauce.

them several times. However, by American standards, a living room and three bedrooms were not exactly sufficient for four people, especially since one of the rooms had to be reserved for their son-in-law's study. The parents just could not bring themselves to crowd them so.

Tongfu and his wife lived in their daughter's house when they visited America the first time. Then, she had only one child, Cathy, so they took the child's room and she slept in her parents' room. One day his wife rose early and noticed her son-in-law coming sleepily out of his den. Only then did she realize that he had been going to the den to spend the night. The old couple felt very sorry about this. Later, they accidently heard their daughter say that John's parents always stayed in a hotel when they came for a visit. Since then, whenever they travel to America, Tongfu insisted on renting another house nearby.

In all fairness, Tongfu felt that his American son-in-law was not a bad person at all. He treated their daughter well and also treated his in-laws politely. He had even learned several courteous Chinese sentences such as "How are you," "I'm fine," and "Thank you." Though he could not speak their language, he always smiled to greet them, and often shared a cigarette or a drink with the old man. He was also very appreciative of his mother-in-law's cooking. Before, his wife had cried her heart out upon hearing that her daughter wanted to marry a foreigner. Now she considered him a precious darling and cherished him as her own son.

Still, Tongfu was somewhat afraid of seeing his son-in-law, especially when the young couple was together.

When he remembered seeing the intimacy between his son-in-law and daughter for the first time, he still felt embarrassed. That was the second day after they arrived in America. When his son-in-law came home from work, he held his wife tightly in his arms the instant he saw her; he kissed her and bit her, and would not separate himself from her body for a long time.

Tongfu had been married for over forty years. He could also be passionate with his wife, after the lights were out; but in front of other people, they had never even held each other's hands. Instantly he had been embarrassed, not knowing where to hide his face. He felt as though he had driven a car and passed through a red light, and his heart fluttered with shame and apology. He congratulated himself on the strong love between the young couple, but preferred to avoid them.

"I'll call brother this evening and tell him that we've found a suite that's good and cheap. I bet he'll urge you to move there immediately!"

When his wife called them to the table to eat the noodles, his daughter's mind was still lingering on the idea of renting the apartment. Hearing Xiaomei say that she wanted to call her brother, his wife's eyes suddenly brightened.

"Is today Friday?" she asked the old man. Without waiting for him to answer, she eagerly added, "If it is, Maomao will call us!"

Their son was already thirty-eight, but in his mother's eyes he was still a small hairy head that would never grow up.

"Today is Friday; he'll probably call," Tongfu replied

Old papa was confident that his son would call. When the two elders were in Taiwan, their son sent an aerogram home each month. And while they were in America, he phoned every week; it was something he had always done. The old man understood that life in American life was very busy. Therefore, he felt they should not expect too much.

"Mom, this year the prices of real estate skyrocketed again; brother and sister-in-law must have made a fortune!" his daughter said enviously. "In two years, they'll no doubt become millionaires!"

"Ah, what's the use of making a fortune? It cannot match raising two fat babies," his wife grinned with pleasure, but also desiring the best of everything, she heaved a sigh.

"It is high time they have children," his daughter agreed with enthusiasm. "At least they'll have less taxes to pay."

"Try to persuade him. Even if our mouths ache from talking, he won't listen to us."

"Okay, I'll tell him tonight: if you want to be a good son, have a baby soon!" declared Xiaomei, giggling.

The Dandan noodles were so spicy that Mr. Lin's nose started to run. He was busy looking for a handkerchief when Cathy approached him and jostled against her grandfather, asking him to look at the color drawing she had finished.

"Good! Cathy did a good job!" He raised his thumb to compliment her. Their granddaughter was overjoyed. She pressed a kiss on his face before leaving him looking as happy as a hopping sparrow.

What bliss it was to have children! He could not understand why his own son and daughter-in-law were so stubborn and would not have children yet. They lived in Wisconsin, a cold northern part of the country. When the young couple went to work in the day time, the two elders had been confined in the house. Without children around, the desolation and loneliness had seemed even harder to bear than imprisonment in the deserted Cold Palace.[7] The only time they had stayed at their son's was that once, when they fdirst came to America. Afterwards, their son always came to see them in California.

Although Tongfu did not say so openly, in his heart he agreed with his wife and could not wait to have another grandchild. His daughter had married a foreigner, so if his son did not beget children, the situation would result in the extinction of the Lin name. For several years now this worry had made his heart heavy. Unfortunately, his daughter-in-law, who originally came from Hong Kong, was even more radical in thinking than his son; she

---

[7] It was a common historical practice for some Chinese emperors to imprison their respective empresses that they no longer favored in the Cold Palace.

did not want to have children, but instead wanted to amass as much money as possible first. Then after making quite a bit of money, she had been afraid of heavy taxes as well as inflation, so she had invested all of it in real estate. His son told him that they bought an apartment by Lake Tahoe, owned woodland in Oregon, and a house somewhere else....The young couple had really become "land owners."

Because the young couple was so busy with real estate, they of course did not have time to tidy their own house. To save themselves the trouble, they lived in a plain apartment. His daughter spoke correctly, it was very probable that his son and daughter-in-law would be millionaires in a few years. However, presently all their capital was invested in real estate, and every month they were at their wit's end trying to make their mortgage payments, often having problems with cash. Their burden did not seem to be any lighter than their father's.

Their son wanted to be a dutiful son; he told his parents again and again of his pleasure in having them live in his home.

His daughter-in-law had also said several times, "If your parents are not used to living in an apartment and want to live in a house by themselves with a yard, that's fine. If they just notify us a month in advance, we'll tell the tenants to move out, and it'll be no problem."

Tongfu did not have the heart to ask his son and daughter-in-law to expel tenants for his own short-term stay. He would rather put up with high rent and stay close to his daughter in Southern California.

"Papa, can you believe it? Soon brother and sister-in-law will have earned enough money to be able to retire at the age of forty-five!"

"Retire at forty-five? Tch, tch!"

The old man shook his head disapprovingly. He thought, *I retired at sixty-five and still opened a restaurant just so I could have something to do; if I retired at forty-five, I'd be bored out of my mind! Young people who come to*

America all change!

In the afternoon, the old couple helped their daughter tidy her backyard, and then played with their granddaughters for a while. Noticing the sun descending in the west, they rose from their seats to return to their own apartment. When their daughter saw them off at the door, she stuffed a small roll of bills into her mother's hand.

"Mom, this is a little money for you to buy fruit to eat. Wait until I go to work and I'll be able to send you money regularly every month."

Her tone was mixed with apology and gratification. She sounded comforted, as if she had given too little in the past and from now on she would be able to give the filial gifts her parents rightfully deserved.

His wife did not suspect a thing, but he silently dwelled on his daughter's words all the way home. He was puzzled. Was Xiaomei forced to go to work because they would be staying so long? They had never heard her talk about going to work, and now suddenly she was changing everything and planned to leave her two small girls to the care of outsiders. To work so strenuously-- could it be to send money to us "regularly?" If so, Tongfu felt he would be even more afraid of seeing his son-in-law in the future.

As soon as they entered the gate of the apartment building, his wife asked him, "Have you checked the mailbox today?"

Nine times out of ten whenever he checked the mailbox it was empty, so he was not very interested. But since his wife was reminding him, he fumbled for his key to open it, and to his surprise, there was an aerogram.

"Ma Rongsheng sent us a letter again."

While speaking, he waved the letter in his hand at his wife. Ma Rongsheng had worked in "Little Chengdu" for almost a year. At first, he worked part-time, doing the purchasing, but later he took charge of the accounts as well. Recently, the old couple, preparing to leave for America, promoted him to manager, in charge of all the money coming in and going out, trusting him with the whole restaurant. He was very responsible and wrote Boss Lin a letter every week to report on the business situation.

"He sent a letter just the day before yesterday; why is he writing again so soon?"

His wife had an excellent memory; she distinctly remembered every letter she received.

"This Ma is quite industrious."

Among the several purchasers Lin Tongfu had hired and replaced, Ma was the most to his liking. He was in his early fifties and still single. Although he was rather reticent, when he saw people, he always nodded and bowed as if he knew that "amiability makes fortune." He did his work in earnest and was very sharp with the accounts. After returning to Taiwan this time, if everything had gone well, Tongfu planned to put the restaurant under Ma's care, and he himself would become supervisor.

After going inside, Tongfu put on his reading glasses and opened the letter.

"He says that business is not bad...," he said, reading the letter and at the same time passing its contents on to his wife. "Merchandise prices rose again; this is hardly news either! What, listen to this...."

His wife quickly moved over and sat shoulder to shoulder with her husband, listening to him read the letter.

"Manager Shen urgently needs the seven thousand dollars you borrowed from him. Respectfully, I hereby inform you that I collected two thousand dollars from our account for him."

The old man read the letter again and again; his face became red with anger, hot like a scalding black wok.

"This old Shen is not a real friend at all!" he shouted, throwing the letter and beginning on a tirade to his wife. "He and I made an agreement that we would borrow his money for one year at the interest rate of three percent annually. We have not treated him badly! Can he be afraid that we will run away with this small sum of money?..."

His wife was more prudent, and she rushed to placate him, "Don't be so angry yet; maybe he has a problem with cash flow. But really, what's the rush! If he wants to get his money back, it's us he should ask; how can he ask Manager Ma?"

The two had a short discussion and then quickly made a long-distance call to Shen. He was not home, so they called his furniture store and were informed that Shen and his wife had gone to Malaysia.

Since they could not speak English, they were not able to ask the operator to call Shen person-to-person and had to dial the numbers in Taibei directly. Not having succeeded in contacting him, they had just wasted their money on two long-distance calls. After Tongfu hung up, he was both angry and sorry about the money; he collapsed lifelessly on the sofa as though he had suddenly fallen ill.

"We'll call Ma Rongsheng tonight; Xiaomei can help us call him person-to-person," his wife suggested. Fearing that the old man was suffering some ailment, she hurried to heat a bowl of Chinese soup for him to eat.

In his seventy years, Tongfu had never been pressed by anyone to return money. The more he thought about it, the less freely he could breathe. Taking the soup that his wife was offering him, he ate without tasting anything. Once, he had to borrow money to get the deposit needed for his son to study abroad. He gave all the money back and it was over with smoothly. It was not like the present situation at all -- his debtee knocking at his door, demanding the money back before he had even settled down in America.

"When you run a business, you should not be absent every other day. You see, the moment we step out the door, people at home stop knowing us!" he said to his wife. Blaming and pitying himself at the same time, he sighed

256

heavily.

"From now on we'd better come here every year," his wife replied, implying that it was never too late to mend the fence after some sheep were lost. "If we stay for a shorter period of time, the impact on our business won't be so great. If only we had come here last year as we always do."

He gave his wife a severe sidelong glance and remained silent. His cold, hard, face showed no sign of penitence; on the contrary, it was full of arrogance.

Last year he would not come, partly because his restaurant was busy, but mostly because he was mad at America. President Carter announced that America had established diplomatic relations with mainland China, and unilaterally broke off diplomatic relations with Taiwan. This made him furious. For the good of the one billion fellow countrymen on the mainland, he was not against America's decision. What made him angry was Carter's erratic behavior, it seemed as though he meant to insult the Taiwanese people; this provoked his rage. He slapped the table and would not go to America for all the world. This year, if he had not been threatened by the possibility of the green card becoming null and void, he would not have come either. He was trying to run a business and to let it go for half a year was indeed more than he wanted sacrifice.

"Let's give up the green card!" he said tentatively, pushing away the bowl of soup and watching his wife.

"We've made such an effort over the years; what a pity to give it up!" the old woman replied reluctantly. "Maomao and Xiaomei keep asking us to move to America. Once the green card becomes invalid, I've heard the reapplication process is extremely difficult."

Alas, Tongfu thought, *the green card has become almost like chicken ribs, too tasteless for the tongue and too wasteful for the garbage can.*

Miserably, the two waited for time, to pass, until eight that evening.

Xiaomei, after having prepared and served dinner, left her children to her husband and rushed over by herself.

"Papa, sell the business," she advised her father as soon as she arrived. "To keep a restaurant at your age, isn't it too much of an ordeal? You might as well move to America."

Tongfu evasively hemmed and hawed. He remembered seeing some old men and women sitting in the sun at the park. Sometimes, they sat there half a day without moving a muscle; you could hardly tell whether they were awake or asleep. Did she want him to give up running "Little Chengdu" and move to America so that he could sit on a cold bench?

He shook his head heavily from side to side.

Xiaomei called Taibei but Manager Ma could not be found.

"Call again, anyone will do; I just want to ask about it."

He was determined to get to the bottom of the matter. Calculating the time difference, he knew that it was half past two in the afternoon in Taibei. All of his employees should have been at work for half an hour now, and surprisingly Ma was not there. He was puzzled and even a bit disturbed.

The telephone call soon went through, and the cook, Old Wang, answered the phone.

"Manager Ma is on leave for the third day straight," said Old Wang, not wasting a minute in unloading his complaints to the boss. "There is no telephone in the place where he lives and we can't find him! You don't know how busy we've been in the restaurant! I'm the cook and sometimes the waiter, too...."

Boss Lin could imagine the commotion and confusion in the restaurant and also began to cry out into the receiver. "Why did he take leave? Why didn't he...."

"He didn't tell us; although I've heard rumors...."

Old Wang suddenly stopped short in mid-sentence, and old Lin almost

258

stamped his feet in anxious anticipation, "Hello, hello, Old Wang, speak, what did you hear?"

"Well, I don't know whether it's true or not; somebody said that Manager Ma was getting married, and that he was going south for the wedding."

Tongfu was dumbfounded. Getting married was a good thing; why did Ma keep it a secret and not spread the good news?

"I suppose you know that Manager Shen asked for his money?" Tongfu inquired.

"Manager Shen? Oh, Mr. Shen of The Great Wall Furniture Store? No, I didn't hear anything about it; I mean, I don't know--you know, I am too busy in the kitchen already; I never take care of the books."

"Now who is the bookkeeper?"

"The waiters are doing the bookkeeping, but they haven't come to work yet."

"Look what time it is and they haven't come to work, eh?"

By now old Mr. Lin's eyes were glaring. He was about ready to blow up with rage. Suddenly, it occurred to him that overseas calls cost "one inch of gold per minute," and he quickly shouted out instructions into the receiver, "As soon as Manager Ma comes to work, tell him to call me immediately!" The moment he hung up the phone, his wife and daughter hastily asked him what had happened.

"It's a sloppy mess!"

As he recounted the situation, his chest rose and fell rapidly in anger, "This Ma is a real crook; it turns out that he only has an honest appearance! The moment we turned our backs, he deserted his duty. The two thousand dollars is also a mystery. If things go on like this, I think when we go home this time, we'd better close the restaurant!"

"Papa, don't get so upset," his daughter comforted him. "Manager Ma would by no means run away with a mere two thousand dollars. We'll call and ask again tomorrow."

"We cannot depend on phone calls and remote control!" he shook his head seriously, disagreeing. His wife also sensed something fishy and her heart began to sink. She watched the old man's angry black wok face; it was tightly strained as if ready to explode if someone were to pick up the cover.

"Maybe Xiaomei is right," she suddenly said to him with a hardened heart. "We cannot shuttle back and forth like this; let's sell the restaurant!"

"You're right, we cannot shuttle back and forth," he said, raising his hands. Emphatically, he added, "We should go back to Taiwan without further delay and concentrate on running our business!"

"How...."

His wife was flabbergasted, not knowing whether he was serious or merely angry. She averted her eyes from him to their daughter, only to see her calmly and steadily watching her father's face, appearing to be seriously considering his idea. Surprisingly, it did not seem that Xiaomei had any desire to dissuade her father, not only astonishing her mother but even filling her father with wonder.

While they were looking at each other not knowing what to do, the telephone suddenly rang.

"Maomao's call!"

As if her rescue troops had arrived, Tongfu's wife quickly glanced at her husband as if to tell him, "Hear what your son has to say."

Tongfu scowled, his heavy brows furrowed, and sat motionless in spite of the thunder and lightning he felt welling up inside him.

Xiaomei answered the phone and indeed it was her brother calling.

In detail, she told him about looking for apartments during the day and what had happened at the restaurant in Taibei.

"Papa wants to go back right away to take care of the business...um, can only give up the green card....Oh, okay."

She handed the receiver to her father.

Taking the telephone from her, Tongfu immediately tried to get the upper hand, announcing to his son, "Maomao, we're not going to move; we'll go back to Taiwan this minute! Without our own management, sooner or later Little Chengdu is going to fold!"

To his great astonishment, his son had no objections and even seconded his decision.

"Papa, since you two are used to living in Taiwan, maybe it's best that you live there. Sister and I can take turns going to visit you. If you want to run a business for fun, that's alright, too; in the case that it becomes too strenuous for you, just sell it and go traveling...."

"We're not going to sell it! We're not going to sell it!" his father protested without stopping. "The restaurant is just now becoming renowned because of our efforts; how could we think of selling it?"

His son did not insist on his own opinion either, "Then hire more people to help. Dad, next week is Thanksgiving and we'll have four days off. We booked our flights today; we'll come together to visit you and Mom."

Upon hearing that both his son and daughter-in-law were coming, his father was very happy. His son and daughter had surprised him by accepting his decision to return to Taiwan; feeling enormous gratification, he suddenly had the urge to fly back as swiftly as an arrow.

"Maomao, why don't you cancel that flight and use the money instead to come back to Taiwan for Lunar New Year?"

"All right," answered his son without hesitation. "The last few years, since you and Mom have been coming regularly to the States, we stopped going back to Taiwan. We'd like to return and see Taibei."

Then, after chatting with his mother for a few minutes, he finally hung up.

As if a weight had been lifted from his shoulders, Tongfu felt light and agile, and thought that he would like very much to walk around in the living room. He also wanted to rearrange those flowerpots again.

Suddenly his wife's long face grasped his attention. Looking at him, she said, "Tongfu, you decide to leave just like that, but what about the green card....After we've kept it all these years, so painstakingly, isn't it a pity to invalidate it!"

"Invalidate it, so what! We should never have tried to get a green card in the first place."

"But, if Taiwan...."

"You worry about Taiwan every day, but isn't it still safe and sound? On the contrary, for several years now, because of that green card, we ourselves have been kept constantly on the run! If we keep doing this, we'll become bankrupt long before we get ruined by the communists!"

The next day, Xiaomei happily made reservations for their flight back to Taiwan.

Morning Encounter with a Stranger: A Monologue

Editor's Notes:

"Morning Encounter with a Stranger: A Monologue" is the most introspective piece in this collection. It represents a revelation of the "psychological" Chinese-American emigres' inner landscape, one charged by the driving spirit of the American Dream, and typified by growing feelings of existential disillusionment and alienation. Written in monologue discourse, Chen Ruoxi offers us a novel exploration of literary borders and the boundaries of therapeutic technique.

In this story, an outsider is given the psychologist-like privilege of listening to the confession of the narrator's innermost feelings. Singling out two issues that are particularly emblematic to the malaise of contemporary Chinese life in America, divorce and familial discord resulting from new cultural imbalances, Chen raises several other issues. Where integration into new cultural surroundings must take place, there arises new hopes and expectations, leading to new sources of conflict and resentment in everyday life. Here, we must ask ourselves how much must one compromise their hopes and expectations without compromising their values and those of whom are dearest to them? And, if the inevitable changes in expectations and reality do not meet with compromise, is it not herein that the cultural and generational split lies?

MORNING ENCOUNTER WITH A STRANGER: A MONOLOGUE[1]

Good morning. When I saw you from afar I knew you were Chinese. Here, whenever Americans see an Asian-looking face, they just assume that they're Japanese. They're probably mesmerized by all those Japanese cars they see everywhere. Are you a student at Chico State?

You work hard indeed--even on Sunday morning you're taking a book to read in the park.

Yes.

Born on Chinese New Year's Day, just turned three years old. Come here and say hello to auntie. Tell auntie what your name is.

Cadi is his nick name; his Chinese name is Bu Kaiming. I'd already chosen the name before he was born--a boy would be named Kaiming and a girl would be named Kaili. You know, my son Zhiming was already forty-two when he became a father. He was so excited that he went out and bought a big Cadillac for his wife. She especially liked Cadillacs, so she started calling her son Cadi. Well, I should've seen earlier on that all she cared about was cars, as though she didn't have a son at all. O.K., O.K., you can ride your bike around on the road,

---

[1] "Morning Encounter with a Stranger: A Monologue" (Yujian mosheng nuzi de natian shangwu) was translated by Xincun Huang with the permission of the author and the publisher, and is published here in English for the first time. The translation is based on the story's first appearance in *Zhongguo shibao* (China Times), Literary Supplement (March 10, 1988).

but don't go too far away. Grandma wants to talk with auntie.

I'm from Hunan--I've got a heavy accent, don't I? I lived in Taiwan for over twenty years. I've been in America for ten. I'm really ashamed that I still can't speak standard Chinese well. Where are you from? I haven't even asked you your name.

You're also from Jiangsu. Do you know Annie Hu? She used to study at Chico State.

She's the mother of this child. She's from Xuzhou. Xuzhou is close to Lianyun Harbor. I thought you might know each other.

Oh, you came here only last year, no wonder you didn't meet her. She left the year before last. It's been peaceful ever since she left, you know. She created quite a scandal here in town just to get a divorce. People who don't know the truth of the matter would think we'd treated her badly. Our restaurant really is one of the best in Chico. It would've been such a pity if we'd sold it. If we had, Zhiming and I would've already moved away from here.

"Hunan Diner"--I'm sure you've heard of it. It's the one at the intersection of Main and Watts.

Thanks for the compliment. It's just a small place. We depend on everyone's support. Oh, so you like spicy food, too. The barbecue beef noodle is what I make the best. I use a prime cut of beef with an original sauce. Zhiming insists on selling a good product at a fair price--not frying up some chopsuey to fleece a few Westerners! He believes that Americans who really appreciate Chinese food want more than just sweet and sour pork. When I first came here, the customers were mostly Orientals, but now the situation has completely reversed. It really hasn't been easy. From busing at restaurants while in school to starting his own business, Zhiming has put so much energy into this. If we sold it, wouldn't it be like taking a knife and stabbing him in the heart? But, at the time, Annie was trying to create the impression that we were selling it, so a lot of people called us asking about the price. Zhiming didn't know whether to laugh or cry--he couldn't even concentrate on his business.

My son's a terribly honest man. Even though he only wears loose t-shirts at home and doesn't talk much, the moment he steps into the restaurant, he's a completely different person, dressing very neatly and always greeting people with a smile. But, during their divorce, he changed completely--he was weak and distracted. When he sat behind the counter, he'd just stare blankly into space. It took the customers waving their money in front of his nose to make him snap out of it. Oh! Cadi! Come back! Behave yourself! Just ride your bike here on the road, don't go to the other side of the grass. Behave yourself now, Grandma will give you something tasty to eat later.

Why would we have to sell such a nice restaurant? Well, she wanted half of our property. Haven't you heard? The law in California says that a husband and wife have to divide their property evenly when they get divorced.

There's a Chinese saying: "A fall into the pit, a gain for your wit." I really learned a lot from this. The very day after she moved out, she made her demands. It was Zhiming who picked up the phone. I didn't hear him say anything but his face suddenly darkened. "What's the matter?" I asked him. To tell you the truth, I thought that their separation simply meant that they were quarreling with each other. I didn't expect that they would really get a divorce--and then to have to divide the property! At that time, I, too, felt like I'd been struck from behind. I was so angry and irritated that I almost fainted. You know, I have high blood pressure and can't take any excitement.

It was I who first took a fancy to Annie. She seemed perfect in every way, so I asked someone to introduce her to him formally. They went out a little over four months and then got married. Such a perfect match--who would've imagined they'd change so fast. Even now, I still feel that I did a disservice to my son. Divorce is common enough in America and the eighties, but the Chinese community in Chico is small, and we've got a business to run. Although we weren't exactly afraid of losing face, we still couldn't afford to get involved in a lawsuit. It would have been impossible to do business. Of course, in the end, we could do nothing but take some advice from friends, hire a lawyer, and prepare to go to court with her.

No, how could she get away with <u>that</u>? The law is, after all, reasonable. What they say about dividing the property actually means that the increase in property value after a couple gets married is what gets divided in half. They were only married for a year or so, and the value of the restaurant didn't increase too much during that period. We even asked someone to appraise our house. Chico is a small town, so house values don't increase too much, not like big cities such as San Francisco. At that time, just taking an inventory of our property--the restaurant and house--raised a huge commotion, not to mention how upset we were. The Bu family has never been taken to court, not in recent generations. People always say that Americans love to file lawsuits, but they are Americans! You see me now telling the story so calmly...but then, I was worried sick--with a headache and an irregular heartbeat--I felt like I would faint any minute. I didn't dare tell Zhiming about my symptoms. Secretly, I took some medicine and forced myself to go out and find someone to help me with the baby. Zhiming wasn't afraid of going to court. He said to let the lawyer take care of everything, that it was no big deal. My son is by nature an extremely quiet person. I believed he meant what he said. But what I really worried about was the way he kept quiet. He had a worried look on his face all the time. It wasn't just that he didn't feel like eating or drinking--it was how he looked, like he'd lost all his spirit. I had to shout at him to get his attention. When he finished work and came home at night, the first thing he would do was go see his son. He would stand before the cradle for half an hour, crying a little. Of course, I knew what he was thinking--that mother and child are one in their hearts. He loved Annie so deeply...he was so enchanted by her. I asked someone to go talk to Annie and ask her to come back to stay for another couple of years. The child was still so small. But, she insisted that they could never get along with one another and that she couldn't stand to live with him even one more day. Two months passed by, and my son became so thin his clothes looked enormous draped on his frail body. I had to go beg Annie myself, without any regard for my own dignity! If only she would've agreed to come back, I wouldn't have hesitated to move out and live elsewhere, by myself. But she just kept repeating that there was such a gap in their ages, and they didn't get along well.

Thirteen years. I agree that he was much older, but she wasn't a young girl any more either. She was already twenty-eight. And, if she hadn't wanted to get married, could anyone have forced her to go to the alter?

I don't blame you, of course someone might think that was the real problem. The reason I wanted to move out was so that I wouldn't interfere with the newlyweds. I became a widow when I was only thirty years old. Zhiming is my only child. But, I know that this is America, and people believe in a small family. I wanted to get out of the way. I'm not crippled--I can work and move around fine by myself. I didn't need to stay at my son's house, don't you agree? I'm not short of money, either. When I retired in Taiwan, I received fifty thousand dollars. It's still in the bank, and there's no way to spend it all. All I wanted was for my son to live happily and for them to get along with each other well. I really liked Annie. Even though they're divorced now, I don't want to say bad things about her. She had beautiful eyes and an oval face, and her figure was exquisitely delicate. When she smiled, a pair of dimples lit up her face, really pretty. She graduated from a teacher's college. She knew how to say all the right things, probably because she'd been a teacher; she understood older people very well. She lost her mother when she was very young, so the second time she saw me, she wanted me to call her my adopted daughter. She could be so adorable. Zhiming also liked her from first sight. He said she was very sweet. She was calling me "mom" even before they got married--it really made me so happy. I don't know why, but it seems they weren't fated to be together. That day I went to see her, I started crying while I was talking. Isn't that a sin? She *was the daughter-in-law I chose myself. At the time, in order to find a wife for my son, I really put all my heart and soul into it. I went any place where there were Chinese....*

No. She said that I didn't have to move out because it didn't have anything to do with me. It was because the two of them didn't get along. She said a lot about how they didn't get along, but I don't understand. Older husbands always dote on younger wives. Zhiming fulfilled her every desire. People say that Zhiming is very devoted to his mother, but, at that time, he was devoted only to his wife. For instance, she didn't like the clothes in Chico, or even in Sacramento. She thought the styles were too unsophisticated--the only place to buy clothes was San Francisco. You know, our restaurant is open seven days a week, and employees rotate their days off, but the boss doesn't get a day off at all. Zhiming used to go to San Francisco several times a year to buy supplies. But, after he got married, he would take her to San Francisco once or twice a month. Five hundred dollars for a single outfit--I didn't dare show how shocked I was! Young ladies do treasure beauty, I understand that. I'm old, but my mind isn't. I didn't want there to be a generation gap in my family.

Oh! Look at me! I've drifted away from our original conversation. I wasn't this long-winded before, but these years have worn me down....I don't want to talk about it any more. As for the property dispute, we settled out of court. We gave her cash for the increase in property value. We also satisfied all of her other demands, such as giving her all the alimony at once instead of paying her monthly. The new car also went to her. We'd purchased it on an installment plan and didn't finish making the payments until last year. At that time, she still hadn't received her permanent residence card. We were afraid that she wouldn't be allowed to stay in the United States if they were divorced, so they separated the property first, but didn't finalize the divorce until after she'd received her permanent residence card.

Well, we had no other choice. Zhiming said that they'd been husband and wife, so they shouldn't make the separation more difficult for each other. She was also the mother of his child, and that was a major consideration. I know too well that he was hoping for the day when Annie would change her mind and come back. But, she left Chico right after she'd finished the legal proceedings, without telling us a thing. We didn't know that she had disappeared until the letters we forwarded to her were returned. See how cruel-hearted she was!

Child? No, don't mention it! Oh! Cadi! It's O.K., it doesn't matter. Come here, let Grandma look at it. It's O.K., you didn't cut your hand. Don't ride your bike any more, just sit here and Grandma will give you some sugar cake to eat. Here, you should offer it to auntie first.

You're welcome, this is a type of Cantonese dim sum we've started to make recently.

Yeah, we have to start selling it. You don't know how competitive running a restaurant is! The popularity of eating dim sum came to America from Hong Kong. It started on the coast, in places like San Francisco, then slowly worked its way inland. Nowadays, even small towns like Chico can't resist its influence. "Hunan Diner" also serves dim sum during weekends. Zhiming specially hired a cook from Hong Kong and is trying to learn how to cook a little himself. It's not easy being the boss. You have to learn a little of what the cook is good at, that way, the cook won't have control over you.

Of course we do! Shaobing² and youtiao³ are very popular! There aren't many Cantonese here.

I'm not used to drinking milk, either. You like soybean milk, well then, I'll treat you to a bowl some day, we have it both at the restaurant and at home. We use soybeans and make it ourselves--we never use soybean powder--we want

---

² Shaobing is a kind of cake with sesame seeds sprinkled on top, commonly eaten for breakfast in China.

³ Youtiao is another common Chinese breakfast food, made from strips of dough which are deep-fried.

to be sure it tastes fresh. We haven't been able to keep up with the demand since we started selling it. You don't know how good business was yesterday--we sold more than half of what we'd planned to sell today. Zhiming had to soak more soybeans so that we could make more after the restaurant closed. Filtering, boiling ...he didn't come back until midnight last night. Even though he was really tired from work, when he woke up this morning and saw the sun shining, he thought it would be a good business day. So he sent us to the park without even having breakfast. He loves his son, but he has no time to play with him.

I think so, too. The feelings between a father and son have to be developed when the child is still young. Zhiming is so quiet during the day. Only when he sees his son will a smile appear on his face, and then he'll play with him a bit. But, if they're together a little longer, he drifts into a trance, his eyes just staring at the child, his face numb, obviously not with us any more. See how self-contradictory I am! I want them to be together, but I don't want Zhiming to think about the past....It's really so difficult for me!

You want another piece? Tell me, what is this called? I'll give you another piece when you tell me what it's called. "Sugar cake"--how smart you are! Just eat a small piece. If you eat too much, you won't eat your lunch when we go back.

Thanks for the compliment. You have to teach children Chinese while they're still young, then they won't forget it the rest of their life. Human beings are like that--natural things become habits, and those habits never change. Speaking Chinese isn't the only thing, eating Chinese food is the same. It's important to exert this subtle influence on the child, giving him Chinese food when he's young. That way, when he grows up, he'll have to marry a Chinese girl so that he can eat Chinese food.

We've hired a Mexican maid, but I try to take care of Cadi all by myself. Luckily, with Cadi's company, I have someone to talk to, otherwise I'd feel terribly bored staying in the house. My English is almost good enough to read *newspapers, but I can't speak it. I can't talk with the Mexican maid at all.*

No. We've never heard anything from her since she left. Her lawyer only has the number of a post office box in Los Angeles. Just a second, Cadi, behave yourself, clean your hands when you're finished eating. It's not easy for Grandma to get a chance to talk with a nice lady. Go play with your ball. Here, just stay on the grass--don't run away.

Thanks for the compliment again. He just recovered from an illness, or his complexion would be ruddier. His eyebrows are like his mother's, but the lower half of his face is exactly like Zhiming's. His personality is like Zhiming's, too. He's quiet and understanding, not a pest, but a real darling. I treat this grandson of mine like a treasure. I've nothing to complain about. You just asked me whether Annie cares about her son, well, I didn't want to talk about his mother in front of him. He's already three years old. Do you understand? The heart of their problem was actually the child!

Annie doesn't like children.

Even now I can't understand, being a woman, how she could've been so afraid of having a baby. When she learned that she was pregnant, her personality suddenly changed. At first she said that a child would interfere with her studies, so she wanted to have an abortion. In our Bu family, during the last several generations, there has only been one male to pass on the family name. Zhiming was already in his forties--any man that age, without a child, would want to kneel before the Buddha and burn incense to pray for one. Now that she was pregnant, there was no reason for her to get rid of the child. I absolutely wouldn't allow it. Zhiming always yielded to his wife, but he couldn't be heartless in this matter. Seeing that she was unable to dissuade us, Annie changed her tactics. Even though she'd never exercised after they'd gotten married, all of a sudden she started to play tennis and go swimming. Early every morning, she'd either go out running or jump rope, before Zhiming got up. You should've seen the way she whipped that rope around, as if she wanted to break it. *I was so worried that my heart almost jumped out of my mouth. There was no way to stop her. She said she was accustomed to physical labor in the countryside and wasn't worried. I'm not a Christian--in the six years I'd been here I'd only gone to church once, that was for my son's wedding. I was so afraid she would have a miscarriage that I went to church every Sunday to pray. Finally God helped us, and the child survived.*

She did mention that before their wedding. She was very dedicated to her work. She said she wanted to get her master's degree first and didn't want a child for at least another two years. Zhiming loved her so much that he complied with her every whim. To tell you the truth, that child was Heaven sent--one hundred percent the will of Heaven. At first, Annie was on the pill, but it made her throw up day and night, making her life miserable. As soon as she changed contraceptives, she immediately became pregnant--wouldn't you say it was the arrangement of Heaven? Of course she didn't see it that way--she insisted that it was her husband trying to keep her from finishing her degree. She squabbled and fussed all the time. All Zhiming could do was say he was sorry, that he would comply with her every wish except for having an abortion. He would have given her anything she asked for, even the moon....if he could have brought it down, he would have given it to her!

No, she didn't. But it was entirely her own fault that she didn't finish her degree. When her belly began to show just a little, she was so embarrassed that she wouldn't go to school. She stayed home all day writing letters, corresponding with someone named Ouyang Han in Anhui. I don't know what their relationship was. She very seldom talked about herself, and after she got pregnant, she didn't want to talk with us at all. Whenever Zhiming said something, she would get mad and find something to quarrel about. After quarreling several times, they started sleeping in separate rooms. We thought that it was the pregnancy that changed her temper, but looking back on it, her feelings had already changed. Not only was Zhiming unsuspicious, but he continued to

*try to find all kinds of ways to please her, such as taking her out to buy clothes
and jewelry. One time, she suddenly said that American cake didn't taste good,
it was too sweet, she wanted to eat the cakes sold in Chinatown. Without saying
a thing, he put aside his business, drove all the way to San Francisco--five hours
round trip--just to buy cakes for her. I also spent a lot of time helping her,
making her tonic, changing the dessert often, always afraid that she wouldn't eat
enough--she was the daughter-in-law that I picked. Oh, Cadi, don't chase it,
Grandma will get the ball for you.*

    *Sorry to bother you, thank you. I'll hold the book for you. Cadi, auntie
went to get the ball for you. Wait here.*

    Don't thank me, I should thank you. <u>Human Behavior</u>--is this a novel?

    Psychology? Why are you reading psychology? What are you studying?

    *Terrific! It's unbelievable that such a delicate and pretty girl like you is
studying sociology. No wonder you are so attentive, and don't mind me being
so long-winded. This society is so diverse, you must have studied all of it. So,
you're majoring in sociology and also studying human psychology--can I ask you
a favor?*

    Would you help me analyze my son?

    *He's too depressed. After the divorce, he's become even quieter, as if all he
has to say has already been said at the restaurant. He turns into a mute when
he comes home. Sometimes, when I sit with him watching TV all night, it gives
me the feeling that I'm sitting with a block of wood. He stares at the screen, but
his vision isn't focused, he's obviously not there. At the beginning, I could
understand. I thought it was the divorce that hurt him a lot, that it was natural
for him to get upset and even discouraged. No one could endure that kind of
sadness. But three years have passed...why is he still like this? He wasn't that
way before. There was nothing between us that we couldn't discuss. After he lost
his father, he became very obedient. He would tell me everything and always
asked me for advice. Even things like trying to steal our neighbor's papayas, he*

never hid the truth from me. Now he's become a completely different person, closed the door on me. Although we live in the same house, we seem to live in two separate worlds. I really can't describe my feelings!

He's not much better to his son. Of course he loves Cadi, he always wants to hold him and play with him when he comes home. But sometimes, when he's looking at the child so fondly, he suddenly frowns, pushes him aside and walks away. He acts as if the child is in his way. It was after Annie's pregnancy that she started to quarrel with him. Maybe Zhiming's scars have never healed.

Probably...but it doesn't matter whether he still loves her or not. She didn't even want her own son, how could she possibly still think of Zhiming? It's absolutely impossible for her to come back to him.

I also thought of what you just said, but it's no use. He doesn't want to talk about a second marriage. Nor does he want anyone to be introduced to him. I already told him that if he gets married again, I will move out with Cadi so the child won't suffer either. Isn't that right? He just disagrees. I became a widow when I was young and I've made it through all these years. I have a grandson now, and he's everything to me. For the sake of the child, I'd like him to stay single, but I also want him to be happy! I heard that nowadays one can find partners using computers. They say that choosing a person to date according to personalities and interests gives people a better chance of success. I told Zhiming about this, he just smiled and remained silent. What's he thinking? Even arguing with me is much better than this silence!

It's not that serious. He's not mentally ill, so why should he go see a psychiatrist? That doesn't sound good if it gets around. And if the doctor hospitalizes him and doesn't let him out, isn't that worse?

Yes, it's better to try to analyze it. I said I wanted to talk with you about this for that very reason.

It's hard to know what to say about mixed-marriages, because some people get along well and some people don't. I want to make it clear that I'm not *racially prejudiced, really.*

There are two mixed couples in Chico--both are Chinese wives with American husbands. They come to our restaurant frequently.

As for Zhiming, he's very Americanized. To tell you the truth, if it hadn't been for my opposition, he would have married an American woman!

Of course he did. I never met the first one because I was still in Taiwan at the time. It happened after he received his master's degree and started to work at an insurance company as a broker. She was a typist at the same company. I did see her picture once. She had thick eyebrows, big eyes, and hair the color of creamy coffee braided into a pony tail. Her smile was charming. Have you seen the movie "The Wizard of Oz"? She looked like the leading actress in that movie.

I had to oppose it. I sent him three telegrams, one right after the other, to force him to give up the idea of marrying her.

Of course I thought it wasn't appropriate at the time. He already had a girlfriend in Taiwan. They were not just friends. Before he left, I held an engagement ceremony for them and had a ring made for her. The two of them went to America at the same time to study, but unfortunately they didn't attend the same school. That was the problem. Zhiming was studying economics and working at a restaurant at the same time, so of course he graduated late. The girl didn't want to wait that long, so she returned the ring and married a man with a Ph.D. in electrical engineering. That was a real blow to Zhiming. He didn't write home for a long time. I was so anxious that I almost became sick. I retired earlier than planned and traveled thousands of miles to America, only because I couldn't stop worrying about him. I was afraid that something would happen to him. Have you ever seen Zhiming?

Yes, that was him. If there are too many customers, he comes out and seats them himself. If you've seen him before then you know that I wasn't exaggerating. He's medium height, has fine features, never smokes or drinks or becomes rude to others. *To tell you the truth, his personality and manner are both gentle and modest. His father was like that when he was alive--they seem to have come from the same mold. He was good at everything, so how could he be without ambition? Just because one woman had a change of heart, is that enough of a reason for him to hastily marry a foreigner? Don't you agree? They say that a man should get married when he is old enough. He was over thirty years old already, but since he'd gotten by for all those years, there was all the more reason for him to be careful with his choices. For men and women alike, marriage is life's most important event.*

Of course, I felt it wasn't appropriate...and also not convenient. The Bu family has had only one son for each of the last several generations. When it came to Zhiming's generation, if we had...a child of mixed race, that really wouldn't have been acceptable. Moreover, he is my only son, and I have to live with him. If he'd married an American woman, we wouldn't have been able to communicate, and our customs would have been different. How could we have lived together?

Not just two, there was still a third one! At least to my knowledge, there were three of them. I knew the two later ones, one was named Jenny, the other May. Jenny was a waitress at our restaurant. When I first got here, the two of them were already very close. At first glance, I could tell it was the girl that was chasing him.

It's not that. We have to look at what she was chasing, the money or the person. Even though I'm old, I'm not that conservative. These days who cares who's chasing who? I just thought it wasn't appropriate. There are so many Chinese girls, and many of them are good-looking and well-educated. Why would Zhiming want to date an American girl who was only seventeen or eighteen, who'd never finished her last year of high school? She was good-looking, sweet, and always smiling. She would pull me aside and chatter at me, without it occurring to her that I couldn't understand anything she said.

Of course, she was warm-hearted, but she wasn't at all reserved--she was almost frivolous. She dared to kiss and be affectionate in front of everybody, without any sense of modesty. Her eyes were really unrestrained. She would stare at Zhiming all the time. Even when he turned around, she would still stare at his back. After driving her home every night, as soon as Zhiming arrived home, she'd phone him. She really didn't give Zhiming time to catch his breath. The most terrible thing was that when I first arrived here, I found out that the two of them were already talking about getting married. I made up my mind that I wouldn't agree, no matter how they begged me. I'd never accept her as a daughter-in-law, over my dead body!

She's married now, to the manager of a gas station here.

He was all right. He just kept quiet for a couple months. He also knew that it wasn't right. Speaking about appearances alone, she was half an inch taller than him, and he was twice her age. What do you think--would that have been a good match?

He did have feelings toward Jenny, but he wasn't that involved, not like his feelings for May. The way he treated May...he even wanted to adopt her son.

Yeah. Her ex-husband would get drunk and beat her, so she divorced him. She was living alone, and raising the seven-year-old child by herself.

She didn't need to be formally introduced. She applied for the position that used to be Jenny's. Since she'd learned accounting and had done cashier work before, Zhiming hired her immediately. The first day she came to work, our cook had the day off, I was helping in the kitchen, so I met her. My impression of her wasn't bad. She was generous and poised, and her voice was softer than cream. She spoke as if she was afraid that if she spoke any louder she would frighten someone. She would hand me the orders herself every time, and called me "Mrs. Bu," "Mrs. Bu" all the time, very politely. She was thin and ordinary looking. She had thick brown hair, hanging to her shoulders. Later on, for the sake of work, she put her hair in a bun...actually, it made her look better and matched her large eyes and mouth. She wasn't young. When she smiled, you could see some wrinkles around her eyes. She kept her age a secret, but you could guess she had to be between twenty-five and thirty. She did look a bit pale and old though. Her son was named Tom, really cute and bright. He always called me Grandma when he saw me, a real darling.

He was seven years old. Zhiming lost his father at that age. If it wasn't for...that, I could've really loved the both of them dearly.

Zhiming hid it from me for a whole year!

I never went to our restaurant when it wasn't necessary, so I didn't find out earlier. I just felt lucky that Zhiming found such a helpful employee. I told him to give her more pay because she would come to help him check the accounts--even on her days off--and sit in the office the whole day. May was very devoted to her work. She was the oldest among the five waitresses, but she worked the hardest and earned the biggest tips. She was also trying to learn Chinese. One time, I heard her reading the menu, and several Chinese customers complimented her.

Of course it was Zhiming who taught her. He said that May loved Chinese culture, Chinese food, and Chinese clothes. That's right, after a while she even started to wear a Qipao.

Who can make a Qipao here? It was Zhiming who asked someone to buy it at some place called the "Friendship Store" in Peking. It's strange that a wax-printed, one-size-fits-all cotton Qipao, which was cut so simply, looked so pretty on an American woman. I don't wear one now, but I used to wear one everyday in Taibei when I was working. I am not very sure about other things but I think I'm quite an expert in judging whether a Qipao fits or not. Have you ever seen an American woman wearing a Qipao?

You should take note of it next time. If their figure is slender, they can look very attractive in a Qipao, and if they also wear high-heels, it's quite graceful and charming.

Sorry, I've strayed too far from my topic again. Yes, I asked everyone to introduce girls to Zhiming. There were more than a dozen of them. Some of them lived here, some were from the Bay area. The last one was named Miss Zhang, she came here from Oregon, by plane, especially to meet Zhiming. After she went back, she still wrote to us. She was in her thirties, good-looking, just a little bit conservative. I thought she was fine, but they just weren't fated to be together.

Yeah, don't you think it's strange? None of them seemed to meet Zhiming's standards. I really racked my brain for nothing!

At first, it didn't seem as if he was only going through the motions just to please me--I would've found out. Zhiming went out with them in all sincerity. Even on weekends, when the restaurant was very busy, he would still go out with them, leaving the business to May and the cook. But when he came back, whenever I asked him how it went, he would either shake his head, or say "Not right," and try to convince me by saying, "Mom, you just can't rush into these kinds of things." I was so anxious that I didn't notice he wasn't very serious about meeting the last two. I didn't suspect the slightest bit that he was already involved with someone! I really should have noticed earlier. May used to wear high heels when she first came to work, but soon she started wearing shoes without them. That way, when the two of them stood together, they looked about the same height. Tom used to call Zhiming "Mr. Bu," but then he started calling him "Uncle." Zhiming would drive him to swimming classes, skating lessons, and they also played tennis together. They were very close. Sometimes when Zhiming didn't come home until two or three o'clock in the morning, I merely thought that he'd stayed after hours at the restaurant to check the accounts and didn't ask him any questions. During the three days when Miss Zhang stayed in Chico, he didn't come home for a couple of nights. I was a little suspicious at the time, but I thought that young people nowadays all want to seem so open-minded, especially here in America. They're really so different from my generation, aren't they? I just turned a blind eye to what was happening. But, now I know it had nothing to do with Miss Zhang--I blamed an innocent person.

May told me.

You also think it's strange, don't you? I'm sure it was Zhiming's idea. One day, May came to my house and told me in Chinese, with a western accent: "I love Zhiming, I want to marry him." At first I thought she was just practicing her Chinese, so I nodded and complimented her on her Chinese. But when I heard it the second time, and saw the serious look on her face, her bright eyes staring at me, I suddenly realized what she was saying and I shouted, "NO!"

No, no, it doesn't mean that I look down upon divorced women. I just thought it wasn't appropriate. If he could marry an American woman, he would have married one already, why should he wait until now? It didn't matter that she was divorced, but she already had a child. I couldn't imagine it--there would be white and yellow--all mixed together in our family. Wouldn't it have been like the United Nations? I did like Tom, I gave him toys, and I made Yuanxiao[4] a couple of times for him. Ah, where is Cadi? Hey, come back! Bring the ball here, Cadi. Oh, it's already twelve o'clock, I forgot the time while I wuas talking. We have to go back now. Cadi, take a rest, look at how you're sweating.

No, he didn't mention it. It was I that mentioned it first. He didn't talk for four days. When he came home, he either hid in his room and made phone calls, or fell asleep after getting drunk in a bar. I understand he was just using wine to numb the sadness, but I couldn't understand why he wouldn't talk with me. Now I have Cadi to talk with, but at the time, who did I have to talk to? The seven rooms upstairs and downstairs were quiet and somber, as if the house was a graveyard. I only asked him to obey me in this one matter. I said, since your father died when you were seven years old, I haven't asked you for anything. This once, only this once, I would like you to listen to me. I felt so wronged that I started to weep as I was talking. Silent tears also rolled down his face. This

---

[4] Yuanxiao is a sweet dessert made of glutinous rice flour.

282

was the first time I'd seen him cry in over ten years. It made my heart ache. So, I made up my mind to find a wonderful wife for him. Now, Annie has left, but he still has many chances for a good marriage. But, he is so obstinate. Do you know what he could possibly be thinking?

You want to give me suggestion, good! Go ahead.

I should go to see a psychiatrist? What do you mean? You do like to joke around! Well, we have to leave now, or that Mexican maid at home will be anxious and start a fuss. Cadi, let's go!

It's Your House, But It's My Home!

Editor's Notes:

For many Chinese, Berkeley is a symbol of America, a symbol of freedom and democracy for all people, regardless of skin color, social status, or beliefs. As such, it attracts a large crowd of idealistic Chinese intellectuals who choose Berkeley as the permanent site to pursue what they envision to be the American Dream. However, influenced by the Beat consciousness of the sixties, Berkeley is a city of dichotomies. Although the sixties are over, the spirit of the sixties has remained the watershed of recent American sociopolitical-cultural history and continues to affect the ambiance of those who reside in Berkeley in innumerable ways. The following story serves as a revelation, exposing the hollow core of Berkeley's bureaucratic system and the illusiveness of its idealistic utopian image. It is a demonstrative example of the impact political activities and decisions have on the lives and feelings of many ordinary people, Americans and immigrants alike.

IT'S YOUR HOUSE, BUT IT'S MY HOME![1]

Truthfully speaking, had we not lived in Berkeley, we would not be returning to Taiwan so soon.

You probably know my husband, Junxiong. While attending National Taiwan University, he was an election volunteer for the non-Guomindang candidates who were pursuing the goal of democracy and freedom. When we met in America, the first time he spoke of Berkeley, he praised it as the symbol of American freedom and democracy. He sincerely believed that Berkeley equated democracy, a synonym for liberty and advancement. Soon after we were married, he received his Ph.D. Among the many job offers and locations, he chose one in San Francisco. His justification was that from here, he could "cast an eye on his hometown on the other side of the Pacific Ocean." But, the truth of the matter was that he yearned to live in Berkeley.

The second day after we moved into our newly purchased home, I clearly remember seeing the "For Sale" sign standing at the edge of the lawn of house No. 15, across the street from us. The house was similar to ours in

---

[1] "It's Your House, But It's My Home!" (Suishi nide fangzi, queshi wode jia) was translated by Hsin-sheng C. Kao with the permission of the author, and is published here in English for the first time. This story is based on its first appearance in *Lianhebao* (United Daily), literary Supplement (November 19 & 20, 1989). Although this story is based on a factual situation, all names contained herein are fictional.

both size and style. Americans call this type of two-story house colonial style with a pointed roof top. The only difference was that this house had a more rugged appearance, with its gray exterior, and a front porch with a wooden fence. Adjacent to the fence, sat an oak rocking chair, imperturbably bathing in the sunset, looking so demurely tranquil as if it had been through all of life's unpredictabilities.

"If we had known that house was for sale earlier, we might as well have bought that one instead," I nagged Junxiong, wishing that I could sit in that rocking chair myself, leisurely inspecting all the people and traffic that would parade on by.

"Um, the structure of this house is quite solid, except that it hasn't been well maintained," said my architect husband, who could easily detect the construction quality of a house. He continued, "It needs some cosmetics. If we throw on a few cans of paint, the house will look like new from top to bottom."

As a first-time homeowner, I loved to compare home prices. I dialed the phone number painted on the "For Sale" sign and was told that it cost thirty thousand dollars less than ours.

"So cheap?!" Even Junxiong sounded a bit distressed. "At that price, it will be snatched up immediately."

"I heard that the owner lives somewhere else and has been renting it to a female tenant. But, what I wonder is why we've seen so many people going in and out?"

"Apparently she sublets it. A three-bedroom house is just too roomy for one person," my husband replied logically.

At that time, I was expecting our first child. Feeling bored sitting at home, I followed the doctor's order and took frequent walks. One day, by coincidence, I saw a realtor showing the house to some clients. The female tenant opened the door, letting them inside to view the house, and then sat outside on the rocking chair to wait. Slightly rocking the chair, she appeared very comfortable and at ease. Between the ages of thirty and forty, she was the visage of an old spinster, her black silk blouse making her look even more flat and dry. She had a determined look about her, with her chestnut-brown hair trimmed neatly to the ears, an eagle-shaped straight nose, tightly closed lips, and no make-up -- all of which made her look pale and fragile at the same time.

"Hi, good morning!" I greeted her with a smile, as I walked to the front of her home.

"Good morning. I'm Sarah," she said, walking down the steps, introducing herself.

"Welcome to the neighborhood!" she exclaimed with the welcoming look of a hostess.

Wasting no time in asking about our background, she continued, "You came from Taiwan? Hum, I once bought a computer made in Taiwan, it's not bad. You know, I've lived in Berkeley for more than ten years and know this place quite well. If you need any help, just let me know."

"Thank you!" I was quite moved by her concern and said, "But, I'm afraid that you'll be moving out soon."

"I don't think so," she responded somewhat disparagingly, and smiled. "This is our home, how could we move out at a moment's notice? They have to give us enough time to find another place to live."

What she said sounded quite reasonable. Originally, I had planned on going inside to take a look at the house. Yet, after this conversation, I decided not to bother her. I went back to our house and watched from inside our living room.

The clients were a white couple. The woman, her belly slightly expanded, was a fragile-looking pregnant lady. The man, wearing a checkered shirt with rolled-up sleeves and a pair of jeans, was tall and well-built. He constantly extended his huge hands to give aid to his wife, showing his concern. It seemed as if they had immediately fallen in love with the house. After getting into the realtor's car, they were still looking at it, pointing here and there. As the realtor drove them away, the husband repeatedly turned around to see the house.

Two days later, the couple came back again and brought along a little girl, about three or four years old. The man supported his wife with one hand and held onto his daughter with another. He seemed like such a good father, every once in a while bending down to listen to the little girl talk.

A couple days after their last visit, a "Sold" sign was placed on top of the "For Sale" sign.

During the transaction period, I got to know my neighbors. On the right side of No. 15 lived a retired postman. He was very fond of repairing cars, and every two or three days, he'd open the hood of his old Ford that was parked alongside the street and tinker with it for a while. On the left side of No. 15 lived two black brothers, who always smiled, exposing their snow-white teeth. The elder brother, Murray, was a commercial artist. The younger one, Peter, was an elementary school teacher. Neither of them were young any more, but they seemed fond of being single. They frequently dated pretty young black women and lived a flashy bachelor life style.

The people who lived in No. 15 were rather complicated. Sarah, was an adviser at some sort of consulting firm and seldom left the house. Besides her, there was also a couple and an University of California Berkeley student.

In the middle of May, the "Sold" sign was removed, which meant that escrow had been completed. A few days went by, and there was still no sign indicating that anyone was moving in or out. I could not help but be perplexed over the reason. One day I saw Murray mowing his front lawn. At one interval, when he turned off the motor, I went over to him and inquired about it.

"Those people are really hard to deal with," Murray said as he uncharacteristically stopped chewing his gum, his eyes open wide. "Especially Sarah, the Communist."

"A Communist?"

Having lived through several decades of Communist fear in Taiwan, I was really shocked to hear that and unconsciously put my hands over my belly.

Murray immediately got rid of his gum and apologized, "Sorry, Mrs. Ma, I didn't mean to frighten you! What I meant is that she acts like a Communist."

Sarah was, in fact, an activist with a rather stormy past. During the sixties, she participated in UC Berkeley's anti-war movement and was involved in the sit-ins. In the seventies, after the war was over, some of these anti-war activists began trying to actively apply Communist Socialism to the city of Berkeley. The existing rent controls are one of their accomplishments.

"I was sympathetic toward the Vietnam Anti-War Movement, too," Murray said. "If I'd been in Berkeley, I would have joined them. I also support some of their beliefs, such as their concern for the welfare of minorities and the poor, but I just can't agree with their rent-control policy-- especially the unequal rigid control here in Berkeley. Now that I'm a property owner, I personally know how these restrictions really hurt property values and victimize middle-class people like you and I. Sarah is one of those rent-control activists and is extremely aggressive. So, Peter nicknamed her 'The Communist.'"

This conversation with Murray made me more aware of what rent control and restrictions could mean to people like my husband and I. A couple of days later, when Junxiong could not start his car, the retired postman came over to help. As we were talking, I really began to realize the magnitude of the problem.

At first, we had thought that this bargain-priced housing was only suitable for our own use as first time homeowners. Compared to adjacent cities, the acceleration of Berkeley's housing market was very low, so in the future, the only way we could sell the house was to keep the price down.

"All of these benefits are bestowed to us by democracy," the elderly postman sounded cynical as well as sarcastic. "If we continue to practice this kind of democracy, eventually Berkeley will deteriorate, losing everything, except its so-called democracy."

It was believed that Berkeley had a population of less than one hundred twenty thousand. Among them were thirty thousand university students, all of whom could obtain the right to vote after one year of residency in Berkeley. The students constituted nearly half of the eligible voters. Young people, always full of ideas, supported propositions that advocated wealth-sharing or those that benefitted the poor. Their votes were the gambling chips of the elected liberal politicians. However, the students only lived here temporarily, and they did not know much about the long-term effects of city planning. Since cheap rent was their immediate benefit, they strongly supported the issue. Ever since the city's implementation of rent control a few years ago, landlords could hardly make any profits. And their inability to reinvest often left them no choice but to allow the apartments to deteriorate. Worst of all, the situation had brought down the values of all properties in the area. The lousy real estate market in turn affected the city's tax income, making public construction and the city's overall future take a downward turn.

The retired postman pointed out, "Eventually, the students became victims of this fiasco as well. Now they have a tough time finding a place to live."

That's true. Students who left the area during winter and summer breaks could not afford to keep an empty apartment. These cheaper apartments were then snatched and occupied by working people. When school started again, many students were forced to live in adjacent cities, suffering the long-distance commutes and higher rents.

"As long as we live in a real democracy, everything is still hopeful," Junxiong tried to comfort the old man as well as himself. "If the property owners would unite, then together they could change the unfair laws through election."

"I can't see any hope at all," the old man repeatedly shook his gray-haired head. He continued, "The low rent has also attracted quite few jobless people. Haven't you seen those strange looking people on the streets wearing ragged clothes, looking like beggars? Those people have voting power too! They're the backbone of the local Democratic Party. Even if we, the property owners, backed up the Republicans, we would still be overwhelmed by their sheer number. In the long run, I wouldn't be surprised if Berkeley became a slum."

Even Junxiong, always the idealist, was dumbfounded.

From then on, my prior satisfaction of owning a house gradually began to melt away, like a candy bar under the hot sun.

I complained to my husband, "We bought a house in the wrong place."

"Forget about it! It's well enough that we have a place to live. Anyway, we're going back to Taiwan in two years," Junxiong tried to console me. "Berkeley, after all, is the home of the world-renowned UC campus, a gathering place for top-notch intellectuals and scholars. It will be commemorative if our child is born here."

I thought he was right, so I quietly awaited the birth of our baby. Meanwhile, I looked forward to meeting the new mistress of that house across the street, hoping that I would have a friend with whom to raise our child.

One day, about a month or so later, I suddenly heard a stream of ear-piercing noises coming from across the street. I, along with several other housewives, went outside to investigate.

"Open the door! It's the police! Open the door!"

Apparently no one answered the doorbell, and a tall, strongly built police officer forcefully knocked on the door. On the steps not too far behind him, stood the new homeowner, wearing the same checkered shirt and jeans.

The officer continued knocking for a while. The curtains on the windows were drawn closed and no movement came from the inside. Helplessly, he turned to the new owner, and shrugged his shoulders in dismay. Then, he took out a piece of paper from his pocket and posted it on the door with scotch tape. After saying something to the owner, he got in his car and drove away.

The new owner turned around and slowly walked down the front steps of his house. Looking around at us, his face was full of distress and anger.

"Hi everyone! Do you know if Sarah Churchill is at home or not?" he asked us, the curious and nosy neighbors who came and stood around him.

We looked at each other without saying a word, indicating our mutual knowledge of the fact that she had kept her door closed to others as well.

"I'm Ben, Ben Harry, a carpenter," he continued sincerely. "We can't wait any longer to move in here and be your neighbors. You know that my wife is going to have a baby soon. We already bought this house and started to make the payments. But, since we can't move in yet, we still have to pay rent elsewhere. It's a very heavy burden on us!"

"Before you bought this house," asked the retired postman, "didn't you and the seller agree that the tenants would have to move out once escrow closed?"

"The agent told me that the previous owner had notified them of his decision to sell the house, as early as four months ago."

Knitting his thick eyebrows, his honest face perplexed, he sighed, "Who would've dreamed that the tenants would drag something like this out! Living in a house even after it's sold!"

"As far as I know, this house has been rented for the last ten years, and the previous owner was never able to get it back," the old man whispered. "The city government is controlled by leftists! The housing control officers and tenants always stick together. I'm afraid that your house...."

"As soon as I realized something was wrong, I immediately hired a lawyer and filed suit. Now, the marshal himself has come to deliver the 'Eviction Notice', but no one came out to accept it....If she has any problem with moving, I'd like to help," Harry implored, admitting his bad luck. "I'm sorry to bother you. Here's my phone number, if you see her, please tell her to give me a call. If she has any requests, we could talk about it."

Everyone copied down his telephone number. Yet, just by looking at each other's faces, everyone seemed aware that they would be unable to help.

The next day, the Berkeley student moved out. Taking two suitcases and a huge box of books, he drove away in his old Volkswagen Bug. Later I was told that he had finished his final examinations and had gone home for summer vacation. The eviction notice was still posted on the door.

It seemed that Harry intended to make things happen. He came in an old pick-up truck and began to mow the lawn. Avoiding him, Sarah and the other couple left from the back door. Since they continued to act this way, Harry simply started to paint the house. A couple of days later, a policeman came to warn him that the city rent control department had accused him of "disturbing family life and invading privacy," and that he would get himself arrested if he did not leave the premises immediately.

"What?" Harry screamed in anger. "Who has disturbed whom?"

But in the presence of the expressionless police officer, Harry had no alternative but to jump back in his truck and drive away in rage. The scaffold was left standing there, in a corner at the front of the house, a simultaneous symbol of the new owner's steady perseverance and the fruitlessness of his efforts.

Two days later, the couple finally moved out. I was hoping that Sarah would move out, too. However, her light was on every night, and she rarely showed her face during the daytime.

One late afternoon, about a month or so later, Harry appeared on the front lawn again. He shouted out desperately, attracting everyone in the neighborhood to come out and watch.

"Sarah Churchill, come out if you've got any guts. Let everyone be the judge, you S.O.B...."

He banged his fists against the tightly closed door, cursing and yelling endlessly. Every strand of his brown hair was standing on end, as if he had pulled it into that position himself.

"You're occupying our house illegally! You've forced us into being unable to pay rent where we've been staying, now we've been kicked out! Where's your conscience?"

The neighbors looked at him from afar and shook their heads quietly. Knowing that they were unable to help, no one went forward to comfort him.

Receiving no response, he started to kick the door with his feet and then with his head. Unfortunately, none of the tactics he tried were effective. Finally, he staggered on the wooden porch and broke down in bitter tears. Looking at this grown man with tears streaming down his face was like seeing a child suffering a great injustice. When his tears dried up, he started banging and kicking on the door again.

Soon after, the policemen and news reporters came. Harry was put in the police car and driven away.

That night we saw Sarah being interviewed by reporters on television.

"Why didn't you move out after the house was sold?" they asked her.

"Although my landlord notified me of his decision to sell the house, he never received my approval. Besides, I haven't found a comparable place to rent," she shamelessly responded with her truck-load of explanations. She held her hooked nose high enough to hang a bottle on it.

"But no matter what," the news reporter asked her from another angle, "Mr. Harry did pay for this house. Therefore, this is his house, isn't it?"

"This may be *his house*, but it is *my home!*"

Her emphasis of the word *"home"* was deliberately slow and serious, as if it was superlatively holy.

As if he had been hit on the head, the reporter unconsciously turned his face away from her and looked up to the sky, rolling his eyes. Apparently, not knowing how to continue, he ended the interview.

"What kind of law is this!" I said, angrily turning off the television. Thinking of Harry's expectant wife, with a big belly like mine, unable to live in her own house and forced to wander around on the streets, I just could not believe that such a thing could happen in America.

"This is indeed a bad law, a cannibalism of democracy. Still, we can't pass judgement on the entire political system based on one unfortunate incident," Junxiong tried to argue rationally, though admitting that American democracy did not seem so perfect after all.

The most unexpected thing happened the night I was in the hospital giving birth to my son. Harry made the headlines on the evening news.

I had not seen him for three months, and he was almost unrecognizable. Handcuffed and being taken away by two policemen, he was unconcerned with the reporters' microphones. Appearing irretrievable and dissipated, he did not seem to know what he had done wrong. By the looks of his ragged outfit, headful of disheveled hair, unshaven beard, and the leanness of his face, God only knew how long he had been wandering the streets.

"She destroyed my home," he said repeatedly.

According to reporters, Harry waited for Sarah, who was on her way home, and tried to block her way with a gun, beating her with his fists. Right now, she was being treated for injuries at the hospital and refused to be interviewed.

"In recent months, Mrs. Harry has been living in a homeless shelter and, just this morning, was sent to the hospital to deliver her second child."

The reporter continued, "Due to their incapacity to provide care for their first child, she has been taken out of state by her relatives. According to experts, Mr. Harry probably became violent as a result of anxiety caused by family separation. Before bringing any charges against him, the court decided to wait for his psychological report. If the assumption of mental disorder is unfounded, he can be charged with bodily harm, which means he could get a sentence for any where from five to ten years. Having a house is every American's dream. It's a pity that the Harrys' American dream ended on such a tragic note."

That night, after work, Junxiong came to the hospital to see our new-born baby. When he heard about the tragedy of Harry's shattered dreams, he felt it very unfair for Harry and was saddened by the situation. I felt sorry for Junxiong that the sad story had spoiled some of the joy of being a new father.

"Did you buy a house in Berkeley, too?" my wardmate in the hospital asked us sympathetically. She added, "You should blame your agent for it!"

Junxiong only responded with a bitter smile.

"As soon as the baby is one year old," I said to Junxiong, "we must leave Berkeley. I would rather go back to Taiwan."

"O.K., O.K." By now, he was really disheartened. "We didn't anticipate that Berkeley would be like this."

The day I went home with the baby, I saw two rusty cars parked in front of house No. 15. I could hear rock'n' roll music coming from inside the house, as if some kind of celebration was going on. As the evening approached, the entire house was lit up, and from time to time we could hear some kind of queer and clamorous noise.

"What's going on over there? Where did those people come from?" I asked Junxiong.

As I was talking, I heard someone yelling on the street. Junxiong got up to check it out and came back moments later to tell me, "Murray has gone out and complained!"

Thanks to him, I was able to get a good sleep that night.

At noon the next day, I saw Murray coming my way. I immediately went over to him to express my appreciation.

"Don't mention it, Mrs. Ma. Congratulations on your new-born son," he said.

"Thank you! By the way," I inquired, " what happened at No. 15?"

"Um, that Sarah is so vicious!" as he mentioned her name, Murray's snow-white teeth suddenly made a grim chattering sound. "Although she finally moved out, she left the key to a bunch of vagabonds."

As it turned out, there was a law in the city that, after a house remained vacant for a month, allowed the first person who moved in to claim possession of it. They had the right to live there as long as they paid rent and could not be evicted by anyone. These people apparently took advantage of Harry's imprisonment and rushed in to occupy it first.

"If you hear any noise from now on," Murray suggested, "call the police to stop them. We must unite and get them kicked out!"

Being foreigners, Junxiong and I did not want to get involved with the issue, therefore we tolerated it as much as possible. The others' protest only resulted in a short period of peace and quiet, and soon after, they would resume their boisterous uproar. These people were all loafers who did nothing but sleep during the day, while at night, they became energetic, extremely wild and noisy, and disturbed everyone's sleep. Murray insisted that some of them used drugs, and said that he could often smell unpleasant odors in his backyard. Whenever he was fed up with the noise, the retired mailman would also summon the police. However, reporting to the police could only ease the problem temporarily, not solve it permanently. The most lamentable thing was that we had to constantly hear them sing the lyrics from "The Internationale," which went "We have nothing, what we have lost is only the shackle."

One night, they even dared to light firecrackers in the backyard, producing a current of non-stop, thunder-like noise. My son was frightened awake by the noise and started to cry incessantly, not even baby formula or sweet juice could help quiet him.

"You just can't play with firecrackers like this in America," I angrily persuaded my husband. "Call the police!"

While Junxiong was dialing the telephone, we suddenly heard several gunshots.

After the sound of gunfire ceased, we emerged from hiding in the living room darkness and quietly lifted up a piece of the curtain and peeked outside. Under the dim glow of the street light, we saw Murray, with his back to us, frozen in the middle of the street, holding an automatic handgun. His shoulders were shaking as he tried to catch his breath. There were several holes shot through the windows of No. 15, and the glass was shattered like spider webs. Inside the house, the lights and shadows oscillated wildly along with the noise of yelling and screaming, creating a chaotic flurry of confusion.

While we were wondering what we should do next, the sound of piercing sirens emerged from afar. Before long, police cars and their flashing lights all arrived on the scene. Murray gave up his weapon and was immediately led into the police car. From beginning to end, we did not hear any sound of resistance from him.

The gunfire also woke Junxiong from his American dream. Soon after the incident, a job offer arrived from Taibei. Before our baby was one month old, we hurriedly erected a "For Sale" sign in front of our house.

Twenty Thousand Dollars Less....

Editor's Notes:

The technique of interpreting illusion as a theme is by no means a unique convention in modern time. However, Chen Ruoxi's creation of this supercilious, materialistic, and purposefully banal title is perhaps an ironic prefiguration and opportunity for her tongue-in-cheek authorial commentary on the illusive "values" of the American Dream. Thus, the descriptive word "less" may well constitute one of the story's most relevant and meaningful literary components.

To many aspiring immigrants from Taiwan, America is the "Promised Land", a place with endless opportunities for material gain and social advancement. Based on this conviction, many sell all of their possessions in order to come join their family members living in the United States. Yet, the unfortunate truth is that this "Promised Land" is not for everyone, nor can it be molded by one's own imagination. In "Twenty Thousand Dollars Less....", the protagonist, the elderly Mrs. Ke, faces the myths behind immigrant life in America. Like many other immigrants, she must come to terms with the distinctions between reality and myth before the folly of ignorant dreams and beliefs confines her to the negative accommodations of an alien life devoid of meaningful communication and significance.

TWENTY THOUSAND DOLLARS LESS. . . .[1]

Firmly she said, "We had already agreed to the amount of three hundred thousand dollars. This is such a sacrifice! It's impossible, I can't reduce it another twenty thousand dollars....How much is it in Taiwanese dollars?"

In the midst of her disappointment, she suddenly could not convert the figure herself.

Her realtor, also from Taiwan, was very familiar with the exchange rate. The figure immediately came out of his mouth, "Seven million Taiwanese dollars."

"That's all?" she asked unhappily.

Hearing her agent voice the amount out loud, she felt her heart sink in dismay. With her eyebrows furled tightly, she responded, "Ten years ago, I bought it for eight million Taiwanese dollars."

Like a bone lodged in her throat, there was another unspeakable and disheartening fact she had never mentioned. In order to buy this apartment building, she had sold her mansion and land in Dajia. Then, she had

---

[1] "Twenty Thousand Dollars Less. . . ." (*Bu renshu liangwanyuan de hua*) was translated by Hsin-sheng C. Kao with the permission of the author, and is published here in English for the first time. The story is based on its first appearance in *Mingbao yuekan* (Mingbao Monthly), no. 12 (1989): 75-78.

entrusted her friend to exchange the profit into US dollars through the black market at the ratio of forty Taiwanese dollars to one US dollar. It would be impossible to buy back the same property for that amount of money. It was a cold reminder that in her anxiousness to come to America and live with her son, she had exhausted all of her resources.

"Cheer up, Mrs. Ke, the appreciation of the Taiwanese dollar caught everyone by surprise," said the realtor, appraising his client carefully as if trying to discern her every thought.

Recounting his own personal experience, he continued, "If I hadn't emigrated to the United States five years ago, my apartment building in Taibei would now be worth more than ten million Taiwanese dollars. Fate has its own turn. If you want to make money nowadays, you have to go to Taiwan!"

"Indeed, that's true!" Mrs. Ke replied sourly.

She continued, "Still, I can't believe the buyer wants to keep on cutting the price like this. He doesn't even need to make any improvements on the building. And, besides that, he's going to pay the full amount in cash. It's such an easy transaction for both parties!"

"You might as well think it over anyway, Mrs. Ke," the realtor insisted. "Please, call me anytime."

As was customary in their native Taiwan, she politely walked him out to the apartment gate. Moreover, she was thinking that she could use the opportunity to get a little fresh air and to see other people.

It was a fine weekend morning. On the street, the hustle and bustle of the crowd and the noise of the traffic seemed to be livelier than usual. The most riveting sight was all of the children playing on the sidewalks, riding their bicycles, or kicking balls--the stream of their laughter filling up the entire block. She glanced up and down the street. Among the various apartment buildings, hers was the only one with a "For Sale" sign. Under the bright autumn sunshine, the sign's lonely appearance suddenly looked very unpleasant to her eyes.

"I think," said Mrs. Ke, pointing at the sign, "you can remove it now."

Her agent hesitated for a moment, then took off his jacket and started to take the sign down.

"San Francisco's real estate market skyrocketed the last couple years, so the current drop in sales prices actually reflects a normal trend," said the agent, as he pulled up the wooden sign.

"Having lived in Berkeley so many years, you should know that rent control is very strict, probably unequaled!" he continued. "As a consequence, real estate prices are affected. Would you believe that suggestions were made again this spring asking state legislators to restrict housing prices? Of course, this is impossible, but, it succeeded in frightening away property owners, many of whom immediately put their property up for sale. Now the market's saturated. Just trying to sell your building, our company has advertised at least fifteen times during the last four months....The demand for apartment buildings in Berkeley is nonexistent. Truthfully, you're lucky to have a client making an offer, hardly anyone is interested in them."

Still unwilling to completely refuse the offer, she forced herself to say, "I'll think it over again."

After seeing him off, she felt somewhat guilty for spoiling his efforts to make a deal on the only offer she'd received the entire summer. Perhaps she was being overly cautious. Yet, because of the lesson she had learned from her hasty purchase of this apartment, putting the building up for sale scared the daylights out of her.

It all started when she heard her son was going to be transferred from New York to San Francisco. Immediately, she flew from Taibei to San Francisco and looked for a piece of property. In her excitement, she made a down payment after three days of house hunting. The Cantonese realtor, who was introduced to her by a mutual friend, had only stressed the low price of the apartment building. Rent control was never mentioned.

She became disillusioned for the first time after coming to America when she discovered that rent was controlled by the city of Berkeley, not by supply and demand. Two years later this became even more disturbing to her when, after not being able to get along with her daughter-in-law, she decided to move into her apartment complex. However, none of the tenants in the six-unit complex were willing to move out. The reality of her situation made her realize how horrible rent control could be. Her son, who was still alive at the time, hired a lawyer to handle the negotiations for her. Finally, upon agreeing to compensate the tenants, she was able to get one unit back for herself.

          *   *   *

"Good morning, Mrs. Ke!" said the elderly postman, stopping for his daily delivery. Before opening the six mailboxes, he handed her two letters first.

"Hey, not bad, the 'For Sale' sign has finally been removed."

The personable black man always stopped to chat with her. He continued, "Congratulations on selling your apartments."

"No, no," she tried to say, but her poor English would not allow her to explain anything. All she could do was to give him a dry smile and shake her head forcefully.

"Not yet? Oh, that's too bad!" Before departing, he comforted her good-naturedly, "Don't be discouraged. You'll sell it, it just takes time."

After thanking him, she stood in front of the mail box and opened her letters. Even with her poor English, she knew that these two "letters" were so-called "junk mail"--a loan application form and an advertisement. She was always the first person to check the mail, though she knew quite well that people seldom sent her letters. Nowadays, her younger brother's family preferred calling her long distance; and, whenever there was a holiday or a birthday, her daughter-in-law would send her a card, signing her grandson's name, Mingzong. It was now two weeks before Thanksgiving, and thirty days before her birthday--so, unless she called Mingzong herself, there would be no news from him.

A difference of twenty thousand dollars, should I sell it and return to Taiwan? she asked herself silently, her feet feeling as if they were glued to the cement in front of the apartment building. She recalled her younger brother's words over the phone not so long ago, "No matter what the price is, Sis, sell it. The whole family is waiting for you to come back and celebrate your birthday! You have to be here for the elections. There's so much going on, it's really exciting."

She had been considering the idea of retiring to Dajia for a while now. After her son was killed in a traffic accident, her daughter-in-law remarried and moved to Boston with her grandson. The idea of moving still lingered on, but she had not taken any action, partly because of financial constraints, and partly due to her own laziness. More importantly, because she had emigrated to the United States so enthusiastically just years before, she felt that if she were to return to Taiwan by herself, she could not handle the disillusionment she had suffered. There is such a discrepancy between hopes and reality!

Last year, after her younger brother commissioned the construction of a twelve-story apartment building, she began to seriously think about moving. He had taken back three stories for himself to rent out and, among those, reserved a two-bedroom suite for her. She was moved by the generosity and sincerity of his offer.

Since it was her own family, she would not have to pay rent. Yet, she could not allow her brother to pay for her living expenses, too. Thus, her only hope rested with the money she would get from selling this apartment building.

In spite of the world-wide increase in housing costs, only Berkeley's had plunged downward. Owning the property for ten years without making any profit was already a disappointment, and now she was having to consider an offer that was even lower than her original purchase price...this was a hard one to swallow.

I should just forget about it and live here until I die. The rental income is enough to sustain my daily necessities, she thought to herself. She looked up at the blue sky and sighed softly. Drifting in the boundless sky, she saw only a few patches of closely knit clouds and suddenly felt the urge to cry. Alone, without any relatives, and not knowing English well enough to communicate-- it seemed that her later years would be even more isolated and lonely than those few patches of clouds floating in the sky. Only in her dreams could she pursue the scenery of her beloved hometown, Dajia, and the gaiety of a houseful of relatives and friends.

The most agonizing worry was her grandson. Alas! How difficult it was to see him. Last year, she had gone to the trouble of flying to Boston to visit Mingzong and ended up staying in a hotel room arranged by the boy's mother, who simply dropped him off there and hurriedly left for work. They had to call a taxi whenever they went anywhere. It wasn't the taxi fare, but the trouble of waiting for one that had bothered her. Before her departure, the child guilelessly asked her, "Granny, when will you come back to see me again?"

"Next year," she responded, though she actually had no idea when her next visit would be.

Coming downstairs to get her mail, the elderly lady from Hong Kong politely greeted her landlady in Cantonese, "Good morning, Mrs. Ke!"

Wearing heavy make-up, she was dressed in a strikingly daring, sexy outfit. It was a crimson dress with a collar that opened widely to reveal her bare, wrinkled neck--reminding Mrs. Ke of the dry banks of the Dajia river, all rugged and weathered.

"Good morning to you too, Mrs. He," she said, trying to hide her disapproval by offering a compliment instead. "You dress yourself fancier and fancier everyday now!"

Mrs. He was so overjoyed to hear the compliment that, when she smiled, every detail of her face, wrinkles, gold incisor and all, was mercilessly revealed. "Old Chap Zhang is taking me to San Francisco to see a movie called 'The Old Well.' I heard it won some kind of film award."

"Old Zhang is really very nice to you," commented Mrs. Ke. While paying the compliment, Mrs. Ke had, in reality, mixed feelings of revulsion and envy, unjustifiable and despicable.

Mrs. He, whose children lived in Los Angeles, had lived in an one-bedroom apartment for quite some time now. She was about the same age as Mrs. Ke and could be considered a friend as well. Mrs. He never put any savings in her own name so that she could live on welfare. Even her monthly rent of one-hundred-eighty dollars was paid by the city government. Four years ago, she was introduced by a friend to a film director from mainland China. Soon afterwards, they began to live together, with no intention of marrying each other. From time to time, Old Zhang would work in a restaurant, but Mrs. He had lived off the tax-payers' money for years. She did not even have to pay a dime for her medical expenses.

In contrast, the now childless Mrs. Ke had an apartment building that she could not sell. Furthermore, as a property owner, she did not have a chance of getting any welfare from the government. Mrs. He's one-bedroom apartment would rent for six-hundred dollars a month if it were situated in San Francisco. Yet, because of the restrictive rent controls in Berkeley, the rent had only gone up fifty dollars in the past ten years. Then there was inflation. Mrs. Ke's real income earned as landlord had actually lessened because of it.

On the other hand, inflation did not affect Mrs. He at all. Welfare was always adjusted to meet the cost of living. No wonder Mrs. He would boast from time to time, "Now, I depend on the American government to support me during my final days, and when I'm dead, I can count on them to bury me."

Exactly! Unless Mrs. He died, Mrs. Ke could never get the apartment back; and even when she did get it back, she could live in it herself, but could not increase the rent for another tenant. No matter what Mrs. Ke tried to plan, ever since she had become a landlord in Berkeley, she had been doomed to suffer defeat. No wonder the one-time Communist Party Member, Old Zhang, exclaimed: "Berkeley is truly the most democratic city in America, but, in China, this is what we called socialism!"

Such unfairness is called American Democracy? Whenever Mrs. Ke thought about it she would sneer to herself, *This is even worse than Taiwan!*

"Mrs. Ke, have you noticed that the black woman on the third floor is pregnant again?" Mrs. He made a gesture of a big stomach.

"Really? I thought she had just gained some weight." Having said that, Mrs. Ke's eyes suddenly sparkled with a light of hope, "This time they'll have to move to their own house rather than stay here!"

The couple, Mr. and Mrs. Lincoln, both worked as custodians at the UC Berkeley campus. Since living in Mrs. Ke's building, they had gotten married and had a child. It was probably because of Berkeley's low rents that they rented out the house they had purchased four years ago in the neighboring city, Oakland, and lived here instead. The Lincolns were nice people and always paid their rent on time. The only regret was that they had a drinking problem. Whenever they were intoxicated, they became very noisy. Mrs. Ke could not wait for them to move.

"When the new baby arrives, the two-bedroom apartment will be too crowded for a family of four," exclaimed Mrs. Ke happily.

When Mrs. He heard Mrs. Ke saying "too crowded," her own guilty conscience prompted her to change the subject, "Well, it's getting late, Old Zhang and I have to go."

*　　　　*　　　　*

After parting from Mrs. He, Mrs. Ke returned to her apartment and put on an apron to prepare lunch. Almost immediately, she heard a knock on the door. it was the Lincoln's daughter, Jenny, standing there holding a note in her hand.

"Jenny, how's your mom? I heard that she...um, that she... baby?"

Mrs. Ke did not take the time to read the note that Jenny handed to her. She was busy trying to communicate with her by imitating the look of a pregnant woman.

"　ᵔh! Yeah!" Jenny responded excitedly.

"(　! So you...move out?"

Unable to understand her landlady's English, the child nodded her head in confusion. Overjoyed, Mrs. Ke gave Jenny two chocolate candies and sent her off. Then she sat down and put on her glasses to read the note.

It did not read like a moving-out notice. The more she read, the more she could tell that it was not what she had expected. Jenny's mother repeatedly mentioned the refrigerator. Could it mean that something was wrong with the refrigerator?

Immediately, she went upstairs with the note in her hand to see Mrs. He, who was just about to leave with Old Zhang.

"Do me a favor, could you please read this note for me?" Mrs. Ke asked.

"I'll try," Old Zhang said.

Taking the note from her hand, he adjusted his glasses and started to read it carefully.

"Mrs. Lincoln says that the refrigerator is not working well," he translated for her, word by word. "The back corner is always too cold and has frozen her vegetables several times. They had the repairman check it over already. They were told that it would cost more to repair the old one than to buy a new one. She suggests that you buy a large-size refrigerator, because soon they'll have a new family member."

Mrs. Ke was dumbfounded and could only murmur repetitively, "Not moving out...they're not moving out...."

"Moving out? I don't think so," the well-mannered director said trying to analyze the situation for her. "They want you to purchase a new large-size refrigerator. That means they intend to stay here indefinitely."

Tactfully pulling at the corner of Old Zhang's sleeve, Mrs. He interrupted, "Of course, you'll fix the refrigerator if it needs repair. It may even be reasonable to ask for a new one. But, they're going too far demanding a new and larger one. According to the rent laws, Mrs. Ke, you don't have to replace it with a larger one."

Pointing at the kitchen, Old Zhang suggested, "You can buy a medium-size refrigerator like ours. It should only cost you five or six hundred dollars."

"Well...it's not a problem of money...," Mrs. Ke uttered incoherently. "If they keep on having babies...."

"That's right!" exclaimed Mrs. He, expressing her sympathy.

Clucking her tongue through her crimson lips, she continued, "A quiet apartment like ours....Now, we'll have to listen to a baby crying for food! How irritating! Don't you agree, Mrs. Ke?"

Mrs. Ke forced a smile on her face without making any comment. Inside she thought, *Since you, Mrs. He, are supported by the government and a live-in companion, how could you understand my feelings? Everyone who lives in this apartment has found loopholes. And, only I am trapped in this hopeless dilemma.* Yet, she did not want any cheap sympathy. Apologizing for disturbing them, she left immediately.

310

As she walked down the stairs, her feelings became as heavy as her footsteps. With every descending step she took, her previous determination to hold on to the apartments became weaker and weaker. She knew if she did not take this offer of twenty thousand dollars less than her original purchase price, she would be stuck playing the role of a philanthropist. She would have to postpone her plan for a joyful and friend-filled retirement in Taiwan. *Having lived in America for ten years, how many thousands of dollars have I lost already? Is it worthwhile to waste the rest of my life here.*

Returning to her kitchen, she resolutely tore up the note and threw the pieces into the trash can. Then, she phoned her realtor. When his "Hello" came on the line, a rare smile appeared at the corner of her lips.

Ah Lan's Decision

Editor's Notes:

Spring of 1989 was a time of hope in China, a vertiginous period of democratic fervor, both humanistic in its values and spontaneous in its methods. In Beijing's Tiananmen Square, scenes of flags and placards waving in the air, hunger strikers, and throngs of supporters became a familiar sight to the world. People from all walks of life huddled together to defend Tiananmen Square, dedicating their young lives and hot blood. As one student leader, Chai Ling, so aptly summarized: "Our heads can be crushed and our blood shed, but we do not intend to lose the People's Square to the military. Every last person here will fight to the very end...."

On June 4th of 1989, the hardline government of Deng Xiaoping and Li Peng ordered the brutal military crackdown on the weaponless demonstrators. The world watched with horror and condemnation as this tragedy unfolded before their eyes. Using this historically tragic event as the backdrop for "Ah Lan's Decision," Chen acts as a staunch defender of the student democracy movement, denouncing the brutality of the military regime in China. In doing so, two heterogeneous themes emerge in the story, both dealing with failure. The first is Ah Lan's failing marriage, and the other deals with Ah Lan's employees' failing dreams of democracy for China. However, in confronting these problems, the real test of courage and commitment for the characters, and even oneself, is whether or not one can supersede failure and rise to a higher calling that is not governed by personal interest, beyond the dilemma of the self.

AH LAN'S DECISION[1]

Knowing the business hours of the restaurant, he called her at the very moment her last customers were paying their tab.

"Ah Lan, are you going to make it to the three o'clock appointment at the attorney's office?"

She did not say anything. Instead, she pressed her head against the receiver and concentrated on counting the money with both hands.

"Things have gone too far. Ah Lan, we're too old for this! Let's part from each other in a friendly manner...."

She understood her husband's rationale. Their newly engaged son had already declared that he would not interfere with his parents' divorce. Not only that, she was going to be a grandmother soon, it would not be commendable to settle the matter in court.

Her husband had been living with the mainland woman for half a year now, and had voluntarily renounced his share of the restaurant. So, in reality, the dissolution of their marriage was already complete. However, if she didn't go to the lawyer's office to formally sign the divorce papers, she would

---

[1] "Ah Lan's Decision" (Ah Lan de gushi) was translated by Hsin-sheng C. Kao with the permission of the author, and is published here in English for the first time.

inevitably end up in court. Under the circumstances, making a futile public appearance would not result in any gain for her whatsoever. She had promised to go twice before, and missed both appointments. It was as if she had done it out of spite.

"After the Tiananmen Square Massacre, it was impossible for her to return to China. You see...," her husband continued.

Ah Lan let the crisp sound of the cash register answer his question and smiling, she reminded her customers, "Please come back again!"

For a second, her self-proclaimed heart of steel felt weak, listening to his strangely remote, soft whispering; and, simultaneously, she felt a tinge of pain. While she was deciding whether to firmly refuse him or to drag it out, a muffled sound filled her ear. He had already hung up.

Dumbfounded and dejected, she hung up the receiver. Seeing that her customers had left, she arranged the money in the till and locked up the cash register. At last, she found time to leave the counter.

One by one, the cooks and busboys came out and sat together at the big round table closest to the kitchen. Some of them brought newspapers, while others poured tea--they began to enjoy their one hour break before dinner. As usual, Ah Lan joined in and sat next to Mingmei. Among her seven or eight employees, Mingmei was the only waitress; and, at times like this, they always sat together.

"Mrs. Wei, have some tea, please!" Waiter Little Zhao immediately poured some tea and handed it to her.

"Thank you!"

Ah Lan took a drink of the tea and as she swallowed, her throat contracted painfully. She suddenly realized how thirsty she had let herself get.

Mingmei always knew how to make the best use of her break time. She took out her compact mirror and a tiny comb to fix her newly permed hair. While she was looking at her hair, she softly asked Ah Lan in

Taiwanese, "When will you be leaving for your appointment?"

"I don't know!" Ah Lan retorted.

Afraid that she was not strong enough to sustain her will-power, Ah Lan shifted her body slightly and used her shoulder to block Mingmei's gaze.

Swallowing another sip of tea to calm herself, Ah Lan raised her voice and directed a question toward Old Zhang, who sat across from her reading the newspaper. "Broadcaster, what's the news today?"

Old Zhang, a lecturer from an university in the Hobei Province, had been sent to the United States to study for six months. He now worked full-time in the kitchen as a busboy. Originally he had only planned to work three months, long enough to earn the money to buy a color television and VCR to take back to China. Unexpectedly, soon after he had started to work, the Chinese government had sent in the army to quash the student democracy movement. Though the United States was allowing the Chinese scholars to extend their visas, Old Zhang could not make up his mind whether or not to stay. It was for this reason that he was more concerned about current affairs than anyone else. Everyday he diligently read each and every word from several different Chinese newspapers that were sold in the restaurant. Thus, he was the most knowledgeable about current events. The head chef, from Hong Kong, was too lazy to read the newspaper and had given Old Zhang the nick-name, "Broadcaster."

"It's all bad news," he said putting his glasses down along with the newspaper. Old Zhang answered her as if he blamed himself for having to report bad news.

"The Beijing government has, again, executed more people. Now it seems they are practicing a "quick judgement, quick execution" policy. What seems even worse is for them to do this and think they can hide it from the world."

The cook, who took every spare moment to doze off, now opened his sleepy eyes to ask about the fate of a captured student movement leader, "What has happened to Wang Dan?"

Ah Lan anxiously added, "Is he going to be secretly killed?..."

She had never before taken an interest in mainland affairs. Only after having marital problems had she started to pay attention to what was happening. In recent years, the students that came from Taiwan were usually loaded with money and rarely needed to work in restaurants to supplement their income. Reluctantly, she was forced to hire all of her employees from mainland China.

It was under these circumstances that she came to have daily contact with mainlanders and was gradually able to comprehend the situation on the mainland. It helped her face her troubled marriage with a calm and steady attitude. After the Tiananmen Square Massacre, she listened to the news daily. Her sympathy toward mainlanders and the students was deeply aroused. Among the arrested student leaders, Wang Dan was the one about whom she was most concerned. It was said that Wang had contacted a Taiwanese reporter (*referring to Mr. Huang Debei*). But, because the reporter's rental car was followed, Wang Dan's identity was exposed. Subsequently, he fell into the hands of the secret police. Coming from the same province as the reporter, Ah Lan felt somewhat guilt-stricken by this.

"Indeed, there is some news, but it's not necessarily that reliable. A Hong Kong newspaper reports that he has been punished. It's said that he took a severe beating," Old Zhang replied slowly, choosing his words carefully as if he were handling the most fragile and fine china.

Little Zhao, who was young, unsettled, and short-tempered, exclaimed pessimistically, "I don't think Wang has much of a chance. He'll probably be executed."

"Excuse me," the Chef politely nodded to his boss, his tone changing to a complaining one. "Just chasing after a story, this Taiwanese reporter has really stirred up a lot of trouble!"

"That's not necessarily true," Old Zhang said. Ruffling his tousled short hair, he presented his opposite view in an orderly manner, "Wang Dan and the other students were engaged in a peaceful demonstration. If Wang was sentenced to death, it definitely won't win over the hearts of the people. With the entire world watching, the Communist government wouldn't dare do such a thing."

"Don't forget the taxi driver," Mingmei said, looking at the others for sympathy. "He was also involved in the incident. That's really bad luck."

With the exception of Ah Lan and the Chef, the mainlanders had little sympathy for the taxi driver.

"It's obvious that the Taiwanese do not understand mainlanders. The problem, in fact, originated with the taxi driver," Old Zhang said, offering his analysis and judgement in an absolute tone. "It is said that foreign reporters, especially the Taiwanese, were closely watched by the secret police. The taxi driver, who had been driving for this Taiwanese reporter for half a year, either worked with the police, or was tailed by them. By making contact with him, the people who tried to escape were eventually arrested."

The Taiwanese do not understand mainlanders. This statement had struck Ah Lan like an invisible dagger pointed at her heart. It was quite true that it was her idea to hire the woman from China. Ah Lan's husband had not approved of it, simply because the applicant was over forty and not suitable for a waitress job. Once she had been hired, Ah Lan groomed her with the proper clothes and helped make her presentable and attractive. Who would have ever thought that, in the end, she would steal Ah Lan's husband from her. Ah Lan had no one else to blame but herself for this ungrateful act.

"She is not staying with me because I have a green card," her husband once defended the woman. "Married or not, we would still live together."

Ah Lan was originally waiting to see how long they would live together without getting married. Eventually his story lost consistency. Just look how meek and timid he was, begging her for a divorce! She must have really swept him off his feet. Ah Lan was beginning to suspect that if she insisted on dragging it out much longer, she might become the spiteful "third party" herself.

"Oh, here's some good news!" Little Zhao shouted excitedly, pointing at the newspaper. "There's a Chinese-American lawyer who's agreed to help the Chinese couple seeking political asylum. He's even doing it free of charge."

Mingmei cast a quick glance at Ah Lan and then asked Little Zhao contemptibly, "Are they real refugees or alleged ones? In Japan, there are quite a few mainlanders who pretend to be Vietnamese Boat People. They probably couldn't have survived in Tokyo, so they moved to San Francisco!"

Evidently, Mingmei was afraid that the word "couple" would annoy Ah Lan. Actually, Ah Lan did not care about it too much. As a matter of fact, her husband had made a good point. Their marriage had already hit rock bottom, creating the opportunity for a third party to step into their relationship.

Ah Lan turned around to face her employees and said gracefully, "If they're really a pair of lovers, then I hope that they'll get married soon."

"Sure they will!" Mingmei responded, encouraging her with a smile.

After she had broken up with her husband, the entire restaurant staff had changed, with one exception. That was Mingmei, who knew what had happened. Mingmei's previous husband had fallen in love with a white woman. After the divorce was finalized, she had come to work for the restaurant on a temporary basis. During the past few years, they had given her several raises so that she would continue working there. It was because of her own past experience that Mingmei was able to advise Ah Lan, "If your husband wants to leave, you can't do anything about it. If you can get through this divorce, your life will be much happier."

Ah Lan had managed the restaurant since she immigrated from Taiwan. After more than ten years of struggling, her son had grown up and left home, and her husband had left her for another woman. Fortunately, she had Mingmei to keep her company. Otherwise, she would have suffered from severe loneliness and isolation. She usually listened to Mingmei's suggestions; but, on the subject of her marital problems, she could not be swayed.

"It's sad that Chinese people are forced to go to other countries to become refugees," Old Zhang said helplessly, scratching at his hair.

"Don't feel so sad. They have to keep on trying, and sooner or later the situation will have to improve for the better," Mingmei said, comforting Old Zhang. "Look at the Taiwanese people, they're no longer refugees."

Turning to Little Zhao, Mingmei changed the subject, "Isn't there any other news?"

"There's going to be a music concert at San Francisco State tomorrow night," Little Zhao said, turning to the local news. "It's sponsored by Chinese students from all of the California State Universities. The proceeds from the ticket sales will be donated to support the Democracy Movement. This is great! Professors and graduates from the Shanghai Music Conservatory will perform for free."

Being a native of Shanghai himself, Little Zhao read the news with uncontrollable elation. Yet when he came to the performance time, 7:30, he became subdued.

Old Zhang frowned, "I know there isn't anyone to substitute for me."

He continued dispassionately, "As for the Democracy Movement, the money doesn't help much. But I'd still like to show my sincerity to the people who have already escaped from China by making some kind of donation."

"I'd like to make a donation, too," followed Little Zhao.

Suddenly Little Zhao's face lit up with a wonderful idea, "How about this? On the day of the concert, I'll come to work as usual, but I'll donate every penny I make during the day."

The highest earning Chef added, "I'll be glad to donate my one-day earnings to help the mainlanders!"

"I'd like to pledge mine as well," Mingmei conferred, raising her hand.

Immediately tearing a page from the order book that was in his pocket, Little Zhao jotted down the amount that each person was going to donate.

"I'd like to follow our Chef's example and make a contribution."

Saying this, Ah Lan stood up firmly and continued, "I'm willing to give more to support our mainland people."

With a look of tacit understanding, she glanced at Mingmei and then looked at her watch. *It's 2:30.* She still had enough time to get to the attorney's office.

As Ah Lan prepared to leave, Mingmei lauded her with a warm smile and exclaimed, "Isn't it a great feeling to finally let it go!"

SHORT BIOGRAPHY OF CHEN RUOXI

Chen Ruoxi (Chen Jo-hsi), born in 1938, is the pen-name of Chen Xiumei, who also has published in English under the name Lucy Chen. She was born in a rural area of Taibei, Taiwan, to a working class family that had been for five generations Taiwanese. Her father and grandfather were carpenters and her mother was from the peasant class. The family moved to Taibei before she began junior high school. An extremely intelligent child, in 1951 she took the entrance examination and was admitted to the most prestigious Taiwanese girl's school, The First Middle School of Taibei for Girls. In 1957, she entered National Taiwan University, where she majored in English Literature. That same year she made her literary debut in the *Wenxue zazhi (The Literary Review)*, which subsequently published half a dozen of her short stories written during her undergraduate days in Taiwan. During her junior year, Chen Ruoxi and a few of her literary friends, Bai Xianyong (Pai Hsien-yung), Li Oufan (Leo Ou-fan Lee), Liu Shaoming (Joseph S. M. Lau), Ye Weilian (Wai-lim Yip), and others, co-founded the *Xiandai wenxue (Modern Literature)*, and served as one of its editors. After receiving her B.A. in 1961, she worked for a year before deciding to further her education in the United States. In 1962, she commenced studies in English Literature at Mount Holyoke College. That same year, she published her first book in English entitled *Spirit Calling (Zhaohun)*. It contains a number of her original works written in English as well as her translations of some of her Chinese short stories.

The following year, she transferred to Johns Hopkins University, where she studied English Literature and Creative Writing. It was there that she met Duan Shiyao (Tuann Shih-yao), a graduate student from Taiwan, who was studying engineering. They were married in 1964, and she received her M.A. in 1965. Shortly after her husband finished his Ph.D., the couple, fired by patriotic zeal, left the United States in October of 1966 to repatriate to the People's Republic of China. Unfortunately, their dream of serving the motherland during its reconstruction was shattered by the upheavals of the Great Proletarian Cultural Revolution.

They remained in Beijing waiting for teaching assignments from 1966 to 1968, and in 1967 she gave birth to their first son. It was not until 1969 that Chen Ruoxi was assigned to teach English at the Hydraulic College in Nanjing, and in 1970, she gave birth to their second son. Finally, after seven traumatic years in China, the family requested and subsequently was granted permission to leave. They arrived in Hong Kong in November 1973, and the following year, Chen Ruoxi resumed her writing after nearly a decade of silence.

In 1974, the family moved to Vancouver, British Columbia, where Chen Ruoxi worked in a bank and continued her writing. Most of her stories about the Cultural Revolution were written between 1974 and 1978. Then, in 1979, she accepted a position as a researcher for the Institute of Chinese Studies at the University of California at Berkeley, and made Berkeley her permanent residence. During the last few years, Chen Ruoxi has devoted herself to writing and has occasionally spoken as a guest lecturer at several universities throughout the United States, as well as in Hong Kong, Taiwan, and the People's Republic of China. Currently, she is the Chief-Editor of

Square Quarterly (Guangchang), a magazine for Chinese exile literature, and serves as the President of the Overseas' Chinese Women Writers' Association.

Chen Ruoxi's best-known story collection, *The Execution of Mayor Yin and Other Great Cultural Proletarian Revolution Stories* (1976), has been translated into eight languages. She has published seven other collections of her short stories, five novels, seven prose and essay collections, and several volumes of critical writings and translation.

GLOSSARY[1]

I. Titles and Main Characters of the Short Stories:

"Ah Lan de fengxian" ("Ah Lan's Decision)	《《阿蘭的奉獻》》
Ah Lan (Mrs. Wei)	阿蘭
Mingmei	明美
Old Zhang	老張
Little Zhao	小趙黄德北
Huang Debei	
"Burenshu liangwanyuan de hua" ("Twenty Thousand Dollars Less...."	《《不認輸兩萬元的話》》
Mrs. Ke	柯太太
Mrs. He	柯明宗
Ke Mingzong	
Old Zhang	老張
"Guizhou nuren" ("The Woman from Guizhou')	《《貴州女人》》
Weng Dehe	翁德和
Shuiyue (Mrs. Weng)	水月
Abing	阿炳
Weng Wanfen	翁婉芬
Xiluo	西洛
"Ke zi guxiang lai" ("Guest from the Homeland")	《《客自故鄉來》》
Luo Shaoyong	駱少勇

---

[1] The following section only contains Chinese names, titles, and proper Chinese terminology that appears in this collection.

Wang Zhi	汪直
Guan Li	關力
Old Bai	老白
"Luka" ("Green Card")	《綠卡》
Lin Tongfu	林同富
Xiaomei	小妹
Maomao	毛毛
Ma Rongsheng	馬榮勝
Manager Shen	沈經理
"Lukou" ("The Crossroads")	《路口》
Yu Wenxiu	余文秀
Fang Hao	方豪
Ading	阿叮
Yu Wenjuan	余文娟
Wu Weixiong	吳偉雄
Consul Gao	高領事
"Suishi nide fangzi, queshi wode jia" ("It's Your House, But It's My Home!")	《雖是你的房子，確是我的家》
Ma Junxiong	馬俊雄
Mrs. Ma	馬太太
Sarah Churchill	莎拉•邱其兒
Ben Harry	本•哈利
Murray	莫瑞
Peter	彼德
Retired Postman	退修的郵差
"Suyue de chuxi" ("Suyue's New Year's Eve")	《素月的除夕》
Gui Wuqi	桂梧奇
Suyue (Mrs. Gui)	素月〔桂太太〕
Dabao	大寶

Xiaobao	小寶
Mrs. Hong	洪太太
Zhu Ming	朱銘
"Xiangzhe Taipingyang bi'an" ("On the Other Side of the Pacific")	《向著太平洋彼岸》
Su Deqing	蘇德清
Lin Yizhen	林以貞
Su Zhong	蘇中
Su Tai	蘇台
Qiao Jianguang	喬健光
Su Deming	蘇德明
Zhao E	昭峨
Su Lina	蘇莉娜
Lin Yilie	林以烈
Wu Chunfa	巫春發
"Yujian mosheng nuzi de natian shangwu" ("Morning Encounter with a Stranger: A Monologue")	《遇見陌生女子的那天上午》
Mrs. Bu, Senior	卜老太太
Bu Zhiming	卜志明
Annie (Mrs. Bu)	安麗〔卜太太〕
Bu Kaiming (Cadi)	卜凱明〔凱弟〕
May	梅兒
Jenny	珍妮

II. Terminology or Names Appearing in the Short Stories:

Beijing	北京
Chen Yingzhen	陳映真
Choulaojiu	臭老九
Dayuejin (Great Leap Forward)	大躍進

Dazibao (Big-Character-Poster)	大字報
Deng Xiaoping	鄧小平
Diwuge xiandaihua ("Fifth Modernization," or "Democracy")	第五個現代化
Fanyoupai yundong (Anti-Rightist Campaign)	反右派運動
Fu Yuehua	傅月華
Gaoxiong shijian (Kao-hsiung Incident)	高雄事件
Gongchandang (Chinese Communist Party)	共產黨
Guangming ribao (Guangming Daily)	光明日報
"Guojige" ("Internationale")	國際歌
Guomindang (Chinese Nationalist Party)	國民黨
Heiwulei (Five Black Categories: referring to landlord, rich peasant, counter-revolutionary, rascal, and Rightist)	黑五類
Hong Kong	香港
Hongweibing (Red Guards)	紅衛兵
Hu Yaobang	胡耀邦
Hua Guofeng	華國鋒
Jiang Jieshi (Chiang Kai-shek)	蔣介石
Jiang Jingguo (Chiang Ching-kuo)	蔣經國
Jiang Qing	江青
Jiaoyu gaige (education reform)	敎育改革
Lin Yixiong	林義雄
Meilidao (The Beautiful Island)	美麗島
Minzhu qiang (The Democracy Wall)	民主牆
Mingzhu yundong (The Democracy Movement)	民主運動
Nikesen (Richard Nixon)	尼克森
Renmin jiefangjun	人民解放軍

(PLA, or People's Liberation Army)

Renmin ribao (People's Daily) 人民日報

Renquan (Human rights) 人權

Sige xiandaihua
(Four Modernizations) 四個現代化

Sirenbang (Gang of Four) 四人幫

Taidu fenzi
(Taiwanese independent activists) 台獨份子

Taidu yundong
(Taiwan Independence Movement) 台獨運動

Taiwan Ererba shibian
(Taiwan's February 28 Incident) 台灣二二八事變

Tansuo (Explore Magazine) 探索

Tiananmen datusha
(Tiananmen Square Massacre) 天安門大屠殺

Tiananmen guangchang
(Tiananmen Square) 天安門

Tianjin 天津

Wang Dan 王丹

Wei Jingsheng 魏京生

Wuqi ganxiao
(The May Seventh Cadre School) 五七干校

Xiao liuxuesheng
(Junior Chinese Students Overseas) 小留學生

Xiao Taibei
("Little Taipei", or Monterey
Park of California) 小台北

Xidan minzhu qiang
(Xidan's Democracy Wall) 西單民主牆新華社

Xinhuashe (New China News Agency) 新華社

Xuesheng shiwei
(Student demonstration movement) 學生示威

Yanlun ziyou (Freedom of speech) 言論自由

Yashua zhuyi (Toothbrushism)	牙刷主義
Zhao Ziyang	趙紫陽
Zhishi fenzi (The intelligentsia, or intellectual)	知識份子
Ziyou Zhongguo (Free China)	自由中國

BIBLIOGRAPHY

Chen Ruoxi (陳若曦)

I. **Primary Sources**

A. **Novels**

Zhihun 紙婚 *(Paper Marriage)*.
Taipei: Zili wanbaoshe, 1986.
Hong Kong: Joint Publishing Co., 1987.
Beijing: Wenlian chuban gongsi, 1987.

Er Hu 二胡 *(The Two Hus)*.
Taipei: Dunli chubanshe, 1985.
Hong Kong: Joint Publishing Co., 1986.
Beijing: Youyi chuban gongsi, 1987.

Yuanjian 遠見 *(Foresight)*.
Taipei: Yuanjing chuban gongsi, 1984.
Hong Kong: Boyi chubanshe, 1984.
Beijing: Youyi chuban gongsi, 1985.

Tuwei 突圍 *(Breaking Out)*.
Taipei: Lianjing chuban gongsi, 1983.
Hong Kong: Joint Publishing Co., 1983.
Beijing: Youyi chuban gongsi, 1983.

Gui 歸 *(The Repatriates)*.
Taipei: Lianjing chuban gongsi, 1978.
Hong Kong: Mingbao chubanshe, 1979.

B. **Short Stories**

Guizhou nuren 貴州女人 *(The Woman from Guizhou)*.
Taipei: Yuanliu chubanshe, 1989.
Hong Kong: Xiangjiang chubanshe, 1989.

Chen Ruoxi zhongduanpian xiaoshuo xuan 陳若曦中短篇
小説選 *(Selected Short Stories and Novellas by Chen Ruoxi)*.
Fuzhou: Haixia chubanshe, 1985.

Chen Ruoxi xiaoshuo xuan 陳若曦小説選
(Selected Short Stories by Chen Ruoxi).
Beijing: Guangbo chubanshe, 1983.

Chengli chengwai 城裡城外 *(In and Outside the Wall).*
Taipei: Shibao chuban gongsi, 1981.
Hong Kong: Bafang chubanshe, 1981.
Hong Kong: Tiandi tushu, 1983.

Laoren 老人 *(The Old Man).*
Taipei: Lianjing chuban gongsi, 1978.

Chen Ruoxi zixuan ji 陳若曦自選集
(Selected Works by Chen Ruoxi).
Taipei: Lianjing chuban gongsi, 1976.

Yin xianzhang 尹縣長 *(Mayor Yin).*
Taipei: Yuanjing chuban gongsi, 1976.

C. Prose

Qingzang gaoyuan de youhuo 青藏高原的誘惑
(The Temptation of the Tibetan Plateau).
Taipei: Lianjing chuban gongsi, 1989.
Hong Kong: Publications Ltd., 1989.

Xizang xing 西藏行 *(Trip to Tibet).*
Hong Kong: Xiangjiang chubanshe, 1988.

Caoyuan xing 草原行 *(Trip to Inner Mongolia).*
Taipei: Shibao chuban gongsi, 1988.

Tianran shengchu de huaduo 天然生出的花朵
(Flowers Grown Naturally).
Tianjin: Baihua chubanshe, 1987.

Wuliao cai dushu 無聊才讀書 *(Reading to Kill Time).*
Hong Kong: Tiandi tushu, 1983.

Shenghuo suibi 生活隨筆 *(Random Notes).*
Taipei: Shibao chuban gongsi, 1981.

Wenge zayi 文革雜憶
(Reminiscences of the Cultural Revolution).
Taipei: Hongfan shudian, 1979.

D. Works Written in English by the Author

Democracy Walls and Unofficial Journals.
Berkeley: University of California Press, 1982.

Ethics and Rhetorics of the Chinese Cultural Revolution.
Berkeley: Center for Chinese Studies, Institute of
East Asian Studies, University of California, 1981.

"Formosan Literature,"*China Quarterly* (July-September,
1963).

Spirit Calling: Five Stories of Taiwan.
Taipei: The Heritage Press, 1962.

E. Works Translated into English by Others

*The Execution of Mayor Yin and Other Stories from the
Great Proletarian Cultural Revolution,* translated by Nancy
Ing and Howard Goldblatt. Bloomington: Indiana
University Press, 1978.

"The Last Performance," translated by Timothy A. Ross and
Joseph S. M. Lau. In *Chinese Stories from Taiwan: 1960-
1970,* edited by Joseph S. M. Lau, 3-14. New York:
Columbia University Press, 1976.

"My Friend Ai Fen," translated by Richard Kent and Vivian
L. Hsu. In *Born of the Same Roots,* edited by Vivian L. Hsu,
276-302. Bloomington: Indiana University Press, 1981.

The Old Man, edited by John Minford and T. L. Tsim. Hong
Kong: Renditions Books, 1986.

"Ting Yun," and "The Tunnel," translated by Chi-chen
Wang. In*Two Writers and the Cultural Revolution: Lao She
and Chen Jo-hsi,* edited by George Kao. Hong Kong:
Renditions Books, 1980.

F. Novels Translated into Other Languages

Le Prefet Yin.
French translation by Simon Leys.
Paris: Editions Denoel, 1980.

Die Exekution des Landrates Yin.
German translation.
Hamburg: Albrecht Knaus Verlag, 1979.

The Lonely Man in Beijing.
Japanese translation by Minoru Takeuchi.
Tokyo: Asahi-Simbunsha, 1979.

Haradshovding Yins.
Swedish translation.
Stockholm: Atlantis, 1980.

Borgmester Yins Henrettelse.
Danish translation.
Denmark: Albatros, 1980.

Mayor Yin.
Dutch translation.
Amsterdam: B.V. Uitgeverji de Arbeiderspers, 1980.

Mayor Yin.
Norweigian translation.
Oslo: Dreyer Florg, 1980.

II. Secondary Sources

A. Criticism in Chinese

Bai Xianyong 白先勇 [Pei Hsien-yung]. "Wutuobang de zhuixun yu huan-mie" 烏托邦的追尋與幻滅 ("The Pursuit and Dissolutionment over Utopia"). *Zhongguo shibao* 中國 時報 (November 1, 1977).

Cai Danye 蔡丹冶. "Yichu gaishou zuzhou de beiju: Ping Chen Ruoxi de'Jingjing de shengri'" 一齣該受詛咒的悲劇：評陳若曦的〈晶晶的生日〉("A Condemned andCursed Tragedy: On Chen Ruoxi's 'Jingjing's Birthday'"). *Lianhebao* 聯合報 (May 20-21, 1976).

Chun Ren 純人. "Renxing, huigui yu chaoyue: Du Chen Ruoxi de *Zhihun*" 人性，回歸與超越：讀陳若曦的〈紙婚〉("Humanism, Repatriation, and Beyond: On Chen Ruoxi's *Paper Marriage*"). *Wenyi pinglun* 文藝評論, no. 2 (1988): 87-89, 99.

Lan Yu 藍雨. "Dengdai Guotuo: Tan Chen Ruoxi de xingzuo, *Zhihun*" 等待果陀：談陳若曦的新作〈紙婚〉("Waiting for Godot: On Chen Ruoxi's New Novel, *Paper Marriage*"). *Zhongbao* 中報 (December 28, 1987).

Li Yong 李勇. "Guo Zijia de gushi" 郭子加的故事("The Story of Guo Zijia"). *Zhongyang ribao* 中央日報 (October 12-14, 1977).

Lin Shicun 林適存. "Wo du Chen Ruoxi de xiaoshuo" 我讀陳若曦小說 ("Reading Chen Ruoxi's Short Stories"). *Lianhebao* 聯合報 (February 29, 1976).

Liu Shaoming 劉紹銘 [Joseph S. M. Lau]. "Chen Ruoxi de gushi" 陳若曦的故事 ("The Story of Chen Ruoxi"). In *Xiaoshuo yu xiju* 小說與戲劇 (*Fiction and Drama*), 83-98. Taipei: Hongfan shudian, 1977.

Lu Yaodong 逯耀東. "Chen Ruoxi he tade lishi yanyu" 陳若曦和他的歷史言語 ("Chen Ruoxi and Her Historical Rhetorics"). *Zhonghua wenhua fuxing yuekan* 中華文化復興月刊, no. 9 (1977): 59-71.

_____. "Chen Ruoxi yu Lao Duan" 陳若曦與老段 ("Chen Ruoxi and Her Husband; Duan Shiyao"). *Lianhebao* 聯合報 (February 29, 1976).

Luo Qing 羅青. "Lun Chen Ruoxi de 'Didao'" 論陳若曦的〈地道〉("On Chen Ruoxi's 'The Tunnel'"). *Lianhebao* 聯合報 (February 26-29, 1978).

336

_____. "Tan fangong wenxue de chuangzuo" 談反共
文學的創作 ("On the Creation of Anti-Communist
Literature"). *Zhongyang ribao* 中央日報 (April 30, 1976).

Mo Lingping 莫靈平. "Kulian yu wenhao" 苦戀與問
號 ("Bittersweet Love and Inquiry"). *Taiwan shibao* 台灣
時報 (July 29,1981), Section II.

Ni Luo 尼洛. "Jiushi nayang fanfu wuchang: Ping Chen Ruoxi de
'Jen Xiulan'" 就是那樣的反復無常： 評陳若曦的〈任
秀蘭〉 ("Always so Capricious: On Chen Ruoxi's 'Jen
Xiulan'"). *Qingnian zhanshibao* 青年戰士報 (July 29-30,
1977).

_____. "Qingliangshan de fangke: Ping Chen Ruoxi de *Yin
xianzhang quanji* " 清諒山的訪客： 評陳若曦的〈尹
縣長全集〉 ("Visitor from the Cold Mountain: Criticism
on Chen Ruoxi's Complete Collection of *The Mayor Yin*").
Zhongyang ribao 中央日報 (July 5-6, 1977).

_____. "*Yin xianzhang* de shehui beijing" 〈尹縣長〉的社
會背景 ("The Sociological Backgrounds of *The Mayor
Yin*"). *Mingdao wenyi* 明道文藝, no. 38 (May 1979): 79-83.

Pan Yandun and Wang Yisheng 潘嚴墩與汪義生. "Chen Ruoxi
de changpian xinzuo, *Er Hu*"陳若曦的長篇新作〈二胡〉
("On Chen Ruoxi's New Novel, *The Two Hus*"). *Scholars
Book Club* (July 1986): 58-61.

Sima Sangdun 司馬桑敦. "Fang Chen Ruoxi" 訪陳若曦
("Interview with Chen Ruoxi"). *Lianhebao* 聯合報
(December 16, 1976).

Wei Ziyun 魏子雲. "Xuelei zhengyan: Du Chen Ruoxi zhuanji"
血淚証言： 讀陳若曦專集 ("Bloody Witness: Reading
Chen Ruoxi's Special Collection"). *Zhongguo shibao* 中國
時報 (March 17, 1976).

Wu Dayun 吳達雲. "Zizhu yu chengquan: Lun Chen Ruoxi xiaoshuo zhong de nuxing yishi" 自主與陳若曦小説中的女性意識 ("Independence and Fulfillment: Feminist Consciousness in Chen Ruoxi's Fiction"). *Wenxing* (February 1988): 100-108.

Xia Zhiqing 夏志清 [C. T. Hsia]. "Chen Ruoxi de xiaoshuo" 陳若曦的小説 ("The Fiction of Chen Ruoxi"). In *Chen Ruoxi zixuan ji* 陳若曦自選集, 1-31. Taipei: Lianjing chuban gongsi, 1976.

Xiang Qing 項青. "Kongju yu zhengzha: Du Chen Ruoxi duanpian xiaoshuoji, *Yin xianzhang*" 恐懼與掙扎:讀陳若曦短篇小説集〈尹縣長〉 ("Horror and Struggle: Reading about Chen Ruoxi's Short Story Collection, *The Mayor Yin*"). *Shuping shumu* 書評書目 (May 1976): 34-37.

Xiao Jinmian 蕭錦綿 ."Yuankan *Yuanjian*" 遠看〈遠見〉 ("An Objective Analysis of *Foresight*"). *Chuban yu dushu* 出版與讀書 (March 25, 1984): 1-2.

Xin Wu 心吾. "Du Chen Ruoxi" 讀陳若曦 ("Reading About Chen Ruoxi"). *Mingdao wenyi* 明道文藝, no. 2 (May 1976): 153-57.

Yan Huo 彥火. "Suxie Chen Ruoxi" 速寫陳若曦 ("Brief Portrayal of Chen Ruoxi"). In *Haiwai huaren zuojia lueying* 海外華人作家略影 (*Brief Interviews with Chinese Writers Overseas*), 54-71. Hong Kong: Joint Publishing Co., 1984.

Yan Yuanshu 顏元叔. "Ping Chen Ruoxi de *Laoren*" 評陳若曦的〈老人〉 ("Critical Review of Chen Ruoxi's *The Old Man*"). *Zhongyang ribao* 中央日報 (March 17, 1980).

Yang Hanzhi 楊漢之. "Xuerou ninglian de bishou: Lun Chen Ruoxi de xiaoshuo" 血肉凝煉的匕首:論陳若曦的小説 ("The Dagger Sharpened by Flesh and Blood: On Chen Ruoxi's Fiction"). *Zhongguo shibao* 中國時報 (March 4, 1976).

Ye Jingzhu 葉經柱. "Tan Chen Ruoxi de shu" 談陳若曦的書
("Discussion of Chen Ruoxi's Fiction"). *Zhongyang ribao*
中央日報 (June 17-18, 1976).

Ye Weilian 葉維廉 [Wai-lam Yip]. "Chen Ruoxi de lucheng"
陳若曦的路程 ("The Journey of Chen Ruoxi"). *Lianhebao*
聯合報 (November 7-10, 1977).

Zhan Hongzhi 詹宏志. "Yuanze yu liyi: Pingjie Chen Ruoxi de
'Lukou'" 原則與利益：評陳若曦的〈路口〉 ("Principles
and Benefits: On Chen Ruoxi's 'The Crossroads'"). *Shuping
shumu* 書評書目 (July 1980): 11-21.

Zhang Cuo 張錯 [Dominic Cheung]. "Guopo shanhe zai: Haiwai
zuojia de bentuxing" 國破山河在：海外作家的本土性
("Divided Nation, Undivided Land: On Overseas Chinese
Writers' Nativism"). *Lianhe wenxue* 聯合文學 (Unitas) 7,
no.3 (January 1991): 24-28.

Zheng Yungxiao 鄭永孝. *Chen Ruoxi de shijie* 陳若曦的世界
("The Fictional World of Chen Ruoxi"). Taipei: Shulin
chubanshe, 1985.

Zhu Xining et al. 朱西寧等. "*Chengli chengwai* huiping" 〈城裡
城外〉會評 ("Review Committee Report on Chen Ruoxi's
In and Outside the Wall"). *Lianhebao* 聯合報 (January
9-11, 1980).

B. Criticism and Reviews in English

Berstein, Richard. "Mao's Misfits." *Times* (June 26, 1978): 60, 64.

Cohen, Mark. "Three Literary Works on the Cultural Revolution."
Journal of the Chinese Literature Teachers Association,
no. 5 (1982): 127-35.

Dinsdale, Douglas. "Cultural Revolution Revisited." *San Francisco
Review of Books* (November and December 1980): 8-9,15.

Duke, Michael S. "Personae: Individual and Society in Three
Novels by Chen Ruoxi." In *Modern Chinese Women Writers:
Critical Appraisals*, edited by Michael S. Duke, 53-57. New
York: M. E. Sharpe, 1989.

Dunn, Joe P. "In Search of China." *Air University Review* (May-June 1980): 129,133.

Dolezalova, Anna. Review of *Two Writers and the Cultural Revolution: Lao She and Chen Jo-hsi*. *Asian and Africa Studies* 18 (1982): 238-40.

Echevarria, Evelio. Review of *Two Writers and the Cultural Revolution: Lao She and Chen Jo-hsi*. *Modern Fiction Studies* (Summer 1981): 399-400.

Eichwald, Bethea. "A Novelist of the Chinese Revolution." *Chicago Literary Review*(June 1981): 22-23.

Elvin, Mark. "Tales of the New China." *Time Literary Supplement* (June 9, 1978): 629-30.

Goldman, Merle. "Dissent in China." *Problems of Communication* (March-April 1982): 58-59.

Hsu, Kai-yu. "A Sense of History: Reading Chen Jo-hsi's Stories." In *Chinese Fiction from Taiwan: Critical Perspectives*, edited by Jeannette L. Faurot, 206-302. Bloomington: Indiana University Press, 1979.

Kern, William Alfred. "Tales Evoke China's Cultural Revolution." *News Sentinel* (Fort Wayne, Indiana) (October 8, 1984).

Lattimore, David. "Chinese Samizdat." *New York Times Book Review* (July 30, 1978): 10-11, 20-21.

Lee, Leo Ou-fan. "Dissent Literature from the Cultural Revolution." *Chinese Literature: Essays, Articles, Reviews*, no. 1 (1979): 59-79.

Leys, Simon. An "Introduction" to *The Execution of Mayor Yin and Other Stories from the Great Proletarian Cultural Revolution*, translated by Nancy Ing and Howard Glodblatt, xii-xxviii. Bloomington: Indiana University Press, 1978.

Light, Timothy. Review of *The Execution of Mayor Yin and Other Stories from the Great Proletarian Cultural Revolution.* *Chinese Literature: Essays, Articles, Reviews*, no. 1 (1979): 131-34.

McDougall, Bonnie S. Review of *The Execution of Mayor Yin and Other Stories from the Great Proletarian Cultural Revolution.* *Harvard Journal of Asiatic Studies* 39, no. 2 (1979): 469-74.

Pai Hsien-yung. "The Wandering Chinese: The Theme of Exile in Taiwan Fiction." *Iowa Review* 7, nos. 2-3 (Spring-Summer 1976): 205-12.

Roxroth, Kenneth. "Examination of Two People's Republic Writer." *Los Angeles Times* (November 6, 1980), part v: 35.

Tang Jong See. "First Writer to Throw the Book at Mao's Gang." *The Strait Times* (June 9, 1982): 1.

Wakeman, Jr., Frederic. "The Real China." *New York Review of Books* 25, no. 12 (July 20, 1978): 9-17.